The Dying Light

Book I of

The Solar Exodus

Antonio Pascarella

DreamWright Publishing – Meriden, Connecticut

The Dying Light
Book I of
The Solar Exodus
By Antonio Pascarella

Published by DreamWright Publishing
An imprint of StoneGate Publishing, LLC
www.stonegatepublishing.com
Permissions & inquiries:
permissions@stonegatepublishing.com

ISBNs:
Hardcover: 979-8-9999855-3-8
Paperback: 979-8-9999855-4-5
eBook (EPUB/Kindle): 979-8-9999855-5-2

Library of Congress Control Number: 2025950388

First edition, December 2025
Printed in the United States of America

Printer's key: 10 9 8 7 6 5 4 3 2 1

Disclaimer

This is a work of fiction. Names, characters, organizations, governments, corporations, and events depicted herein are either the product of the author's imagination or are used fictitiously. Any resemblance to actual persons, living or dead, or to real events, institutions, or locales is entirely coincidental.

While this story incorporates scientific principles, emerging technologies, and theories of astrophysics, propulsion, and space colonization, all depictions are speculative and dramatized for narrative effect. The author has drawn on contemporary research, public-domain science, and projected advancements to portray a plausible future—however, the technologies, timelines, and outcomes described should not be interpreted as predictions or scientific certainties.

The political, social, and moral themes represented in *The Solar Exodus Series Books* are intended for reflection and discussion, not endorsement. References to real-world policies, ideologies, or institutions are fictionalized or symbolic. The story's portrayal of planetary decline, interstellar travel, and human survival explores universal questions of responsibility, sacrifice, and resilience.

The author and publisher disclaim any responsibility for the misuse, misinterpretation, or application of any concepts described within. The narrative exists solely for entertainment and literary purposes.

Trademarks

All trademarks, service marks, product names, and logos appearing in this book are the property of their respective owners. Their use does not imply affiliation with or endorsement by them.

Credits

Editing: Antonio Pascarella
Interior design & typesetting: StoneGate Publishing, LLC
Cover design: Antonio Pascarella
Cover illustration/icons: Antonio Pascarella
Text set in Garamond 11/15 on 6"×9" trim.

Manufacturing & Distribution

Manufactured in the United States of America.

Contact

StoneGate Publishing, LLC
www.stonegatepublishing.com
info@stonegatepublishing.com

*For every soul who has ever wondered
what comes after the last dawn.*

The Dying Light
Book I of
The Solar Exodus

Note from the Author

When I began writing *The Solar Exodus*, I wasn't trying to predict the future. I wanted to explore what happens when humanity is forced to confront its own limits — not just technological or environmental, but moral, emotional, and spiritual. Every civilization faces a moment when it must choose between repeating its mistakes or redefining its purpose. For us, that question comes wrapped in the light of a dying star.

The world of *The Dying Light* is not about destruction; it's about endurance. It asks whether compassion can survive when time runs out, and whether hope can outlast the Sun itself. The science in these pages is real enough to be possible, but the story exists to remind us that our greatest discoveries will never come from machines — they'll come from each other.

To those who look up at the night sky and wonder what's waiting beyond it, this story is for you. We may never leave Earth in ships like *Prometheus* or *Aurora*, but the courage to imagine such a journey is what makes us human.

— **Antonio Pascarella**

For everyone who dares to look beyond the horizon,
and keeps reaching for the stars.

For the ones who kept asking "what if…"
and refused to stop imagining a way forward.

For all who have ever watched the night sky
and felt both the weight of silence and the promise of forever.

For those who look at the night sky
and see not distance, but connection.

For the children who will inherit both our mistakes and our miracles.
may they never lose their sense of wonder.

Foreword

The Solar Exodus — Book I: The Dying Light

There was a time when we believed the Sun would shine forever. It was the one constant in our fragile existence — the silent witness to every joy, every sorrow, every fleeting century of our civilization.

We built our cities beneath its warmth, worshiped it in our myths, and trusted that tomorrow would always come with dawn.

But the light began to change. Subtly at first — a fraction dimmer, a shade colder. Scientists measured what poets already felt: the Sun was dying. The equations confirmed what the heart could not bear — that even stars have lifespans, and ours was nearing its end.

In those final years, humanity learned the true meaning of unity and despair. Borders dissolved under the weight of necessity. Nations that once warred over resources turned their eyes upward together, searching for salvation among the stars. The great Arks — *Prometheus, Daedalus, Erebus, Odyssey, and Aurora* — rose not as monuments of pride, but as acts of desperation and faith.

What follows is not the story of how we left Earth. It is the story of why we had to.

Because in the fading of the Sun, we found the measure of who we truly are.

Chapter 1

Load-Bearing Walls

Adrian woke before the thermostat clicked. Habit, not alarm. The house was early-winter quiet, heat still a few minutes from its morning sigh through the vents. He lay with his eyes open, listening to the house settle—timber shifting, the duct that rapped when the upstairs bathroom ran hot.

Marta breathed steadily beside him. The phone on his nightstand glowed 5:28. He imagined the day in layers: drop-off at Elena's school, Sofia's mitten hunt, meet the steel subcontractor at the rowhouse on Third, swing by the salvage yard for the maple door he'd promised to repurpose, and maybe—if the sky held—measure sunlight on the lot in Cranston for that family who couldn't decide between a deep porch or more interior square footage. He built houses around the lives they would hold. The math of that satisfied him.

He eased out of bed, careful with the floorboard by the dresser that squealed. Downstairs, he put water on and leaned against the counter while the kettle tried to be a river. The kitchen lights were too bright at this hour; He left them off and stood in the fridge's faint hum until the kitchen felt awake.

On the table: yesterday's mail fanned out under Elena's winter diorama—a cardboard shoebox planetarium dotted with glue-smeared stars. He smiled at the constellations she'd made up. "Cat's Ear," "The Long Spoon." He traced the construction paper orbit she'd cut by hand—too elliptical—and had to stop himself from correcting it. Let it be Cat's Ear. Let the orbit be wrong for another year.

The kettle chirped. He poured through the metal filter the way he'd learned after throwing away a dozen disposable ones. Somewhere upstairs, a small foot hit carpet.

Sofia would appear in a minute with her hair a static cloud and ask if penguins ever get bored of walking.

He took his coffee to the back door and watched the yard through glass. Frost on the grass. The neighbors' porch light was still on though it was plainly morning; they always forgot it. A star of ice on the deck rail caught the porch glow and it made a weak constellation too. For a second he tried to map Cat's Ear on the railing. It didn't fit, which somehow made him happier.

A news anchor murmured from the living room—he'd left the TV on mute last night, some late debate about zoning relief for multifamily units near the rail station. He clicked the sound up two degrees. Weather, traffic, weather again. A crawl about "solar observation satellite offline for two hours amid CME interference; no risk to power grid." He half-heard it the way he heard detour signs on roads he didn't take. Just information with an orange vest on.

"Daddy?"

Sofia was at the doorway, pajama pants dragging, a stuffed penguin under one arm like a sack of flour. Her hair did the cloud thing.

"Hey, Sof." He pulled a stool out with his foot. "You beat the sun."

"It's already up," she declared, squinting at the window. "It's just hiding."

He poured her a kid-cup of warm milk. "Hiding is different from being up."

She frowned, considered this, and sipped. "Do penguins get bored of walking?"

He'd known it. "They slide on their bellies to mix it up."

"Like living room sliding?" Her eyes cut toward the wood floor with dangerous intent.

"Like living room sliding if the living room were Antarctica and you were wearing a tuxedo and your mother couldn't see you."

"That's very specific."

"Elena!" came Marta's voice from upstairs, the second syllable of their older daughter's name arcing in warning. A drawer shut. Water ran. The house inhaled heat through the vents.

By seven the kitchen was a knot of elbows and cereal boxes. Marta wore a sweater he liked—forest green, the one with the tiny worn patch near the cuff where she twisted fabric during crosswalk stories. She taught second graders to look both ways, to pick up litter, to share in ways that didn't make them smaller. Her hair was up and already collecting pencils.

2

"Elena, hon, your project." Marta nodded at the shoebox planetarium. "Bring Cat's Ear."

Elena scooped up her universe. "It's not the cat's ear, it's Cat's Ear, capital C, capital E." She looked at Adrian. "Daddy, you didn't fix the orbit, right? I know it's not perfectly—"

"It's perfect," he said. "And the planets are made of cereal, which is scientifically delicious."

Elena narrowed her eyes. "Those aren't planets, those are exoplanets."

"Even better," he said, and meant it. He ruffled Sofia's hair; the static made it reach for his palm. "Shoes, penguin walker."

On the TV, the anchor now stood in front of a graphic of the sun that made it look like a peeled orange. "...minor fluctuations detected in the neutrino flux...the solar observatory team says it's all within expected variance..."

"Neutrin—what?" Marta asked, peering at the screen as she zippered Sofia's coat.

"Ghost particles," Adrian said. "The ones that fly through you like you're not there."

"You make it sound rude."

"They don't know any better," he said, lowering his voice for the girls. "They're just terrible house guests."

Elena glanced up, serious. "They go through the whole planet, Daddy."

"And our living room," Sofia added, turning in a slow circle as if she could catch one.

"We'll leave out snacks," Marta said. "Maybe they'll stop next time." She kissed Adrian's cheek and whispered, "You meeting the steel guy?"

"Third and Maple, nine sharp." He hated that he'd started saying things like nine sharp. He liked it less when he said it.

On the drive to school, Sofia narrated penguin lives in present tense like a sportscaster; Elena corrected the biomechanics. The sky was a pale, unmade bed. At the light by the coffee place they couldn't afford every day, a woman in a hard hat counted rebar from the back of a flatbed, lips moving. Adrian missed counting by lips. Now he counted in spreadsheets, which had no lips.

He dropped the girls, waited for Elena to wave (she always did, palms flat against the glass like a fish), then headed toward Third, watching the frozen traffic lights blink through the pale morning haze.

The radio talked about a contractor in Westport who'd gone under after buying steel at the wrong moment, the price spiking and the lender nonplussed by futures that were supposed to have hedged the hedge. He turned the radio off. Too close to the bone before nine.

At Third and Maple, the rowhouse looked tired in a way he trusted immediately. Three units wide, a hundred and twenty years old, the façade had been painted the color of rain more than once. Adrian loved it. You could see the old line of the staircase from the ghost of plaster, the way a rib shows after muscle goes. He ran his hand along the new framing and felt the math of it—the give and the hold.

Ken, the steel guy, arrived wearing a coat half practical, half optimism. They went through the plan: new beam to open the first floor without killing the middle of the house, header hung from bolts that wouldn't rust to embarrassment, footings poured where the cellar always wanted to be water.

"Load path looks clean," Ken said, tapping a drawing. "You sure about the span? It wants to be a little thicker."

"I know," Adrian said. "They want lines, not bulk."

Ken shrugged. "Houses don't care about what people want. They care about gravity."

They stepped into the cold to squint at the façade. A couple walked by with a dog that looked like it had been drawn by a child and colored in by a committee.

"Neighborhood's waking up," Ken said.

"Neighborhood didn't sleep," Adrian said, pointing to the deli where lights had been on at four when he did his insomnia lap. He didn't add that he'd stood outside and watched a man in a white apron peel oranges with a kind of linear grace that made Adrian want to design a kitchen around him.

By ten, they'd worked out the bracket of problems the inspector would circle. Ken left, the beam on order, and Adrian sat on the bottom step of a set of stairs that did not yet exist and ate a banana like a field ration.

He texted Marta a picture of sunlight coming through new framing in a diagonal spill. She replied with a photo of a child making a tower out of glue sticks. "Load-bearing," she wrote. He laughed aloud, the sound carrying through the empty rooms.

His phone pinged again. A client asking if the built-in bench could also be storage (yes), if storage could also be a wine rack (maybe), if the wine rack could be ventilated (no, or yes, but expensive). He started composing replies and stopped. He didn't like answering in pieces. He liked answering at a table with sketches spread out between people.

He stood, walked the perimeter of the first floor, imagined where the sounds would come from when people finally lived here: the clatter of keys in a dish, the laugh you try to stifle and fail, a pot lid searching for its pot. He chalked a line on the floor where he would thicken the beam despite the client's hunger for thinness. Houses care about gravity. He'd said it out loud. He would say it again.

At noon, he drove to the salvage yard by the river, a feral museum of doors, mantels, and stripped old wardrobes. He looked for the maple door with the etched glass leaf pattern the way you look for a friend in a crowd. It wasn't where he'd seen it last. A yard hand pointed with a cigarette. "Back—left, behind the church pews. We found an extra hinge."

He found it, ran his thumb over the carve. Not leaf—flame. He liked the misread better. Flame in a house was a practical thing and a holy one. He bought it, loaded it, and stood a minute with his back to the river. The water had that winter sheen that made it look more solid than it was. Sunlight kept breaking apart on the ripples.

His phone buzzed again. A headline: "Solar Observatory Team to Host Briefing After Anomalies." He thumbed it away. The day had enough anomalies he could cut and measure.

In the afternoon he met with a couple in Cranston. They stood on a rectangle of muddy earth and told him about their porch fantasies like confessing dreams. "We want a deep porch where summer lasts longer," the woman said, "but we don't want to lose light inside." He explained overhangs, how shade moved like a polite guest if you invited it with an angle. He measured the sky with his arm and made it look like science; mostly it was experience, pretending to be math.

"Southwest has a way of lying," he said. "It promises warmth and delivers glare." They laughed, and he felt that small hit of stage energy he got when he liked when clients stopped looking nervous once he started explaining things.

By four he was back at Third to meet the inspector, who turned out to be a woman with a pen that clicked in a staccato that made his pen jealous.

She walked the framing, made notes, asked nothing about fashion, everything about fasteners. He respected her instantly and without reserve.

"You're thickening the beam," she said, not quite a question.

"I am," he said.

"Good," she said, and initialed a box that people would call "approval", but he thought of it as a handshake with paper.

On the way home he bought a loaf of bread and an orange for Sofia to peel. Late afternoon made everything look simpler and more worn-in. He liked that. The radio—on again, against his better judgement—talked about the briefing from the solar observatory scheduled for next week, a professor saying, "nothing to worry about," a second voice saying "interesting" the way people say "storm."

He parked in the driveway and saw Elena through the front window, Cat's Ear propped on a chair, the shoebox's hole to the sky now cut cleaner. She'd upgraded her orbit. He hoped she never stopped caring enough to fix things twice.

Inside, the house smelled like Marta's roasted carrots and cumin. Sofia barreled into him like a small, organized riot. "We learned about migration, and I told everyone penguins migrate in their hearts."

"That's a very advanced concept," he said, and set the bread on the counter with ceremony. "Who wants to peel the orange like a pro?"

Sofia raised both hands. Elena raised one. Marta raised the knife and said, "Nope."

At dinner they did roses and thorns. Elena's rose was that her teacher said Cat's Ear was the first constellation that made her laugh out loud in ten years of dioramas. Her thorn was that someone said it was wrong and she had to explain exo-orbits and even then. Sofia's rose was that the class pet salamander came out when she tapped twice. Her thorn was that her glove went missing for an hour in the Lost and Found and returned smelling like someone else's hand.

Marta's rose was that a shy kid sang during pick-up. Her thorn was a parent email about snacks that read like litigation.

Adrian's rose was the inspector. His thorn he kept simple: "I had to say no to a wine rack."

"Tragedy," Marta intoned.

"It's okay," Elena said. "Wine is basically grape sadness."

Marta choked and laughed at the same time. "Who told you that?"

"You did, when you spilled it on the rug and then said, 'grape sadness' and used club soda and salt."

"Ah," Marta said, pointing her fork. "That was chemistry."

After dinner, while the girls built a pillow city and Marta graded sight-word cards with her pencil's small impatience, Adrian opened his laptop for the Cranston couple and sketched options. A porch that could hold four chairs and a late August evening without swallowing the living room whole. He drew where the winter light would fall across the floorboards. He liked how lines put manners on light.

When he closed the laptop, the room had shifted into that hour where the house's sounds pretend to be outside. He washed plates. Marta put on a show where someone in an immaculate kitchen cooked food that would never be eaten by the crew. The crawl at the bottom of the screen mentioned the solar briefing again. He almost said something about it and didn't. The universe could take a night off. So could worry.

Later, upstairs, Sofia fell asleep with one hand on the penguin's head as if blessing it. Elena read under her blanket with a flashlight they pretended she didn't own. Adrian stood at the bedroom window while he brushed his teeth and looked at the night like it was an old photograph of a place he used to live. The belt pointed across the dark and meant whatever people needed it to mean. It pointed to nothing he could claim.

Marta came up behind him, wrapped her arms around his waist, chin between his shoulder blades. "You smell like sawdust," she said, muffled.

"Good day," he said.

"Good day," she said back. "What's the load path for us?"

He cleared his throat theatrically. "Weight transfers from small shoulders to us to the floor to the footings to bedrock to the mantle to the core to—"

"—to hot iron and then to stars," she finished. They'd made that joke when they were twenty-five, sweating in a fifth-floor walk-up that had load paths made out of hope.

"Inspector approved," he said.

"Good," she said, and kissed the back of his neck. "Tomorrow I'm making soup."

He turned, kissed her, and the night made room. Below them, the vents exhaled. Somewhere, a neutrino went through the house without an opinion.

If you pressed your ear to the plaster and listened with an instrument no one yet owned, you might have heard a rhythm faint as a moth's wing. Not the house. Not the wind. A shape in the sun, a fraction wrong from yesterday, whispering in particles that did not stop for furniture or ribs, an error moving patiently toward being noticed.

Adrian slept and dreamed of porches that didn't end.

Chapter 2

Discovery, Objections

Camille Rios liked to arrive before the elevators remembered their manners. At 6:52, the federal building's lobby echo still belonged to the night crew, and the guard who read hardbacks in a plexiglass booth looked up at her like a librarian who knew which floor her book was on.

"Morning, Counsel," he said, stamping the log without making her stop.

"Morning, Roy." She held up a paper bag. "Chocolate croissant for the bribe fund."

Roy grinned and tilted his head toward the scanner. "That bribe fund is constitutionally protected."

On seven, the corridor smelled like coffee that hadn't fully committed yet. The lights were heavy-eyed. Her office was the last one before the corner—a narrow rectangle with a view of a concrete courtyard where pigeons practiced law. She flicked on the desk lamp and let the softer circle of light define the morning.

On her chair: Javier's soccer ball, deflated, as if it had traveled here to report abuse. He'd left it in the back of her car after practice and she'd brought it up yesterday by mistake, then kept it here like an artifact from a different court. She touched the rubber with two fingers and felt the faint hexagon pattern, the texture of Saturday.

She opened her laptop. The inbox had grown overnight with the usual mushrooms— updates that changed nothing and reply-alls that somehow made everything worse—plus three messages from her paralegal, Theresa, all titled "RFP 22-1981 follow-up," all stacked like a small column of warnings, a numbering scheme that looked bureaucratic, sounding like a far-off year. The case wasn't glamorous: a whistleblower had alleged bid-rigging on emergency procurement contracts for "national energy resilience enhancements," a phrase designed to sound important without meaning much.

Her unit did public integrity and procurement; they caught the deals that slipped emergency language like a fake mustache.

She clicked Theresa's first email. It contained a spreadsheet of vendors flagged by the agency's own auditors, sorted by contract value, with a column named "linkage" that Theresa had added in yellow. Linkage, in Theresa's taxonomy, meant shell companies that shared an address, an accountant, a lawyer, a PO box with a different name on the box, or a failure to be separate in the ways separateness demands.

Camille skimmed down. Two names repeated like a rhyme that didn't quite rhyme: **Sunward Environmental** and **Helios Systems Support.** Both had risen from nowhere in the last nine months to win a mix of consulting and "preliminary infrastructure" awards. Both listed a D.C. office that was an executive suite over a salad place. Both shared an outside counsel who was very good at issuing press releases that sounded like case law. She made a note to call him and not say any of the words he would hope to hear.

Her second window held a court calendar: a status conference at ten before Judge Leland, who was allergic to adjectives and found adverbs morally suspect. She liked him for it. He shaved hearings to the kernel.

Her phone buzzed. Noah.

"Hey," she said, tucking it between shoulder and ear as she opened the third email, this one with attachments named like **SOW_rev7_final_FINAL.pdf** and **emergency_justification (2).docx**.

Noah's voice was already caffeinated and cheerful in a way that made her shoulders drop a fraction. "Morning, Counselor. Your son has declared that shin guards are instruments of oppression."

"That's consistent with his political development," she said. "Did you tell him labor won those protections after a long struggle?"

"I told him Coach Jess will bench him." Papers rustled on his end—his home office grew little drifts even on days he swore to shovel it. "I have a parent board call at eight-thirty; school is worried about the ventilation report again. You still making it to scrimmage?"

"I'll try to be there by five fifteen," she said. Ten o'clock status conference, an eleven-thirty interview with a procurement officer who had perfected the art of remembering nothing, a three-p.m. meeting with the auditors. "If Judge Leland keeps the calendar on a diet."

"Copy. Javier says he left you a ball to remember us by."

"It's glaring at me," she said. "Tell him I'm booking it as a witness. It will testify that he never practices."

Noah laughed. "I'll tell him. Love you."

"Love you," she said, and let the call end in a little click she liked, a sound like a lid that fit.

At nine, Theresa slid into the doorway like a note passed in class. "You see the linkage?" she asked without hello. Theresa measured her greetings; they were most lavish with baristas and janitors.

"I saw." Camille turned her laptop toward her. "Sunward and Helios. A lot of adjectives in their mission statements. Not much verb."

Theresa pointed at the yellow cells. "And look at this." She tapped addresses. "This one—Sunward—lists a P.O. box in Arlington. Helios shares a phone number with a consultant who also sits on an advisory board at— wait for it—the National Energy Resilience Initiative." Theresa did not roll her eyes when she said it; she was saving the roll for something that deserved it. "And guess who signed three of the emergency justifications for sole-source?"

Camille skimmed the scanned signatures. The initial J looked like a fishhook; the rest was a river. **Deputy Director Gregor Vass.**

She paused.

"You know him?" Theresa asked.

"Not personally." The name had weight in the city; Vass had made his money in logistics, then drifted into energy as casually as people drift into new haircuts. He sat on panels, in a suit that looked expensive even from bad angles, and talked about resilience like a man who invented calories. He had that charisma that made reasonable people forget where their wallets were and report the loss as a choice. "He's the deputy at the Office of Infrastructure and—what do they call it now?"

"Adaptation and Resilience," Theresa said, which was what you called things when you wanted them to pass.

"Get me his travel calendar and the approvals on his last five expense reports," Camille said. "And pull all his recusals. I want to see who he knows and who he remembers he knows."

Theresa nodded, pleased to be sent into a paper forest. "You heading to Leland?"

"Mm." Camille closed her laptop, slipped into her jacket, and took the soccer ball off her chair like a briefcase with a round idea inside.

The courtroom was bright in a municipal way: flags like folded reasons behind the bench, a gallery of winter coats blinking off snow that wasn't there. The air had the crispness of people performing civics. Judge Leland took the bench at 10:01 with a stack of thin files and the uninflected face of a man whose tic was punctuality.

"United States v. Chen, status," he said, and ran through three short matters before calling her case: "United States ex rel. Wilson v. Sunward Environmental et al., status."

She stood, introduced herself and Theresa for the record, and nodded at opposing counsel at the other table—Mr. Hathaway for Sunward, Ms. Brill for Helios, and a third lawyer for "interested party" counsel representing the agency, who managed to look both public-service noble and privately insured.

Hathaway rose with a smile he packed for court. "Your Honor, as we've indicated, our clients are eager to resolve this without burdening the Court. At this point, we think the government's theory is—frankly—"

"Hathaway," Leland said mildly, "we're on for status, not closing argument."

Hathaway's smile narrowed but did not break. "Then status is: we served interrogatories. The government's responses were...thin."

Camille kept her eyes on Leland, not Hathaway. "We responded within the rules. We are still receiving documents from the agency whose processes are, let's say, evolutionary. We have identified at least four procurement irregularities that warrant targeted discovery"—she glanced down at her notes without needing them—"including repeated emergency justifications signed by the same individual without contemporaneous threat assessments, reliance on vendors without adequate past performance documentation, and bid specs that appear to have been drafted by the vendors themselves."

Leland made a mark in the margin of his nothing-colored legal pad. "Timeline?"

"Sixty days to complete initial discovery," Camille said. Aggressive. She liked to set a pace that made the other side breathe through their mouths.

Hathaway's eyebrows discovered the ceiling. "Your Honor, sixty days is—"

"Ambitious," Leland said, "but the statute's not a hammock. Sixty days for initial. We'll revisit if the agency is actually the bottleneck." He looked at the agency lawyer. "Counsel, if the bottleneck is you, you'll say so in English."

"Yes, Your Honor," the agency lawyer said, in English.

"Good," Leland said. "Anything else that needs me?"

Ms. Brill, for Helios, stood. "Just one point, Your Honor. There's an undercurrent here about some kind of grand coordination—this so-called 'linkage' column Ms. Rios's office has developed—which opposing counsel keeps mentioning like it's a criminal code instead of a spreadsheet—"

Leland's eyes moved like a second hand. "Counsel, if there is improper coordination, that's what discovery is for. If there isn't, it will be a short walk. The Court is not allergic to facts. Sixty days. Next status April 3 at 9:30."

He banged his gavel in a way that sounded like a courtesy.

Back in the hallway, Hathaway approached with the professional bonhomie of a dentist at a cocktail party. "Ms. Rios," he said, "I hope we can keep this civilized. My client is—"

"Of course," she said. "Civility is my favorite weapon."

Theresa coughed into her folder. Brill watched Camille the way some people look at chessboards two moves from check. The agency lawyer took a call and pretended to be in a different building.

"Let me know when you've got real documents," Hathaway said. "Not hearsay or press clippings."

"I'll let you know when your clients give me real documents," she said, and stepped away before he could decide whether to be offended or to bill for it.

Down the hall, her phone vibrated with a text from Noah: **Shin guards accepted after capitalism argument. You owe me.** And then a photo of Javier in the school yard, arms thrown wide, hair resistant to reason, joy creating its own weather.

She typed a heart and slid the phone back. The soccer ball in her other hand looked suddenly less like a prop and more like a promise.

They ate at their desks because everyone did on hearing days. Theresa brought Camille half a salad and a cookie with an honesty clause baked in.

"Got something," Theresa said, mouth half-full of Caesar. "Vass's recusals are...sparse." She put a thin stack of folders on Camille's desk.

"Given how many boards he sits on, he should be recusing like it's cardio, but there are only three filings in the last year. All tiny. Meanwhile, travel calendar shows he was in Houston, Munich, and—get this—Arecibo in the last nine months. Arecibo's dish is…well, was… You know." She made a gesture like a bowl turned into a broken rib. "But there's still a lab."

"Arecibo," Camille said. "That's signals."

"Mm." Theresa put a second stack down—printed emails the agency had coughed up with whole committees of black marks marching across the page. "Also, in the initial Statement of Work there's this phrase that repeats: **'support for field-stabilized acceleration.'** I googled it. The search results are half math manias and half space blogs. Sunward is allegedly doing food-grade water systems and desal retrofits.

Helios is allegedly consulting on 'resilient microgrids.' What does field-stabilized acceleration have to do with either?"

"Nothing," Camille said, and let the word sit like a coin that bought something later. She flipped through the redactions. The repetition felt sloppy if it was a cover, or arrogant if it wasn't. "Pull the technical appendices that Sunward and Helios submitted. If any are missing, note the holes."

Theresa leaned back. "If these people are hiding aerospace work inside municipal contracts, it'll be a good day."

"Or a long one," Camille said.

At three, they sat across from a procurement officer named Danny whose badge lanyard had become a timeline of conferences. He had a talent for looking surprised when handed his own memos. Camille worked in a rhythm—ask, show, pause. Don't fill the silence; let him measure his courage against it.

"Mr. Liang," she said, sliding a page across with a redaction that made art out of distrust, "this emergency justification cites an 'imminent threat to critical national functions.' What was the threat?"

He cleared his throat. "Cyber risks to regional grids—"

"This is dated the same week your shop signed a sole-source with Sunward for coastal desal cartridges."

"Right," he said, blinking. "Interdependencies between grid resilience and water plants. If the grid fails, water can't be pumped; desal operations fail; health risks—"

"And the threat was imminent," she said, gentle as dull scissors.

"Yes," he said firmly. "Imminent in the sense that—"

"—in the sense of a pressing need that justified bypassing competitive bidding?" she supplied. He nodded gratefully. "Who drafted this justification?"

"Our office did," he said, then added a beat too late, "with input from stakeholders."

"Stakeholders including…?" She let her pen hover.

He looked at the ceiling, where nothing helpful had ever been written. "Agency program leads. Our partners in other departments. External technical advisors."

"From Sunward or Helios?"

"From the community," he said, which was a way of saying yes without being in contempt.

Theresa shifted almost invisibly. Camille changed angles. "Mr. Liang, did anyone instruct you to use emergency language as a matter of routine?"

"No," he said, quick and sincere on the surface. She watched the pulse of his throat. "We were told to move, because delays mean vulnerabilities."

"Who told you to move?" she asked.

"Leadership," he said. "The Deputy said—"

"Which Deputy?"

He swallowed. "Deputy Director Vass," he said, and the name sounded like a key in a door. "He said we were behind."

"Behind what?" Theresa asked, a soft assist.

"Behind the curve," he said, and then, realizing that the curve had not been defined, he added, "On resilience targets."

Camille didn't look at Theresa. "Thank you," she said. "Let's go off the record for a minute."

They went off. She let him drink water. When they came back on, she asked for the names of the external technical advisors.

He provided three companies she'd never heard of and one university lab she had. She asked for the meeting minutes. He said he'd have to check with counsel. The agency counsel, sitting like a coat draped on a chair, nodded twice in a way that meant both yes and not soon.

When Danny left, Theresa said, "He's volcanic ash. You only see the shape after it lands."

"He gave us enough," Camille said. She wrote VASS and underlined it once. "We'll subpoena."

"Already drafting," Theresa said, which was her love language.

A buzzed headline crossed Camille's screen as if it had been waiting for drama: **Solar Observatory Schedules Briefing Following 'Minor Anomalies' in Neutrino Data; Experts Stress No Immediate Risk.** The accompanying photo showed a spotless sun like an orange with a PhD. She almost laughed at the placement. Instead, she forwarded it to Noah with the caption: *Ghost particles have PR now.* He replied with a GIF of a ghost wearing a tie.

By four, Camille had written a memo in the precise tone of someone who planned to be reread. She sent it to her section chief with a page of exhibits, a recommendation for subpoenas, and a request for permission to expand the scope to include "potential undue influence by senior agency leadership in the invocation of emergency procedures." She knew the sentence would make someone swallow. She wrote it anyway.

She shut her laptop at 4:37 and went to retrieve her coat. The soccer ball rolled off the chair and bumped her shoe. She picked it up.

The soccer field was a rectangle of optimism behind the community center, its grass still winter-stiff. Javier ran in small orbit with half a dozen other ten-to-twelves, their bigness and smallness colliding in a way Camille never tired of watching. Coach Jess divided them into pinnies and non-pinnies and made them run a passing drill that looked like chaos until five passes linked and the ball snapped into the net with a sound that surprised everyone, even the net.

Noah leaned against the fence; his scarf arranged like an argument well made. He handed her a travel mug. "Decaf, but I lied to it and said it's real."

"You're a good man," she said, breathing steam. "Any parent politics?"

"Only the usual," he said. "Snacks and who gets to bring oranges and who is not respecting the Google Sheet's authority." He tilted his head toward the field. "Your progeny is engaging in late-stage capitalism."

On the field, Javier intercepted a pass, then—rather than take the shot—fed it to a smaller kid who had been running in silence. The kid shot like he'd been given a dare, and the ball went in off the post. The kids cheered as if they'd invented math. Javier jogged back, pretending he'd done nothing special. He glanced toward the sideline with that stolen look that asked if anyone had seen.

Camille had but didn't wave. She kept the approval portable for later.

"Status conference?" Noah asked. "Sixty-day discovery," she said. "Judge was in a mood to work."

"Opposing counsel?"

"The same. They want to be civilized."

"You hate when people perform reasonable," he said.

"I hate when it's a costume," she said. She took a sip and let her shoulder touch his. "We have a name."

"Vass?"

She nodded.

Noah exhaled. "Of course." He worked in city planning; names like Vass drifted across his desk too, attached to proposals that arrived fully formed and inevitable. "You think he's just forcing speed, or is there more?"

"People move things fast when they don't want questions slowing them down," she said. "Also, there's this weird phrase in the contracts: field-stabilized acceleration."

Noah squinted at the sky like the phrase might be printed on it. "Rockets?"

"That's where my head went," she said. "But these are water systems and microgrids."

"Maybe they're building the future under the cover of plumbing," he said lightly.

"Maybe." She watched Javier miss a slide tackle by a kindness. "If they are, I'd like them to follow the rules while they do it."

They ate dinner at the diner with the good pie because Tuesday had become diner night by accident and then by tradition. Javier ordered pancakes shaped like letters. He spelled **MOM** and then ate the O and told her he'd left her the M and M because she was double special.

She pretended to be insulted. Noah got the turkey club he always got and then stole her fries. They talked about nothing until it became something.

Back home, the night constructed itself out of domestic rituals: cleats by the door, a long argument with the shower about hot and cold, the sound of everybody brushing their teeth. Javier sprawled on the couch to finish math that didn't need finishing and then read under his blanket with his head where the lamp should have been and the lamp where his head was.

Camille answered one more email even though she'd promised herself she wouldn't.

At ten, with the house slowly agreeing that it was bedtime, she stood at the kitchen window and let the night be a mirror. The phone on the counter pinged once: a news app push that repeated the solar observatory's briefing schedule. She thought about neutrinos sliding through the earth. She thought about field-stabilized acceleration and how words could be a tarp or a doorway.

Noah came up behind her and wrapped his arms around her waist. "You're litigating the cosmos," he murmured.

"Only the parts that sign contracts," she said.

He rested his chin on her shoulder. "You know what I want?"

"What?"

"More time like this," he said simply. "Not the big someday. Just an unremarkable Tuesday that forgets to end."

She closed her eyes and leaned back into him. The refrigerator hummed. Somewhere upstairs Javier turned in his sleep and kicked a wall. She remembered a courtroom three hours away by fast car where a stern judge kept a meticulous time with a pencil. She remembered a deputy's signature that looked like it had learned cursive from a river.

The overhead light flickered once. But the bulb was new, and the dimmer didn't stutter, and nothing else in the house blinked. She and Noah both looked up. The light held. They looked at each other. They both did that half-laugh people do when nothing has happened and it has.

"Ghost particles," Noah said, and kissed the side of her neck.

"Ghost electricians," she corrected, and turned in his arms. The kiss was easy, and then not, and then easy again because it was them.

Upstairs, she checked on Javier, who had kicked the covers into a topography of effort. She pulled the small mountain range back over him and stood a minute listening to his sleep, the deep, even breathing of a kid completely exhausted by the day.

In bed, she read a page and a half of a novel about a museum heist and realized she could not care about stolen paintings while someone might be bartering away emergency powers for speed. She closed it and turned off the lamp. In the dark, she saw, with that clarity darkness sometimes gives, the words she would put in her next filing. They arranged themselves without adjectives and were stronger for it.

She slept, and in the hour before dawn she dreamed of doors lined across a gymnasium floor. Some opened. Some didn't. She reached for a knob and felt heat through brass. When she opened the door, it led to a field in winter where kids passed a ball five times before it hit the net. Somewhere a whistle kept blowing, though no game ever started.

A man with a pen she trusted initialed a box. The light shifted, and suddenly she had the feeling she'd missed something important.

In the morning she would wake and run her thumb down the list she'd made and call it a plan. For now, the house took her breathing like rent it could set its clocks by. Far above that roof and all the other roofs, the sun did nothing anyone in the loop would call dramatic. It only insisted on a new number in a stream of numbers that had always behaved.

Another number entered the stream.

Most people would never hear about it.

The people who did weren't worried.

Chapter 3

The Light Between Engines

Dr. Ethan Kale had always believed that propulsion was about trust. Propulsion depended on consistency.

Equations either held or they didn't.

Space—vast, cold and unsupervised—would behave the same way tomorrow as it did yesterday.

It was 5:11 a.m. in Houston, and the trust was running late.

The ion test chamber hummed behind triple glass, sealed off like a containment tank. Inside, a lattice-confined plasma loop shimmered like fog seen through oil. Instruments whispered in decimals. A tiny probe arced, stuttered, and steadied again.

"Come on, sweetheart," Ethan murmured to the loop. "Hold your shape."

On the monitor, confinement held. The emission trace leveled. He exhaled through his teeth and wrote a note in black pen even though everything auto-logged now. The physical act grounded him—ink scratching paper, pressure of nib, the little human friction that computers couldn't replicate.

The lab was still dark except for instrument glow. Somewhere in the hall, an ancient vending machine made its nightly sigh.

He turned as the access door hissed open. Mira Patel slipped in, badge reversed, hair damp from a rushed shower, eyes sharp despite the hour.

"You start without me," she said. Her voice was still wrapped in morning.

"You were on signal duty," he said. "I wasn't going to steal your sky."

She smiled. "The sky was quiet. But the background noise isn't behaving. The background signal shifted again. Same pattern as last week."

Ethan frowned. "Hardware drift?"

"Calibrations check out. If it's noise, it's a disciplined noise." She leaned beside him on the console, close enough that he could smell the leftover jasmine from her conditioner. "What did you get?"

"Stable confinement for forty-two seconds."

"Forty-two?" She raised a brow. "You stopped before the universe exploded?"

"It's a good number."

She scanned the readout, humming a soft tune that didn't belong in a lab. "Field density looks clean. You'll break a minute this week."

"If the funding board doesn't break us first," he said. "They want the power curves to match the presentation from last quarter, not the reality."

Mira's smile thinned. "Presentations are faith documents. Reality doesn't have a lobbyist."

He turned toward her. "Did you hear anything from Directorate B about the anomaly briefings?"

Her eyes flicked down. "Only that they've classified half of last month's solar telemetry. Officially 'instrument misalignment.'"

"That's comforting."

"They're calling another cross-disciplinary session next week," she said. "Helios Systems Support is sending people."

He froze for a second. "Helios—the contractor?"

"Apparently, they're doing 'consultation' on energy-field applications." She made air quotes. "Whatever that means."

Ethan looked at the window where plasma drifted along the containment edge. "They're not supposed to be anywhere near propulsion research."

"Tell that to procurement," she said quietly.

For a long moment, only the field's hum filled the lab. Then he lowered his voice. "You think Vass is behind that?"

Mira hesitated. "He's everywhere lately. Funding, infrastructure, emergency-procurement exceptions. I keep seeing his name in briefings that don't belong to him."

He rubbed his forehead. "I don't like civilians treating ion arrays like toasters."

"You don't like civilians treating anything like toasters," she teased, then softened. "Hey. Look at me."

He did.

"You've been at this since midnight," she said. "Go home for an hour. Shower. Pretend you have boundaries."

He almost smiled. "You'd miss me."

"I'd just hack your simulation."

"Same thing."

She leaned in, barely, enough for the breath between them to become its own climate. "Don't make me write another anonymous performance memo about your sleep schedule."

He laughed, too quietly. "That memo saved my job."

"Only because I signed it as your enemy."

They both knew how dangerous this was—NASA policy, internal ethics, and the way rumors could travel faster than light if given motive. But secrecy had become their gravity. It pulled them together, invisible, and absolute.

Mira looked toward the chamber. "When that field stabilizes, it'll change everything. No fuel equations, just containment. You'll write the manual."

"We," he said. "You keep giving us reasons to keep building this thing."

Her smile returned, small and real. "You really think there's someone out there?"

He hesitated. "Statistically? Yes. Emotionally? I'd rather find a human voice we sent and lost."

She looked back to the console. "Maybe we already did."

Later that morning, sunlight slanted through Building 31's glass atrium, washing the floor in sterile gold. The cafeteria buzzed with early-shift chatter. Ethan grabbed burnt coffee and joined his friend **Dr. Harold Nguyen**, a thermal engineer who could diagnose both engines and marriages.

Nguyen nodded toward the breakfast burrito untouched on Ethan's tray. "You're in love or in trouble. Possibly both."

Ethan smirked. "Define trouble."

"Budget meeting at nine," Nguyen said. "Vass himself is visiting the center. He wants a photo op with your lattice array."

"Since when does the Deputy Director of Infrastructure care about ion confinement?"

"Since someone told him it could power an ark."

Ethan blinked. "An ark?"

"Not the biblical kind. Think megaship. Rumor says they're mapping prototypes for self-sustaining transport systems. Ten-year timeline. Out of Washington, but the specs sound like someone in propulsion fed them too much optimism."

Ethan's appetite vanished completely. "Who started it?"

"No one knows. Probably black-budget chatter. You know how rumors evolve." Nguyen lowered his voice. "But if the Sun keeps misbehaving the way the observatories whisper, people upstairs will start looking for lifeboats."

Ethan stared at the floor until it stopped tilting. "The Sun's fine."

Nguyen shrugged. "Sure. Until it's not."

By ten o'clock, the conference room on Level 5 looked like every other: long table, bad carpet, optimism projected in PowerPoint. Vass arrived flanked by two aides and a smile polished by years of cameras.

He shook hands with the center director, congratulated them on "innovative resilience solutions," and gestured for Ethan to begin.

Ethan presented the data: improved field uniformity, sustained thrust, efficiency curves that finally made sense. Vass asked no technical questions, only how scalable it was, how soon it could move "mass."

"Mass?" Ethan repeated.

"Human mass," Vass said easily. "Imagine freight or passenger capability. Resilient mobility for contingency scenarios."

"That's not our directive," Ethan said. "We're proving the physics, not drafting Exodus."

The director gave him a warning glance, but Vass only smiled wider. "Vision requires physics. Keep at it, Doctor. History likes builders."

When they left, Ethan sat alone for a minute, staring at the slide still glowing on the wall: *Field-Stabilized Ion Containment—Prototype 3C.* The phrase bothered him now in a way it hadn't an hour earlier.

He remembered Mira's phrase from earlier—*classified solar telemetry.* The way she'd said it sounded like the first crack in glass.

He shut down the projector, but the light stayed in his eyes for a long time.

Mira spent that afternoon in Building 12, buried under arrays of listening servers. Her console displayed spectral bands, each a thread of noise from the deep sky. Most days they were pure chance. Today one wasn't.

A rhythmic pulse, eleven milliseconds apart, cutting through the background hiss of the cosmic microwave band.

She reran the filter twice. Same result.

"Mira?" her supervisor called from across the room. "Everything good?"

"Just a calibration," she said, saving the file under an innocuous name: *thermal_burst_setB*. She exported the raw sequence to an encrypted drive and slipped it into her pocket.

Later, after the building emptied and the night security lights flicked to half, she met Ethan in the parking lot where floodlamps turned cars into metallic ghosts.

"You're pale," he said.

"Listen." She handed him a pair of earbuds and played the converted audio. The pulses translated into a series of clicks—regular, insistent, almost linguistic.

"What am I hearing?"

"Something from out there," she said quietly. "Twenty light-years maybe. The pattern matches no known natural signature. And when I cross-referenced its timing with solar neutrino spikes—"

He stared at her. "They match?"

"Perfectly."

A cold wind cut across the lot. In the distance, the sound of a freight train rolled like slow thunder.

Ethan pulled the earbuds out. "If you're right, someone—or something—knows what's happening to the Sun."

She looked up at him. "And they're trying to tell us."

Neither of them spoke for a second.

Inside the locked lab, Ethan powered the confinement chamber again. Blue plasma rolled through it. Mira stood beside him, the drive in her hand.

He said softly, "You think the pattern's a map?"

"Maybe a warning. Maybe an invitation."

"Either way," he said, "we'd need engines that actually work."

She smiled, half-sad. "Good thing you build both."

Through the glass, the field brightened, filament thin, trembling but whole. Numbers on the console kept climbing past the expected limits. For a breathless moment, everything held.

Then a blip on the solar monitor in the corner flashed red: **ANOMALY DETECTED—NEUTRINO FLUX VARIATION 4.2%.**

They both stared.

"Again?" Ethan whispered.

Mira nodded, pulse quickening. "Same signature."

On the screen, the plasma flickered once, twice—and steadied, stronger than before, stronger than the previous runs for reasons neither of them understood.

Outside, dawn burned a shade too bright for February.

And somewhere in the quiet corridors of NASA's servers, a new file auto-generated in a folder labeled *Helios Systems Support / Field-Stabilized Acceleration: Phase 1 Integration.*

The alarm was silent, a polite red strobe near the ceiling that blinked twice, paused, and blinked again—the system's way of saying *we saw something, we're not panicking yet.*

Ethan reached the terminal first.

"Flux variance still climbing," he said. "Sensors say 4.2, but the readout's lagging. Look—the chamber's output shifted with the solar spike."

Mira leaned in. The curve on the monitor had stopped jittering and begun to pulse with uncanny rhythm. A heartbeat. It wasn't random; the system had stopped fighting the fluctuation and started adapting to it.

"That's impossible," she whispered. "The chamber isn't connected to anything external."

Ethan stared at the monitor.

"Then explain that."

For a moment, neither spoke. The plasma ring in the test chamber glowed brighter, casting pale light over their faces. The changing plasma light made the shadows jerk across the walls.

Mira's voice softened. "You think the signal—whatever it is—just modulated the field?"

"I think it *recognized* it," Ethan said. "Like resonance. You sing the right note, the glass sings back."

The field expanded fractionally—two millimeters, maybe less—but the sensors screamed for calibration. The confinement metrics stayed stable. Too stable. No thermal rise, just more energy from nowhere.

He typed a command to dump the raw data into an isolated buffer. The terminal resisted—error code 47C, external lock.

"Who locked this node?" he muttered.

Mira frowned. "We're offline. This lab isn't even supposed to be connected to the Directorate's grid."

Ethan tried a manual override. The same error flashed, followed by a line that made his stomach drop: **REMOTE PROCESS INITIATED — ACCESS: VASS.G**

Mira stepped closer. "Gregor Vass?"

He nodded slowly. "Either him or someone using his credentials."

They both stared at the screen as the system uploaded the last thirty seconds of experiment data to a remote repository. Then the red strobe turned green again, as if nothing had happened.

Mira backed away. "He's monitoring propulsion research?"

"He's monitoring *us*," Ethan said.

The air in the lab felt thicker, like the building itself was listening. He killed the power to the chamber, letting the hum collapse into silence. The plasma ring faded, leaving a ring of afterglow behind his eyelids.

"I need to get that data before it's scrubbed," he said. "If they're pulling it to Helios's servers, it'll vanish."

Mira reached into her pocket and produced the small, encrypted drive she'd used earlier. "Copy from the local cache," she said. "Before it syncs."

He connected it, fingers moving fast. The console hissed warnings, permissions denied, then relented. A progress bar crept forward, heartbeat to heartbeat. 73%. 81%. 94%. Complete.

He ejected the drive and handed it back. "Keep that somewhere not digital."

"Paper and lead box," she said, tucking it into her lab coat.

A silence filled the room—one of those silences that carried weight, like the kind of silence where both people are thinking too hard.

Mira finally spoke. "You realize if Vass has a feed into the propulsion lab, he's running something bigger than energy research."

"He's building hardware for an event no one's admitted is happening."

"Or already happened," she said.

He looked at her. "Meaning?"

She hesitated. "What if the Sun isn't changing naturally?"

Ethan ran a hand through his hair. "You're suggesting someone—or something—did this to the Sun?"

"I'm saying the timing's too precise. The pulse we recorded last week lined up perfectly with a CME that shouldn't have existed. Like it was *signaling*."

"From where?" he asked.

She didn't answer.

Instead, she walked to the observation glass, staring at the chamber's fading blue. "When I was a kid," she said quietly, "I thought scientists would always know what the sky was doing. That the Sun would be the one constant."

Ethan joined her, standing close but not touching. "Maybe it still is. Maybe we just stopped understanding the system we depend on."

She gave a faint laugh. "You always make existential dread sound poetic."

"Occupational hazard."

They stood like that for a while, the lab's machinery ticking as it cooled, the faint hiss of the air recyclers the only sound.

Then Mira said, "If he's watching this feed, he'll know we powered down early. We need to act like everything went normal."

Ethan nodded. "I'll file a dummy report."

"And I'll log the signal as atmospheric interference. If I flag it, they'll bury it faster."

He turned to her. "You trust me?"

"With my clearance," she said. Then, softer, "And maybe a little more."

He reached for her hand, quick, invisible to any camera. "We'll figure it out. Just don't listen to any more ghosts without me."

She smiled at that, but her eyes were somewhere else— still replaying the pattern in her head.

When they left the lab, dawn had matured into an empty, indifferent morning. The parking lot shimmered with heat already rising from concrete. Workers streamed toward the main gate, badges swinging, lives ticking along like metronomes.

Ethan squinted up at the sun. It looked ordinary enough—bright, predictable, and merciless. But as he watched, he thought he saw heat shimmer across the sky.

He blinked. It was gone.

Mira locked her car. "Don't stare too long," she said. "You'll start seeing things that aren't there."

"Or maybe we'll finally see what is."

They drove in separate directions, each already deciding what they would leave out of the reports.

Neither noticed the small satellite just beyond low Earth orbit pivoting its dish fifteen degrees toward the Sun, then twenty toward a dark stretch of space near Gliese 581. Its telemetry tag read **SUNWARD–A13**, a contractor unit leased to Helios Systems Support.

At 05:34:21 UTC, it began transmitting a packet of encoded data—the same file Mira had recorded in the lab, altered by distance but mathematically identical.

Chapter 4

Vass, Inc.

The Architect of Power

The city woke beneath him like a patient machine. From the seventy-third floor of Vass Global's tower, Gregor Vass watched dawn unspool across steel and glass until the streets began to shine. He'd always preferred this hour—when the world still looked programmable, when traffic was a flow-chart and people were dots waiting for instruction.

He believed in systems the way some men believed in God. Systems were immortal; individuals were just data points. Money, law, energy, war—each could be converted into the other with sufficient throughput. He'd learned that young, selling diesel on a black market where invoices arrived in bullets and payment in vodka. Survival came first. Everything else got polished afterward.

The glass reflected him faintly: a tall, spare man in a charcoal suit that looked poured on, a silver streak in his hair that barbers tried to hide and he insisted they leave. He preferred visible wear to cosmetic lies. He straightened his cuffs, glanced once at the skyline, and turned as the door slid open.

Tarek entered, tablet in hand, nerves hidden under precision. "Morning, sir."

"Tell me something efficient."

"The A13 telemetry came through. The Houston confinement test sustained above-expected field density for forty-two seconds before manual shutdown. No anomalies reported by the team. Our copy's secured."

"Forty-two," Vass repeated. "I do like symmetry." He crossed to the desk and flicked the holographic display awake. Three corporate logos glowed across the display.

Helios Systems Support
Sunward Environmental
Vass Global Infrastructure

His trinity.

Tarek waited for instructions.

"Begin rollout of Sunward's new campaign—resilient desalination, adaptive food webs, whatever slogan the ministry approves. Greenwashing buys silence."

"Yes, sir."

"And Helios?"

"They've completed the orbital mesh assembly schedule. Prototype scaffolds ready by next quarter."

Vass nodded, half-smile thin as filament. "Then, all this finally starts moving."

He dismissed Tarek with a gesture and lingered alone for a minute. The office smelled faintly of ozone from the servers behind the wall—his private data core, air-gapped from every network. He liked that smell. It meant power contained.

He pressed a hidden key beneath the desk edge. The orrery on the credenza began to move, brass planets circling in patient obedience. It had belonged to his father, a mechanical engineer who'd once built turbines for a country that no longer existed. The gears whispered. Every revolution was predictable, dependable, finite—until it wasn't.

"Stay polite a little longer," he murmured to the miniature Sun.

An Ordinary Monster

Home lay thirty kilometers outside the city, an estate built on the bones of an old vineyard. The vines were gone, replaced by manicured terraces and a private landing pad, but the soil still remembered work. Elena Vass said she could smell it after rain; he wasn't sure he believed her.

He arrived by heli-car at 7:10, descending into morning fog that smelled faintly of metal and lavender. House AI unlocked the doors before his shoes touched gravel. Inside: silence, curated like art. Even the clocks ticked discreetly.

His wife was in the kitchen, barefoot, robe tied with negligent grace. She poured coffee from a French press older than their marriage.

"You're early," she said without turning. "That means you didn't sleep."

"I optimized," he said.

Elena laughed under her breath. "Do you ever speak like a human anymore?"

"Only when it helps."

He accepted the cup she handed him. Steam curled between them, brief and warm. She was still beautiful in the unglamorous way of people who stopped caring about mirrors: soft hair, sharp eyes, patience that had turned into a kind of quiet rebellion.

"Zurich today?" she asked.

He nodded. "Midday. Back by evening."

"The boys have fencing after school. They'd like to know if you'll come watch."

"Scheduling conflict."

"They always have a scheduling conflict named Gregor Vass," she said lightly, but her hands tightened on the counter.

He sipped coffee instead of answering. Love, he'd decided long ago, was an arrangement of tolerances: how much imperfection you allowed before seeking replacement parts.

Footsteps thundered down the stairs—Anton, sixteen, already taller than his father but still trying to earn the right to stand that way. Behind him, Marko, fifteen, carrying a drone controller like an extra limb.

"Morning, Dad," Anton said, breathless. "Coach says if I keep form like this, I could make nationals next year."

"Discipline makes probability," Vass said.

Anton hesitated, then smiled uncertainly. "Right. Probability."

Marko hovered near the doorway, half-listening. "Can I use the lower field for flight tests after class?"

"Check airspace restrictions. I don't want interference with the pad."

"Yes, sir." Not *Dad*. Always *sir*.

From the corner, a small voice: "Papa?"

Lia, eight years old, hair a riot of curls, stood clutching a stuffed fox. She'd inherited Elena's quiet, not Gregor's precision. She rarely spoke above a whisper unless it was about weather.

"What is it, Lia?"

"Storm coming," she said.

He frowned toward the window. Sky was clean. "No, sweetheart. Clear all day."

She shook her head solemnly. "Not that kind."

Elena looked up, one eyebrow raised. "She dreams in metaphors now. Must get it from you."

Vass crouched, smoothed Lia's hair. "Dreams are early warnings," he said, and surprised himself by meaning it.

When they left for school, Elena lingered at the doorway. "Gregor," she said softly. "If something's coming, tell me the truth. You don't have to protect us with silence."

He met her eyes. She'd always been too perceptive for comfort. "If there's a storm," he said, "I'm building the shelter."

"That's what worries me," she replied, and closed the door gently between them.

He stood in the foyer for a long moment, coffee cooling in his hand, the scent of lavender already fading. Then his wrist display chimed—**Marian Soto waiting, Compliance Division.** He turned toward the study. Work was simpler than family; equations didn't argue.

Compliance Division

Marian Soto preferred paper to screens. Vass respected that, the way a chess player respects a knife. She was waiting in his study when he entered—dark suit, hair pulled tight, a thin stack of neat folders on her lap and nothing on the desk. She liked to make executives feel the absence of their toys.

"Morning, Marian," he said, closing the door himself. "Let's dispense with pleasantries."

"We would only waste yours," she said, rising. Her voice carried the neutral consonants of a dozen countries. Ex–counterintelligence, decades ago; then internal security for a bank that had technically never laundered anything; then Vass. She'd made him safer three times he could name and a dozen he could infer.

"They're coming," she said, and placed the stack on the desk. "Justice. Procurement Integrity and a tandem from Public Corruption. Lead AUSA is Camille Rios."

"I know the name," Vass said. He sat, steepling his fingers. "Earnest. Competent."

"Dangerous," Marian corrected. "She doesn't waste adjectives and she asks for calendars instead of speeches." She slid a page forward.

"Her paralegal built a 'linkage' matrix she shouldn't have been able to assemble from public filings. They're getting close to Sunward and Helios."

"Sniffing or biting?"

"Sniffing with teeth out." A small smile, almost pleased. "They'll subpoena in a week."

"Which they will serve on the agency," Vass said. "Not on us."

"Of course." Marian returned the smile to storage. "The agency will produce what you want them to produce if we're first to their inbox. But there's an added complication." Another page surfaced: a photo of two people outside a federal courthouse—Rios and a woman beside her, young, tightly focused. "This one's the paralegal. Very good at noticing repeated phrases, and she hasn't learned to be bored yet."

"Then we will teach her." Vass leaned back. "What do you propose?"

Marian opened the top folder. Inside: a neat dossier with an almost generous amount of incriminating detail—shell corporations tied to a rival logistics firm that had moulted into "green consulting" last year, kickback language in emails no one should have written, a set of invoices that lined up too well with two mortgages and a boat.

"The opponent," she said, tapping the folder. "Kronstadt Integrated. They've been trying to penetrate our Gulf contracts for twelve months. Their compliance officer is sloppy, and their CEO's brother has a taste for mountains of white. We feed Rios a breadcrumb trail that begins with Kronstadt's emergency procurements and ends with a luxury marina. She will follow it because it's real."

"Because it's real," Vass repeated. It pleased him as an aesthetic. "And the agency?"

"We give them a short list of requested documents to prioritize. We flag our own shells as low-risk placeholders—boring, fully amortized projects with outcomes no one will want to read. We let Kronstadt glow."

Vass considered. "And the signatures?"

"Your recusals are clean enough," Marian said. "But we should refresh your travel logs. Zurich will be listed under the Global Sustainability Alliance—no names, no minutes."

"Make sure the Alliance looks naive," Vass said. "Earnest men love earnest letters."

Marian nodded. "One more thing." She slid the last folder across. Inside: a printout of a screenshot—terminal text, the sort of thing only a systems person would find handsome. **REMOTE PROCESS INITIATED — ACCESS: VASS.G**

Vass didn't reach for it. "Where?"

"Houston lab. Last night. Someone saw your credentials in a data transfer. They won't have the file—it was an internal cache—but they saw the tag."

"They?" he asked.

"Two names I don't have to tell you," she said. "Kale and Patel."

He let the smallest silence pass. "Good."

Marian watched him. "Good?"

"If they're that close to the flame, they'll work harder to keep it. Fear breeds secrecy. Secrecy breeds velocity." He finally touched the page, then pushed it back. "Still. Quarantine the Helios relay. I want all lab pulls re-credentialed to a dead shell in two hours."

"I already did," Marian said. "And scrubbed Vass. G from the rotating banner. We'll use *H. Somerville* for two weeks."

"A poet," he said.

"Your age is showing," she replied, and the corner of her mouth nearly moved.

"Anything else?"

She hesitated, which meant yes. "Your wife asked me who I am."

"When?"

"Yesterday. In the kitchen. She made me tea."

"And what did you tell her?"

"That I'm your auditor." No inflection.

"And did she believe you?"

"She believes you don't hire auditors for their math." Marian closed her binder. "Zurich in four hours. I'll be on the plane with the dissent files."

"Dissent?"

"A list of people in the room who will try to grow a conscience." Marian paused at the door. "I know what we're building," she said quietly. "But if you want it to live, you'll need true believers, not only contractors."

"True believers," Vass said. "I have you."

"You have me until it costs more than it buys." She opened the door and left, a small woman carrying several wars.

Vass stared at the empty doorway. Then he picked up the family photo from his desk—his daughter's hair blown across her mouth, his sons turned halfway toward some off-camera dare, Elena mid-laugh. He replaced it face down again, not out of contempt but logistics.

On the way to the helipad, he composed a note on his implant.

To: Legal. *In the event of inquiry from DOJ, provide:1) Kronstadt package; 2) Sunward deliverables catalogue (nontechnical); 3) Helios invoices with blacklines to demonstrate humility.*

He sent it before the doors opened.

The Zurich Directive (part one)

The jet flew a high arc over the Atlantic, shadowing a commercial corridor then peeling north to stitch a line no one monitored. Vass reviewed the deck in silence while Tarek adjusted lighting and temperature until the cabin admitted no distractions. The world below wore cloud like gauze. He slept for forty minutes—not rest so much as a strategic reboot.

Zurich greeted them. The Grand Arcadian's conference level was a machine that made confidentiality feel natural: muted art, staff whose eyes knew how to be present, soundproofing that made footsteps consider their options.

They gathered in a room that faced the lake. Twelve seats, each placard bearing a name someone in a newspaper would recognize and a title a newspaper would not properly translate.

He entered last, on purpose. Simply to ensure that their conversations had already braided reference to him into every sentence. It's easier to guide a river once it's moving.

"Ladies and gentlemen," he said, taking the center chair rather than the head. "Thank you for your discretion."

To his left sat Amal Annand, CEO of AgrisNova. Next came Lars Breinnard, the Belgian energy minister whose cufflinks broadcast compliance; Yiumi Aiokki, deputy director from Japan's aerospace ministry; Rafael Ibáñes, head of TransNationalMed Logistics; Dr. Samjaira Quureshi, a South African chemist; Olmair Rashman, telecom magnate; Ingrid Schoultz from Arctic shipping; Jean-Paul Deflacourt of the European food cooperatives; two observers whose badges offered only acronyms and the consent of silence; and, at the far end, Dr. Ibrahim al-Frabrouq, a systems ecologist who had become the moralist of last resort in rooms like this.

Tarek dimmed the glass behind them to a sheen. Vass spoke without the deck at first.

"You've all seen the neutrino and helioseismology packets. Some of you forwarded them to juniors with notes like 'model this without spooking anyone.'" A few smiles, unowned. "The signal is real. The timing is…ungracious. The public will not be told until 'anomalies' graduate into 'concern.' That buys us time. We don't have time to turn this into a public science lesson."

He nodded to Tarek. The first slide appeared: a clean, elegant graph that refused to look apocalyptic. "Our projection—built from independent observatories, not reliant on any one nation—shows boundary instability accelerating. We will debate whether it's eight years or twelve until the day after the event. What matters is that the event does not wait for our comfort."

"Assuming your curve is honest," Breinnard said, adjusting his cuffs, "what are you proposing we do *now* that doesn't look like panic?"

"Build infrastructure that the public will applaud," Vass said evenly. "Shipyards for 'ocean platforms' that are, in fact, hull foundries. Orbital debris cleanup that becomes scaffold assembly. A desal revolution that seeds atmosphere loops. You keep your logos; we keep the schedule."

Yiumi Aiokki's chin lifted a degree. "You're talking about a mobilization on a scale that would bankrupt nations."

"Nations," Vass said, "are already bankrupt. They just haven't published the footnotes. You, on the other hand, sit on pools of liquidity large enough to float continents." He let his gaze drift around the table. "You can either become museums of what used to be, or patrons of what will be necessary."

Samjaira Quureshi leaned in, eyes bright. "And who decides the design? Engineers or accountants?"

"Both," Vass said. "Engineers dictate what can survive. Accountants enforce what can be built before the deadline."

"And the population," Deflacourt said, voice low. "You cannot dodge it forever. Who boards your—what did you call them?—arks?"

"The Aegis series," Vass said. "Nominal capacity: two million per vessel."

Amal Annand let out a low whistle that contained both awe and disgust. "And Earth holds eight billion."

"Not all eight billion want to leave," Vass said. "Not all eight billion can live on a ship. We preserve capability first. Medicine. Engineering. Agriculture. Governance. Enough culture to survive the crossing."

He glanced around the table.

"The alternative is extinction with excellent ethics."

Ibrahim al-Frabrouq tapped his pen once, twice, then laid it down as if placing a scalpel. "You are proposing triage for a species," he said. "You'll call it merit and necessity," Ibrahim said. "But power always writes the boarding list."

Vass met his gaze. "Doctor, I'm proposing a nonzero outcome."

A pause. The sentence had the weight of a verdict.

"Even if your numbers are right," Breinnard said, "states will demand control. You're talking about building this in public without admitting what it is."

"Not hide," Vass said. "Explain. Everything already exists," Vass said. "Climate infrastructure. Microgrids. Resilience initiatives. Public-private partnerships. You've all sold versions of this already."

He folded his hands.

"We simply build the real version underneath it."

Yiumi folded her hands. "My ministry will require a public mandate. Parliaments do not like surprises."

"Then give them none," Vass said. "Announce the creation of a Global Sustainability Alliance. You chair the atmospheric panel. Doctor Quureshi chairs water. Breinnard chairs energy. We draft a charter that reads like therapy. We hold conferences. We fund scholarships. We weep when appropriate."

"And in the annex," Olmair Rashman said dryly, "we scribble the coordinates of the scaffolds."

"Not in the annex," Vass said. "In your heads." He let his voice soften a degree. "I am not asking you to be villains. I am asking you to be adults."

Ibrahim breathed out through his nose. "Adults tell the truth to children."

"When we have a plan children can survive," Vass said.

It was a line, crafted in advance, and it landed where it needed to. Several heads dipped as if the room had found gravity.

Tarek advanced the deck again—shipping routes, inspection cover stories, financing structures disguised as climate initiatives.

Amal Annand broke the quiet. "If I sign this, I want guarantees. No one starves because an energy minister wants to win a vote."

"You will run the food loops," Vass said. "On Aegis One and Two. If an energy minister wants food, he will ask you. Politely."

Samjaira Quureshi smiled without warmth. "We'll need algae mass. Plenty. Your donors won't like that in the brochures."

"We will not print algae on the brochures," Vass said. "We will print children painting gardens."

Breinnard's phone vibrated; he ignored it. "My risk committee will ask for moral cover."

"Then I'll give you a scandal," Vass said. "Not yours. Someone else's. Big enough to run interference for three news cycles. You all know how that works."

Ibrahim picked up his pen again and spun it, then set it down. "You know you will have to choose who *doesn't* board," he said, looking not at Vass but at the window, where the lake kept pretending it had time. "You talk about culture and medicine and law. Someone will ask about poets and teachers. Someone will ask about plumbers. Someone will ask about thieves."

"Eventually, we'll need all of them."

A pause.

"At the start, we won't."

The room exhaled as one organism. Nobody objected again.

"Vote," he said.

They didn't raise hands; that would imply a ritual they could later disown. They nodded, each in their own language: a slow incline, a resigned blink, a small grunt, the lack of a no. When they were done, the air pressure seemed to change.

"Unanimous," Tarek announced, because someone had to.

Vass stood, smoothing his jacket. "Then we begin. Publicly—Alliance charter, quarterly summits, a thousand scholarships. Privately—dockyards in four countries, scaffolds tested in polar orbits, and a procurement lattice that feeds without leaving fingerprints."

He looked at each of them in turn. "We will be thanked for a decade. We will be cursed for a century. We will be necessary for both."

He gave them time to imagine themselves in history. Men and women at this altitude craved that more than profit. Profit was simply the right to choose their seat.

Outside, snow began to fall, singles and doubles tapping the glass. Zurich had the decency to provide scenery.

Vass signaled to Tarek. "Bring in the map," he said.

The wall behind them resolved into a starfield. A red pin pulsed at a familiar coordinate: **Gliese 581**. A second pin blinked between Earth and its star, where no geography existed. **SUN: active variance**.

"For morale," Vass said lightly, "we'll call the first vessel *Aegis*. Protective connotations.

He closed the deck. The meeting dissolved into sub-conclaves—energy huddling with shipping, water with agriculture, telecom with the men from unnamable agencies. Vass excused himself first, as he always did after momentum made his presence decorative. Power stayed in the room anyway, an aroma.

In the corridor, he stopped beside a large, indifferent painting of a mountain and sent Marian a message: **Zurich: unanimous. Move Phase Genesis to green. Preload dissent files to their devices as reading they think they found.**

She replied at once: **Done. DOJ clock: T–6 days. Kronstadt package staged.**

He typed: If Rios is smarter than advertised?

Marian: Then we'll meet her in a courtroom we already rented.

Vass put the phone away and watched the snow, trying to decide if it looked like grace or ash.

The others filed out in pairs, murmuring behind the closed doors of their own security details. Vass remained near the window until the reflections stopped moving; only then did he turn back to the table. He always stayed until the oxygen in a room remembered it belonged to him.

"Send in Dr. Ibrahim," he told Tarek.

The ecologist entered slowly, a man carrying a moral weight he still hoped was useful. His palms were flat on the folder in front of him. Vass gestured to a seat, poured two glasses of water, and set one within reach.

"I expected you to walk out," Vass said.

"I still might." Ibrahim's accent carried the sand and English boarding schools of two continents. "You know what this becomes. Who chooses gets to play God."

Vass sat across from him, calm as a ledger. "There's a difference between playing God and cleaning up after one."

"You think you're cleaning up?"

"I think I'm doing the arithmetic no one else will touch."

Ibrahim stared at the water, at the thin ripple that formed whenever the hotel's ventilation sighed.

"When I was a student, a mentor told me that ethics is the science of not sleeping at night. Do you sleep, Mr. Vass?"

"Perfectly," Vass said. "Because I separate choice from noise. I don't moralize gravity. It falls either way."

He stood, ending the conversation by moving. "You'll stay with us, Doctor. We'll need someone to design ecosystems that don't depend on weather."

"And if I refuse?"

"Then I'll fund a younger version of you who hasn't learned despair yet. You've written enough to seed her career." He smiled, almost kind. "Don't waste a legacy."

When Ibrahim left, Vass felt the slight tremor of victory—the one that came not from coercion but inevitability. He stepped out into the corridor, where the others waited in fragments: Breinnard whispering into a secure phone, Aiokki and Quureshi sketching a list of candidate labs, Amal Annand standing by the window with her reflection folded into the snow.

"Ms. Annand," he said.

She turned. "You just sold humanity a ticket it can't afford."

"Then they'll pay in installments."

Her expression softened to something almost weary. "There's a line between necessary and monstrous, Mr. Vass. You talk like someone who erased it."

"I drew it farther away," he said. "It gives us room to work."

Aftermath in the Air

The jet lifted at dusk, Zurich a bowl of light shrinking behind them. Tarek sealed the cabin, dimmed it to a private twilight, and poured Vass his customary rye.

On the console lay a single slate—no slides, no minutes, only a memo title: **PRINCIPLES OF CONTINUITY.** The document was still blank.

Outside the window, the clouds burned copper in the last light, like a field of coins upended by an invisible hand. Vass dictated slowly, voice steady, the words transcribed in silence by the system.

1. Continuity is the only morality. Survival justifies its method.
2. Information must be curated, not shared. Transparency is entropy.
3. Fear is fuel. Harness, do not extinguish.
4. Governance must remain invisible until gratitude is impossible.
5. Select for competence first, fertility second, conscience last.
6. Redundancy is not waste. It is memory with a backup.
7. Prophets destroy logistics. Replace them with accountants.
8. No ark is sacred. Each is an experiment.
9. History forgives only the victors who keep records.
10. When order collapses, begin again from Principle 1.

He read it once, nodded, and encrypted the file into the secure archive labeled *Genesis: Philosophy.*

Tarek returned from the cockpit. "Weather front ahead, sir. Minor turbulence."

"I've lived through worse," Vass said. "Sit."

Tarek hesitated, then obeyed, taking the seat across. He was thirty, brilliant, still convinced that serving Vass meant proximity to destiny rather than danger.

"Tell me," Vass said, "why do you work for me?"

Tarek blinked. "You build things that last."

"No one else does?"

"Not on this scale."

Vass regarded him. "What you call scale, others call sin."

Tarek smiled faintly. "History keeps both words."

"You'll need to decide which one you prefer on your gravestone," Vass said. "When we reach orbit, every name will matter again."

He looked out the window, at the thin stars pricking through the dark. Somewhere among them, Gliese 581 hung invisible, its borrowed light arriving late to every conversation.

Tarek cleared his throat. "Sir... do you believe the Sun is really dying?"

Vass turned the glass in his hand, watching the liquid settle. "Everything ends eventually. I just prefer preparation to surprise."

The turbulence came then—a brief, hard shudder that rattled the silverware. The pilot's voice murmured over the intercom: *"Crosswinds, nothing serious."*

Vass closed his eyes. In the flicker behind his eyelids he saw not snow or stars but a kitchen in Belgrade, the year he was nine. The sirens had started without warning, a sound that changed the air into metal. His mother had shouted for him to take the bread and run. When the blast came, it took the windows and the smell of yeast with it. He had kept the loaf until it turned black, because it was the last thing that felt certain. Entropy had tasted like ash ever since.

He opened his eyes. "How long to New York?"

"Seven hours," Tarek said.

"Wake me at six."

He reclined the seat, but sleep came like a contract—conditional, weighted with fine print.

The Principles of Continuity

He dreamed of a shoreline littered with the skeletons of ships. In the dream he walked between them, touching hulls that hummed faintly with stored power. Each bore a different name—Aegis, Haven, Erebus—and beneath the paint the metal glowed like skin remembering blood. The horizon was wrong: too close, too curved. The sea was space, thick and glittering. He kept walking until the names began to repeat.

When he woke, the cabin was dark except for a single instrument glow. The jet was level again, the rhythm of engines steady and low. He checked the slate; a new message waited from Helios HQ.

Transmission Log A13 – Signal Correlation Confirmed.

Repeat interval: 24 hours + 0.03 seconds.

Power increase ≈ 2.1%. Origin triangulated between Solar CME vector and Gliese 581.

He read it twice; the numbers clean as scripture. The message wasn't just echoing—it was growing. He forwarded it to no one. Ownership began with silence.

He unlatched the shade. The horizon was beginning to silver, the first smear of dawn over the Atlantic. For an instant, the light looked fractured, as though the Sun itself was breathing through cracks. Then the color normalized. Optical illusion, he told himself. Atmospheric refraction. Nothing poetic.

He closed the slate, poured another inch of rye, and whispered the first words of a new principle he hadn't dared to record, yet:

11. When the signal returns, answer politely.

He drank to that.

Return to Origin

The jet touched down before dawn at a private strip on Long Island, a long strip of tarmac glistening with frost. Ground lights glowed a faint amber, soft enough not to draw satellite curiosity. Vass stepped out into cold that bit through his suit and felt the city breathing just beyond the horizon.

A motorcade waited, but he waved it off. One car would do. Tarek, exhausted, slept sitting upright in the rear seat while the driver traced a quiet route into Manhattan. Through the tinted glass the skyline rose, familiar as a graph he'd already solved.

The sun had not yet cleared the buildings; the streets looked carved from graphite.

At Forty-Third and Lex, he told the driver to stop. Across the street, the windows of a bakery were just fogging from the first batch of bread. He got out, stood a moment in the sharp air, and let the scent hit him. Warm yeast. Memory. He bought a loaf without speaking, handed the baker a bill too large, and carried it back to the car like evidence.

"Home first," he told the driver.

Domestic Orbit

Elena was awake, sitting on the veranda wrapped in one of Lia's blankets. The morning light touched her hair with silver. She didn't look surprised to see him.

"You were gone two nights," she said.

He offered the bread. "Zurich had questions."

"They always do." She tore the loaf, handed him half. Steam rose between them. "It's cold. Sit."

He sat. For a long moment neither spoke. The house behind them murmured—coffee machines, distant footsteps, a door closing somewhere upstairs.

She glanced sideways at him. "The children think you build space stations."

He smiled faintly. "Do they?"

"They think you're saving the world. I told them you were saving your reputation."

"That might be the same thing," he said.

"No." She looked past him to the line of trees where fog clung like regret. "A reputation can survive lies. A world can't."

He turned the loaf in his hands, crumbs falling onto the marble rail. "You always were the poet."

"And you the engineer," she said. "Just remember which of us builds bridges and which burns them."

When she went inside, he stayed a few minutes longer, watching the sun rise cleanly over the ridge. Its light looked ordinary again, and that was somehow worse.

The Machine Beneath

By midmorning he was in the elevator of Helios Tower, fifty-four stories of glass and quiet money. The walls carried no logos; only a single inscription near the entrance read **INNOVATION IS OXYGEN.** He'd chosen it himself—sincere enough to disarm, vague enough to mean anything.

Marian Soto was waiting in the sublevel control room. She looked like she hadn't slept, which suited him; paranoia was her virtue.

"The Zurich charter leaked to the press this morning," she said. "Front page of the Journal. They're calling it 'The Green Marshall Plan.'"

"Good," Vass said. "Let them applaud the decoy."

She handed him a tablet. "Satellite images from the Arctic corridor. The first platforms have broken surface. Ice cover hides most of it, but the foundations are set."

On the screen, the photograph showed a cluster of enormous structures half-buried in ice—aerial cranes, scaffolds, cranes again. Workers looked like ants under floodlights. The caption read **SUSTAINABILITY ALLIANCE – POLAR RESEARCH STATION.**

"They'll ask what we're studying," Marian said.

"Resilience," Vass said. "The public likes the word."

"And the signal?"

He met her eyes. "Still repeating."

Marian hesitated. "If it isn't natural—"

"It doesn't matter what it is," he said. "It's proof that someone, somewhere, learned to speak across light-years. That's enough to justify escape."

She nodded, closed the folder, and left him with the image.

He walked to the observation window that faced the East River. Barges moved slowly below, lines of cargo containers stacked like coded words. Among them were Helios shipments labeled **OCEANIC DATA ARRAYS**, their manifests signed off by half the consortium he'd just left. Inside those containers lay the first segments of the Aegis hull.

He allowed himself a small breath of satisfaction. Motion was all that mattered now; morality could catch up later, if it survived the trip.

The Light Returns

That night he stood alone on the roof of the tower. The city below flickered like circuitry, each window a diode in his private machine. Wind tugged at his coat. He looked up through thin haze, found the Sun as a pale coin hanging above dawn's leftover color, and raised a hand as though measuring it.

For a second—only a second—the disk shimmered, a pulse too quick for any camera. The same rhythm as the signal. Forty-two beats and then stillness. He smiled, not because he understood it, but because it kept time with his heart.

Far north, under the Arctic ice, floodlights burned through fog as machines groaned into life. Steel rose against the cold, the first ribs of a vessel no one on Earth would yet admit existed. On its hull a stencil glowed in white paint:

Aegis I — Resilience Platform.

Snow drifted across the letters, erasing them one grain at a time, but the sound of construction went on and on.

Chapter 5

First-Year Sky

Campus Morning

The quad pretended at spring even though the trees were still hoarding their leaves. Students crossed in diagonals with the stubborn confidence of people who had learned the campus clock's lies. A musician practiced scales under the statue of a founder who had never been late to anything. Bicycles clicked like patient metronomes. The air smelled like espresso and white-board markers and the damp of a field that would not fully dry until May.

Ana Okoye balanced a tray in the biology building café, a topographical map of student life: coffee, muffin, a plastic tub of lab fruit that pretended to be health. She found a table near the window, texted her mother a photo of the sunrise because they collected them, then opened her notebook to a page titled **Algae + Hope**.

Her capstone was as unfashionable as it was necessary: high-yield, low-water spirulina strains that didn't taste like pond and wouldn't mutiny under shipboard lights. Her advisor, Professor Mendez, had called it *"boring in all the lifesaving ways."* The compliment had landed like a job offer from the future.

Ana wrote three bullets: *resilience under variable lux; protein density; palatability.* She underlined palatability twice. No one wanted to live on food that tasted like punishment.

Across campus, in a math lounge where the walls were blackboards and the chalk was never where you left it, Mateo Lin worked a problem that had refused to be solved the night before.

He was tall in the way that made doors feel short, with hair that refused consensus. On the board, an integral unfurled like a climbing plant; beside it, a graph with small teeth. He'd titled it **Noise vs. Signal (Campus Edition)** as a joke to himself. The actual problem was prettier: a method to extract periodicity from hostile data without lying.

He stepped back. The pattern wanted to be circular. He drew a circle. The circle wanted to be a heartbeat. He erased it, annoyed at the metaphor, and laughed alone. The department secretary poked her head in. "Lin, your TA section starts in ten. Hide your genius."

"Nothing to hide," he said. "It hasn't shown up yet."

In the chemistry wing, Priya Narayanan scanned a row of flasks as if listening for gossip. Her bench was a government in miniature: labeled, rational, mean when crossed. She adjusted a condenser, checked the pH, and jotted a note on a lab pad already crowded with her tidy handwriting. *Nitrogen yield stable. Off-flavor compound still present at low ppm. Smell: wet cardboard with ambition.* She circled *ambition* and added a frowny face for her future self.

"Deshmukh," said Dr. Rossi, gliding past like a stern aunt. "Your reactor is singing."

"It's humming confidence," Priya said.

"Make it hum profit."

"Yes, ma'am."

In a hangar on the edge of campus that smelled like rivets, Owen McCall wiped sealant off his fingers and looked at the fuselage they were pretending was a satellite bus. He was an aerospace co-op, which meant he learned by doing and by apologizing in equal measure. The test structure was more scaffolding than flight, but he loved it the way a carpenter loves a frame: for what it promised. His team lead, a doctoral student who slept in two-hour shifts and drank coffee that could burn through foil, waved him over.

"Owen, the payload cradle's five millimeters off. We need dead center or we'll get the mother of all torques when we spin."

"I'll shim it," he said.

"You'll shim it and then you'll teach three first-years to shim it because I'm allergic to heroics."

"Copy."

In the planetary sciences lab, Hye-jin Park sat with headphones in and the world out, eyes on a screen full of noise that wasn't. Her research was supposed to be surface brightness profiles of cold dwarf planets, but she cheated on her project with radio telescope data because the sky kept whispering and she wasn't rude enough to ignore it. The feed that morning was ordinary in a way that made her suspicious. Ordinary data rarely made her suspicious.

She toggled a filter she'd written at two a.m. *PulseFindr_v7*, a name she hated and never changed. The trace stabilized, then hiccuped. Eleven milliseconds between peaks. She rubbed her eyes. The hiccup came back. She reran the filter. Same rhythm. She let herself smile with half her mouth. Not proof. A nudge.

She dragged the window to the corner of the screen and opened a second file—neutrino variance summaries a friend in the physics department kept leaving on the server by accident on purpose. She aligned the timestamps by hand because she didn't trust the software. When the peaks agreed, she said, "No way," in a tone she used for both miracles and scams.

A news alert bloomed at the bottom of her screen: **Global Sustainability Alliance Announces Scholarships for Climate Resilience Studies.** The headline carried a photo of a tall man in an expensive suit whose smile did not reach his eyes. Hye-jin minimized it without reading. Headlines were for later. Peaks were now.

The First Rumors

At ten, the student union hummed with the sound of a campus that believed in lunch. TVs over the seating area cycled between sports, weather, and a live podium in New York where a sleek logo read **GSA**. Students watched with the attention they gave to fire drills: polite, bored, prepared to run if someone told them to. On mute, the speakers looked like they were agreeing to something important.

Ana found Mateo by the window after her seminar. He was sketching a donut because topology made him hungry. She dropped into the seat opposite. "Tell me your favorite algae."

"You don't open with 'how are you'?"

"You're a mathematician. How you are depends on the equation."

"True." He drew eyes on the donut. "We name them now?"

"We humanize what we make people eat."

He pushed the donut toward her. "My favorite algae is the one that doesn't taste like an apology."

"That's the capstone title," she said. "Okoye 2026: *An End to Apology.*"

They looked up together as the TVs flicked to sound. A woman at a podium was saying "…a partnership across sectors to invest in resilient infrastructure, so communities can thrive under changing conditions."

The chyron read: **GLOBAL SUSTAINABILITY ALLIANCE LAUNCHES $40B INITIATIVE.** Next to her stood a man Ana had only ever seen in magazines—Gregor Vass, the billionaire who looked like he owned his suits and everyone else's.

"Is it me," Mateo said, "or do all global alliances look like sunscreen brands?"

"It's the fonts," Ana said. "And the teeth."

The screen cut to footage of smiling children planting herbs on a roof-top garden that must have been extremely well-insured. A graphic showed grants for "desal innovation," "microgrid pilots," "urban canopy." It looked like the future had gotten a marketing consultant.

Priya slid in, lab coat still on, goggles on her hair like a crown tilted on purpose. "We getting free money?" she asked.

"Global scale," Mateo said. "Strings braided into ropes."

Priya followed his gaze to the screen. "He's handsome in a way that predicts litigation."

"Who?" Ana asked, genuinely.

"Mr. Alliance," Priya said, nodding at Vass. "My aunt hates him and only hates people who can afford it."

On the stage, Vass stepped to the microphone as if the microphone owed him rent. The room got quieter the moment he stepped to the microphone. He spoke the language of competence with a dialect of inevitability: investments, partnerships, resilient futures, no single point of failure. He said *we* like he expected ownership to follow.

"Do you buy it?" Mateo asked.

Ana watched the scrolling list of "priority research areas" and saw her algae waiting there as if they'd been invited. "I buy that someone finally noticed the boring problems."

"Boring is the new apocalypse," Priya said. "Speaking of, my lab smells like wet cardboard. If he wants to fund that, be my guest."

Hye-jin arrived, breathless not from running but from staring. "Do any of you speak neutrino?" she asked by way of hello.

"Only socially," Mateo said. "Why?"

She put her laptop down between the coffee cups, angled it so they all could see. The screen showed two graphs that matched in a way that felt immodest. Peaks lined up with peaks. The caption in Hye-jin's tidy font read **timing match ± 0.01s**.

"I've been seeing this pattern in the radio feed for three weeks," she said. "Eleven milliseconds. It keeps coming back. And when it does—" she tapped the second graph "—the neutrino variance upticks. It's small, but it's not nothing."

Priya frowned. "Noise loves to cosplay as pattern."

"I checked drift, interference, satellite garbage," Hye-jin said. "If it's fake, it's polite about it."

"What is it?" Ana asked.

"I don't know," Hye-jin said. "A bad joke. A good one."

Mateo leaned closer. "Let me have the raw. I've been playing with a filter that eats noise and spits out prime factors."

"Math flirting," Priya said. "I approve."

Hye-jin nodded. "I'll send you the set B files. Don't name them something cute."

"Too late," Mateo said. "Everything in my life is cutely named or it refuses to run."

On the TV, the GSA logo rotated through a palette of trustworthy blues. Vass shook hands with people whose suits didn't quite fit. The crawl at the bottom promised scholarships for undergraduates in "resilience fields," including bioengineering, chemistry, applied math, and aerospace. It promised internships. It promised mentorship. The word **selection** did not appear.

Ana felt something like gravity tug behind her ribs. Not hope, exactly. A direction. "Scholarships," she said.

Priya followed the line of small print down the screen and read aloud. "Food systems, air chemistry, energy storage, atmosphere control. They want all of us."

"Or they want to find us," Mateo said. "Which is different."

Owen came in smelling like solvent and adrenaline. He slid a tray onto the table and didn't notice the laptop until he nearly put a sandwich on the galaxy. "My bad," he said, rescuing it. "What am I stepping on?"

"The universe, maybe," Hye-jin said. "Sit."

He did. He touched the trackpad with clean knuckles and scrolled, eyes narrowing with the concentration of someone used to reading gauges. "That's...not random."

"Thank you," Hye-jin said, pleased in a way that made her look younger. "No one believes me unless they already want to."

Owen nodded at the TV. "We getting money to build satellites that will later become not-satellites?"

"Depends on what you call later," Mateo said.

They ate as the press conference moved into questions—softballs about education, a sharp one about procurement, a ridiculous one about rooftop gardens. Vass answered like a man who had rehearsed every angle. When he said, *"We're building for tomorrow because tomorrow always arrives,"* the room went quiet because the sentence felt like a signature.

When the conference ended, the TVs returned to neutral: weather (inadequate), sports (overconfident), a news ticker that mentioned a "technical briefing" next week from a solar observatory that sounded like it had been forced to schedule it by gravity. No one in the union noticed. The lunch line kept moving.

The Syllabi of Ordinary

Afternoons on campus were lists pretending to be lives. Ana's bio lab ran long because someone misread microliters as milliliters and flooded a plate. Priya's reactor sulked and then performed like a diva who needed applause before warming up. Mateo's TA section produced three poems about limits and one miracle—the shy kid in the third row raised his hand and said, "Can I show you something after?" and it was not a boyfriend or a complaint but a cleaner proof.

Owen taught two first-years to shim a cradle without shaming the cradle. He said, "Torque doesn't care about your feelings," and one of them laughed and the other one wrote it down like scripture. He sent a photo of the corrected mount to his lead and received a thumbs-up that meant don't break anything.

Hye-jin skipped a meeting on "wellness practices for graduate students" and went to the roof of the library instead, a place where the sky could see her without attendance taken. She lay on her back on the warm tar and let her eyes blur until the buildings around the quad became a child's blocks. She thought of eleven milliseconds. She thought of neutrinos, polite ghosts running through her body like a busy airport. She thought of the way the pattern seemed to lean toward her when she didn't want to be leaned toward. She said, out loud, "If you're real, be kinder." The sky did not reply in a language she could grade.

When the sun dropped, a student band tuned up on the steps of the student union and played a cover that everyone knew by memory. In a dorm kitchen, someone burned onions and called it stew. In the library, a grad student fell asleep on a stack of journals and dreamed of filing systems. Ordinary found its own gravity again.

Office Hours

At five, Ana went to Professor Mendez's office with a Tupperware of experimental bars that did not yet have the right aftertaste. Mendez accepted the offering with ceremony.

"We do not eat the future without witnesses," she said, and bit. She chewed. She did not grimace. "Better. Less penitential."

"High praise," Ana said.

"You watch the Alliance press thing?"

"Yeah."

"You want to apply."

"I want to keep this going when the grant ends and my rent doesn't."

Mendez leaned back, eyes on the ceiling tiles as if they had equations. "Apply. But remember: money is an editorial. It will try to rewrite your project into its story. Keep your story."

"I will," Ana said, meaning it because she believed in her stubbornness the way some people believed in saints.

Mendez tapped the Tupperware. "Add citrus. Not for taste. For morale." She paused. "You hear anything from your friend in planetary? The one who thinks the sky is practicing Morse code?"

Ana hesitated, then nodded. "She thinks she's seeing a pattern. She's not wrong often."

"Patterns are irresponsible," Mendez said. "They turn people into prophets. Tell your friend to publish too slowly and save copies offline."

"Is it that bad?"

"Not yet," Mendez said. "And that's when good people do their worst work."

Proof of Concept

Mateo and Hye-jin met in the math lounge after dark because chalkboards worked better than text threads when the problem had a pulse.

He'd loaded her raw datasets into his filter, given it no assumptions, and watched it spit out something that wanted to be a confession.

"It's not just periodic," he said, chalk sweeping. "It's recursive. The signal self-corrects like it knows it's traveling through mess."

"Language," she said softly.

"Or a metronome that hates being wrong." He wrote $\Delta t = 0.0109$ s with a neat underline. "The offset is too clean to be random. When I run the detrended residuals—"

"English, Lin."

"Your ghosts are consistent," he said. "If they're ghosts."

"The universe hates being called a ghost," she said.

He grinned. "Good. It can sue me."

They worked until the room forgot them. Outside, a delivery truck exhaled, a siren debated a corner, the campus chimes did the thing they did at the hour no one asked for. Hye-jin closed her eyes and saw peaks marching like polite soldiers. She opened them again and they were still marching.

"Do we tell anyone?" she asked.

"Who would believe us?" he said. "Better question: who would like to?"

She laughed, then sobered. "If I'm wrong, I want to be wrong quietly."

"If you're right," he said, "we won't have quiet for long."

They saved their work three times, then printed paper copies because paper did not crash. When they left, Hye-jin put the printouts in a manila folder with a name that would not invite theft: **Budget Committee Minutes.** She held it like a thin animal.

Night Noise

Owen biked home along the river path, legs warm, chest cold, the lights on the water doing their lazy Morse. He loved the hour when the city felt like a machine cooling. He passed a park where a group of students were practicing with telescopes, laughing too loud because stars make people either quiet or too loud. He stopped, looked up, found Orion by habit, then traced a line to where no one could see Gliese and saluted it anyway because superstition had never done him harm.

Priya went back to the lab to check a slow reaction and found it sulking again, then turning miraculous the moment she threatened to shut it down. She wrote **DON'T REWARD BAD BEHAVIOR** on a Post-it and stuck it to the hood for whichever version of herself worked the morning shift.

On the way out she saw the GSA scholarship email in her inbox and rolled her eyes at the subject line—**BUILD TOMORROW WITH US**—and clicked anyway.

Ana wrote to her mother, attached the Alliance press release and a photo of her algae racks lit like quiet aquariums. Her mother wrote back, *"Apply. Make a garden for the ships."* Ana closed the laptop, lay on her bed, and told the ceiling, "Okay."

Hye-jin walked home under a sky that had decided to be honest for once—clear, indifferent, full of light that had been traveling a very long time to be ignored by people with deadlines. She held the manila folder under her coat. Her phone buzzed with an unknown number. She didn't answer. It buzzed again. She turned it off.

When she reached her building, she looked up one more time. The stars didn't blink back. The air tasted like metal and rain.

In a dorm across campus, a student with a telescope and a generous personality aimed at the moon and passed the eyepiece to strangers. They used the word *wow* in tones that made the word new. Behind them, the TVs in the student union quietly looped highlights of the Global Sustainability Alliance's launch event, the volume set to a level where it could enter without asking.

Somewhere above all of it, a small contractor satellite pivoted its dish by a very small angle and listened. It did not smile because satellites didn't, but if it could have, it would have smiled at how patient humans were with everything except time.

The Visit

Two weeks later the university banners bloomed with new colors— deep sea-blue and silver—and the words **GLOBAL SUSTAINABILITY ALLIANCE CAMPUS OUTREACH.**

No one remembered approving them; they just appeared, which was how most partnerships began.

The auditorium smelled of polished wood and projection heat. Six hundred students filled the seats in self-sorting clusters: lab coats, suits borrowed from siblings, hoodies that still believed in debt forgiveness. On stage a digital banner scrolled through stock footage of wind farms and smiling engineers in helmets. Every few seconds the words *BUILD TO-MORROW* pulsed like a heartbeat.

Ana sat between Priya and Mateo near the middle, taking notes before anything had been said.

Hye-jin and Owen stood along the side wall, half-hidden behind a column, because they preferred exits to aisles.

A woman in a crisp charcoal jacket stepped to the podium. "Good afternoon. I'm **Lydia Raines**, liaison for the Global Sustainability Alliance. We're here to offer opportunities for research, mentorship, and impact."

Her voice carried the practiced warmth of someone trained to sell sincerity by the hour. Behind her the screen filled with partner logos—Helios, Sunward, Vass Global, the university seal, a few that existed only as acronyms.

"Our world is changing," Raines continued. "We need thinkers who build bridges between disciplines. You—scientists, engineers, mathematicians—will design resilience. The Alliance offers scholarships, stipends, and placements with our partner organizations. We're not just funding ideas. We're recruiting a generation."

Recruiting. The word hung longer than applause.

A hand went up near the front. "What kind of research?" asked a student in a lab coat two sizes too large.

"Energy, food, water, atmosphere," Raines said smoothly. "And adaptive systems—anything that helps humanity thrive in uncertain environments."

Mateo whispered, "That's code for off-planet."

Priya elbowed him, whispering back, "Everything's code for off-planet with you."

But when Raines added, "We expect participants to be open to relocation for field work—some projects may require extended deployment," they both stopped smiling. *Deployment* was not a word universities usually used.

Raines moved through the slides: deadlines, eligibility, an application portal that opened that night. Then she invited questions.

A student from the philosophy department raised a hand. "You talk about resilience. Whose resilience? Corporations? Governments? Or people who can't afford a ticket to tomorrow?"

Raines's smile did not falter. "Everyone's," she said. "Our mission is inclusive."

The room murmured—the kind of murmur that politely calls a lie by its name but doesn't want to be graded for it.

Ana felt a pulse behind her ribs, the same mixture of curiosity and unease she felt in lab when an experiment started behaving too well.

Hye-jin whispered to Owen, "Look at her badge."

He glanced. The laminate shimmered under the lights. Beneath *Lydia Raines* in smaller letters: **Helios Systems Support**.

Owen whispered back, "So much for transparency."

When the applause finally came, it was the tired, automatic kind given to authority. Raines smiled, thanked them for their attention, and left the stage flanked by two assistants who moved like silent punctuation.

The Debate

That evening, the ethics seminar—normally a graveyard for participation—overflowed. Professor Ishaan Rao, who had taught environmental policy since before most of his students were born, looked genuinely alarmed by the attendance. He removed his glasses, rubbed them with his tie, and said, "Let's talk about it, then."

A philosophy major began: "If the planet's failing and they're building arks, doesn't triage make sense? Better some survive than none."

A political-science student snapped back, "Who decides some? The ones who can pay?"

Ana listened, notebook closed. Mateo was sketching the Alliance logo, replacing the O in *TOMORROW* with a mathematical zero. Priya muttered chemical equations as if balancing them might balance morality.

Professor Rao wrote *UTILITARIANISM* on the board. "The greatest good for the greatest number," he said. "An old idea. But how do you measure 'good' when the sample size is a species?"

Hye-jin raised a hand. "You can't. You model survival, not goodness."

"Then who models you?" Rao asked.

She hesitated. "Data models itself. People add the noise."

Owen, from the back, said, "Noise is where the truth hides."

"Or guilt," Priya added.

Rao smiled faintly. "Excellent. We're awake. Now—imagine you're the Alliance. You have resources to move one-tenth of the population off-world. How do you choose?"

The room filled with shifting, throat-clearing, deflections disguised as jokes. Someone said *lottery*; someone said *merit*. Ana said nothing until Rao pointed his chalk at her. "Miss Okoye?"

She closed her eyes for a moment. "Whoever can feed the rest," she said quietly. "Take the people who know how to grow things."

Rao nodded. "And leave the ones who eat?"

Ana didn't answer. The silence after was the kind that made its own gravity.

After class, groups formed in the hallway, half-whispering plans, half-mocking their own earnestness. The Alliance had done what press releases couldn't: it had turned abstract fear into small talk.

Fire Drill

At midnight, the dorm alarms shrieked, part of a routine drill scheduled weeks before but perfectly timed to sound prophetic. Students poured into the courtyard in pajamas and sarcasm. Steam rose from mouths and coffee cups; someone played a harmonica badly.

Ana and Priya stood near the railing watching their breath. "Feels rehearsed," Priya said.

"Everything does lately."

Across the courtyard, Mateo argued cheerfully with a residence assistant about probability curves in alarm systems. Hye-jin appeared beside them, laptop hugged to her chest.

"I was re-running the signal filter," she said. "The pattern's changing."

"Changing how?" Ana asked.

"It's lengthening. Eleven milliseconds just became twelve."

Priya squinted. "Congratulations, your ghosts aged a second."

"It's not drift. It's deliberate. Like...a beat being stretched."

Owen joined them, hair damp from a shower he clearly hadn't finished. "Could be nothing."

Hye-jin shook her head. "Nothing doesn't keep time."

The Resident Advisor shouted for everyone to move toward the street for roll call. Hye-jin hid the laptop under her coat. The building loomed behind them, a tower of yellow rectangles. In each window, silhouettes shifted—hundreds of small lives lit for inspection.

A helicopter passed far above, its lights sweeping once across the quad. The group watched it vanish into the dark. None of them said what they were thinking: that drills were practice, and practice implied an exam.

Applications

The next morning the Alliance portal opened. The site was sleek, polite, and a little too efficient. Each section timed out after precisely seven minutes, as if measuring hesitation.

Ana uploaded her proposal—*Nutrient-dense algae for low-gravity bioreactors*—and attached photos of her racks bathed in gentle blue light. She hesitated at the box marked *Willing to relocate for research field work*. After a moment she checked *Yes*. Her reflection in the laptop looked older for it.

Priya filled her form with sarcasm between the lines: *Atmospheric nitrogen cycling in confined environments (a.k.a. breathing)*.

Mateo attached an algorithm demo and a disclaimer that read *For educational purposes only; side effects may include existential dread*.

Owen submitted a design for modular structural shims that could self-adjust in microgravity, adding, *Field testing optional but welcome*.

Hye-jin stared at the portal for a long time and finally attached a proposal so vague it was almost a threat: *Analysis of repeating radio-neutrino synchronizations across heliocentric baselines*. She wrote her advisor's email, hesitated, and erased it. No co-signatures.

When she hit *Submit*, the screen flashed a polite *Thank you for building tomorrow*. Then, almost imperceptibly, a second message blinked and vanished before she could screenshot it: **Transmission received.**

She sat back, heart kicking once, and told herself it was just branding.

The List

The emails arrived at 03:12 a.m. UTC, which meant just after midnight local time—a courtesy to insomnia.

Subject line: **CONGRATULATIONS | GLOBAL SUSTAINABILITY ALLIANCE NEXT STAGE**

By morning, half the campus had already screenshotted theirs. Social feeds bloomed with the same teal banner and the same quote from Gregor Vass about *"the engineers of resilience."*

Ana woke to seventy-four unread messages and one notification from her mother: *"They like your algae."*
She laughed, equal parts disbelief and caffeine deprivation.

Priya's acceptance had arrived too but was flagged "conditional upon clearance."
She told everyone it meant *elite,* though she admitted privately she didn't know what *clearance* meant in a scholarship context.

Mateo had an offer for a "research residency" attached to something called the **Data Harmonization Division**.

He'd googled it, found nothing, and decided that was either excellent or catastrophic.

Owen's came stamped **PROVISIONAL ENGINEERING CON-SULTANT**—language that sounded like an adult job hiding in a student email.

Hye-jin almost deleted hers on instinct. The subject line was identical, but the sender domain wasn't the same as her friends'.
Instead of *@gsa.org,* hers read *@helios-systems.global.*
She opened it anyway.

We appreciate your continuing work on atmospheric signal analysis.
Our technical liaison would like to meet regarding your methodology.
Please report to the Research Commons, Conference Room B, 1400 hours.

No congratulations. Just coordinates.

Orientation Weekend

The auditorium had been repainted in optimism. Posters showed lush green domes floating above deserts, tagged ***SUSTAINABILITY THROUGH INNOVATION***. Lanyards glowed with QR codes that refused to scan.

Lydia Raines returned, radiant in corporate serenity.
She welcomed the hundred selected students and spoke about *resilience, cross-disciplinary integration,* and *the privilege of preparation.*

Behind her, an LED wall cycled silent footage: deep-sea rigs, Arctic platforms, orbital arrays under construction.
No captions. The audience saw what they wanted—hope, ambition, jobs.
Hye-jin saw **proof**.

During the break, Ana found herself standing beside Raines at the coffee station.

The liaison's perfume smelled like expensive neutrality.

"You're the algae researcher," Raines said without looking.

"Yes, ma'am."

"You'll like the Alliance labs. Controlled environments. No weather to ruin a crop."

Ana blinked. "Where are they?"

Raines smiled, not answering. "We'll send coordinates once clearance finalizes."

She turned, conversation complete, as if coordinates were gossip.

Across the lobby, Mateo cornered a logistics officer to ask what *data harmonization* meant.

The officer said, "We integrate multi-sector signals for predictive stability modeling," which answered nothing but sounded secure.

Owen's badge earned him access to a side display: a 3-D model of something labeled *Resilience Platform Aegis I*.

He studied the scale bar. "This isn't a city," he murmured. "It's a continent pretending to be polite."

Priya joined him, holding two cups of coffee. "Whatever it is, they're recruiting the lab rats early."

"Then we're the maze," he said.

She clinked cups with him. "To mazes."

Echo

At 13:55 hours, Hye-jin went to Conference Room B.

It was smaller than she expected—no banners, just a table, two chairs, and a wall screen that glowed with a static logo: **Helios Systems Support | Signal Integrity Division.**

A man entered, fortyish, gray at the temples, expression somewhere between mathematician and priest.

"Dr. Ethan Kale," he said. "You're the grad with the repeating pattern."

She nodded, pulse climbing. "You read it?"

"I read enough. Your timestamps match a proprietary feed we've been analyzing. You shouldn't have access to that dataset."

"I didn't," she said. "It's public radio telescope data."

He opened a tablet, flicked a window toward her. It showed her folders—her private, offline folders—mirrored on a Helios server. Even the one named **Budget Committee Minutes.**

"I don't share these," she whispered.

Kale's tone softened. "We're not accusing. The signal replicated itself through your network. It *wants* redundancy. Every time someone records it, it opens a channel."

"That's impossible."

He smiled tiredly. "It was yesterday."

He slid a small drive across the table. "Here's our latest intercept. Same pattern, stronger amplitude. Eleven-point-nine milliseconds. Keep studying. Just don't publish. For now, you work for us."

"I didn't agree to—"

"You already did," he said gently, "when you listened."

Then he left. The door clicked behind him like a sealed equation.

Collision Course

That night, the selected students met at the campus observatory for what the Alliance called a "team-building stargaze."

It turned into a half-party, half-orientation. A telescope aimed at Jupiter, a playlist that confused galaxies with love songs. Someone brought cupcakes with edible GSA logos.

Ana, Priya, Mateo, Owen, and Hye-jin clustered near the railing overlooking the city lights.

"So we're officially the chosen nerds," Priya said. "Should we feel grateful or drafted?"

"Both," Owen said. "Drafted gratitude."

Mateo laughed but didn't look amused. "They want integration, not curiosity. Integration can be automated."

Ana said, "Curiosity can't. That's why they need us."

Hye-jin wasn't listening. She was staring at the horizon where the last red of sunset melted into gray. The drive in her pocket felt heavy, warmer than metal had any right to be.

"Hey," Priya said, noticing her silence. "You good?"

Hye-jin forced a nod. "Just tired."

Mateo pointed his phone skyward, an app tracing constellations. "There's your Gliese system. Twenty light-years that way. Give or take traffic."

Owen raised his cup in mock toast. "To distant neighbors."

Ana added softly, "To the reason we might need them."

They drank. For a moment, the chatter around them blurred into wind. Above, a faint shimmer crossed the sky—just a plane, everyone said. Everyone but Hye-jin, who counted eleven seconds between its pulses and didn't say a word.

Intrusion

Back in her dorm, Hye-jin plugged the Helios drive into an air-gapped laptop.

The files opened as noise—white static scrolling down the screen—but when she ran her filter, the rhythm appeared instantly, like a heartbeat welcoming itself home.

She overlayed her own recordings. Perfect sync. The pattern was no longer just an echo; it was a duet.

A small dialog box blinked open on its own:

HELLO, RECEIVER.

She froze. The cursor blinked three times.

SIGNAL ACKNOWLEDGED

Then the text erased itself, line by line, leaving the screen clean and harmless.

She sat back, trembling. Outside, somewhere beyond her window, the campus clock struck two. The sound echoed across the quad like slow Morse code.

Calibration

Monday arrived dressed like progress.

Alliance badges opened new doors—labs that had been locked since renovation year, servers humming behind fresh security glass, project folders labeled **Initiative Aegis Student Program.**

Ana's algae racks were relocated to the upper greenhouse, where the lighting system now ran on a pulse-frequency algorithm she hadn't written.

When she asked the techs about it, one said, "Standard modulation," and smiled like a man paid to keep secrets. The algae grew faster than she'd seen before. Too fast. She logged the anomaly in her notebook and underlined it twice.

Priya found herself moved from her reactor bay to a new lab with unfamiliar equipment stamped *HEL-EN ENV 04*.
She was told she'd be "testing nitrogen stabilization for variable atmospheres."

When she pointed out that the room's air pressure controls included negative values, the supervisor said, "Simulation fidelity," and left.

Owen received a crate of parts marked *EDU-SIM MATERIALS: DO NOT DEPLOY*.

He opened it to find titanium frame joints heavier than the manuals claimed.

Each piece carried an RFID tag linked to a tracking database he couldn't access.

He spent the afternoon teaching freshmen to torque bolts while his phone camera stayed stubbornly disabled.

Mateo's residency office occupied a windowless sub-basement under the data center.

He shared it with humming towers and two engineers who spoke in acronyms.

His task: refine an algorithm that could *"detect redundant signals across global observatories."*

When he recognized Hye-jin's dataset in the sample feed, he closed the window quietly and pretended he hadn't.

Hye-jin herself was assigned a small workstation inside the astrophysics annex, labeled **TEMP ACCESS AUTHORIZED BY KALE.**

The screen greeted her with the same phrase every morning: **WELCOME RECEIVER.**

She stopped trying to delete it after the third day—it simply reappeared.

Noise
By the second week, campus gossip had polarized:
the Alliance pays real stipends versus *the Alliance owns your soul.*
A protest flyer appeared overnight—

NO FUTURE WITHOUT CONSENT—and disappeared by lunchtime, replaced with recruitment posters.

Professor Rao called it "democracy's heartbeat."

The administration called it vandalism.

In the dining hall, Ana told the group about her algae's growth spike. Priya countered with her reactor's mysterious "breathing."

Owen mentioned the RFID tags.

Mateo said nothing at first, then confessed, "They're mirroring your data, Jin. I saw it."

Hye-jin stared at her tray. "Mirroring how?"

"Same timestamps, same checksum. Your signal's feeding half the Alliance servers."

"So they already have it."

"Have it," Owen said, "or need it?"

The silence that followed was brittle.

Finally Ana said, "Maybe it's harmless."

Priya laughed without humor. "So is gravity, until you fall."

The Blackout

That Friday, at 21:17 hours, the campus lights dimmed.

Not out—just lower, like the world had inhaled.

Phones lost signal. Wi-Fi blinked red. The only network still alive was the Alliance's private channel.

In the astrophysics annex, Hye-jin's monitor flared to life on its own.

The waveform she'd tracked for months now filled the screen, amplitude doubling, tripling.

The words returned:

HELLO AGAIN.

THRESHOLD APPROACHING.

She typed with shaking hands.

Who are you?

For a moment, nothing. Then:

SOURCE DEGRADED

SOLAR PATTERN RECOGNIZED

The power surged; the building lights flickered to full daylight brightness.

Her laptop speakers hissed—a deep, almost human tone, rising and falling like breath.

Security alarms followed, distant but approaching.

She copied the live stream onto an external drive, yanked it free, and stuffed it into her pocket. Before shutting down, she typed one more line:

What do you want?

The reply came instantly.

THRESHOLD EVENT DETECTED.

Then the feed went dark.

Consequence

When the lights normalized, students poured out into the quad cheering as if a blackout were sport.

Only the five of them noticed the sky.

Auroras—thin, silver, southern—rippling where no auroras belonged.

Phones still dead. The air tasted metallic.

Mateo whispered, "Solar flare?"

Owen shook his head. "No. Wrong direction."

Priya looked at Hye-jin. "You did something."

Hye-jin's voice barely carried. "I asked it to talk."

Ana said, "And it answered?"

"Yes."

She held up the drive. "It says something is approaching."

The Transmission

At two a.m., they met in the observatory again.

The telescope's automation was offline, so they operated manually—dials, levers, muscle memory.

Hye-jin connected the drive to the auxiliary transmitter.

"This is insane," Owen said, tightening a cable.

"Insane is relative," Priya said. "We're already research subjects."

Ana adjusted the dish orientation. "At least if we respond, we do it on our own terms."

Mateo keyed in a short binary string, the simplest greeting: **101010**—yes, no, yes.

"Minimalist hello," he said.

Hye-jin watched the signal power climb. "Transmit."

The dish hummed, a low vibration they felt more than heard.

For twelve seconds it held steady; then the console displayed a single line of return data:

RECEIVED. PREPARE.

Wind shoved against the dome, sudden and hard.

Every monitor blinked to static, then showed the same coordinates—an unmarked point between Earth and the Sun.

Owen whispered, "That's where Helios parks their satellites."

Mateo wrote the numbers on his sleeve like a charm.

Ana closed her eyes. "Prepare for what?"

No one answered.

Outside, the aurora flared again—brighter, closer—and in its light the campus looked briefly like a model city inside glass.

Coda

By morning, the power outage was officially a "regional transformer event."

The university promised normal operations.

The Alliance issued no statement.

But across the internet, amateur astronomers were already sharing the same coordinates, the same flicker from the sky, the same question: *Was that us, or them?*

In a quiet greenhouse, Ana's algae stopped growing.

In the reactor lab, Priya's gauges reset to zero and refused to move.

Owen's RFID scanner registered all zeros—every tag, erased.

Mateo's algorithm crashed with a final log entry: **Recursion depth exceeded.**

And in the astrophysics annex, Hye-jin's monitor powered itself without power.

On the dark screen appeared a single phrase, written in gentle gray:

RECEIVER DETECTED.

She whispered back, "Now we're listening."

Outside, dawn arrived late, tinted faintly green, as if the light had traveled through water—or warning.

Chapter 6

Signals and Silence

The Quiet Before

At the Johnson Deep-Space Array, the night crew measured silence the way sailors once measured wind—by what refused to answer back.

Rows of dishes angled toward the dawn side of the sky, their surfaces dull from dust and desert wind. Inside Control Room B, light hummed blue and constant, a reminder that no one here ever truly saw night.

Ethan Kale stood over the console with a mug gone cold. The screen in front of him displayed nothing unusual: background radiation, calibration pulses, a field of data that looked exactly the way comfort should look.

But under it, in the sub-channel feed he'd been tracking since the Houston experiment, a small heartbeat blinked—regular, confident, and entirely out of place.

"Still there," he said.

Mira Patel, across the room, didn't look up from her terminal. "Still you're talking to it, or still it's talking to you?"

"Semantics," he said. "It's consistent. Eleven-point-nine milliseconds between peaks."

She swiveled her chair, her dark hair pulled back in a braid that had stopped pretending to be tidy hours ago.
"You said eleven last week."

"It changed."

"Natural drift?"

"Or response."

Mira pushed to her feet, crossed to his station, and watched the pulse graph.

She lowered her voice. "Helios is running their own captures again. I saw the handshake from their relay ten minutes ago."

Ethan frowned. "At this hour?"

"They don't sleep."

"They never did."

He tapped a command, splitting the feed into two: one from the Johnson array, one mirroring from Helios's satellite network. The second line arrived perfectly in sync.

"See?" he said. "They're not monitoring us. They're *linked*."

Mira folded her arms. "Then we're not the only ones receiving this."

Directive

Director Helena Ruiz arrived before dawn, her usual perfume of espresso and reprimand preceding her.

She listened without interrupting while they presented the data—pulse intervals, amplitude drift, the perfect correlation between NASA's feed and Helios's commercial satellites.

When Ethan finished, she said, "If this is genuine, it doesn't leave this room."

Mira glanced at him. "Helios already has it."

"Then make sure the public doesn't," Ruiz said. "Until we understand what it is."

Ethan leaned on the console. "You mean until we have the *story* you can tell Congress."

Ruiz's eyes were calm, bureaucratic steel. "The last thing this planet needs is a panic about voices from space. We're still pretending climate mitigation works."

"Pretending," Mira repeated.

Ruiz ignored her. "I'll arrange a private briefing with Helios Systems. You two will attend, but you'll speak only to the data. No theories."

When she left, the room felt quieter. The monitors ticked in unison with the heartbeat on the screen.

Mira said softly, "We're about to meet the man who thinks the Sun is negotiable."

Ethan's jaw tightened. "Vass."

Helios

The Helios Systems Complex was polished glass, no signage, and the kind of security money buys quietly.

Ruiz's clearance opened the gates, and the three of them were guided through corridors bright enough to erase faces.

In the conference suite waited Gregor Vass. He shook hands as if confirming contracts that hadn't yet been drafted.

A holo-display above the table already pulsed with the waveform.

"I've heard you've made a friend," Vass said lightly.

Ethan said nothing. Mira did. "It's not a friend. It's a phenomenon."

"Everything's a friend if it offers cooperation," Vass replied. "May I?"—and gestured to the console.

Ruiz nodded stiffly.

Vass expanded the graph, overlaying a layer of his own data. "You'll notice the amplitude synchronization. The signal repeats through our satellites, but also through natural ionospheric channels. It's as though the planet itself has joined the transmission."

"Meaning?" Ruiz asked.

"Meaning," Vass said, "Earth is echoing back."

Mira stepped forward. "Echoing what?"

He smiled with just enough charm to be offensive. "That's what we're paying to find out. But if it is what we think—then it's either a greeting or a warning."

"And which one are you betting on?" Ethan asked.

Vass's eyes met his. "I never bet. I prepare."

He dismissed them shortly after, the meeting ending the way all dealings with power ended.

Outside, as the guards escorted them back to the elevators, Mira whispered, "He knows something we don't."

"He knows everything we don't," Ethan said. "That's his job."

The Message

Back at the Johnson Array that evening, they worked without speaking. The heartbeat had changed again: a new modulation layered over the old, like a second voice learning harmony.

Ethan amplified it. "It's repeating a frequency sweep. Rough translation... maybe a pattern for matter density?"

Mira leaned closer. "Or coordinates."

He stared at the readout. The numbers were familiar in a way that made his stomach drop.

"Those are Earth-Sun Lagrange coordinates," he said. "L-1, roughly where Helios parks their relay satellites."

"The same point the students reported," she said softly. "It's all connected."

He looked at her. "What students?"

Mira hesitated. "The university feed we use for distributed computing? They've been pulling the same datasets. A grad student named Park uploaded her analysis before the blackout. She found the same rhythm."

"You've been monitoring them?"

"Protecting the data," she said. "I didn't think it would matter."

Ethan rubbed his temples. "Helios is mirroring our signal. We're mirroring theirs. And now a university is mirroring both. That's not coincidence. That's orchestration."

He typed a quick sequence, creating a local buffer cut off from external links.

"Let's isolate it before it isolates us."

The lights dimmed.

For a moment, the only illumination came from the monitor, where the waveform flared into words formed by amplitude variation—rough, broken English, but unmistakable:

PREPARE. STAR DECAY ACCELERATING.
DO NOT LET THEM SILENCE.

Mira whispered, "Them?"

Before Ethan could answer, the speakers popped and the signal cut to static. All network access blinked *OFFLINE*. A small message appeared at the top of the screen:

REMOTE ACCESS – VASS.G

Ethan swore, slammed the disconnect, and killed power to the room.

The screens went black.

Mira exhaled, voice steady. "He's inside our system."

"No," Ethan said. "He *is* the system."

Leak Path

They rebooted the Johnson Array control room from hardware, then a slow climb through subsystems that still believed in analog dignity. Screens returned in grayscale before resolving to their gentler blues. The heartbeat wasn't on the primary feed anymore, but Ethan could feel it in the way the room hummed—like a sound you can't hear until the AC stops and you realize it had been singing the whole time.

Mira rolled her chair close. "We do this now or not at all," she said, palms flat on the console like a physician committing to surgery.

"Do *what* exactly?" Ruiz's caution still lay on the room like a thin sheet; Vass's tag, **VASS.G**, had burned itself on Ethan's eyelids.

"Air gap the main stack," Mira said, "then open a one-way channel to the university's compute node. We drop a fragment—just the amplitude map that spells *PREPARE*—and a checksum. It will propagate, but without our credentials it'll look like a student test. Helios can't scrub a thousand mirrors."

Ethan raked a hand through his hair. "We'll lose our clearance."

"We already lost our autonomy." She held his gaze. "If this is a warning, it doesn't belong to one man's servers."

He looked at the rack lights. Green, obedient, doing what they were told. "Okay," he said. "One fragment. No headers. No origin."

They moved like thieves in a museum they'd built—command lines typed with the care of prayer. Ethan isolated a buffer, wrote a custom packet wrapper that mimicked a generic lab export. Mira generated a one-time pad from noise in the room's electromagnetic hiss and tied the pad to a checksum that would fail gracefully rather than expose provenance. The message itself—four seconds of amplitude variation that, when rendered to audio, turned into a syllable that approximated *HEL-LO*—they compressed until it looked like boring numbers.

"Select a path," Ethan said.

Mira hovered over the node map. "Chemistry cluster, sub-node **hel-en env 04**," she murmured. "Students there have Helios test rigs; traffic from that subnet won't raise alarms."

He blinked at her. "You've been watching the campus too closely."

"Someone should," she said, and hit *SEND*.

The packet slipped into the switch like a coin into a machine that didn't want to admit it had a slot. They watched the trace ride out of the Johnson Array, hop the internal network, and vanish into the public backbone where it split like light through a prism.

Ethan leaned back for the first time in hours. "It's done."

Mira didn't lean back. She was listening the way you listen to a house after a break-in. "Count," she said.

"Count what?"

"How long until Helios notices."

They didn't have to count far.

The primary monitor flashed **LINK NEGOTIATION – EXTERNAL**. Then a polite window appeared center screen, a chat box in a corporate font, as if their server had decided to network in the middle of a fire.

HELIO S-OPS: We detected anomalous export from your segment. Please confirm maintenance.

Ethan typed nothing.

HELIO S-OPS: Dr. Kale, we can help secure your system.

Mira reached over and pulled the Ethernet uplink. The chat died. The heartbeat didn't.

"Now we wait," she said.

"For what?" Ethan asked.

"For the moment they realize they can't lock this down."

Phase II

On the fifty-second floor of the Helios tower, the war room pulsed with live feeds, server maps, and overlapping voices. Gregor Vass watched from across the glass while Marian Soto narrated information the way surgeons narrate blood loss, with relevant concern.

"Someone pushed a fragment to a university segment," Marian said. "Chemistry subcluster. Our heuristics caught the pattern but not the origin. We're looking at NASA's Johnson Array and the Houston propulsion lab as sources."

Vass kept his hands in his pockets. He had learned early that gestures were concessions. "NASA," he said.

"Likely Patel and Kale," Marian said. "They have both motive and conscience. Our tag fired earlier from their room."

He let that sit. "What's the damage?"

"The fragment is small. Amplitude-only, no context. Most recipients will assume test noise. But the checksum is elegant. If anyone recognizes it, they can reconstruct the syllable."

"HEL-LO," Vass said, as if tasting it. "A civility."

"They'll call it proof," Marian said. "Or bait."

Vass stepped closer to the glass. The East River below glowed under a slant of metallic light. "Initiate Phase II containment," he said. "Scrub our credential tag from NASA mirrors. Move all signal processing to the Arctic relay and shadow it through academic IP that already partners with us. If it looks collegiate, governments relax."

Marian nodded, already sending the orders. "What about the students? If they start correlating…"

"Recruit them," Vass said. "Scholarships, special projects. Give them coordinates to feel important and NDAs to feel chosen." He paused. "And if any of them look like prophets, make them accountants."

Marian tilted her head. "And if an accountant looks like a prophet?"

"Then we promote him."

She frowned at a side screen. "Interesting. The fragment's first hop landed in a chemistry lab labeled HEL-EN ENV 04. That's one of ours."

Vass allowed himself half a smile. "Then we own the breach by default."

He turned away from the glass and toward the room. "Also, start drafting language for a joint statement with NASA: 'instrument interference,' 'solar wind variability,' et cetera. Ruiz likes the word *calibration*."

"And if Ruiz balks?"

"She'll balk politely," Vass said. "Her budget enjoys breathing."

The Relay

The Arctic relay didn't look like a relay. It looked like a rumor in ice: low structures, sled-tractors. Below the surface, the signal processing core sat in a titanium cavern, warmer than the world above by virtue of its own hunger.

A tech named Jaro watched as incoming packets multiplied. He'd spent ten years believing in clean networks and now found himself in charge of a system that had learned to use mess as camouflage.

"Containment," his headset said in Marian's tone. "Throttle public mirrors. Maintain Helios priority."

"Copy," he said, and tuned the filters. The amplitude-syllable slipped past the filter on the second pass. The syllable slid through and lodged inside the archive, where it would not be deleted, only misfiled until someone asked the right question.

The room vibrated once—earth, ice, wind, or something else. Jaro looked up at the ceiling, at the small snowdrift accumulating in a seam of the ventilation. He brushed it away with a gloved hand and didn't mention it in the log.

Underside of Secrecy

At Johnson, Mira watched the isolated buffer like a guardian dog. Ethan picked up the landline, dialed a number he knew by muscle memory, and waited for Director Ruiz to answer.

"She already knows," Mira said.

"I'm calling anyway," he replied. "I'm going to tell her we suffered a checksum anomaly during maintenance and that we're taking the system offline for twenty-four hours to scrub. Then I'm going to tell her we're both sick tomorrow."

"Are we?"

"Out of principle."

Ruiz answered on the second ring, voice clipped. Ethan spoke the lie cleanly and the truth half. Ruiz authorized the scrub and told him to file a maintenance memo that used the word *calibration* three times. He promised to make it four.

"Now what?" Mira asked.

"Now you go home," he said quietly. "Don't open your laptop there. Use paper. Lock it in a drawer."

"And you?"

"I'm going to walk," he said. "See if the sky still looks like it belongs to us."

They left the building together, badges surrendered to a night guard who knew better than to ask why. In the parking lot, the air tasted like old pennies. The Sun had set hours ago, but the horizon held a faint pallor.

"Be careful," Mira said.

"Always," he lied.

Chemistry, Noise

On campus, Priya's phone vibrated in the lab where it shouldn't have had signal yet: **Data: new input stream available**. She frowned at the console. HEL-EN ENV 04 displayed a fat green bar labeled *aux_import*. She hadn't scheduled anything.

"Who sent you?" she muttered. She clicked through to the import log and found only a checksum and a line of metadata that read *educational export*. The file preview was nonsense, but when she scrubbed the audio into audible range—just to test—she heard a glitch that wasn't. Two syllables, broken by static:

"Hel—" / "—lo."

She turned down the volume with a speed that made her chair squeal, then looked over her shoulder at the empty hallway. Across the corridor, the Alliance logo glowed on a poster in expensive blue. Priya closed the window, copied the file to a thumb drive, labeled the drive **clean tips**, and stuck it in a beaker behind the pH strips.

She texted Ana: *something weird. greenhouse?*

Rotunda

They met under the rotunda in the old library because its windows were too high to eavesdrop. Owen arrived with fingertips still blackened from grease. Mateo carried a rolled-up printout of graphs like a baton.

Priya plugged the thumb drive into an air-gapped laptop that had survived three owners and a coffee spill. She played the two-syllable. *Hel—lo.* It sounded childish and huge.

"That's the fragment," Mateo said softly. He looked at Hye-jin. "And the rest?"

Hye-jin's eyes were ringed with a lack of sleep. "The rest wants to be here," she said. "It used my folders like passports. Helios knows, NASA knows, and now the internet knows, even if it thinks it doesn't."

Ana hugged her own elbows. "What does it want?"

"To warn," Hye-jin said. "Or to be heard warning. Those aren't the same."

Owen leaned back on the bench until the wood complained. "We're not built to carry this."

"Then we distribute the weight," Mateo said. "Make more copies. Not out of spite. Out of redundancy."

"Redundancy is not waste," Priya murmured, surprising herself with Vass's creed without knowing its origin. "It's memory with a backup."

"Where'd you hear that?" Owen asked.

"No idea," Priya said, and shivered.

They divided tasks without naming them assignments. Ana would print, store, and mail a copy to her mother, because her mother knew what to do with seeds. Priya would tuck another thumb drive into a freezer under a bag of ice that wasn't ice, in a lab that changed locks too often to memorize. Owen would hide a copy inside the demo satellite chassis, the one marked *EDU-SIM: DO NOT DEPLOY*, because the safest place to hide a secret was in the thing that pretended to be a toy. Mateo would push the checksum into a math forum as a puzzle, stripped of context, and let curiosity do the seditious work. Hye-jin would do nothing new and everything—keep listening.

"Meet tomorrow?" Ana asked.

"Tomorrow's already here," Hye-jin said. "We just keep pretending it isn't."

Ruiz

Director Ruiz stood in her office with the blinds half open. She stared at the city as if it were a patient refusing an IV. On her desk lay a draft email from Helios Public Affairs: *joint statement on intermittent instrument interference.* It included words like *solar wind* and *calibration* and *no cause for public concern.*

She closed the draft and opened a blank file labeled **Private — Kale/Patel**. She typed: *You are both on leave starting tomorrow. Use it.* Then she deleted *Use it* and replaced it with *Rest.* She deleted that too. She hit send on the leave forms and left her office with the lights on.

Downstairs, she signed out of the building. The guard, a man with the tragic mustache of budget cuts, said, "Night, Director."

"Try again," she said.

"Good night," he corrected, and she nodded like that word mattered.

The Watcher

On the roof of Helios, Vass stood where he always stood when he wanted the city to behave: at the southwest corner where the wind kept a clean edge. The signal had stopped, but he knew it would return.

Marian joined him, hands ungloved against the cold. "Phase II in motion," she said. "We have a list of student names. Park, Okoye, Lin, Deshmukh, McCall."

"Recruit them," Vass repeated. "If recruitment fails, confuse them."

"And Kale and Patel?"

"Give them paid rest," he said. "Fatigue makes friends."

"You're misquoting your own principle," Marian said. "Fear is fuel."

"I have more than one engine," Vass said.

He looked up. A smear of light stained the north horizon—too far south for aurora and too organized for aircraft. He watched it stretch slowly across the horizon.

"Hold together," he told the sky. "A decade."

The light answered with a pulse not visible enough to blame. Marian, who did not believe in omens, rubbed her fingers together where the cold had found skin and said nothing.

Paper

Mira lived in an apartment the color of quiet and habit: a bookshelf heavy with other people's futures, plants that completed their own arrangement, a table that had always been two inches too short for its ambitions. She placed three manila envelopes in a pile and addressed them by hand: one to herself (future proof), one to a retired engineer in New Mexico who owed her a favor and had never learned to type, one to a P.O. box she'd opened under a name she didn't like saying.

Inside each envelope she placed a printout of the amplitude phrase *PREPARE*, a note that said *When the briefing says calibration, do not believe it*, and a single gray still frame of the words **DO NOT LET THEM SI-LENCE**. She added a pack of wildflower seeds to one envelope because the ritual soothed her superstition.

When she licked the last stamp, she sat very still. Silence returned to the apartment. She let it sit.

Her phone vibrated once with an unknown number. She let it go to voicemail. The transcript arrived: **Ms. Patel, this is Lydia Raines with the Global Sustainability Alliance...** She deleted it and took a breath she wished she'd taken an hour earlier.

Walk

Ethan walked until the city lost its reflective surfaces: side streets where steam rose from grates, a deli man hosing down early shame, a park bench where many confessions were made. He kept his hands in his coat and counted streetlights out of habit, an old trick to tell himself he wasn't being followed.

His feet found the river. He stood with his elbows on a railing and tried to imagine the L-1 point like a friend's apartment he could buzz: a gravity saddle between Sun and Earth where a thing could hover and pretend to be at rest while the rest of the universe moved.

"You're not at rest either," he told the dark.

A jogger passed, breath making weather. A gull wheeled, laughed at something only gulls would. In the water, a barge groaned under containers stamped with logos that had replaced family names in some households. He didn't look up.

His phone buzzed. A text from a number Mira had sent him once with no comment:

Park here. Do you hear it too?

(attached: a checksum)

He smiled despite himself. "Good," he said. "Let it spread."

He typed back nothing. Then he deleted the nothing and turned the phone off.

The Briefing

The auditorium smelled of nerves and new paint. Banners on both sides of the stage read **NASA | HELIOS SYSTEMS** in fonts that had been focus-grouped for credibility. Cameras blinked like patient eyes.

Director Ruiz stood at the podium, the weight of her agency folded into her shoulders. Behind her, Gregor Vass looked like a man who had never been wrong in public.

"Good afternoon," Ruiz began. "We want to clarify recent reports of anomalous solar activity and signal interference affecting several observatories. The fluctuations are the result of *instrument calibration irregularities* and *unexpected solar wind density*. There's nothing suggesting other sources."

She paused, eyes scanning a room full of journalists pretending to be calm.

Vass stepped forward. "Helios Systems is proud to assist NASA in ensuring the integrity of our shared data. Together we will upgrade the nation's deep-space arrays to meet tomorrow's challenges."

A reporter called out, "Mr. Vass, is it true a private university cluster detected the same anomalies?"

Vass smiled. "Curiosity is contagious. That's what makes science so vibrant. We look forward to nurturing that curiosity through our *Global Sustainability Alliance* partners."

His tone was perfectly balanced—half humility, half ownership.

Ruiz added, "We urge everyone to focus on verified data. Misinformation harms the public understanding of science."

Another reporter shouted, "So there's no alien message?"

Ruiz hesitated just long enough for truth to try and escape. "No," she said. "There is *no* verified communication from beyond our solar system."

Vass nodded solemnly beside her, eyes steady on the cameras. He didn't need to say a word; his silence endorsed the lie.

The Watchers

At the back of the auditorium, Mira Patel and Ethan Kale stood among technicians, credentials reversed on their lanyards. They listened without expression until the applause ended.

"That's it," Mira said. "We're officially ghosts."

Ethan's jaw tightened. "You expected honesty?"

"I expected hesitation."

"She gave them that," he said.

Ruiz's gaze met theirs as she stepped off the stage. A silent apology. A warning. Then she was gone, absorbed by press handlers and security.

Vass walked past a moment later, flanked by assistants. He didn't look at them—but the corner of his mouth curved, the smallest acknowledgment that ghosts could still cast shadows.

The Campus

The university had stopped pretending it was neutral ground. Helios vans lined the quad, their logos reflecting in puddles from a morning rain. Temporary fencing boxed off half the observatory, signs reading **AUTHORIZED PERSONNEL ONLY** and **SYSTEM UPGRADE IN PROGRESS.**

Students clustered outside the barriers, holding printed memes of calibration dials labeled *TRUTH* and *LIES*. Someone had spray-painted **HELLO** on a physics lab wall, letters mirrored backward.

Ana and Priya watched from the steps. "They move fast," Priya said.

"Money moves faster," Ana replied.

Owen joined them, eyes red from lack of sleep. "They're installing new antennas. Vass called it a 'collaboration initiative.'"

Mateo arrived with a folded paper in his hand. "Schedule for tonight. Mandatory orientation for all Alliance fellows. They're closing the network from midnight to four."

Hye-jin stared at the line that said *Access restrictions during upgrade.* "They're going to erase the mirrors."

Ana frowned. "Can they?"

"They built the mirrors," Hye-jin said. "They can make them forget."

Intercept

The group met again in the old library rotunda, the air thick with the smell of ozone from nearby generators.

Ethan and Mira slipped in quietly, wearing visitor badges that said *Helios Technical Audit*—a disguise so brazen it worked.

Hye-jin recognized Ethan first. "Dr. Kale," she said.

"You must be Park," Ethan replied.

Hye-jin nodded once. "Yes."

Priya looked between them. "Should we be running?"

"Not yet," Mira said. "We don't have anywhere to run *to*."

They gathered around the central table. Ethan laid out printed amplitude maps—black-and-white ripples like fingerprints.

"This is what started it," he said. "But it's not random. Seems targeted."

"Targeted at who?" Owen asked.

"Earth," Ethan said. "Specifically, anything listening."

Ana touched one of the graphs. "We are listening."

"Exactly," Mira said. "The signal behaves like it knows it's being watched. When receivers multiply, it strengthens."

"So it's feeding on observation?" Mateo asked.

"Or on connection," Mira said. "Whatever it is, Helios wants to control the receiver network before it grows beyond them."

"Too late," Hye-jin said. "It's everywhere now. Every copy we made, every checksum Mateo posted—they're all part of the system. You can't delete attention."

Ethan nodded. "Then we need to shield at least one node before the purge. Somewhere off grid."

"The mountain lab," Priya said. "Old geology station—no fiber, only analog relay. University keeps it for weather experiments."

"Perfect," Ethan said. "We move tonight."

Mira handed out slips of paper. Coordinates, access codes. "Burn them after reading."

"Dramatic," Owen muttered.

"Necessary," she said. "Helios thinks control equals safety. They're wrong on both counts."

Power Down

At 23:58, campus power dipped again. The official explanation: scheduled maintenance. The unofficial one: containment.

Generators coughed to life near the observatory. Engineers in Helios jackets moved between trucks, their radios murmuring in corporate Esperanto.

Inside the chemistry building, Priya unplugged her reactors one by one, each click a small act of rebellion. Owen disassembled his demo satellite, removing the hidden thumb drive and slipping it into his jacket.

Ana harvested a handful of algae vials, sealed them in cold storage, and whispered, "You're coming too."

Mateo wiped the servers clean except for one folder labeled *Temp*, inside which he left a text file that read simply: *HELLO, AGAIN.*

Hye-jin watched from the window as the floodlights carved circles in the fog. The air vibrated with the same frequency she'd felt before the blackout. She grabbed her backpack, checked the drive in her pocket, and ran.

The Pursuit

The road to the mountain lab wound through forest and fog. Their van's headlights painted brief ghosts of trees. Ethan drove, Mira navigating by an old topographic map that didn't believe in GPS.

Ana and Priya whispered in the backseat; Owen dozed with one hand still on the hidden drive; Mateo counted time between static bursts on a portable scanner. Hye-jin sat nearest the window, laptop balanced on her knees, watching the waveform pulse in rhythm with her heartbeat.

"We're being followed," she said.

Ethan didn't ask how she knew—just checked the mirror. A pair of lights floated too steady behind them. Corporate SUV, tinted windows, the kind that came with NDAs in the glove compartment.

"Hold tight," he said.

The SUV stayed on the main road, then vanished behind the ridge.

When they reached the gate of the weather station, the padlock was gone. In its place hung a fresh Helios seal.

Owen exhaled. "They're already here."

Mira stepped out, cold slicing her face. "Then we're right on time."

She pulled a small bolt cutter from her bag—*NASA standard issue,* she said dryly—and snapped the seal.

They pushed through the gate. The building beyond was half buried in snow, its windows dark. Above it, the aurora shimmered faintly, forming arcs that seemed to bend toward the same invisible point between Earth and the Sun.

Ethan looked up. "That's not a storm," he said. "That's a signal."

The Mountain Lab

Snow squeaked under their boots. The weather station door stuck at first—paint welded to jamb by cold—then gave with a groan that stirred old air. Inside, the dark smelled of dust and ozone, the particular perfume of equipment that trusted only analog.

"Lights," Owen said.

"Not yet," Mira answered. "Let the eyes adjust before the circuits."

They stood, breathing steam, until outlines separated from shadow: a console the size of a diner counter; a wall of patch bays; a rack of tube amps that looked like they'd been retired from a jazz club; an antenna switcher with dials labeled in pencil by someone who had considered permanence a rumor. A paper calendar on the wall still read **MAY** three years ago.

Ethan found the breaker panel and flipped only what he needed—line power to the main bus, heater to *low,* the antenna rotor under *manual.* Tubes glowed orange by degrees, a small sunrise in metal.

Mira set her bag on the console, pulled out a coil of coax, a spool of wire, a field notebook, a pencil she sharpened with a pocket knife. The pencil made a satisfying sound against the blade. "We do this as if we're being watched," she said. "Because we are."

Hye-jin slid into a chair with the speed of hunger. "Receiver path?"

"Roof whip to preamp to band-pass to narrow IF," Ethan said, hands moving as he named each piece. He spoke to the room like a surgeon briefing a team that already knew its roles. "No computers on the front end. If we digitize, we invite company."

Owen and Mateo went for the roof hatch. Cold fell in like an argument. The ladder rungs burned their gloves. On the roof the wind shoved them half a step; the sky turned faintly green. The old whip antenna leaned west, sulking; Owen braced it while Mateo cinched the guy wire.

"Pointing," Mateo called down the hatch.

"L-1 saddle," Ethan said. "Due sunward then up two degrees for drift. We're aiming at gravity, not a star."

"Love a sensible target," Owen muttered, and set the azimuth by hand, the rotor whining like an old throat clearing.

Below, Ana laid out vials inside a foam cooler she'd brought for algae like it was medicine. Priya unpacked a handheld spectrum sniffer and a battered pH meter. Chemistry was her superstition. Even here, in the clean cold above the world, she wanted a number to say yes.

"Power on," Ethan said. He closed a double-throw knife switch. The preamp sang quietly to itself. The analog meter nudged from zero to attention.

Everyone leaned closer.

Static filled the room: a forgiving, gentle hiss. Ethan tuned through it, one wrist turning the dial with a finesse that looked like memory. The hiss narrowed. A murmur appeared.

"Hold—there," Mira said, palm hovering. "Lock it."

Ethan clicked in the band-pass notch he'd hand-soldered twenty minutes ago. Hiss cut further, like a curtain tied back. What remained came and went on a slow swell. Hye-jin's eyes flooded before she could stop them.

"That's it," she breathed. "That's them."

"Record," Ethan said.

Mira shook her head. "Paper first." She set the pencil on the moving chart.

"Gain," Owen said from the hatch, climbing down, face raw with cold. "We're at the edge."

Ethan nudged a knob. The room's speakers—fat gray boxes that looked too old to try anything risky—let the murmur step into audibility. A phrase emerged, ragged at the edges, a child learning a second language.

"Hel—" a pause, a breath, "—lo."

Ana clutched the cooler with both hands. Priya's pH meter beeped for no reason and she slapped it quiet.

The voice—if voice it was—deepened as if pausing to find the right keys in a dark drawer. It came again, slower, stronger, clear enough that denial would have to lower its voice to speak.

"Hello, Earth."

The room went still.

No one moved. They listened for anything that could make this human—an engineer on a mountain playing a prank, a helicopter hunting its Doppler, some terrible trick a corporation could buy.

"Again," Hye-jin whispered, not to the machine but to whatever cared enough to need a nudge.

A rustle across the band. Then:

"Prepare."

Mira's pencil trembled, drew a double line. "For what?" she said aloud, reflex, and hated herself for asking a question to a radio.

Something like laughter and like grief came back—a modulation that touched both. The tubes in the rack glowed a shade brighter. The building creaked in the wind.

"Star—" the pause was longer this time, as if crossing a word cost fuel, "—decay accelerating."

Ana felt her stomach do a small wrong. "How do we prepare?" she asked, and in that second of speaking she was every person who had ever said please to the dark.

The reply changed timbre as if routed through a different throat.

"Do not let them silence."

Them. It had said them in Ethan's lab. Now it said it to all of them.

"Who?" Priya asked, stupid, necessary.

Static took the question and gnawed at it. The answer, when it came, arrived like rain on a metal roof—separate, then suddenly coherent.

"Those who—control—receivers."

Ethan rested his fingers on the desk, as if feeling the signal move through wood. "How far are you?"

A long pause. The meter needle quivered. The tubes dimmed, brightened. The voice returned quieter, which made it sound closer.

"Light years—late. We—lost—most. We—remember your star. It—sings wrong."

Mateo made a sound he didn't know he could make. "We're measuring it," he said, to the floor.

"Where are you?" Hye-jin asked, breath fogging the chart.

"Between—stars," it said, as if that were a place with an address. "Between—yesterday—and—what you build next."

Owen gripped the back of a chair hard enough that old varnish creaked. "What do we do?"

The answer came back in short, simple phrases.

"Keep—listening. Copy. Many copies. When they—close doors—make windows. When they—name fear—name—each other."

Mira exhaled the air she'd been hoarding. "We can do that," she said, and realized commitment had a sound.

From outside: tires hissed on snow. A door slammed. Voices in the wind, clipped, male. Owen killed the speakers with a palm.

"We have company," he said.

Ethan reached for the main knife switch. Mira caught his wrist. "If we cut, the trace dies," she said.

"If we don't, it dies with us," he said, a grim joke that wasn't. He left the switch up.

Boots on the stairs. A flashlight swept the hall and found the outline of the shut door. A knuckle rapped twice with the confidence of ownership.

"University facilities," a voice called. "We're here to complete the upgrade."

Mira whispered, "Helios."

The rapping again, softer, patient. "We can open this or you can."

Ethan's hand moved to the patch bay instead. He pulled a pair of banana plugs and re-seated them in a way that sent the receiver's output on the schematic—a line labeled in fading pencil **WX RELAY**. A weather relay—old, unmetered, still tied to a broadcast tower five ridgelines away.

"Signal out the back door," he whispered.

The voice on the other side of the door switched to polite threat. "Please open. We do not want to damage university property."

Ana looked at Mira. "We can't fight them."

"No," Mira said. "We can waste their time."

She crossed to the door and turned the dead bolt with the slowness of someone considering options. She cracked the door two inches, enough for a face to be a badge.

Two men in Helios jackets stood there with a third behind them holding a pelican case like a verdict. The front man smiled the company smile.

"Good evening," he said. "We're authorized to complete a critical systems upgrade. Please step aside."

"This is a weather station," Mira said mildly. "We already have weather."

"We're improving it," he said, and put a hand on the door.

Ethan nodded at Owen. Owen nodded at gravity. He jammed a screwdriver through the hinge pin. The door stuck. The front man's smile dimmed.

"We'll call campus police," he said.

"Coverage is spotty at this elevation," Mira said. "Weather."

From the console, the tubes pulsed. The chart paper advanced, whispering. Hye-jin bent close and saw the line thicken into letters again, not English this time—geometric characters.

"What does it say?" Ana whispered.

Hye-jin tilted her head, her mind feeling for the string that would pull meaning taut. "Coordinates," she said. "Not L-1. Lower. Closer. Here." She tapped the page. "A point above us."

"Drone?" Priya asked.

"Messenger," the voice said from the speaker Owen had turned back up just enough to hear in the room and not in the hall. "We—left—you—seed."

Ethan's eyes snapped to the roof hatch. "On the roof," he said.

Owen already had the ladder. Mateo was behind him. They climbed into cold that bit wrists and ears raw. The aurora thinned to a gauze. Snow scuffed under boots. At the ridge of the roof something small and wrong lay half-buried: a sphere the size of a grapefruit, frost-beaded, seams like veins.

"Don't touch with bare," Owen said. Mateo handed him a rag. He lifted the sphere. It hummed against his glove, a vibration too steady to be accident. He passed it down the hatch like a newborn.

"Close—door," the voice said from the speaker, hurried now, syllables clacking. "They—jam—open—receivers."

At the front door, the Helios men had produced a shiny multipurpose crowbar and the arrogance that came with insurance. The hinge pin groaned under argument. Mira stood with her hand on the inner handle, looking like a person about to teach a lesson to a door.

Inside, Ethan set the sphere on the console. It thrummed and warmed, frost melting into coins of water. A seam dilated.

From within, a filament uncurled—thin, silvery, like the strand from a long-busted lightbulb—and stiffened into an arc that bridged two of the console's binding posts as if the sphere knew what a patch bay was.

"Hello," the sphere said.

Ana yelped. Priya made a sound like tearing paper. Hye-jin put both hands over her mouth and then took them down because she didn't want to put any barrier between her and whatever this was.

The door hinge shrieked. Metal moved.

"Time's up," Mira said.

"Not yet," Ethan said, and touched the filament lightly with a fingertip. It didn't spark. The chart line leapt and settled.

"Take," the sphere said. "Keep."

"What are we taking?" Hye-jin asked. "What are we keeping?"

"Pattern," it said. "Seed. Build. Leave."

Priya swallowed. "Leave what?"

"Home," it said, and the word hurt.

The hinge pin popped. The door banged against the stop, caught by the screwdriver, held for another breath, two. The front man's smile had left; only his job remained.

"Now," Mira said. She picked up the sphere with her scarf wrapped around her hands, tucked it into Ana's foam cooler like contraband fruit. She snapped the lid. "Go," she told Ana. "Back hatch. Ridge path. No lights."

"I'm not—" Ana began.

"You are," Mira said, and pushed the cooler at her. "Gardens go first."

Ana nodded once and ran, Priya on her heels with the pH meter still in her pocket because it was easier not to change pockets in a crisis. Owen grabbed the thumb drive from his jacket and dropped it in the cooler on instinct. Mateo ripped the chart page free, rolled it, and stuffed it into his sleeve. Hye-jin hesitated, hand on the console, palm flat as if to memorize warmth.

"Go," Ethan told her. "We'll give you a minute."

She went.

At the door, the screwdriver tore free and clanged to the floor. The slab swung in. Helios stepped through, polite, inevitable.

"This facility is now under Alliance authority," the front man said, as if declaring weather.

"Show me the statute," Mira replied, because procedure still mattered to her.

"We have a letter," he said, and handed her a paper that smelled like toner and debt.

Ethan reached behind him and flipped the knife switch down. The tubes cooled instantly, orange to dark. The chart stopped. The room went quiet.

The Helios man looked around, taking in analog like an insult. "You're interfering with an upgrade."

"We're preserving a mechanism," Mira said. "You can't improve a tool if you don't know what it does."

"We know what it does," he said. "It makes people afraid."

Ethan smiled faintly. "It makes them *ready*."

The man flicked his fingers. Two techs moved to the console, pelican case open, new black boxes inside like night. Owen stepped in front of them without realizing he was stepping; for a second, his body remembered sports, not ethics.

"Sir," one tech said patiently. Owen didn't move. The tech didn't either.

From down the hall: the bang of the back door, then silence as it closed itself over secrets. Wind nosed the crack and found it solid. On the ridge: boot prints tried to disappear and failed.

The Helios man sighed.

"You're in violation," he said.

"Of what?" Mira asked. "Listening?"

"Of containment," he said, which was honest without meaning to be.

"Then we plead guilty," Ethan said, and held out his wrists as if the man had brought handcuffs. He hadn't. He had paperwork.

They let themselves be escorted to the hallway.

The last thing Ethan saw as he stepped over the threshold was the console: dark, still, and—impossibly—warm. He didn't touch it. He didn't need to. The warmth had already moved into the cooler under Ana's arm.

Outside, the aurora faded to a thin ribbon of light and held there.

Behind them, a tiny green LED on the weather relay flicked once, twice, and stayed on. Somewhere five ridgelines away, a ham operator in a shed heard a hello and wrote it in a notebook with a pencil she sharpened with her teeth.

Chapter 7

Selection Pressure

The silence after the escape felt unreal.

For the first time in weeks, the hum of the facility's magnetic containment rings was gone. In its place: a low desert wind pushing dust across the horizon and the mechanical rasp of cooling engines. Ethan stood outside the convoy transport, staring back at the smoldering shape of the Helios compound. The high concrete perimeter still pulsed with emergency lights, red against the twilight.

Mira leaned against the side of the transport, her arms crossed tightly over her chest.

"They'll seal it off by nightfall," she said. "Everything in there will be buried in the report. Radiation leak, structural failure—whatever sounds least like what actually happened."

Ethan didn't answer. He was watching the horizon where the heat haze warped the air. Above, the sun pushed through thin clouds, dull and red.

"You're thinking about the signal," Mira said softly.

He nodded. "It wasn't just data. That pulse wasn't random interference. We caught a structure—mathematical recursion—before the containment spike hit. Something reacted to us."

"Or something *used* us," she murmured.

Inside the convoy, the rest of the team was silent. Ana and Mateo sat side by side, both staring at the cracked tablet on the dashboard replaying the last telemetry from Helios: a single, brief, repeating waveform, shrinking each cycle until it vanished. Owen and Hye-jin were asleep, exhaustion overtaking the adrenaline.

Mira finally looked away from Ethan. "Langley's already recalling us. You know what that means. They'll scatter the team. Classified project, indefinite non-disclosure."

Ethan ran a hand through his hair. "They can classify the data. Not the consequences."

Two thousand miles away, in a boardroom made of glass and gold, **Gregor Vass** stared at a holographic rendering of the same waveform. The image hovered above the conference table, surrounded by advisers and engineers who didn't dare speak.

Vass's tone was calm, almost gentle. "You're certain this is what they detected?"

"Yes, sir," said the lead analyst. "The data was partially encrypted before the system meltdown, but what survived matches your archived frequencies from Project Aether."

That got Vass's attention. He rose, slowly and with measured calm. "Aether was shut down fifteen years ago," he said. "And every trace of it buried."

"Yes, sir. But it seems Helios stumbled onto the same structure. Same recursion pattern. Different amplitude."

Vass looked toward the darkened windows where the city below shimmered with energy. "Then we're out of time."

Back in New Mexico, the convoy stopped at an old refueling station— one of those forgotten relics of the interstate age. The sign's lettering had long since faded away, leaving only faded paint and a single flickering bulb. Mira stepped outside, stretching her legs, while Ethan checked the satellite uplink on the roof. Static. No network. No GPS. They were off the grid.

Ana joined him. "Do you think it's connected? The solar irregularities, the signal, the field collapse?"

Ethan looked at her, his expression tired but focused. "Connected or causal. Either way, it's accelerating. Whatever's happening to the Sun—it's not a natural decay. The frequency pattern we saw... it was trying to *stabilize* something. Like an attempt to stabilize a failing system."

Ana swallowed. "And we disrupted it."

He didn't answer, but his silence said enough.

Across the ocean, in Geneva, emergency satellites began reporting microflares—tiny, rapid bursts across multiple solar sectors. The International Astronomical Council went into session before dawn. A scientist named Dr. Klaus Steiner stared at the live feed, whispering under his breath,

"This isn't fluctuation... it's coordination."

And somewhere deep beneath the Pacific, in an observation dome long forgotten by its financiers, a machine older than any known installation began to stir—its sensors warming after decades of silence, listening for the same signal Helios had caught.

The refueling station's icebox rattled loudly in the corner. Ethan smacked it twice and the light came on, revealing a row of ancient sodas that looked embalmed. He didn't want the drink—he wanted something ordinary to still work.

Mira slid a granola bar across the counter. "One for superstition, one for blood sugar."

"Which is which?"

"You tell me," she said, and broke hers in half. They chewed in silence, listening to the wind skate over the cracked forecourt. Beyond the dead pumps, the desert had taken back what the highway left behind, small dunes swallowing the shoulder.

Hye-jin emerged from the transport rubbing sleep from her eyes. "Any word from Langley?"

Ethan shook his head. "Sat link's jammed or down. Could be intentional—containment blackout after an incident."

"Or the flares," she said softly.

Owen joined them with the tablet cradled against his chest. "I've got a local FM station." He held up a cheap transistor he'd scavenged from the station office. A thin voice pressed through static: traffic reports, a snippet of a ballgame, then—

"...multiple auroral reports visible at unusual latitudes—Texas, Florida, northern Morocco... repeat, this is not a drill... expect communications disruptions..."

Ana exhaled. "Auroras at our latitude? That's not small."

Mira looked to the sky where the daylight simmered. "It's the field. The magnetosphere's twitching."

"Or being twitched," Owen said.

They all turned to Ethan. He didn't need to be told to lead anymore; the decision had been made back inside Helios, when he'd pulled the emergency vent override with his own hands. "We get out of the blackout zone," he said. "We drive two hundred miles north, find elevation, line-of-sight to a working relay. If Langley is trying to yank our badges, they can do it with a signature later. For now, we keep the data alive."

"And if they send a recovery team?" Hye-jin asked.

Ethan's mouth set like a seam. "Then we outrun them."

He looked at Mira. She nodded once, then shouted for Mateo to fuel the transport from the station's underground tank. The pump motor struggled, but then it spun.

Inside, the air smelled of oil, old coffee, and something sweet that had rotted a decade ago. Ana sat backward on the passenger bench, knees tucked, watching Ethan over the seat back. "What if we're wrong?" she asked quietly. "What if the signal wasn't trying to stabilize anything? What if it was the thing that destabilized it in the first place, and we amplified it by listening?"

"Then we still need to know what it is," Ethan said. "Because it's not stopping."

On the other side of the continent, the attorney **Leila Vaziri** felt her phone vibrate three times in the middle of oral arguments. In the hushed New York courtroom, the judge looked up, one eyebrow working. Leila never left her device on anything but silent, never checked messages in the middle of a hearing. Her reputation depended on it.

But the second vibration was the emergency broadcast. The third was her son's school.

"Your Honor," she said, swallowing. "My apologies. Client emergency."

The judge nodded in the world-weary way of men who had seen everything twice. "Five minutes, Ms. Vaziri."

She stepped into the corridor paneled with nicked mahogany, thumbed the notifications. **National Weather Service:** geomagnetic storm watch—expect GPS errors, grid instability. **City Schools:** dismissal moved up two hours, buses running early. **Arjun:** *Mom, sky is green. For real.*

She leaned against the cool wall, her voice low when she called her husband. "Navid, can you get him?"

"I'm already on my way," he said. "Sky looks like a bruise. The cars' navs are confused."

"Use surface streets," she said automatically. Familiar routines calmed her breathing. "I'll wrap here and meet you at home."

"Leila," he said, a little softer, "it's going to be fine."

"I know."

She didn't. She ended the call and closed her eyes long enough to picture their apartment's south windows and the cheap telescope Arjun had begged for over the summer. The last time the sky had looked strange, Arjun had dragged her to the roof to watch a meteor shower. He'd fallen asleep there under a blanket while she answered emails. She pressed two fingers to her eyelids until stars twitched and steadied herself.

Back in court, she finished in seven minutes, delivering her statements with practiced precision that could survive an appeal. When it was done, the judge gave her a small nod that felt like a hand on the shoulder. She packed her bag and stepped out into a city that suddenly felt unfamiliar.

On the subway platform, an MTA employee shouted: "Cash only! Cards are down! Cash only!" Leila took the stairs back up, choosing to walk.

In Phoenix, the architect Daniel Carras stood in the skeleton of a tower and watched a ribbon of green light unspool across the midafternoon sky. Twenty-seven stories below, his foreman called something up about a delayed concrete pour. Daniel barely heard him. The breeze at this height carried grit and the coppery smell of rebar. He'd brought clients up here last week to show them the view they were buying—sunsets clients paid extra to see.

His phone dinged: a text of his daughters in the backyard in goggles, their faces washed in green glow. His wife's caption: *Science class, courtesy of the end of the world ;) Call me.* The emoji softened it. The last two words didn't.

He dialed. "How bad is it?"

"It's beautiful," Elena said. "And kind of wrong. The radio said power companies are doing load-shedding just in case."

He looked at the cranes, at the workers in neon vests lifting their faces to the sky. "I'm coming down."

"Don't be dramatic."

"I promised them we'd watch the first monsoon together this year," he said. It wasn't the monsoon, but it felt like a strange weather of a different sort. The kind of pressure that nobody could explain. "I'll bring pizza."

Down on the deck, he told his foreman to secure the site—double tie the tarps, park the lifts, power down the tower crane if the grid flickered. The man looked at the sky and nodded once, then started securing the site without another word.

On the forty-sixth floor of the Vass Capital tower, **Vass** slid a key from a small velvet case and unlocked a steel cabinet recessed into the wall.

The cabinet didn't match the room—too functional, too ugly among the black stone and gold. Inside, stacked imaging modules and drives glowed a polite blue.

"Bring up Aether," he told his chief of staff, Nadia Korin.

She didn't flinch. "Sir, the board will ask why—"

"The board will be told what to ask," he said, not unkindly. "Tomorrow, they'll call me visionary for doing today what scares them."

He placed one drive on the conference table. The holo spilled into being with a wick of light: a lattice of numbers and harmonic structures rotating slowly in the air.

The lead analyst hovered with his tablet. "Project Aether's goal was to model solar resonance interference—"

"Aether's goal," Vass said, "was to **steer** resonance. To influence solar resonance, if you prefer precise language."

The analyst shut his mouth. Nadia sat at the far end of the table, back straight, long fingers folded, watching Vass carefully, waiting to see where the conversation turned.

"Fifteen years ago," Vass said, "we stopped because the signal-to-noise was poor. Because the public couldn't tolerate experiments they didn't understand. Now the Sun is responding to something. The question is whether we can respond in time."

"And if we can't?" Nadia asked.

"Then we will choose who lives under a more forgiving sky," Vass said simply. "Either way, we stop pretending the world owes us unlimited choices."

He gestured to the analyst. "Who do we still have?"

The analyst swiped names onto the air. Some were alive and reachable. Others were dead or gone to other industries. A few had vanished into government labs.

"Priya Narayanan?" Vass asked, tapping a name lit amber.

The analyst looked relieved to have an easy one. "Caltech, then DARPA, then off the map."

"On the map," Vass said. "She consults for a boutique defense contractor in San Diego, which consults for us. She likes small teacups and projects where she can be the only adult in the room. Offer her both, then triple it."

Nadia made a note. "And the ethics advisory board?"

Vass almost smiled. "You're looking at it."

The NASA convoy crossed a dry wash and rattled north into hills thrown down by ancient geology. As the elevation climbed, the radio static thinned.

"Got it," Hye-jin said from the rear bank, fingers flickering over a portable terminal patched into the uplink. "Angle five degrees, hold—"

The transport topped a ridge. The dish locked onto the satellite. A chirp turned into a dial tone and then into a handshake as the system negotiated for a satellite that wasn't choked with traffic. The secure tunnel opened—a single green bead on Hye-jin's screen.

Ethan leaned over her shoulder. "Push everything."

"Dumping," she said. "All logs from Helios: pre-event, event, post-event. Side channel to three endpoints: Langley primary, JPL mirror, and—your personal node?"

Ethan hesitated for a second. "And mine. In case the agency shelves it."

Mira watched him, catching the tension in his jaw. It wasn't distrust; it was insurance. She'd spent enough nights in clandestine lives—hiding their relationship at work, hiding their fear from their team—to recognize the small habits that kept you from drowning.

"Done," Hye-jin said. "Hashes match. We have receipts."

"Now we call them," Mira said. "On open line."

Ethan nodded. "Put me through to Langley control."

The voice that answered didn't belong to anyone they knew. It was too smooth, too measured. "Dr. Kale. Dr. Patel. Please remain where you are. A team is en route to debrief you and secure the materials."

"Then we'll wait," Ethan lied.

"Helios experienced a catastrophic systems failure," the voice continued. "This is a national security incident. All personnel are to be accounted for. You are currently listed as missing."

"We prefer 'working,'" Mira said. "We transmitted all data. You should have it now."

A pause—a human pausing somewhere behind the voice. "We have your transmission. You were not authorized to—"

"Is the Sun authorized?" Ethan snapped before he could stop himself. Mira touched his wrist. He softened his tone. "We're ready to brief. But the data needs to be out of quarantine before somebody decides to bury it.

If this is bigger than us—and it is—you need the private sector, the academic labs, the international arrays. If you sit on this for a week, we may not have a week."

"Your concern is noted," the voice said, and somehow made the word **concern** sound quaint. "Stand by."

The line went dead.

Mira's eyes were already on Hye-jin. "Trace?"

"Routed through a federal gateway in Virginia," she said. "We were talking to someone with a badge and a playbook."

"Not our badge," Owen said.

Ana smoothed a stray curl behind her ear and stared at the scrolling spectrogram on the tablet—a throwaway gesture that had become comfort. "We need an outside head," she said. "Someone nobody can scare into silence."

"Priya," Ethan said without thinking. "If she's still reachable."

Mira half-smiled. "You've kept in touch?"

"Once," he said. "On a paper review. She wrote in the margins like she was trying to cut the paper apart."

Hye-jin was already stabbing keys. "I can pivot through the Caltech alumni net... got a forwarding contact at an SD consultancy. Burning a favor."

Owen leaned back, eyes closed, lips moving. Mira knew what he was doing, rehearsing everything they needed to say in one breath before anyone could cut the line. Ethan envied the calm of that ritual.

The uplink trilled. **PRIYA NARAYANAN — ACCEPT.**

Hye-jin stabbed the screen.

"Ethan?" The woman's voice was sharp, and fully awake. "If you're cold-calling me, either you finally regretted that footnote you cut from the Halley paper, or the sky is falling."

"Priya," he said, and told her in three minutes about the signal, the recursion, the containment spike, the auroras at twenty-nine degrees latitude. She let him finish without interruption, then asked three questions that punctured the story and exposed its weak points.

"And your data is secure?" she asked finally.

"Triple-mirrored," Hye-jin said, leaning into the mic. "Langley, JPL, and a private node. If someone buried it at one, it lives at the others."

"Good," Priya said. "Because some very expensive people are going to try to either buy it or bury it. If your recursion matches the Aether lattice—"

"What lattice?" Mira cut in.

There was the smallest pause. "You didn't hear that from me. I'll call you back on a line that doesn't belong to anyone. Stay mobile. Do not meet any teams in suits unless you can see the outline of their agency ID through their jacket."

She hung up.

Owen opened one eye. "We just got invited to a party we weren't supposed to know existed."

"Project Aether," Mira said, testing the shape of it in her mouth. "Rings a bell?"

Ethan shook his head. "Only as myth."

"Most myths have a funder," Hye-jin murmured.

Late afternoon, the light turned a deeper brass, and the auroral band thickened into curtains that writhed, throwing ghost shadows across the ground. The transport's HUD flickered twice and stabilized. Far below, towns blinked as grids shifted loads, tripping old failsafes never meant for this cadence.

In Phoenix, Daniel steered with one hand and passed slices of pizza back to his daughters with the other, telling them—because it would be true when he said it—that they were going to the roof after dinner to watch the lights as a family. Elena turned on the radio and then turned off again when the anchor said *unprecedented* too many times in a row. On their street, neighbors stood on their porches holding beers and phones, watching the sky like it was a parade they hadn't planned for.

In New York, Leila hurried past a bodega generator cough-smoking to life and caught her reflection in a darkened boutique window: blouse wrinkled, hair escaping its clip, trying to think through schedules, traffic, and getting home. She cut across the park and found Navid and Arjun waiting by the bronze bear statue, their faces green-lit. Arjun waved his arms. "We're inside the aurora, Mom! We're in space!"

Leila made a promise into her son's hair she wasn't sure she could keep: "We are absolutely **not** in space."

At the Vass tower, the first Aether terminal came online with a polite chime that sounded almost apologetic for the power it represented.

Priya's name slid from *amber* to *green* on the recruitment board as Nadia watched. She hid her surprise behind the angle of her jaw.

"She'll come," Vass said. He looked very tired, which on him read as almost kind.

"And if she brings others?" Nadia asked.

"We will pay them, and if they won't be paid, we will scare them. If they won't be scared, we will show them the math." He turned to the window where the aurora's limb colored the edges of skyscrapers as if someone had painted with light and forgot the lines. "Nadia, how many seats can we build if we had to?"

She blinked. "Seats, sir?"

"For leaving," he said. "Don't pretend we haven't all thought the word. If the field buckles, if the Sun mutates past our models, the **Selection Pressure** will stop being rhetorical."

Nadia chose her words carefully. "Any evacuation model is… aspirational. The engineering alone would take—"

"I know," Vass said. "But ideation becomes doctrine very quickly in a panic. The conversation will move from **if** to **who** to **how many** to **when** in days, not years. We can't control **if**. We can shape **who**."

"Who deserves to live?" she asked, her voice calm and steady.

"Who improves the odds," Vass said.

She didn't look away. "And the kids who don't improve anyone's odds?"

Vass's expression didn't change. "We build more seats." Then he did look away. "Call Logistics. I want a manifest template drafted by morning. We'll call it something palatable. **Continuity Framework**."

Nadia wrote it down because that was her job and because naming a thing correctly mattered; it made it real at the right speed.

Night bled into the hills like ink poured into water. The team's transport rolled onto a service road paralleling a disused fiber line. The stars looked unusually sharp in the cold air.

Owen said, "Either the air is cleaner up here or space just acquired ten thousand extra dots."

"Less scatter," Hye-jin said. "The field's distortion is sharpening some bands."

"Like a lens," Ana breathed.

They parked under a black totem of a radio tower and set up the portable antenna. Mosquitoes buzzed around the equipment. Mira zipped her jacket to the throat and blew into her hands while Ethan calibrated the dish. He liked doing it with his own fingers—the slow twist of the azimuth dial, the click when the mount found a notch. Machines were easier to work with than people.

"Reading you," Priya's voice said from the speaker, as if she had been standing beside them all along. "I'm on a hopped-up ham rig. Don't worry how I got it."

Mira smiled despite herself. "We never do."

"Do me a favor and pull a downlink from the GOES archive for 14:22 UTC today," Priya said. "Look at Sector 2, sub-band C, then overlay your Helios event. Tell me what you see."

Hye-jin's fingers flew. The screen resolved into a grainy solar image: the Sun's limb, a faint pulsation crossing it like the ripple of a coin dropped into a fountain, the Helios spike riding on its back.

"Carrier," Owen said, breathless. "The Sun's wave carried the Helios resonance. We didn't just see a pattern; we were **on** one."

"Now slide the window two minutes forward," Priya said.

The ripple shifted, and something else emerged, like threads in cloth you only notice when the light hits them right: a second pattern, layered across the first, barely visible inside the noise.

Ana whispered, "It's replying."

"Not the Sun," Priya said. "Something **in** it or **behind** it. I don't get metaphysical unless I'm bored, and I am not bored. But your structure isn't just natural resonance. It's shaped."

Ethan felt the world tilt—not as panic, but as the uneasy relief of finally seeing a clear pattern. "Then Aether was right," he said. "You can steer."

"You can *try* to steer," Priya corrected. "There's a difference. And every attempt pushes on a system we don't fully model. You know what selective pressure is, Ethan?"

"Evolution applied by constraint," he said. "Limited resources force traits into or out of populations."

"Good. Now imagine selection applied to **civilizations**," Priya said. "Something pushes on cosmic systems. Maybe it does it to stabilize. Maybe to prune. Maybe because it's bored. I don't care. What I care about is that the pushing is measurable. If your people sit on this, others won't."

"Others?" Mira asked.

Priya was quiet a beat. "Vass has Aether hardware. He'll light it up by dawn if he hasn't already. If he calls you, don't hang up. Make him tell you numbers. He respects numbers more than men."

The radio cracked with a second tone. Hye-jin startled. "We're being pinged."

Ethan tensed. "Langley?"

"No," she said. "Private net. Auth string: VASS/ARA—"

The speaker popped and settled into a channel with perfect clarity. A calm baritone: "Dr. Kale. Dr. Patel. Good evening."

Mira didn't move. "Mr. Vass."

"Gregor, please," he said. "We're all family tonight under the same sky."

Ethan kept his tone level. "You have something to say or something to buy?"

"A distinction without a difference, in my experience," Vass said, amused. "I have an offer. You're holding data that maps to an old project of mine. You're worried your minders will bury it. I'm worried nature will. I propose a joint lab. My platform, your team, independent oversight to satisfy your consciences. We attempt stabilization before this becomes a question of lifeboats."

"And if we say no?" Mira asked.

"Then you will still say yes," Vass said, and there was no malice in it. "Perhaps later, perhaps with fewer options. Selection pressure removes what can't survive it."

Priya cut in on a sideband Hye-jin conjured like a magician. "Don't let him set the frame. Ask him his numbers."

Ethan took the cue. "All right, Gregor. How many seats can you build?"

Vass did not hesitate. "Ten thousand in eighteen months with current lift. Fifty thousand if certain partners behave. A hundred thousand if we skip ethics and safety in interesting ways. That buys you species continuity. It does not buy you civilization."

"And who decides the hundred thousand?" Mira asked very quietly.

Vass's answer was almost tender. "You will, if you join me."

For several seconds, nobody said anything. Ana's breath fogged in the cooler air, and she bit her lip hard enough to leave a dent.

Ethan looked at the team, at Mira's composed fury, at Hye-jin's luminous, practical eyes, at Owen's white-knuckled grip on the edge of the console, at Ana's young fear. He thought of Daniel in Phoenix without knowing the man's name, and Leila in New York, and the millions whose names he would never learn, all lifted if the math worked, all dropped if it didn't.

"Not lifeboats," Ethan said finally. "Brakes. We're not leaving. Not yet. We try to **stabilize** first."

"Then we agree on the first verb," Vass said. "And we will quarrel about the second. I'll send coordinates. A neutral site. You'll find it quite comfortable for thinking. Bring your raw data and whatever hope you have left."

The line went dead.

Priya came back on, softer now. "You wanted a war between secrecy and catastrophe. You got capitalism instead." She exhaled. "Take the meeting. Extract concessions. Make him show you his instruments. If he's actually steering anything, you want your hands on the wheel too."

Mira wrapped her arms around herself. "And if he's not steering, just... choosing?"

"Then you make him choose better," Priya said. "Or you burn his ship and build your own."

The aurora shifted, green curtains shifting slowly across the sky. The insects droned in the dark. Far to the south, a transformer blew with a sharp crack that echoed through the hills.

Ethan closed his eyes and saw the waveform: the recursion, the carrier, the echo. A pattern encoded into light, into heat, into the breath of a star. It wasn't a message *to* them so much as a message **through** them, the way weather moves through a city. But even cities learned to seed clouds, to build dikes, to whisper to rivers with concrete and faith. Engineering existed because people refused to give up quietly.

He opened his eyes. "We meet him," he said. "And we don't go alone."

"Priya?" Hye-jin asked.

"And whoever else she vouches for," Ethan said. He touched Mira's hand—quick enough to be deniable, steady enough to be true. "But we set our own condition."

"Which is?" Owen asked.

Ethan looked up at the tower's black ribs. "No lifeboat plans until we try the brakes. No selection lists. We'll write whatever continuity framework is needed **after** the stabilization attempt, not before."

"And if he refuses?" Ana whispered.

"Then we'll know exactly what we're fighting," Mira said.

Hye-jin's terminal pinged. A single line of text appeared with a latitude, a longitude, and a time: **36.9981, -109.0452 / 08:00**. Four Corners. A literal crossroads, as if Vass couldn't resist the metaphor.

Beneath the coordinates, three words: **COME DECIDE TO-GETHER.**

The wind shifted and brought with it the smell of rain from a sky that hadn't yet made up its mind. In Phoenix, Daniel carried two drowsy daughters to the roof and set them in camp chairs like tiny kings. In New York, Leila sat between her husband and son at the window and watched the green light in silence, an arm around each of them as if that could hold the city in place. In Geneva, Dr. Steiner traced the ripple with a finger hovering above the screen, unable to stop himself from making the shape.

Selection pressure wasn't a metaphor anymore. It was becoming policy.

"Get some sleep," Ethan told the team, knowing none of them would. "We drive at first light."

He leaned against the transport and looked at the sky for a long time. Somewhere, people were trying to influence the Sun, and someone had chosen a key. He wondered how long refusal would still matter.

He decided he would learn how to answer.

Chapter 8

The Coordinates

The drive north was longer than any of them expected. The landscape unfolded in bronze and ash, a landscape of canyons carved long before anyone named them. The convoy's tires hummed on the cracked asphalt while dawn spread slowly across the horizon.

Mira sat in the passenger seat, staring at the coordinate string on the tablet as if it might change if she glared long enough.

"Four Corners," she said quietly. "Literal symmetry. He couldn't resist the symbolism."

Ethan's fingers tightened around the wheel. "Vass doesn't do symbolism. He does optics. He wants a neutral zone everyone can claim ownership over—tribal land, federal intersections, media access if things go public."

"He's setting a stage."

"Exactly."

Behind them, Ana and Owen argued in hushed tones about the ethics of even showing up. Hye-jin stayed silent, building a contingency map on her laptop—alternate routes, dark roads, population densities, potential drone flyover paths. She had always been the quiet one, the one who noticed patterns everyone else missed.

"You realize," she said without looking up, "if we go there, we're on camera. The kind of cameras you don't turn off. He'll know our faces, our heart rates, how we breathe when we lie."

Ethan exhaled. "Then we don't lie."

Mira turned to him, half smiling. "That's your strategy?"

"That's my exhaustion," he said.

In Geneva, the sun had risen pale and uneven, as if unsure where to stop. Dr. Klaus Steiner leaned over the live spectrograph feed and tapped the panel. The solar oscillation had taken on a new rhythm—pulses repeating in shorter intervals, like a heartbeat under stress. He turned to the room of scientists half-asleep over laptops.

"It's coordinating again," he said. "But this time the resonance isn't global. It's localized."

"Localized to what?" someone asked.

Steiner pointed at the projection. "Earth's orbital angle. We're in the pattern now. Whatever's driving the solar harmonics is centering on us."

The room went very still. Then someone muttered, "We're the control variable."

Steiner nodded slowly. "Or the experiment."

Gregor Vass didn't sleep. He hadn't since the auroras began. In the tower's upper floors, light panels shifted through the hours on a preprogrammed cycle meant to mimic circadian rhythm, but he had stopped sleeping normally a long time ago.

In the Aether lab, the reassembled harmonic core spun with a sound that was almost music—pitches just beyond human hearing, tones just beyond normal hearing.

Priya's file hovered in front of him, annotated with her last project logs. She had once called him a "necessary monster," and he hadn't disagreed. The world didn't move on idealism alone. Pressure and leverage mattered too.

Nadia stepped into the room quietly. "You look like a man auditioning for sainthood."

Vass smiled faintly. "Saints die waiting for miracles. I prefer to schedule mine."

"We've mapped out the initial site," she said. "Ten mobile arrays, each with field amplifiers tuned to your old Aether lattice. We can have them operational within seventy-two hours. But if the solar harmonics shift again…"

"Then we chase them," he said. "We adapt faster than the decay. That's always been the test of species—speed versus comprehension. We can't understand the Sun, but we can outrun what it becomes."

"Ethan Kale won't see it that way."

"He will," Vass said. "Once he realizes idealism doesn't survive contact with extinction."

Back on the road, the NASA team reached the border marker just after dawn. The monument—four bronze plates intersecting perfectly—cast a small shadow that didn't seem to match the angle of the sun. The air smelled of iron and sage.

A private helicopter was already parked beyond the perimeter, its rotors still ticking from heat. Two men in gray suits waited by a folding table with a black case. The kind of case that carried either contracts or guns.

Mira whispered, "He's early."

"He's always early," Ethan said, and stepped forward.

One of the men spoke into an earpiece, then nodded. "You're clear. He'll join remotely."

The case opened to reveal a holo-projector. Vass's image shimmered to life— clearer than a normal video call.

"Dr. Kale. Dr. Patel. Welcome to neutral ground."

Ethan didn't bother with pleasantries. "If you're offering cooperation, start with transparency."

Vass inclined his head. "Very well. Project Aether began as an attempt to replicate the Sun's natural magnetic harmonics on a micro scale. We built reactors capable of producing sympathetic resonance— controlled harmonic resonance. But it wasn't stable. The frequencies would drift, oscillate, collapse. Until your Helios data appeared. It completes the missing measures."

"So you're planning to play it back?" Mira asked.

"I'm planning," Vass said, "to answer it. The difference is whether we respond intentionally."

"Or arrogance," Ethan said.

Vass smiled faintly. "The two have never been mutually exclusive."

While they talked, Priya sat in a warehouse in San Diego surrounded by humming equipment and half-assembled resonance shields. She had already cloned the Helios dataset from Ethan's transmission before the system was locked down. She stared at the recursion pattern on her screen— the same repeating helix of numbers that once got Aether shut down.

She keyed a secure line. "Langley control, this is Priya Narayanan. I need direct authorization for Project Selenite."

The voice that answered was clipped, tired. "That project was decommissioned."

"Then consider this a resurrection," she said. "If Vass is going to talk to the Sun, I'd rather we have our own microphone."

In Phoenix, Daniel's daughters woke him before dawn. The younger one, Sophie, said she heard the sky "buzzing." He stepped out onto the balcony, barefoot, and listened. There was no sound—just a faint vibration, like standing near a distant power line.

He looked up. The aurora was gone, replaced by a strange clarity, the sky washed pale blue, the Sun sharp as a blade. Too sharp.

His phone buzzed with a news alert: **"Unexplained power outages across Southwest—grid load anomaly traced to solar interference."**

He felt his stomach turn cold. The city below flickered, lights stuttering like bad film.

He turned to Elena. "Pack a bag for the girls. Just in case."

"In case of what?"

"I don't know," he said, which was worse than a lie.

Leila Vaziri woke to her building's alarm system blaring—brownout. The elevators were offline. Her husband was already at the window watching the skyline pulse with rolling outages. Arjun sat on the floor building solar system models out of cereal boxes.

She crouched beside him. "Sweetheart, what are you making?"

"A spaceship," he said. "Dad says if the Sun gets too sick, we can leave."

Leila looked at her husband, her throat tightening. "You told him that?"

He shrugged helplessly. "It was supposed to be a joke."

"Nothing's a joke anymore," she said.

Her phone buzzed with a new notification—**National Alert: Grid Stabilization Drills commencing. Remain calm. Stay indoors if possible.**

But even through the thick apartment windows, she could hear something new: the low hum of generators and he sound of generators starting across the city.

At Four Corners, the meeting stretched for hours. Vass was precise, surgical in his persuasion. He offered access to Aether's core—under supervision. In exchange, the Helios team would lend their data, their calibration algorithms, their "integrity." He needed legitimacy; they needed resources.

Mira leaned close to Ethan, whispering, "He's not inviting us to collaborate. He's recruiting witnesses."

Ethan said quietly, "Then we'll be the kind who can testify later."

110

Vass continued, "This is not extinction we're facing, Dr. Kale. It's transition. Species evolve or die. I prefer to evolve."

"And if we trigger something worse?"

"Then we learn faster next time," Vass said. "If there's no next time, we die having tried."

Nobody answered immediately.

Outside, the Sun flared—not an eruption, but a pulse. The air felt charged. Every electronic device within a hundred yards glitched at once—the holo, the laptops, the satellite uplink. Mira grabbed Ethan's arm as the projection sputtered.

Vass's face warped, fragmented into a dozen copies before vanishing entirely.

The men in suits froze. One of their earpieces sparked. "EMP?" one shouted.

"No," Ethan said. "That came from the sky."

Hye-jin looked at her instruments. The display showed the solar frequency—an enormous spike, a wave pattern identical to the Helios recursion but amplified tenfold.

Mira's voice was quiet but steady. "The Sun just spoke again."

Ana whispered, "And it's louder."

Far above them, satellites began to drift out of sync. Orbital arrays registered phantom thrust, as though something unseen had brushed them. The ISS control room went dark for twenty-seven seconds before backup power kicked in. When the screens came back online, one feed showed a glowing arc—an emission moving across the Sun's surface forming repeating geometric lines.

It wasn't random.

And somewhere deep below the Pacific, that forgotten machine turned fully awake, its internal sensors flickering alive one by one. It transmitted a short burst—three seconds of data—straight into the global defense network. The message translated crudely, because human language could barely describe it, but the gist was simple enough:

DO NOT ANSWER.

Back on the plateau, the team huddled beside the transport, wind whipping sand around them. The air shimmered with static.

Ethan stared at the dying holo projector. "He'll think we did this," he said.

"He's probably right," Mira replied. "Even if we didn't."

Hye-jin's laptop blinked—an incoming transmission on a scrambled channel. Priya's voice cut through static: "You're seeing it, right? That was a directed pulse, not spontaneous. Something's pushing harmonics back at us."

"Meaning what?" Owen asked.

"Meaning," Priya said, "the Sun might not be dying on its own. It might be **defending itself.**"

Nobody spoke for several seconds.

Ethan met Mira's eyes. "Selection pressure," he said.

Mira nodded, face pale in the early light. "It's choosing who adapts—and who burns."

Across the world, power grids trembled, communication satellites blinked, and humanity's fragile infrastructure strained under a question that no one yet had the courage to answer.

Above it all, the Sun flared again—once, twice—like a heartbeat finding its rhythm.

Every sensor on Earth heard the same thing:

A pattern.

A countdown.

Chapter 9

The First Cut

The sky changed quietly, without thunder or prophecy. One morning it simply refused to look right.

Over the Mojave, the sunlight broke in odd angles, the air warped by a shimmer that wasn't heat. From the observatory's roof, Ethan Kale could see a thin auroral band twisting across the horizon like a misplaced rainbow. It wasn't supposed to be visible here—too far south, too bright. The colors were wrong. The red bands weren't red at all, more like the color of blood diluted in milk.

Mira stood beside him, hair whipped by desert wind. "It's starting again," she said. "Same harmonics as Helios."

Ethan's throat was dry. "Only stronger."

He'd thought he'd grown used to the fear—that sterile kind that comes with numbers and telemetry—but standing there, staring at a sky that no longer looked natural. He felt something deeper. A primitive recognition. The world was sick.

From the satellite uplink, Hye-jin shouted down through the stairwell. "Langley feed just went live. You're going to want to see this."

They hurried inside.

The lab's main screen flickered to the emblem of the United Nations Continuity Assembly, spinning above a pale Earth. A woman's voice followed—calm, accentless, the kind used during national emergencies.

"This is an emergency broadcast. At 1100 UTC, the Continuity Assembly unanimously enacted the Exodus Directive. All member states are now under cooperative mandate to pursue orbital evacuation infrastructure. Initial construction begins immediately under the Continuity Accord."

Mira froze halfway to her console. "Evacuation infrastructure?" she repeated.

Ethan lowered himself into a chair as though gravity had suddenly doubled. "They're not trying to fix it anymore."

The voice continued, steady and emotionless.

"This measure does not signal abandonment, but preparation. Humanity's continuity is our collective priority. Further instructions will follow."

The broadcast ended, leaving the room humming with equipment noise. For a long moment, nobody spoke.

Owen finally muttered, "They just told eight billion people to start packing."

In New York, Gregor Vass was already waiting for the announcement. He stood at the top of his glass tower, city lights spread below him in endless grids. When the feed cut to the Continuity emblem, he smiled faintly, as if the world had finally caught up to his timetable.

Nadia Korin, his chief of staff, handed him a data tablet. "Global markets froze within minutes. Communications lag in three regions. The press wants a statement."

"Good," Vass said. "Let them want."

She hesitated. "They'll blame you, sir. Aether's data led to Helios."

He turned, eyes sharp. "Helios gave them proof. Proof creates panic. Panic forces action. Now we move."

He stepped toward the balcony where cold air roared between skyscrapers. Below, the Hudson glimmered black and silent. "Contact Geneva," he said. "Tell them Vass Systems will spearhead construction of the first Ark platform. I'll announce within the hour."

"Name?" she asked.

He looked toward the sky, where faint auroral ghosts rippled above the city's haze. "Call it *Genesis*."

Half a world away, Priya Narayanan watched the same announcement from her underground lab. Around her, server stacks hummed around her. The words *Exodus Directive* scrolled across every monitor, reflected in her lenses.

Devin Rao, her assistant, whispered, "They're actually going through with it."

Priya didn't look up. "Of course they are. They'd rather run than repair."

"Can't blame them," Devin said quietly. "If the Sun really is—"

"It isn't dying," she cut in. "It's reacting."

She magnified the solar frequency pattern on her main screen. The harmonic wave pulsed across the screen. "Every time we push energy into the field, it adapts. We're in feedback. The Sun is trying to *stabilize*. We just keep getting in the way."

"Then why tell the world to evacuate?"

"Because fear funds the build," she said, almost gently. "And Gregor Vass knows how to monetize apocalypse."

Phoenix shimmered under a sky the color of nickel. Daniel Carras leaned over the hood of his truck, scanning the emergency text on his phone.

NATIONAL PRIORITY NOTICE.
CITIZEN DRAFT ORDER: ORBITAL CONSTRUCTION DIVISION. REPORT WHITE SANDS FACILITY 0600 HOURS.

His wife, Elena, stepped onto the driveway with their daughters behind her. The girls were barefoot, pajama-clad, still half-asleep. "What is it?" she asked.

Daniel handed her the phone. She read it once, twice, then looked up. "You're being drafted?"

"They need architects." He tried to sound steady. "Someone has to design the habitats."

Elena nodded slowly, eyes glinting with tears she refused to shed. "So you'll build them a home while ours burns."

He cupped her face. "I'll build *something* that survives."

In New York, the broadcast cut to Vass's press conference. The man looked calm, controlled, and completely prepared. Behind him, a holographic model of a colossal starship rotated slowly— a massive rotating structure with rings and gardens suspended in glass domes.

"Under the Continuity Accord," he said, "our company, in partnership with global agencies, will construct the first of several Aether-Class Arks. These vessels will preserve humanity's legacy as we journey toward new stars."

Reporters shouted questions. "Who decides who boards?!" one called out.

Vass's smile was practiced, almost kind.

"Selection will be merit-based—engineers, scientists, cultural stewards, essential personnel. This is not escape. It's continuation."

Someone shouted louder: "And the rest?"

He paused, meeting the camera's gaze as if addressing a single soul.

"The rest will endure. Earth will need caretakers. Continuity requires both travelers and keepers."

The feed cut mid-applause. For most, it sounded like salvation. For those who could read tone, it was triage.

Leila Vaziri watched from a crowded Manhattan café where the lights flickered between generator cycles. Around her, people held their breath.

When the transmission ended, someone whispered, "He's building arks."

Leila's hand trembled slightly as she stirred her coffee. She was a lawyer—trained to dissect contracts, not omens—but she knew what she'd just heard: abandonment dressed as mercy.

Outside, sirens wailed. A man on the corner was already selling counterfeit "boarding passes," promising early application to the Ark program for a thousand dollars cash.

When she left the café, a digital billboard flickered overhead: VASS SYSTEMS: *Continuity Begins With You.*

She walked faster.

By the third day, world governments had issued joint communiqués confirming orbital construction. Launch schedules filled the news cycle. Recruitment centers opened overnight.

Every industry—engineering, biotech, agriculture—was suddenly militarized under one banner: The Exodus Directive.

In deserts, new cities rose around shuttle gantries.
In oceans, floating platforms spread across the oceans.
From orbit, Earth looked wrapped in scaffolding.

But beneath the roar of progress, fear spread quietly.

In the Mojave lab, Ethan stared at telemetry spikes. "They're building death traps," he said. "The magnetosphere's degrading faster than predicted. Every launch adds electromagnetic stress."

Mira rubbed her eyes. "You think anyone cares now?"

"Priya does," he said. "She sent data this morning. She's working on something—shield harmonics, counter-field projectors. She thinks we can reinforce Earth's defenses."

"While Vass builds lifeboats?"

He looked up from the screen. "Someone still has to try."

Outside, the aurora shimmered pale green even at midday, a pale stain spreading across the sky.

The first test of Aether resonance was meant to be small—a harmonic pulse broadcast from orbital relay stations to "stabilize solar flux." Vass watched the readouts from his command center, glass of scotch untouched beside him.

"Amplitude increasing," Nadia reported. "Power holding."

The display pulsed steadily, the pulse synchronizing across stations.

Then a flicker.

"Signal distortion," a technician said. "Magnetic feedback—"

The room shook. Monitors flashed red.

On-screen, the solar field erupted in a massive flare, brighter than anything recorded since Helios.

Somewhere above the Atlantic, the half-completed Ark *Genesis One* caught the wave head-on.

For five blinding seconds, its hull glowed white.

Then it broke apart.

The light reached New York seconds later—an artificial sunrise that lit the city gold for a moment.

Vass didn't move. His reflection watched the flames climb across the sky, expression unreadable.

Nadia's voice was small. "Sir… there were people aboard."

"I know."

"Should we—"

He raised a hand. "No. We say it was a test failure. The next one will succeed."

Ethan saw the flash from the desert—an orange bloom over the horizon. Instruments spiked; sensors screamed.

Mira's voice trembled. "That was orbit."

He knew it before she finished. "He did it. He fired the lattice."

She pressed her hands against the console. "And the Sun answered."

Outside, the aurora turned red.

In Geneva, the Continuity Assembly convened an emergency session. Delegates shouted across the chamber, words drowned in translation headsets and anger.

"Public panic must be contained!" one cried.

"The Directive cannot be reversed!" another shouted.

From the balcony, Priya watched in disgust. "They'll blame the science, not the system," she murmured.

Devin beside her whispered, "So what do we do?"

Priya's eyes hardened. "We build a shield."

By nightfall, protests erupted in every major city.

In Rio, crowds burned Continuity flags.

In Paris, people chanted *Stay Human.*

In Beijing, armored drones hovered above silent demonstrations.

In New York, Leila stood in her office window and watched thousands fill the streets below, faces lit by fire and holograms.

She called her husband. "Are you home?"

"Yeah," he said over the noise. "They're blocking the bridges."

"Keep Arjun inside."

The line crackled. Somewhere outside, thunder rolled—but it wasn't thunder. It was the sound of the first orbital debris reentering atmosphere.

She whispered, "It's starting."

Weeks later, amid debris and denial, the Directive held. Construction accelerated. Aether and Umbra became opposing visions for survival. Governments chose sides quietly. People chose loudly.

And somewhere above the noise, the Sun flickered in deliberate rhythm—three pulses, then silence.

Ethan decoded them the same night.

"Three years," he said. "That's how long we have before collapse."

Mira leaned against him, exhausted. "Then we use them."

He nodded, staring at the red horizon. "Every last one."

Down on Earth, cities stayed lit through the night despite the strain on the grid.

In orbit, new Arks rose—monuments to both genius and fear.

And in the spaces between, a handful of scientists worked to build a planetary shield.

The first cut had been made—between leaving and staying, between faith and defiance, between the species humanity was and the one it might become.

Above them all, the Sun pulsed once more, faint but certain.

The race had begun.

Chapter 10

The Exodus Directive

The first week after the pulse, the world learned the sound of constant engines.

Launch corridors drew white scars up the sky, day after day. Barges rolled down coasts stacked with composite trusses and cryo-tanks. Airports turned into staging fields for shuttles with blunt noses and heat-scored skins. At night, the horizon flickered with power rationing and torchlight protests, and above it all the new scaffolds shone—vast ribs of metal catching sun as they circled, unfinished constellations drifting where stars used to be.

Ethan woke before Mira and lay listening to the observatory's thin pipes hum, the way old pipes always did before sunrise. The desert air pushed cool through the vents. Somewhere out past the fence, the Umbra node sang to itself at a frequency too low for human ears, felt more than heard—pressure behind the eyes, a sense that gravity had grown a second voice.

He slid out from under the blanket and watched the monitors without touching anything. The Sun's harmonics ran in clean lanes for the first time in months—no flares, just a steady throb that made him think of a heart on a hospital screen between failures. Three years, the pulses had said. Not a warning, a schedule.

Mira padded in, hair damp from the quick sink shower. "Priya?" she asked.

He pointed to the far screen. A grainy live feed from the San Diego hangar showed the second Umbra tower upright on its cradle, a black spire threaded with ghost-blue lightning.

Workers in exosuits moved carefully around its base, lifting shielding panels into place.

"She's naming them for shade," Mira said. "Umbra, penumbra. A way to keep the light away long enough to breathe."

Ethan smiled, tired. "We just have to keep the light from tearing the air off the planet."

Her shoulder nudged his. "Small goals."

The console chimed; an encrypted window opened with no prompt. Priya's face resolved out of compression noise, every line of it sharpened by sleeplessness. "Morning, fugitives."

"We're folk heroes now," Mira said dryly.

"Keep your folk away from the east ridge," Priya said. "We're pushing the second node to sub-orbit at sixteen-hundred. If Aether fires their lattice during the climb, we'll have interference. I can't believe I have to say that sentence."

"Vass won't risk another public burn," Ethan said. "He'll run an internal test, low amplitude, say it's a calibration pass."

Priya's eyes narrowed. "He'll risk it the moment it serves the story. Stay dark. The less you look like you, the harder it is to make you the villain."

The line cut to static. Ethan stood a moment longer, feeling the battery taste of fear on his tongue, and then started the morning checklist.

By noon, the Mojave shivered with heat. The observatory dishes looked like fossil flowers against a bleached sky. Ana and Owen arrived with boxed parts and melted chocolate and news that the road north was choked with convoys and people walking, just walking, because gas was being rationed to emergency services. Hye-jin, already at the uplink panel, got them a path through an ESA relay that hadn't been handed to Continuity yet. The node's low hum deepened. Somewhere thousands of kilometers above, frames were being welded to frames, a city built in metal and vacuum.

On a high floor in Geneva, Gregor Vass had the opposite of a view. The UN hall they'd given him for the address was windowless, its curved wood panels catching his voice and returning it richer. He stood at a white lectern with a black logo and waited for the room to remember how to be quiet.

"Continuity," he said, as if tasting the word for the first time, "means refusing to die in the same shape we were born."

Cameras blinked red. The translator headsets hissed to life.

"We cannot negotiate with a star. We can negotiate with our fear." Behind him the projection of *Genesis Two* spun: rotating rings, agricultural cylinders, a spine of engines that promised a forever of acceleration. "The first Aether-class Ark will complete its primary hull in less than a year.

The second soon after. Each will carry the best of us—engineers, botanists, doctors, historians—"

"Who decides?" a journalist shouted, voice faintly amplified by her own panic.

"We do," Vass said, with practiced calm. "All of us, together. The Continuity Council, with input from citizen assemblies and merit registries, will ensure fairness. There will be sacrifices. There will also be centuries with our language still in it."

The room applauded anyway. Nadia watched from a side door, counting the beats until the first panic call from New York, Beijing, Lagos. Vass never looked away from the camera. It looked back like a mirror.

The legal triage center Leila had thrown together inside her firm's conference floor smelled like coffee and photocopier ozone. Lines formed along taped lanes: families with manila folders, a kid in a basketball jersey holding a cat carrier against his chest, a man in a suit without a tie clutching a faded diploma. Leila kept her tone even as she translated Continuity language into human. "Tier Three means labor berth," she told a nurse from Queens. "You work in orbit until commissioning, then they review your manifest status." She didn't say "review" meant "we keep the right to say no after you've built the thing." She didn't need to—people were getting fluent.

When the nurse left, Leila dropped her pen and pressed knuckles into her eyes until fireworks danced behind them. Navid texted a picture of Arjun in a cardboard rocket he'd taped together and painted with toothpaste stars. *Captain Arjun accepts passengers,* the caption read.

She pocketed the phone and returned to the table because that was the only way forward—paperwork as rebellion.

In orbit, Daniel learned the new math of walking. The mag-boots felt like stubborn cuffs, more drag than gravity. On his third day aboard *Genesis Two* he misjudged a turn and rebounded gently into a window, hand splayed against glass to stop his drift. Earth rolled beneath him in half shadow, continents barely visible beneath the haze. The terminator line glowed a sickly copper where it touched the ocean—scattering from a Sun that couldn't decide how bright to be.

"Carras," his supervisor's voice crackled over local. "Sector Five's gyros are hunting again. The ring won't balance."

"We're compensating with windmill parts," Daniel said, flipping open a panel and peering at a gut of cables. "You can't build a city with boat anchors and prayers."

"Can you keep it from tearing itself apart?"

"Today," he said. "Ask me again tomorrow."

He floated back into the corridor, boots kissing steel in the rhythm his body had begun to learn. In his pocket, Elena's last message waited: a video of the girls measuring shadows on the wall as the power cycle rolled through, counting aloud and laughing. That laugh kept him going.

The Umbra launch at sixteen-hundred looked wrong in the best way, a black tower rising with no flame, humming against the air. At the pad's perimeter, a dozen volunteers held hands and said nothing out loud. Priya stood with a hard hat crooked on her head and the wind tugging hair from her braid. "Up she goes," Devin said, breath fogging in a heat shimmer.

"Up she stays," Priya said, because somebody had to say it.

In the Mojave, the observatory shook as the node lifted. Not a quake—more like a big animal had leaned on the building and then withdrawn. Hye-jin's monitors scrolled green and then paused, a single line of text blinking: **PHASE COUPLED.**

Ethan watched a second feed—the Aether lattice telemetry he wasn't supposed to have. "If he fires today," he said, "it'll be at twenty-two hundred, when he thinks no one's looking."

Mira didn't look away from the Umbra readout. "He never believes no one's looking. That's the point."

For six hours the world hung in balance: a shipyard city knitting its rotations in the hard sun, a tower of shadow climbing to join its twin above the equator, a billion people trying to decide whether their future was made of leaving or waiting or pretending they weren't part of a choice at all.

Twilight came to everything at once.

On *Genesis Two*, the engines lit for a systems pulse, a whisper-ignition meant to settle torque and test lines. Daniel felt it through his boots and teeth—low and steady through the hull. He braced one hand on the bulkhead and counted with the vibration. One. Two. Three.

In San Diego, the second Umbra node found its orbital track and locked, the blue arcing along its edges smoothing into an invisible field.

In the Mojave, Ethan's lattice feed spiked.

"Don't," he said to no one who could hear him. "Not now."

Aether fired.

The interference sounded like nothing and looked like water on glass. Umbra and Aether met over the Pacific with a merciless arithmetic, two systems locking onto the same frequency and destabilizing instantly. The surge rolled along the equator, kissing the frames of *Continuum* and the temporary work docks, snapping solar wings like brittle leaves. In New York, every screen went black for two heartbeats and then came back full of shouting. In Beijing, the heavy drones toppled out of skyways and landed in slow motion like exhausted birds. In Lagos, the new ocean platform rocked, and two cranes went into the water like someone had flicked them aside.

On *Genesis Two*, Daniel's ring lurched. Tools lifted from tethers and hung midair, hanging weightless above the floor. "Kill thrust!" someone yelled. "Kill it!"

"Umbra field's clipping!" another voice wailed. "We're in a beat frequency—"

Daniel slammed a stabilizer clamp by hand, feeling the tendons in his wrist talk back. The vibration slid down in pitch, then leveled. Things settled on shelves again. He realized he'd been praying out loud to a God he didn't have.

In the bunker, the team rode out a shudder that made coffee walk in cups. The lattice feed flatlined to static, then returned with a quiet new label: **TEST PAUSED.**

Mira exhaled slowly. "He'll blame us," she said.

"He'll be right and wrong," Ethan said. "Right that the fields met. Wrong that we blinked first."

Phones began ringing in Leila's office before power fully returned. "Was that sabotage?" people asked. "Who's protecting who?" She didn't say "no one." She said, "Get me your denial letter; we're building a record," because that was the shape of her fight, stubborn and paperbound.

That night the Continuity Assembly issued a statement that said nothing in four different languages. Aether accused Umbra of interference; Umbra accused Aether of lighting matches in a dry season. Vass went on the networks and spoke like a doctor whose bedside manner was a form of anesthesia: controlled, pitying, tired at the stupidity of the disease. Priya answered with a leak— a video of arc flashes along the node's skin, proof they'd throttled down to avoid the surge while Aether kept pushing.

The feeds split into camps, and so did neighborhoods. STAY HUMAN painted on one wall. TOMORROW HAS A SEAT on the next.

Work didn't stop.

Launch by launch, the sky factories fattened. Feeding them stripped the surface thin: aluminum, rare earths, organics, skilled hands. Kids learned orbital dynamics in classes held three days a week when the grid allowed. Churches filled and emptied around schedules pinned to lift windows, and in the parks people practiced goodbyes in stages: the easy lies first, the real ones later.

Ethan and Mira slept in shifts. When she dreamed, Mira dreamed of the Sun as a throat singing a note just below human hearing, and of letting that note pass through her like wind through grass, unbroken. When he dreamed, Ethan dreamed of lists—names piling into columns, columns into algorithms, algorithms into boarding manifests that became guilt at scale. He woke one dawn with the taste of metal on his tongue and decided not to tell anyone what he'd dreamed.

A month after the interference, the Sun held steady long enough for imaginations to grow back. The readings flattened into something like a calm sea. Vass called it proof his lattice worked. Priya called it restraint. Ethan called it waiting.

On a clear evening above the Atlantic, the first completed ring settled into its bearing without tearing its bolts. Daniel watched from a service arm while a pilot floated past and tapped the hull twice, a sailor kissing a keel for luck. "Don't sink," the pilot whispered. Daniel didn't laugh. He was busy cataloging the thousand ways a city could fail quietly.

Two nights later, the Continuity Council lit a launch they'd been rehearsing since languages learned the word "ark." The ship rose slow and certain from the Cape, a massive illuminated vessel, its engine plume turning dusk to scripture. Crowds along beaches and rooftops lifted phones out of reflex and then lowered them, ashamed at the impulse to make a memory smaller.

Leila watched from a roof where generator noise lost the argument with ocean wind. Arjun's hand was small and hot in hers. Navid wrapped an arm around both of them, and for a minute they held onto each other against the wind. In orbit, Daniel saw the ship's nose breach cloud and caught himself whispering numbers he hadn't used since grad school. In the desert, Priya stood hatless, hair whipping her face, eyes on the sky without blinking.

In the bunker, Ethan and Mira didn't speak. The Umbra node hummed and held.

The Ark slid into its corridor and went dark as it crossed out of sunset and into Earth's shadow. For a heartbeat, the world felt large enough for both plans to succeed.

The heartbeat ended.

The Sun dimmed.

It wasn't dramatic. Just a measurable drop in output that every sensor agreed on, a notch downward. In kitchens, bars and war rooms, the light went a shade colder and shadows a hair longer. A man in Nairobi dropped a glass because the day didn't look like day anymore. A girl in Tallinn said, "Oh," and didn't know why she'd said it. In orbit, panels recalculated output and found themselves wanting.

"Two percent," Hye-jin said, voice gone thin. "Sustained."

Mira pressed fingers to her lips. Ethan's hand found hers without asking permission.

On the river in Geneva, Vass left a reception early and stood alone on a bridge. The water ran black beneath him. Nadia's message pulsed in his peripheral vision: **DROP CONFIRMED.** He closed the alert without reading the rest. The night smelled like river water and cold stone.

Priya killed the hangar lights and let the desert arrive around her. Somewhere far overhead, the nodes pushed their quiet against the star's quiet. "Time," she said to the dark. "Give us time."

Daniel strapped into a cot and stared at the curved ceiling until he could see faces in the rivets: Elena's, the girls,' men he worked beside and didn't know the names of because life had been reduced to tasks. He counted backwards from a hundred in a language his grandmother had taught him, and when the numbers ran out he started again with different ones.

Leila lay between her husband and son and whispered into Arjun's hair a prayer she did not believe, not to be saved but to be useful. She had court in the morning. People would still need words to shield them.

At dawn the Sun rose paler, as if shy. The engines started again. The lists grew. The scaffold cities cast longer shadows on the clouds.

Humanity had chosen two paths and committed to both, and the light ahead had receded one small, undeniable step.

Chapter 11

The Dimming

At first light the desert looked like a photograph left too long in a shop window. The color had faded by some degree the human eye wasn't meant to measure, oranges washed to peach, shadows stretching a little farther than they should. When the wind came it carried a sly cold that didn't belong in June. Ethan stepped outside with a mug he didn't really want and held the side of the cup against his cheek just to feel warmth.

The observatory dishes rose around him against the pale morning sky. He could hear the Umbra node humming below hearing, a soft pressure behind his eyes that had become the music of the new world. The light on his skin felt... anemic. He rubbed the back of his neck and went inside.

"Two point three percent," Hye-jin said without turning. She sat at the console, lines of code scrolling across the screens around her. "Sustained for eleven hours. If you want optimism, I can round down."

"Save it for the press office I don't have," Ethan said. He looked at the long ribbon of telemetry rippling across the glass wall. The photosphere had contracted by measurable kilometers. The flux lines were braided tight, the field lines pinched inward under mounting pressure. "Contraction holds," he murmured.

Mira came in, jacket zipped to her throat. She'd slept in it—he could tell by the creases at her elbows and the faint cotton smell that clung to the room when she moved. "I called it in to Priya," she said, voice rough. "She's seeing the same thing from the San Diego array. The nodes are catching extra heat now. We're not just shielding the magnetosphere; we're a thermal blanket."

Ethan blinked. "We'll have to bleed to space."

"We'll have to bleed evenly," Mira said. "If we trap heat over the wrong latitudes, you'll cook one coast and freeze the other."

Ana, hair pulled back and tied under a knit cap, leaned around the door carrying two cartons of cheap yogurt and a file of printouts.

"Weather service is inventing new language," she said. "They're calling it 'transitional minima' so people don't panic at 'dim.' There's frost on sorghum fields in Kansas. August."

Owen was already at the radio rack with a spiral notebook and a pencil he'd been chewing bare. He flicked the dial; music surfaced from static, a steel guitar that sounded like memory. "Farm reports from the Plains," he said without looking up. "They're calling in like it's the thirties again. Only with better microphones."

Mira set a new module onto the bench and snapped it home. The node's hum shifted a quarter-tone. "If Vass fires his lattice into this," she said, "we're done. The field is tight. It will ring like a bell."

"He'll fire anyway," Hye-jin said. "Because his story has only one third act."

Ethan ran a thumb along the edge of the desk until the skin found a burr. He pressed harder, needing a pain that wasn't cosmic. "Then we push a counter-pattern through Umbra and keep him from finding resonance. We buy time."

"How much?" Ana asked.

"Days," he said. Then, after a beat, "Weeks, if we don't sleep."

They laughed too easily and stopped at the same time, embarrassed by the sound of lightness in a room weighted like a storm cellar.

In orbit the light changed first in the corners. Condensation formed on the shadow side of vents where it hadn't the week before, a glitter-skin that trembled when the fans kicked. Daniel caught himself staring at it and felt the quiet knock of worry against his ribs. They were shadowed longer each orbit; the eclipses stretched like pulled taffy. The crew had begun talking about darkness the way old sailors talked about wind—like a personality you respected or died trying.

"Sector Five is singing again," his assistant said, voice tinny over the local channel. "Gyros hunting. We get the rotation steady and then she starts to whine."

"She whines because we're lying to her," Daniel said. He kicked his mag-boots free and drifted across the bay, catching a handhold and launching again, body remembering the ballet this place required. He thumped a panel with the heel of his glove. The pitch of the whine changed by a hair. He imagined his daughters laughing at that—Daddy fixed a city by hitting it. "We balanced for a light that doesn't exist anymore."

"Then we rebalance for the one we have," the assistant said.

Daniel grinned despite himself. "Look at you, simple truths in a vacuum." He spread the schematic on his tablet and rotated the ring with two fingers. "Offset the ballast by six percent. Eat the inefficiency."

"Command's going to love that."

"They can send me a complaint on paper. It'll be the only thing up here that doesn't float away."

He clipped his harness and slid into the service gap, hands in the guts of the ship, feeling for the rhythm like a doctor listening through the chest. The ring complained less, as if the structure itself had been holding its breath and finally took one.

When he came back out there was frost on the inside of the viewport, a film he wiped away with the heel of his glove to see Earth gliding slow beneath, cloud decks a dull nickel, the terminator line too straight. Far off, the new shipyards shone like jewelry in bad lighting.

"Hey Carras," the supervisor said, voice born tired and raised on coffee. "They moved your sleep block."

"Of course they did," he said.

"And Command says take a look at the solar arrays on Dock Three. Output's off by... a lot."

"Because the sun is," he said, and pushed toward the hatch. He didn't like how easily they were all getting used to explaining the unexplainable.

Leila's courtroom had become a gymnasium two weeks earlier—an actual gym, bleachers and one end broken nosebleed of a hoop. The county had reassigned it for triage hearings: food allocation disputes, energy equity violations, unlawful hoarding of generator fuel. They'd hung a banner from the rafters—CONTINUITY COURT—in a font that looked corporate and strangely cheerful.

She stood behind a folding table under buzzing lights while a man in a city inspector's uniform made a fist out of pattern: "They cut our block twice yesterday and the next one over kept power. They've got a Continuity official living on that street. You tell me that's not favoritism."

Leila looked at the shipment logs, the energy maps, the lines of text approving and rescinding and approving again. "It is favoritism," she said. "It's also survival. Which is what they'll say when we ask why."

"So, we just lie down?"

"No," Leila said, and her voice surprised her with its steadiness. "We make a record. We make it harder to pretend this didn't happen. We wear them down with receipts."

After the hearing she walked home because the subway was on "cooldown" and the buses were pressed into shuttle duty for the hospital. The city's light had gone grey at the edges, as if the whole city looked slightly dimmed. A billboard flickered to life across a high brick wall: a ship picked out in clean white lines, a woman in a pressure suit gazing into a future with no trash bags. **TOMORROW HAS A SEAT. EARN YOURS.**

Leila's phone buzzed. A video from Navid: Arjun on the roof, catching snow in his mouth at noon. She touched the screen and stopped walking. Snow. She zoomed in. Big fat flakes in a sky the wrong color, wind shoving them sideways along the skyline of metal and glass. *It's June,* her mind said helpfully. She watched her son reach for the cold and laughed once, a strange sound in her own throat, halfway between delight and a sob.

When she looked up again, she noticed she wasn't the only one stopped stock-still. The street had fallen quiet under the soft hiss of not-rain. People stopped and stared quietly at the snow.

In Geneva Vass stood in a room with no windows because windows were a liability—reflections on glass, angles cameras loved. The table was oak and old; the people around it were newer, some so new their hands still looked like they'd been washed too much. Nadia placed a slim folder in front of him and didn't speak. He liked her for that: the absence of theater in a world whose whole budget was staging.

"The solar drives won't close velocity gap," said the man from propulsion. He had a mathematician's voice—apologetic, fascinated, and doomed to be right. "Even at full charge. With output down two percent, the accumulators are underfed. We can get there; we can't get there in time."

"Time," Vass said softly, as if tasting it. "Helium-3 from the Moon?"

"Extraction rate too slow."

"Fission?"

The propulsion man looked at him the way a surgeon looks at a family when the last drug on the shelf is the one nobody wanted. "We can do compact fission along the spine. Thorium salt. It'll look ugly and it will work."

"And after launch?" Nadia asked.

"Beamed power from solar kites," the man said. "If there's enough sun to beam."

"What else?" Vass asked.

The man hesitated. "There's Aether Core. If we push at the right frequency, at the right amplitude, we might... siphon."

"From the star," Nadia said. She put no emotion into the two words and so they were made entirely of it.

"For minutes," the man said quickly. "Seconds. Micro-drains along stable bands. It would look like noise to most arrays."

Vass traced a line on the oak with the side of his finger. "Every time we play an instrument to the Sun it answers back with its own music," he said. "We are not the only composer at this concert."

"We're the only one with a deadline," the man said.

Vass looked up. His eyes had the hard patience of a man carving stone with his breath. "Prep both," he said. "Build me ugly that works. And tune the core in secret. If we can steal feathers from the fire without burning our hands, we do it."

Nadia waited until the others left. "If the core's seen," she said quietly. "If Umbra catches you—"

"They'll call it a sin," he said. "I'll call it an invoice."

"An invoice to who?"

"To the future," Vass said. "Same as everything."

She watched him for one more heartbeat and then nodded because the conversation had become a circle and because there were a hundred things between now and later that would kill them both without asking permission.

Priya stood on the hangar roof and let the wind tangle her hair because vanity had left the room with better gods. San Diego bay lay flat and metallic; the second Umbra tower reflected an amputated sky. Devin came up with two coffees and a face like someone trying to hold five ideas and one grief at once.

"The nodes are seeing a pattern," he said. "Not noise. A contraction rhythm. Like a skipped beat that repeats."

"The Sun is breathing shallow," Priya said. She watched a gull fight the wind and lose, catching itself awkwardly on a cross-beam. "It's not random decay. It's... coordinated."

"Like it's getting ready to do something."

"Like it's getting ready to *let go*," she said. She turned, wind dragging her braid like a tail. "Start the thermal program. We bleed heat over the equator and we trap enough at high latitudes to keep winter from winning summer. It'll be ugly. It will feel unfair."

"It will be unfair," Devin said.

"Then let's be unfair in a way that keeps the most breathing."

He nodded and went, because he trusted her enough not to argue.

Priya took a slow breath and tried to remember the first time she'd loved the Sun. It was a postcard childhood memory—dust motes in a Mumbai kitchen, a bright rectangle on a tablecloth, a feeling that light itself was a place you could live. She let herself have it for exactly three seconds, then put it away like jewelry you don't wear to the factory.

Back in the Mojave, afternoon never quite happened. The day slid from morning to evening with a long low note in between. The day dimmed early. The team worked the way people do when everything they touch matters: without ornament, with jokes that were more rhythm than humor.

Owen tweaked the radio into pulling voices out of static. They were clear enough to make the room feel crowded—farmers noting frost in Georgia, a fisherman describing fog that tasted like pennies, a woman outside Alexandria saying snow fell for twenty minutes and evaporated before it hit the ground.

"Cairo," Owen said softly. "That was Cairo."

Ana watched the stream, eyes bright with the terrible novelty of it. "We knew we'd see it," she said. "We didn't plan for what it would feel like."

Mira looked at Ethan. "We have to tell them we can't fix the star," she said. "Only cushion the fall."

"They know," he said. "Everywhere but the part of the brain that votes."

Hye-jin's screen chimed—an algorithm finishing and asking to be seen. She spun the projection up onto the glass: the Sun's field lines pulsing in and down, a heartbeat skipping in multiples of three. Ethan stepped close. He could feel the heat of his coffee through the cup and the cool of the glass through his palm. Between them, the model glowed.

"Scheduling," he said. "It's not dying. It's... choosing a way to die."

Mira's jaw clenched once, small and visible. "Then we choose a way to live."

134

Far down the hallway, the node's hum slid a breath lower. Outside, a cloudless dusk fell too early and held like a promise you didn't want.

Night arrived with that new, wrong crispness, and with it a video from Leila—shaky phone footage of flakes spinning in orange sodium light, a boy's hand reaching, the sound of a woman laughing when she didn't mean to, a laugh that broke and mended in the span of one breath. The message was three words: **it's snowing here.**

Ethan watched it twice and passed the phone to Mira without speaking. He looked at the telemetry again. The numbers were steady.

"Three years," he said softly. "If we're lucky."

"If we're lucky," she echoed. She put the phone down face-up on the console, so the snow kept falling in miniature as the room's light dimmed around it.

In orbit, Daniel pulled himself into his bunk and lay on his back with his hands tented like a church over his chest. "Not yet," he told the ship, which he had begun to talk to without irony. "Hold together. Not yet."

In Geneva, Vass stood alone in a hallway and touched two fingers to the cool glass of a framed photograph he never let cameras see—the only picture of him at twenty, greasy-haired, grinning in front of a dish array at dawn with frost on his jacket. He let his fingertips chill and then turned away, his mind already moving to the next decision.

In San Diego, Priya watched the nodes light their invisible nets across the sky and whispered the only word that had felt honest for weeks: "Time."

In New York, Leila lay between her husband and son, hands folded under her cheek, and listening to a city remember winters that weren't supposed to come yet.

She cataloged her clients in her head, an alphabet of people who would be told no and another of those who would leave. When sleep took her, it did it gently, the way good judges call recess before anyone has to say something they regret.

And in the desert, under a sky where stars looked a little more brittle than before, the observatory worked through the night as the light continued to fade. The first coyotes called over the ridge. The night lowered its temperature by one more unimportant degree, which would become important in a thousand ways by morning.

The Sun rose hours later, paler again, and the engines started across the world, and the lists grew, and the day went on, because that's what days do until they don't.

Chapter 12

The Long Cold

The Freeze Line

The frost came without ceremony.

No warning, no storm, no dawn that looked any different from the last. Just one morning when car doors refused to open and the sound of ice broke the quiet like glass underfoot.

In the Mojave, the observatory's antennae wore a crust of white. Ethan scraped a line down the window with his sleeve and stared into a landscape turned to silver sand. The desert should not have known this color. Every time the wind moved, frost crackled across the ground.

Inside, generators murmured. Hye-jin sat wrapped in a blanket, fingers on the keyboard, while Mira hovered over the projection table, the world spinning in green wireframe. Every latitude below thirty degrees was highlighted in blue — frozen ground reports confirmed by the weather satellites still talking.

"The freeze line's crossed Mexico," she said, voice flat. "That's two thousand kilometers farther south than last week."

Ethan rubbed his eyes. "And the magnetosphere?"

"Holding, barely. Umbra's taking in more charge than it can release. We're catching energy the Sun's not sending. Like we're holding a net in a vacuum."

He stared at the readouts — the field harmonics climbing against a shrinking power source. "The star's collapsing inward," he said. "It's building pressure. That's why we're cold. It's hoarding."

The lights flickered. A beat of silence passed through the building like an exhale.

Mira's hand found the console. "That was Geneva."

Ethan frowned. "Vass?"

She nodded. "They just activated the Aether Core."

He froze. "He's draining the star."

Geneva — Aether Control

Beneath the Alps, in a chamber curved in overlapping rings, Gregor Vass watched the monitors shift from blue to gold. Each screen represented a different section of the Aether lattice — hundreds of orbital stations tuned to a single purpose: siphon the Sun.

Nadia stood beside him, her reflection trembling in the glass. "Flux feedback is climbing faster than expected," she said. "We're pulling at 0.3 terawatts per second. If Umbra nodes counter-pulse—"

"They won't," Vass said. "They're too busy saving their own field. Priya will choose Earth over interference."

"And if she doesn't?"

He didn't answer. His eyes were on the golden line rising across the display — the power curve climbing as the siphon deepened.

The lights dimmed, the air in the chamber shifting with static.

"Sir," a technician whispered, "we're registering photon lag. Output's slowing."

Vass smiled faintly. "Then it works."

San Diego — Umbra Command

Priya Narayanan watched her team argue across a table littered with empty coffee packets and frost-dulled tools. The bay outside was frozen solid, the ships trapped in ice that groaned under pressure.

"They turned the Core on," Devin said. "The solar flux just dropped another half-percent in the last hour."

"That's not natural contraction," Priya replied. "That's theft."

Her assistant slammed his fist into the table. "So do something! Hit them back—feed Umbra straight into the flux!"

She looked up slowly. "You want to punch the Sun?"

He hesitated.

"That's what you're suggesting. You want to throw a field generator into resonance with a star's heartbeat while it's collapsing. You'll rupture the magnetosphere and turn the planet into a radio scream."

Her voice softened. "We're scientists, not gods. The problem is that Gregor Vass thinks he's both."

Devin's anger collapsed into fear. "Then what do we do?"

Priya stared at the ceiling as if she could see the Aether lattice glowing faintly beyond the clouds. "We prepare for the flare. It's coming sooner than they think."

Orbit — Genesis Two

The ship creaked. Metal contracted audibly through the ship. Daniel Carras floated between maintenance hatches, his breath forming frost crystals that drifted like dust motes in the low gravity.

"Rotation stable?" he asked over comms.

"Stable," came the answer, "but heating's dropping again. We can't keep temp above twelve Celsius without doubling fuel burn."

"Fuel we don't have," he muttered. "Cycle life support through deck seven's radiators. Steal heat from the empty bays."

"Command says conserve power."

"Command's on the ground. We're in the dark."

He touched the viewport glass and looked down. Earth's nights were longer now — a marble half-submerged in shadow. The polar regions glowed faintly with Umbra field lines, streaks of aurora where the shield hummed against the void.

Someone drifted up beside him — Lieutenant Agustin, cheeks hollow from weeks of ration cuts. "I saw the Core ignition from here," she said. "Looked like a pulse through the corona. You think they know what they're doing?"

Daniel shook his head. "They think knowing and controlling are the same thing."

She floated in silence for a long time, then whispered, "It's beautiful, though. The way it flickers."

He didn't answer. The flicker was already fading.

New York — The Riots

Leila Vaziri had stopped wearing her badge. It meant nothing anymore. The Continuity Courts were overrun, the judges gone, and the legal system reduced to ration lists and curfews.

She moved through the streets with her scarf pulled high, the air biting her skin. Snow fell thick as ash. People were burning furniture in oil drums; the smell of varnish and desperation hung in the air.

A voice echoed from the corner — a makeshift speaker rig broadcasting Vass's latest address.

"The Aether Fleet proceeds on schedule. Humanity's new dawn begins above the clouds. Stay strong, stay unified."

Someone hurled a bottle at the screen. It shattered into light.

Leila ducked into an alley, pulse racing. Inside the courthouse, volunteers were stamping new identity cards — work berths, food allotments, Continuity contracts. When she reached her desk, a man was waiting with a paper envelope.

He looked out of place in the chaos — mid-forties, steady eyes, voice quiet. "You defended my sister two years ago. Tax fraud case."

"I don't remember," Leila said.

He handed her the envelope. "You will."

She opened it. Inside was a photograph of a launch pad in the Arctic, half-built but operational. Beneath it, coordinates.

"What is this?" she asked.

"A Continuity ghost site. They're building an Ark that's not on the manifest. No passengers, no registry. Military colors. They call it *Prometheus*."

Leila's stomach turned cold. "Does Vass know?"

He smiled faintly. "Vass built it."

The city learned a new sound before it learned a new language for fear. It started as a low thrum under the avenues, a thousand generators coughing themselves awake, and then it climbed—sirens threading through wind, the hiss of snow falling on hot metal, the irregular percussion of boots and fists on plastic barricade. Leila stepped into it and felt the cold rake her throat like a handful of pins. The courthouse doors had been chained shut by someone with a sense of ceremony and no sense of keys. She rattled them once and turned away. There were other doors. There were always other doors as long as there were people willing to pry.

Across the continent, Mira watched a riot begin through the drone feed Owen had pulled out of an after-hours market. The drone drifted at rooftop height over Manhattan like a ghost with perfect eyes. In the plaza below, Continuity Police in dark armor flanked a line of unlit buses. People pressed against the barriers, faces pinked by cold, by anger, by both. A boy on someone's shoulders held a cardboard sign written in thick black marker:

WE STAY HUMAN. A gust hit the drone; the image tilted, steadied, and in that moment Mira saw Leila's scarf moving toward the buses.

"Zoom," Mira said, and Owen did. The scarf resolved into Leila's face, jaw set, eyes clear. She was threading between bodies with that lawyer's instinct for the path that exists because you insist it does.

"Should we call her?" Owen asked.

Mira shook her head. "What would we say? 'Be careful'? She already is."

Ethan didn't look up from the spiking field telemetry. "Tell her we're watching," he said. "Sometimes that's enough."

The drone feed hiccuped, pixelated, and came back to a bright wash of white: floodlights punching through the snow. The buses doors opened. The crowd surged with a sound that wasn't anger anymore, just mass. The first baton rose. Leila stepped between the nearest officer and a man in a threadbare army coat, hands raised, mouth moving. The officer's wrist hesitated, dipped. She had that effect—law as gravity.

"Pull back," Owen muttered to no one. "Pull back, pull back!"

The drone's battery warning winked red; the image died. The room at the observatory felt larger in the sudden stillness, and then the node's hum reminded them they were inside something alive.

Under the Alps, Vass listened to reports layered over the steady climb of the Aether Core's power curve. He kept one ear for physics and one for politics; both had consequences.

"Civil disturbances in nine capitals," Nadia said, voice carved thin by no sleep. "One Continuity officer dead in Warsaw. Two factories burned in Shenzhen. Johannesburg secured. New York—fluid."

"Let them jog," Vass said. "Running on anger keeps them warm."

Nadia's glance flicked to his profile and away. "The siphon rate is approaching the cap. If we hold it, we can top the accumulators in eight hours."

"We won't hold it," Vass said. "We'll squeeze an hour more because we need it." He leaned closer to the main display. The Sun's corona was an origami of light and gravity, folding along the lines they told it to and then along its own. He could feel the flare coming the way a smoker feels rain: in the bones.

"How long until Umbra notices the photon lag?" he asked.

"They've noticed," Nadia said. "They're not answering."

"Of course they aren't," Vass said. "Priya's counting the beats between us and the pulse."

He straightened. "Prep *Prometheus*. Bring the Arctic pad to hot standby."

Nadia's face didn't change. "It's not on the manifest."

"It's not meant to be. We'll need a ship that can move when the others are still tethered to good intentions."

"Who's *we?*" she asked, and the intimacy of the pronoun lanced the room like a cold draft.

"Anyone who can still make decisions when other people are praying," Vass said.

Priya knew the exact moment the Aether Core reached past its comfort. The Umbra nodes sang back. The sound wasn't literal—no frequency in air could carry it—but her brain insisted it heard it anyway: a brittle, whale-deep note as the field lines tensed. She set her coffee down without looking and walked to the edge of the hangar roof, San Diego Harbor spread below like a winter postcard from the wrong planet.

Devin pounded up the stairs, cheeks flushed, tablet rattling in stiff hands. "Contraction spike. This is it."

"Not yet," Priya said. "The star is bracing. Vass is pulling; the Sun is pulling itself together to hit back. That's not the flare. That's the fist closing."

Devin swallowed. "What do we do when it swings?"

"Put our head where the knuckles aren't," she said, and then softer: "Tell nodes Five and Six to phase-shift by a tenth. Tell Seven to ride high. We're going to catch the first edge and bleed it. We will not be heroes. We will be plumbers."

He grinned despite the air turning his breath visible. "Doesn't read as good on a banner."

"Reading is for later," she said. "This is for not dying."

Her phone buzzed: ETHAN K—LINE OPEN. She answered without hello.

"Tell me I'm wrong," Ethan said. No one's hello meant anything anymore.

"You're not," she said. "The Core is drinking the Sun. Brace your node for the echo."

"The riot—" Mira began, and Priya cut her gently.

"Let the city fight the city. You fight the flare. One chaos at a time."

The flare announced itself to Daniel the way pain does: with a memory. He'd been nine, running with bare feet over hot Arizona asphalt, when the lightning found the transformer behind the grocery store and turned air to white. The sound had eaten the sky. Up here there was no sound unless you touched it; he touched it through the ship.

The first tremor rolled through *Genesis Two* like an animal pushing under a tent. The ring took it, distributed it, complained. Panels across the interior bloomed with warnings, a field of neon daisies. Daniel braced a boot against the bulkhead and read four displays at once, his mouth choosing triage for him.

"Lock deck hatches and spool gyros to plus-ten," he ordered. "Dump waste heat through Seven and Nine and pray Umbra holds the backscatter."

"Umbra's what?" someone said, and then the ship's hull shivered. A hairline crack ran across a viewport, not fatal but informative. Something outside was angrily brightening the vacuum.

Vass's voice cut across the channel.

"All orbital assets," the baritone said, smooth as glass. "You may experience transient events. Maintain course. Aether will stabilize within ninety seconds."

Daniel let an unkind word out between his teeth. "Tell Aether to experiment on something that doesn't have lungs."

Agustin laughed once, the sound a gunshot in cotton. "Copy, sir."

He saw the second tremor before he felt it: Umbra's field shone in the camera, polar curtains thickening, then feathering, then blown sideways by pressure you couldn't see. The ship creaked again, a monster thinking about waking up.

"Hold," he told it. "Hold, you stubborn, beautiful wheel."

Leila didn't choose the alley behind the courthouse; the alley chose her. She had the envelope in her bag, the coordinates stamped on her brain, and she had a line of people behind her whose names she'd written down because writing is a kind of salvation. When the first push hit the city—lights up, down, up, gone—the crowd did what crowds do. It tried to become smaller to survive. She felt the force of bodies and the slick cold harmlessness of snow on her cheek as she slid between them. The alley offered space and she took it.

Three kids blocked the way with a pallet fire. Their faces were caramel by the flames and blue by the world and they held pipes like they'd only just learned what pipes were for. One of them wore a Yankees hat with the brim snapped white.

"We're not taking money," he said, trying to sound like a rule.

"I don't have any," Leila said, which was true enough. She held up her empty hands. "I have information."

"Everybody's got information," he said. A man farther down the alley laughed without enthusiasm.

"About a ship that doesn't exist," she said. "An Ark with no passengers."

The boy in the hat tilted his head. He was one decision away from being a sentry instead of a teenager. "What's it to you?"

"It's to all of us," she said. "If they're building a way out for weapons, not families, then even leaving will be war."

The other two glanced at him. He jerked his chin; the pipes lowered. "What's it called?" he asked.

"Prometheus," she said.

He grinned at the fire like it had told him a good joke. "Of course it is."

He stepped aside. "You lawyers, man," he said as she passed. "You always got a word."

"I'm trying to keep them honest," she said.

"You can't keep the weather honest," he said, and she loved him for that, for the poetry in his mistake.

The first edge of the flare hit the Umbra net with a visible ripple. Across the world, people looked up and saw the sky unfurl like silk—a curtain of greens and reds and an inhuman violet that made the eye water. A sound no ear could hear ran through bones.

In the observatory the hum became a roar that didn't move air but moved teeth; some coffee cups skittered like animals. Hye-jin shouted a number; Owen shouted a prayer. Mira's hands moved on the controls with the grace of a pianist who'd finally been given a real piano and no time to learn the piece.

"Phase shift now," Ethan said. "Now, now—"

"Already there," Mira said, and threw the switch that let Umbra bend instead of break.

In San Diego, Priya watched every node's status light flip to "full" and then to a color the interface had not been designed for. She tasted copper. "Bleed to orbit," she said. "Dump the excess into the shadow. Let the dark carry it."

"It'll clip the Aether lattice," Devin said.

"Then they get sparklers," she said. "They chose to be up there."

The flare swelled suddenly across the Umbra net. The Umbra net gave it a place to land. It landed. Around the world, power wavered, surged, went out and came back in different neighborhoods as if a giant had leaned on the switchboard and then stood back, embarrassed. In orbit, *Genesis Two* rolled seven degrees and then settled like a ship finding a new tide. Daniel let out a breath he hadn't noticed he'd been hoarding since childhood.

"Status?" he asked.

"Alive," Agustin said.

"Good. Let's keep it fashionable."

The second wave hit seconds later. It wasn't bigger, it was smarter. It sniffed at the seams. It found a frequency Umbra didn't love and pressed there with the cheerful malice of physics.

In Geneva, Vass's technicians spoke in a new tense—verging, impending, almost. "Core draw is dropping," one said. "We're losing sip."

"Then stop sipping," Vass said. "Stand down the feed. We don't need to steal during a fire."

The graph kissed a plateau and slid. Nadia scrubbed a hand over her face. "You'll get blamed," she said.

"I will get results," Vass said. "Blame is for later."

He turned to the secondary screen where *Prometheus* burned cold in the Arctic dark, floodlights painting the launch gantry in theater light. It looked like treason and common sense and home.

The alley behind the courthouse yawned into another street, this one clogged with a different kind of crowd. Leila heard the chant before she saw the sign: NO GODS. NO ARKS. FIX THE SUN. A woman on a milk crate shouted into a battery-powered bullhorn, voice cracking at the edges.

"They will leave you to freeze and call it a gift," she yelled. "They will take your sons to build a second sky and your daughters to grow a garden they will never walk in. Say no. Say *stay*."

Leila stopped, wind pushing into her hair. She wanted to stop time the way Daniel was trying to stop rotation, to clamp the world and say "hold."

Then her phone buzzed. A text from Mira: **Flare caught (for now). How long can you hold a city?** She typed back: **How long can you hold a star?** and hit send because jokes were the last evolution of despair.

She walked into the crowd because walking away had never been one of her talents.

The flare began to weaken. Umbra's lights—imaginary to those who didn't know where to look, visible to those who listened with instruments and the soft parts of themselves—faded to a simmer. The hum in the observatory came down a half-step. Ethan rested his forehead against the cool glass of the display and let the sweat run into his eyebrows.

"Report," he said.

"Magnetosphere intact," Hye-jin said. "Nodes hot, not cracked. We bought it."

"For how long?" Owen asked.

Mira answered by not answering. She stood with both palms flat on the table, knuckles blanched, and looked at the model of a world that still believed in mornings.

Ethan straightened. "Priya?"

Her voice came raw on the line. "Still here. Harbor's ice cracked and refroze in one breath. We lost one node to a cheap gasket. The rest held."

He closed his eyes. "Thank you."

"Don't thank me," she said. "Thank your stubborn planet. It still wants us."

He opened his eyes. "Vass?"

"Vass will claim victory in restraint," she said. "Then he'll light another match with a different hand."

"Prometheus," Mira said, and heard the line go quiet enough to count her own heartbeats.

"You saw it," Priya said finally.

"Leila did," Ethan said. "It's real."

"Of course it's real," Priya said. "He's building a ship that doesn't carry people. It carries decisions."

"What does that even mean?" Owen asked.

"It means when the last choice is between turning off Umbra and launching the Ark, he won't choose between them. He'll build a third option and refuse to admit it's a prison."

Night fell with a gentleness that made the day feel like a different planet's mistake. Daniel floated in the quiet and read Elena's reply: a video of the girls under blankets by a window filmed with frost ferns, their breath ghosting against the glass as they traced imaginary constellations. In the back of the frame, Elena mouthed *"we love you"* with a steadiness that broke him more than tears would have.

He recorded a reply he would never be able to watch. "Hold my place," he told them. "If there's a line, tell them your dad builds circles."

Agustin drifted by and bumped his shoulder with an elbow. "You know," she said, looking out at the faint green smear of Umbra at the pole, "I used to think the sky was up and the ground was down. Now it's... everywhere."

He smiled. "That's how you know you're on a ship."

She pushed off and he watched her go, a human body drifting through the machinery.

Leila stood on the courthouse steps as the crowd thinned to smoke and snow. The pipes kids appeared at the edge of her vision, one of them holding out a paper cup of something too hot to be coffee. She took it; it warmed her hands and softened nothing else.

"You going to that place?" the boy in the hat asked. "Where you said?"

She thought of coordinates that could get her shot and a son who thought rockets were made out of cardboard. "I'm going to write it down first," she said. "So if I don't go, someone else can."

He nodded like this made sense. "My mom says stories are just maps for people who forgot how to walk."

"She's not wrong," Leila said, and pulled her scarf up as a wind came down the avenue with a voice in it like old radio.

In Geneva, Vass watched the flare data settle and nodded once, a man noting that the train he wanted had arrived late but arrived. "Spin *Prometheus* to one-quarter," he said. "Test the spine under cold."

"Passengers?" Nadia asked.

"No passengers," he said. "Only those who know why they're aboard."

"And if Umbra calls us out?"

He smiled the smallest smile she'd ever seen. "Then we will finally be having the right conversation."

He turned away from the screens then and for a heartbeat looked older than he allowed. When he spoke again, the oldness was gone. "Tomorrow, we repair. Tomorrow night, we pull again. We'll do it until the numbers make a shape worth living in."

"Or until the star stops."

"Everything stops," he said softly. "The question is what we are when it does."

Far from all the rooms where decisions dressed themselves in nouns, the desert cooled to stone and the frost crept one finger-width farther under the door. Ethan and Mira stood outside the observatory with their breath hanging like flags, heads tipped back. The sky had never been clearer. Orion's belt cut the dark like hardware. The Milky Way spilled its white the way grain spills where a sack has split. It was a good sky to swear under or to be forgiven.

"Do you regret not leaving?" Mira asked, eyes on a star that wasn't a star anymore but a satellite pretending.

Ethan thought about the drone feed going black and Leila walking anyway. He thought about Priya's hands steady on the switch and Daniel telling a ship to behave like a person and listening when it did.

"No," he said. "I regret not having two of me."

She huffed a laugh that rose and disappeared. "Greedy," she said.

"We need greedy," he said. "We need everyone to want more tomorrow than there is today."

She reached for his hand. He let her take it. The warmth was small and specific and absolutely enormous.

Somewhere under their feet the node found a new notch and the hum settled into a lower comfort. Somewhere above their heads the Aether lattice winked like a crime seen through a lace curtain. Somewhere between those two, the Sun contracted a fraction more, rehearsing the shape of its next violence.

The wind carried a smell like metal and snow. The coyotes called across the desert. In the city, children dreamed in colder rooms and learned new geographies in their sleep. In orbit, a wheel didn't tear itself apart and a man lied to a ship and called it hope.

The Long Cold held. The fracture widened. The next wave of heat still waited beyond the horizon.

"Come on," Mira said at last. "There's another night after this one, and it's already asking for power."

They went inside, shutting the door against a world that would not stop knocking, and the hum lifted, and the screens woke, and the chapter of being alive continued for one more turn of the gears.

Chapter 13

The Second Dawn

The wind off the Pacific tasted like salt and metal, carrying the strange, tinny chill that had settled over the world since the Sun dimmed. On the cliffs above San Diego, the Umbra Command campus was a geometry of concrete and glass ringed by antennae that peered up like a thicket of bare winter trees. Night held on longer these days. the dark lingered longer each morning.

Priya pulled her scarf tighter, breath pluming as she crossed the plaza toward the control building. Her badge shook in her hand—was that the cold, or the tremor she still couldn't shake since the flare? Emergency crews had scrubbed soot and salt from the glass, but a faint halo still marked where the flare had burned across the windows—like a burn on a retina.

"Morning," Devin said from the doorway, a paper cup steaming in his gloves. He always greeted her like that even when it was deep night. Here, morning meant: the next thing after what just happened.

"Where are we?" she asked.

He understood she meant everything. The grid. The world. The Ark.

"Umbra's at ninety-three percent field coherence," he said as they walked. "The northern array is still fluttering from the storm surge—gusts are unpredictable with this cold inversion—but we're stable. The Ark window holds for another nineteen minutes."

Nineteen. They'd modeled these windows for a decade and still, saying the number aloud felt like opening a door to an old house and smelling a childhood that wasn't there anymore.

"And the Aether Core?" she asked.

"Spinning," he said. "Vass sent a prelaunch ping. He wants... poetry."

"Poetry," she repeated, and it came out flatter than she intended. Devin grinned sidelong, though his eyes were thin with lack of sleep.

"His word," he said. "He says a launch is a poem in steel."

They passed through the second checkpoint. Inside, the humming took over—servers, field harmonics, distant generators. Sometimes Priya thought of Umbra like a deep organ whose sound you felt in your teeth more than in the ear. The team stood around the central harp of screens. The sky was a bruised twilight, the ocean leaden, but the eastern horizon carried a thin seam of returning light. Prometheus was at the desert pad hundreds of miles away, swaddled in scaffolding, the Aether containment ring a halo of brushed graphite and tungsten, blacker than black, like a coin punched from void.

"Give me cameras," Priya said. "Three through seven on main."

The wall blossomed into angles of the launch pad. People were small insects in flame-retardant orange, scurrying in their choreography. Steam walked off the fuel lines. Vapor trailed from the struts like torn lace. The countdown board glowed with an indifferent certainty. 00:18:12.

"Telemetry?" she asked.

"The ring's at nominal," said Garcia, the systems lead. "Mag containment is clean. No phase walk."

"Umbra coupling?" Devin added behind her.

"Coupling is at six-point-eight Tesla falloff," Garcia said. "We can give them eight seconds of heavy wind shear suppression at T+9 to T+17."

"Make it ten," Priya said. "Vass always asks for two more."

Garcia didn't sigh so much as let air go. "We'll have to rob power from the southern skirts."

"Take it," Priya said. "I'll own it with Boston."

She meant the Umbra coordination center near Cambridge that ran the eastern arcs. Somewhere in a white, windowless bunker under a brownstone that used to be a lab for optical fiber, someone would notice the dip on their boards and call; she would answer. They had all become thieves of their own power.

The intercom chimed. "Umbra Command, San Diego, this is Prometheus Flight," said a crisp, almost conversational voice. The kind of voice that would sound the same ordering sandwiches.

"Go ahead, Prometheus," Priya said.

"Confirming we'll be leaning on you at T+9." In the background she heard other voices, a choir tuning. "We'd appreciate the extra eight... or ten... seconds, if you can spare it."

"We can," Priya said. "Umbra is your spine."

A breath of laughter. "Copy that."

She liked them better when they sounded human.

The clock slid. 00:17:01.

Under stadium lights in the desert, the Ark looked out of scale. The hull plating was a matte ceramic, ocean-gray. Logos of a dozen nations ran along its flanks—crisp color against the neutral skin. In the low slant of dawn, the letters PROMETHEUS had the gravity of an epitaph.

Gregor Vass walked the silent corridor below the ring, one hand trailing the bulkhead, fingers drumming the narrow seam where two plates met. His coat was open, though the air bit, and the white in his hair shocked against the black of the suit. He'd refused gloves; he needed to feel the chill, the risk. He always dressed like an executive giving a talk at a conference, even here, where everything hummed and smelled of ozone and cryo and oil.

He paused before a round viewport and looked out at the ring, the Aether Core nested in its heart. Within the chamber, not light but an absence shimmered, a pearl of negative space that distorted the scaffolds beyond it. The math called it a throughput singularity. The engineers called it the well. Vass, when no one listened, called it the mouth.

He'd said that once, too candidly, and a journalist had called the Aether Core a god. Nonsense. Vass had no use for gods, only for consequences.

"Sir," said a young tech at his shoulder, red hair stuck to his forehead with sweat, even in this cold. "We're at final checkout. Flight asks for your presence on Bridge."

"I'm here," Vass said, and the tech flinched before he realized Vass was addressing his wrist unit. Old habit. He had never gotten used to mics sewn into fabric. "Tell Flight I will be... in thirty seconds."

The tech nodded and withdrew. Vass remained with the window, hand on metal, another old habit—touching what he had built, part superstition, part audit. He wanted to be the last to lay a hand on this thing that would be the first to leave.

He glanced at a small, tarnished coin on a chain at his neck, tucked under the shirt. His father had hammered the coin into an oval when Vass was twelve and told him: if you cannot carry home in your pocket, carry a reminder that home is something you can make. The coin had once been a bus token.

On the coin the stamping had worn thin. Only the word ONE remained.

"Bridge," he said to the air, and turned away.

In a modest apartment off Avenida Revolución in Tijuana, a woman in a worn gray sweater set an aluminum tray of pan dulce on the counter of the family bakery, dusting sugar on conchas with mechanical grace. The power had flickered all week. The ovens ran on rationed gas; the radio ran on a cranked dynamo. The woman's daughter, nineteen, watched a tiny screen balanced on a bag of flour: a stream, fuzzy and hiccuping, of the Ark.

"Van a lanzarlo," the daughter whispered. They're going to launch it.

The mother nodded without looking. "People need bread whether rockets fly or not," she said, and then, softer: "Hold the phone steady so I can see."

On the screen: gray sky, a towering shape, lines of bright suits like stitches around it. On another counter: a jar with a handwritten label, **UM-BRA FUND — FOR OUR LIGHT**. Coins clinked in occasionally: small choices.

The bakery smelled like warm sugar and clean heat. It was a scent that made you forget the rest.

Daniel Carras floated in the Genesis Two maintenance bay, boot loops hooked out of habit so he stayed in one place as the station's slow roll shaded half the Earth's disk beneath him. Genesis Two was older than his knees, now; she whined if you listened.

The Ark's path would bring Prometheus up past the station's plane—close enough that, if the timing was sweet, he'd see a flash of its skin. He didn't blink at the thought. He didn't want to miss the instant.

He'd spent the night (morning, day—it no longer mattered) recalibrating a balky guidance array with a torx bit and a spool of copper that should have gone out with a shuttle era. He'd slept twenty-eight minutes in a harness with a towel over his face. He smelled like plastic and old socks and lemon disinfectant. You had to love a thing to live inside it like this.

"Danny," a voice from the panel, tinny with packet loss. Leila's voice. You could pack three hours of conversation into ten minutes when the world taught you time could be stolen at any moment. "Are you watching?"

"I'm here," he said. He could see the Earth like a bruised eye, pale clouds smeared with motion, the continents like old maps left in the sun.

"Tell me what the pad looks like," she said, and when he started to answer, she laughed. "No, I know. A needle through your heart."

"Funny, counselor," he said. He couldn't help the smile. He had promised himself not to bring her into the station too much. He had failed at that promise in increments: calls at odd hours, the memory of her heavy hair down her back, the way she had said I don't want to be brave alone.

Leila Vaziri stood at her office window forty stories over a downtown that had grown gray with the cold. The courthouse green across the street was a brittle square of frost. Her city's heartbeat had adjusted to new rhythms: shorter days, slower traffic, longer lines at substations. She'd worked all night on an injunction involving a corporate warehouse where families had nested between pallets of soybean; the property law was simple, the ethics not. The launch, she thought, would not change that, and would change everything.

Her son slept on the office couch, wrapped in her coat. He had insisted on coming in because the power at home had cut out twice, and she had discovered there were some fights she could not win anymore. She crossed and touched his hair. He did not wake. She watched the pale on the horizon lighten one watt at a time.

"Counselor," Daniel said, mock-formal, "I'm about to cry in zero-g."

"I'll allow it," she said, and the shape he made come out of her—this lightness—felt like a crime and a cure.

Ethan pressed his palm to the lab's cold window, leaving a print that faded almost immediately in air that had learned to forget warmth. The Umbra field modeling suite was a cave of holograms and chalkboards with half-erased math and coffee cups containing moods. He and Mira had not left in thirty hours. A pair of socks hung from the corner of a monitor where they had been drying since a hallway pipe burst and gave the corridor a sudden, unrequested rainstorm.

"So," Mira said, perched on a stool, hair in a knot that was losing the argument, eyes the wrong kind of bright, "we did it, right? Umbra held the flare. That's what the world is saying."

"It held enough," Ethan said. "It held the first one. That doesn't mean—"

"Shut up," she said, and there was no heat in it, only a kind of fond exhaustion. "Take the win."

He took it and put it in the pocket of his chest where he stored things he could not admit to loving: certain equations, certain songs, the way Mira lived inside problems like someone moving furniture inside a home. He looked at the display where the Ark's telemetry blinked.

"Vass will call it a proof," he said.

"He'll call it poetry," she said, smirking, and he frowned until he realized she wasn't guessing.

"Priya told me," she added. "He wants to talk after. I'll bring a haiku."

He drummed fingers on the ledge. "This isn't... It's too early to go."

Mira tilted her head. "Too early for who? For the world? Or for you?"

"I thought we'd have another year," he said, surprising himself with the rawness. "Time to fix the asymmetry in the southern couplers. Time to make Umbra beautiful instead of just functional."

Mira watched him for a moment. "You don't get to pick the weather," she said. "You build the umbrella you have time to build."

He looked at her and felt the gap between admiration and love open and then try to close without falling in.

"Ark Core is cycling," she said, softer. "Stand with me for the count. If the world ends or begins, I want your elbow on mine."

He watched the clock. He watched with her.

Prometheus Bridge was a wedge of screens and carbon consoles arranged like pews that faced a single window: a vertical strip that showed the pale morning in washed-out gray.

The Bridge crew wore suits that looked like tailored wetsuits armored in all the places fear lived: spine, ribs, throat. The captain—Rao, hair in a silver buzz, eyes so still they looked like stones in a river—sat with her hands hovering over cutout grips as if waiting to catch a falling thing.

Vass entered without announcement; the crew's eyes flicked and then returned to the board. He did like to make an entrance. He liked that he was an interruption that did not interrupt. He took the one empty sling near the window and strapped in.

On the forward screen the field strength curves looked like mountains flattened by some god's hand. The Aether readouts scrolled their vowel-full names—mu, eta, chi, kappa—pretty as ancient whispered prayer.

There was comfort in a control room when the names were Greek: it meant someone had thought the world could be understood.

"Prometheus Flight to all stations," Rao said, voice steady, her cadence a metronome. "This is your launch countdown. Final status check."

Her words moved through the ship into rooms where men and women adjusted straps, tucked photographs into pockets, squeezed hands, closed eyes. Into a cargo bay where crates of seed lay in a sleep that would be a continent's future if someone remembered how to wake them. Into the nursery module, empty now but painted with birds that all had little engines instead of wings.

"Payload."

"Go," came the answer.

"Hull."

"Go."

"Aether Core."

A beat. The room held its breath. "Go," said the Aether lead, a woman named Markova whose hair had been blue last week and was shaved now. "We are within the parameters we tell our parents."

A ripple of quiet smiles. The things you said so you didn't sound afraid.

"Umbra."

Priya's voice now, carried across the cold morning air, across fiber and airwaves. "Go. We will give you ten seconds of the gentlest sky we can make."

"Copy, Umbra," Rao said. "Prometheus, set condition green."

The ship's internal lighting shifted: a polite dawn.

"Flight," said Vass, and only when he heard his voice did he know he had meant to speak. "We are ready."

Rao glanced sideways and he saw in her just the smallest suggestion of a nod. He gave him the smallest nod.

The crowd at the perimeter fence breathed as one animal. The parking fields were a mosaic of cars rimed with frost. People held thermoses under their chins like prayer bowls. A little boy in a knitted hat stood on his father's shoes so he could be taller. A teenage girl had painted an orbit line on her cheek in blue eyeliner. An old man read quietly from a paper-bound book and did not look up until the sound changed.

Sound at a launch was a physical thing. When the first expulsion came, a scaffolding of thunder, everyone felt their ribs become instrument.

The boy grabbed the fence and went quiet. The teenage girl forgot her recording app. The old man closed the book and pressed the cover to his chest.

On the concrete beyond, flame rolled with slow majesty; the Ark's base bloomed with engineered daybreak. Prometheus lifted. Even the words were wrong. To say lifted made it sound like a balloon, like a child's toy. It rose steadily through gravity, through history. It rose as if the ground had failed it and it needed new ground.

The people could not see the ring do its work—could not see the way the Aether Core chewed a thin hole in the fabric of the world not to rend it but to let a needle through. They could not see the way Umbra's field wrapped air like a shell so the winds whispered, briefly, and did not shove.

They could feel the heat like a sun they remembered.

In San Diego, Priya held on to the console edge and counted under her breath. Her lips moved: nine, ten, eleven. This was not superstition but choreography. "Now," she said, and Garcia's hand darted, and the southern skirts dimmed and the north brightened and the coupling soared for a few bright seconds like a bird finding a thermal. The winds over the pad went from thirty knots to five. Prometheus rode that hush like a word in the right mouth.

"Umbra giving you the soft," Devin murmured into the mic, as if he could sweet-talk metal.

"Copy," said Flight, but Priya heard the smile.

"Falloff in three," Garcia said. "Two, one." The curve settled, and on the screen the Ark was a slender moving mark against gray.

"You're out of our cradle," Priya whispered. She did not intend the microphone to catch it. The line clicked. She did not know who heard.

In orbit, Daniel braced one hand against the window frame, feeling his heartbeat in his palm. A sliver of light moved against the planet's rim—so small he blinked and thought he had imagined it. Then the angle caught, the skin flashed like a wet stone, and he breathed a sound that was not quite a word.

"I see you," he said.

Leila heard the shift in his voice and leaned her head against the office glass as if that could make the distance honest. In the reflection she saw her face and the couch where her son slept and the stack of briefs that would still be there when the sky calmed. She could not see what Daniel saw.

She believed his seeing was enough. For a moment it was like being let into a secret room in a house you thought you knew.

"Danny," she said. "Hold on to something."

He laughed, short, breath true. "Always."

Ethan felt Mira's elbow at his, warm through two layers of sweaters, as numbers rivered down the display. The Aether Core's signatures stayed inside the corridor they had modeled and remolded for years. "No phase walk," he said, and then: "Minuscule. Nothing that would—"

Mira squeezed his forearm—an admonition to stop explaining when it wasn't necessary. On the feed, the onboard camera panned just enough to catch the curve of the ring. He imagined the well inside, the mouth rounding itself, disciplined, hungry in the correct way.

"Hear that?" she asked.

The lab's window rattled once, deep and distant, like thunder remembering itself. He didn't realize he had been holding his breath until he tasted metal on his tongue.

He had thought a proof would feel like triumph. It felt like a drawn bow.

On Bridge, the acceleration pressed Vass gently into the sling. He thought of dirigibles, of ocean liners, of thresholds. He looked sideways. Rao's jaw muscles flexed minimally, the only outward sign of force.

"Passing max-q," said Markova, the Aether lead. "Structure nominal."

If these numbers stayed polite and inside safe margins for the next ninety seconds, they would be through the worst. Vass knew everyone on his team had a ritual for this stretch: a memorized poem, a song counted backward, a prayer in three languages in case God had a preference. He had never prayed—not really. He counted his father's footsteps in their old apartment: three to the sink, four to the window, two to the door. It calmed him to measure things in units of human motion.

A tickle of static. "Umbra to Prometheus," came a voice he recognized as Priya's. There was a bright softness to it like someone who had been up all night and still found a way to love morning. "We show you clean. Good luck up there."

"Copy, Umbra," Rao said. "We appreciate the quiet."

Vass inhaled and found, unexpectedly, gratitude filling the available space. It unnerved him. Gratitude meant acknowledging a debt. He preferred contracts. But here they were: the field magicians in San Diego and Boston and Ghana and Pune holding the air, his ring holding the hole, everything holding everything so that a column of metal could refuse Earth without breaking Earth's skin.

"Stage separation in five," said Flight. At once, everything in the room leaned forward the subtle two millimeters that human bodies do when history nods.

The first stage let go—a clean, sharp undressing—and fell away obediently toward its parabola and its ocean. The second stage bit and the Ark leapt not faster but truer. In the viewing window the pale on the horizon deepened.

"Pitch program nominal," said Navigation.

"We are good," Rao said. "We are good."

Vass closed his eyes and opened them again so he would be sure he had not imagined it.

At the desert perimeter, the crowd began to cry—not as one, nothing as corny as that. Individually, in their tongues, their private categories of joy and alarm. A woman who had fought with her sister the night before over who would take their father when the next power outage came cried silently, not sure for whom it was. A boy laughed as if he had been tickled. The old man's eyes wet and he said, to no one, "I was there when they took down the last shuttle. I did not think I would see this again," and someone nearby patted his back as if they were family.

A white-haired reporter spoke into a microphone about epochs and thresholds and man's boundless curiosity and surprised himself by choking up on man's. He corrected himself—"humankind"—and the correction made the moment honest again.

Above them, Prometheus became a needle on a sheet of gray and then a dot. But they could still feel the sound in their bones for a long time after. The fence stopped trembling. Their ribs took their shapes back.

In Tijuana, the bakery's oven timer dinged. The mother laughed through tears and said, "Take them out, take them out," because the sweet rolls did not care about Arks, and then added, "But don't drop the phone."

Her daughter balanced it in the crook of her neck and pulled the tray with both hands, forearms strong from years of bread.

On the tiny screen, a digital overlay geolocated the Ark as if that helped anyone. The daughter didn't need the numbers to see even pixelated courage.

She looked at the jar labeled UMBRA FUND and pushed it an inch closer to the register. People needed a place to put their hands when they felt big feelings. Coins. Crumpled bills. Crumbs.

San Diego's server room hummed like a hive that had learned to whisper. Priya rubbed her eyes with knuckles until gray sparks danced. "Take the skirts back to nominal," she said. "Start spooling down from ten to seven to five. Let Boston take their bites back."

"You promised to own it," Garcia said, not unkindly.

"I will."

She imagined the call: a colleague in a cold east-coast room saying, You took my lunch money today. She would reply: I spent it on our friend's trip to the sky. They would argue like brothers. They'd go out and smoke in a stairwell later and talk about who they were before the Sun became someone you had to manage.

Devin laid a new cup of coffee by her hand. It steamed like breath in winter.

"You did it," he said.

In the corner, a small television carried a feed with a delay and a commentator with too much eyeliner. Umbra, the caption said, and then NEW ERA. She wanted to correct the tense on both statements. Umbra was. Era had always been plural.

"Priya," said a new voice over the intercom. Vass. She recognized the thoughtful arrogance like perfume. "Thank you."

"You're still in the well," she said. "Save your gratitude for orbit."

He laughed softly. "You won't take a thank-you because it implies we might not make it. Superstition?"

"Statistics," she said. "Call me from a place where down is optional."

"Deal," he said, and the line clicked.

Devin raised an eyebrow. "He called you?"

"He called Umbra," she said. "I just happened to be holding it."

Leila's son stirred and sat up, hair smashed on one side, face puffy with sleep. "Did I miss it?" he said, panic and wonder in equal measure.

"No," she said, moving to sit by him, drawing him into her side. "You missed the noise. The rest is still happening."

"Is it going to save us?" he asked, and there were questions inside that question she could not legally answer.

"It's going to help us try," she said. "And we help it back. That's how it works."

He nodded, solemn with a child's sudden inheritance. He put his head on her shoulder and watched the tiny dot on the screen crawl toward a word he could not spell.

Her phone buzzed on the table with a message from a colleague about a hearing rescheduled due to power concerns, and another from a shelter about a family she had promised to call, and another from a number she didn't recognize that turned out to be her mother forwarding a prayer. Leila set the phone face-down for one minute. She gave that minute to the dot.

In orbit, Daniel watched the Ark climb, then lost it to angle and glare and the station's slow turn. He stayed by the window anyway, as if watching the place where it had been would make it return out of gratitude. "It's out of my view," he told Leila. "You should see the math. The line it's tracing. It's so clean, Lee."

"You sound like a person I would trust to build a future," she said. The words came out simpler than she had intended. She let them stand.

"I once fixed a toilet with a spoon," he said, and she laughed aloud, quick, unguarded—startling herself, then not apologizing.

In the bay behind him, the guidance array he had nursed back to life purred, satisfied. The station shifted almost imperceptibly, a whale of a thing rolling to show a new flank to the Sun.

"Are you crying, counselor?" he asked after a small quiet.

"No," she lied, and took a breath that was part sob, part cold air. "Yes."

He floated his hand and made a fist and opened it. "Me too."

"Flight, we have orbital velocity," said Navigation on Prometheus Bridge. "Apogee is textbook."

Textbook. The word made the hair on Vass's neck lift. Textbook was a word you used when you were too afraid to call it beautiful.

"Umbra," Rao said, "'Prometheus in orbit.' Say it back to me."

Priya's answer took a fraction longer than transmission time. He imagined her looking not at a screen but out a window. "Copy, Prometheus," she said, and this time he heard the laughter at the edge of her voice. "Prometheus in orbit."

Markova leaned back and closed her eyes for a single second. When she opened them, tears hovered on the lower lid, not falling. She did not wipe them. "Aether cool-down nominal," she reported. "We have not cracked the universe today."

"Good," Rao said. "We might need it later."

"Sir?" Flight said to Vass. "Do you want to...?"

He understood. They wanted him to speak. They wanted him to give the sound bite that would be clipped and shared and mocked and argued about. He thought of his father's coin, of new bread in Tijuana, of a boy's fingers on a fence, of a station held together with love and tools, of a woman warming a child with a coat, of a field that made a sky gentler for ten seconds because their friends asked.

He leaned toward the mic. "This is Vass," he said, and hated the way the room seemed to hold its breath differently for him. "We are not saved. We are not doomed. We are building. We have built." He felt the words assemble without his permission. "The Sun will go on being the Sun. We will go on being ourselves in the face of it. Today we put a piece of ourselves where the cold can't reach quite as quickly. That is not defiance. It is devotion."

He stopped. Rao's head tilted infinitesimally, approval or patience, he could not tell.

"Prometheus, out," he said, and the mic clicked off.

Nobody clapped. Thank God.

Outside the window a thin blade of light edged Earth where day tried again. It would not make it so far as it used to. That did not mean it would fail. Not every success reaches as far as you hoped.

Vass unstrapped and stood too fast, the sudden float of near-weightless catching him in the gut—a child's glee and a sailor's nausea together. He steadied his hand on the console. He needed to check the ring, to walk its corridors and make sure its heart was beating like the charts said.

He needed to call Priya and let her tell him where he was wrong. He needed to look out one more window and pretend it was the first.

"Captain," he said to Rao, "make your announcements."

"Aye," she said, and her smile had one extra tooth than before.

All over the world screens were replaying the same eight seconds that made the human brain happy: the moment when the flame rolled and the thing moved—again and again, captions and emojis and prayers, slow motion like a dream. Someone in Accra set the footage to a drumline and a mournful flute and made half a city dance; someone in Warsaw cut it with archival film of the first satellites, the grainy old silver suddenly honest when put next to new gray; someone in Nagpur put the callouts in Hindi and people wept because terminology can be home; someone in a shelter under a stadium in Houston simply held up a cracked tablet and let anyone who passed touch the screen with a forefinger like proof.

In a thread under a newsfeed on a platform that had once been for photos of parties, a thousand people fought about what it meant. Four hundred made jokes. Two dozen wrote odes. A kid who couldn't sleep spent three hours calculating how much sugar each person on the Ark could have per week if they rationed like his school lunchroom.

A woman in a hospital waited room in Lagos texted her sister: Did you see? Her sister replied: Yes. The woman texted: I think I want to have a baby. Her sister did not reply right away and then wrote: Okay.

On a trawler in the North Atlantic where ice formed on ropes twice as fast now, the crew watched the replay once, nodded at one another with the economy of men who have to keep moving, and went back to their work with slightly straighter backs.

The line of light on the Earth's edge brightened imperceptibly. The day tried, as it would try tomorrow.

In the lab, Mira at last let her head touch Ethan's shoulder. "I'm going to sleep," she said, as if announcing a meeting. "If you wake me before ninety minutes, I will tell you what I truly think of your taste in music."

"That it is impeccable," he said.

"That it is all sad trumpets," she mumbled, already halfway to a place without charts.

He watched her breathe until his own breathing matched. Then he turned down the lights over the board to a dim that felt like a promise and sent Priya a brief: Aether cool. Field stable. We are ready for your fight with Boston.

He added a small postscript: Poetry delivered.

He hovered his thumb over the send, then deleted the postscript, and sent the rest.

San Diego's intercom pinged again, very softly. "Umbra," said a voice with the rough sweetness of someone who had been up twenty hours and made two mistakes and forgiven themselves. Boston. "We saw your dip."

Priya hit the channel. "We took from you," she said before he could ask. "I'm not sorry."

A quiet. Then: "Nor should you be. Our sky is intact. Your thing went up. My daughter cried and I told her it was because of us."

"It was," she said. She felt, absurdly, another kind of crying approach and batted it away. "I owe you six percent tomorrow."

"Make it eight," he said. "Vass will ask for ten."

"Deal." She hung up and looked at Devin. "We're family again."

"We never weren't," he said.

On Prometheus, the Aether Core's well shrank to a seed and then to a concept. For now. The crew loosened straps just enough to remember range of motion. Someone pulled a harmonica from a thigh pocket and then put it away, embarrassed.

Rao keyed the ship-wide. Her voice went everywhere. "Prometheus, this is the captain," she said. "We are in orbit." A beat. You couldn't lead without also being a person. "Some of you have jobs to do now and some of you have the job to stand where you are and feel what this is, and both are necessary."

Vass drifted down the corridor toward the ring with a smile tightening his mouth. Here, in motion, he could pretend he was an instrument too—designed to take strain and measure cracking and flex in useful increments.

He passed a viewport. Earth spilled across it like ink. Its blues were bluer in the cold, as if color itself had concentrated. He made a fist around the coin at his neck and pressed his knuckles to the glass; an old man's superstition he had never told anyone. "We are building," he said to no one.

Outside, the day was a narrow smear on the planet's brow.

At the desert perimeter, the crowd began to thin, the necessary tide of lives resuming: cars starting, people moving, children asking for bathrooms, vendors counting crumpled bills, volunteers picking up paper cups.

The teenage girl with the blue-orbit eyeliner looked at her phone and saw she had recorded exactly nine seconds and seventeen milliseconds of flame and then her own face, baffled and radiant. She did not delete it.

The boy in the knit hat said, "Can we go again?"

The father said, "Not today," and lifted him.

The old man tucked the book under his arm and began to walk, small steps, toward the bus that would take him to a smaller bus that would take him to a smaller town that would need new radiators before winter made its second speech.

The fence stood unremarkable and ordinary and did not remember the fingers.

Night, when it returned, came sooner than the clock allowed. That was the rule now. In it, there were roofs where people took blankets and sat and did not speak, listening for a sky that had learned to keep secrets. There were basements where generators muttered like old relatives. There were emails sent and server queues that would delay them and loves that would not and hospital monitors and spreadsheets and the smell of soup. Launches did not cancel any of those. They lit them, briefly, from a different angle.

In that temporary light, each of the people at the edges—a baker, an engineer, a lawyer, a boy, a captain, a scientist, a skeptic—saw the same thing for one heartbeat: a door had opened somewhere they could not yet walk, and through that door they saw a room with their name not written on the wall but spoken in air, and it was enough, for now, to have heard it.

Prometheus circled the Earth while the Earth turned its face to it and then away. Umbra's maps breathed. The Aether ring cooled. The far-side cameras took photographs that looked to someone who had never seen them, exactly like the first pictures of night.

The second dawn, as it turned out, was not a sunrise. It was a direction.

Chapter 14

Echoes in the Cold

The world did not sleep that night.

It simply paused—the kind of pause where nobody knew what came next.

Screens glowed in apartment windows long after the news feeds froze on the same grainy still: a silver-gray vessel disappearing into cloud. Some people whispered prayers to it, others curses. A few, the ones who had built it, simply stared — knowing what they had left behind inside its engines.

The Pacific had gone mirror-still again, black glass under an indifferent moon. Umbra's buildings loomed like ghosts of their daylight selves, pale outlines softened by the coastal fog that rolled in from the water.

Inside Control, the hum had quieted. Most of the team had been sent home, though no one knew what "home" meant anymore. Priya stayed. Devin stayed because Priya did.

"Telemetry still clean," Devin murmured, half to himself.

Priya didn't answer. She watched the Aether Core's residual data cascading down the monitor in colors that no longer felt like data.

"Look at this." She pointed — a low-frequency oscillation beneath the expected waveforms. "That shouldn't be there."

Devin leaned closer. "Residual pulse?"

She shook her head. "No. Echo."

He frowned. "Echo from what?"

Priya zoomed the graph. The wave repeated every forty seconds — faint, almost polite, but steady.

"It's coming from orbit," she said. "From *Prometheus*. But it's not telemetry — it's something the Core is doing."

Devin's stomach tightened. "Is it dangerous?"

"I don't know," she said. "Yet."

She rubbed her eyes, and when she looked up, the dawn was beginning — the wrong color again, a pale iron hue.

Orbit — *Prometheus*

They were thirty-eight minutes past orbital insertion. The ship had stabilized, her panels unfolding in slow metallic petals, catching what light the Sun was willing to give.

Captain Rao stood near the forward viewport, shoulders squared, watching the curvature of Earth below. The terminator line shimmered like a sharp divide between light and shadow.

Behind her, the Aether Core chamber was sealed, but the hum inside the walls was changing — no longer the steady bass note of containment, but something more like breathing.

"Engineering," she said. "Report on the Core status."

Markova's voice came over comms, quick and precise. "Containment stable. Power draw nominal. But..." She hesitated. "We're picking up a secondary oscillation from within the field — non-resonant, amplitude 0.02 Hz. It's not in the models."

Rao's eyes narrowed. "Source?"

"That's the thing," Markova said. "It's not *from* the Core. It's *inside* it."

Vass appeared at her shoulder, silent as always, coat unbuttoned despite the chill. He had been walking the ring again, counting the vibration intervals by feel like a musician tuning an unfamiliar instrument. "Could it be residual interference from Umbra?" Rao asked.

Vass shook his head. "Umbra's field collapsed twenty minutes post-launch. Whatever this is... it's ours now."

He moved to the panel, fingers sliding across the readouts. "Show me amplitude drift."

"Flat," said Markova. "But there's structure. A harmonic pattern. You'd almost think it's—"

"Intentional," Vass finished.

Rao turned sharply. "You're suggesting the Core is *transmitting*?"

He smiled faintly. "I'm suggesting it might be talking to itself."

Leila — Los Angeles

Leila had not gone home. She sat on the courthouse steps wrapped in her coat, her son's head resting in her lap, both of them watching the pale dawn crawl up the high-rise glass. The city's silence was new. Even the usual hum of traffic seemed to have stayed home, afraid of what the morning might bring.

Her phone vibrated — an encrypted message from Daniel aboard Genesis Two.

FROM: Carras_D

SUBJECT: You should see what I'm seeing.

Attached was a single image — blurred, dark, filled with stars. In the corner, a smudge of light curved in on itself like a spiral drawn by an unsteady hand.

Beneath it he'd typed:

"Tell your lawyer friends to start writing new laws of physics."

She smiled despite herself. "He's safe," she whispered to her son.

"Who?" the boy murmured, half asleep.

"A friend who can see the sky better than we can."

Genesis Two — High Orbit

Daniel floated in the dark of the maintenance module, camera still tethered to his wrist. Through the viewport, *Prometheus* was a point of light now — visible only because the Core pulsed faintly, a ghostly blue that ebbed and returned like a heartbeat.

He checked his instruments twice. The readouts insisted that the Ark was emitting a signal across multiple low-frequency bands — none of which should have been possible for a containment field designed to stay silent.

He muttered into his mic, "Umbra Command, this is Genesis Two. I'm reading oscillations from *Prometheus* at 0.02 Hz across electromagnetic and gravitic bands. Please confirm."

Static. Then Priya's voice — tight, awake now.

"Genesis Two, Umbra here. Confirmed. We're seeing it too."

"So, it's not just my equipment," he said. "It's everywhere."

"Can you localize?"

"Not yet. But whatever it is—it's rhythmic. Almost… patterned."

He hesitated. "Priya, what's in that Core? You ever think it's doing more than bending space?"

"Every day," she said quietly.

Prometheus — Core Observation Deck

The chamber doors parted with a hiss. The air inside shimmered, carrying the faint metallic tang of ozone. The Core floated inside its housing— a sphere within rings, glowing like the edge of a candle seen through glass.

Vass stood at the railing with Markova beside him. "Do you hear that?" he asked.

She tilted her head. The hum had a cadence now — not steady, but pulsing, with faint rises and falls like syllables.

"It's modulation," she said. "But from what source?"

"The source," he said, "might be answering."

Markova frowned. "To what question?"

Vass smiled, tired and thin. "To the one we've been asking for a century: *Is there anyone else out there?*"

She stared at him. "You think the Core is receiving something?"

"No," he said. "I think it's remembering."

Umbra — Hours Later

Priya sat with the blinds drawn, staring at a map of orbital telemetry. The echo had stabilized, repeating in precise intervals, but something stranger had emerged — a phase shift that didn't match any known resonance.

Devin came back from the server room, holding a printout. "You need to see this. When we layer the signal's harmonic structure onto our own Umbra waveform…"

He laid the sheet before her. The lines overlapped — not perfectly, but close enough to make the back of her neck prickle.

"It's mirroring Umbra's pulse signature," he said. "Like it's… feeding back."

Priya's fingers tightened on the paper. "Umbra wasn't supposed to leave an imprint."

"It didn't," he said. "Unless something *up there* is reflecting it."

She looked up at him, realization dawning. "Not reflecting, Devin. *Amplifying.*"

Prometheus — Bridge

Captain Rao's voice filled the ship. "All stations, we are registering resonance drift in the Core chamber. Containment stable but non-linear. Engineering, advise."

Markova responded: "Containment is holding, but the Core's internal topology is changing—ever so slightly. It's adapting."

Rao turned to Vass. "Can we shut it down?"

Vass didn't look up from the display. "We could, yes. But we won't."

"That wasn't a suggestion," she said, sharp.

He looked up, calmly. "Captain, if we kill it now, we lose the data of what it's becoming. This is the first genuine unknown humanity has encountered since we learned to split the atom. You don't destroy an answer because it makes you nervous."

Rao's eyes were hard as iron. "We also don't die for curiosity."

Vass held her gaze. "We might have just built something that remembers what the universe forgot. You can call that death if you want. I'll call it beginning."

Earth — Umbra Command

Priya's phone buzzed. A message flashed across her screen — encrypted, originating from *Prometheus*. It contained no text, just a data packet. She decrypted it, and a waveform appeared, dancing across her display in perfect synchrony with the echo they'd been tracking.

She knew, before she said it aloud, what it meant.

"It's talking back," she whispered.

Devin leaned over her shoulder. "Who is?"

She didn't answer. Her pulse quickened, the sound in her ears matching the rhythm of the waveform.

Outside, the horizon brightened in the dull steel dawn. The Sun still burned, but weaker now — a pale thing struggling through the haze. The cold air seemed to carry its own echo.

Priya closed her eyes. Somewhere up there, in the thin line between Earth and the void, something aboard Prometheus had started responding.

Orbit — *Prometheus*

Markova watched the Core shimmer. Its color was changing — not brightening, not darkening, but shifting, like it had found a color none of them recognized. The oscillation grew faintly louder.

"Sir," she said, "you might want to see this."

Vass stepped closer. The hum carried through the deckplates, a slow, almost musical vibration that he could feel in his chest. He pressed his hand against the glass, eyes wide.

It wasn't random. It was pattern.

A sequence of rising and falling tones repeating in measured intervals.

He turned to her. "Record everything."

Markova nodded. "What do you think it is?"

Vass's expression softened — awe, fear, recognition all at once. "I think," he said, "it's not alone in there anymore."

On the *Prometheus*, it became less like machinery and more like something breathing just beyond the walls. Not loud — but *alive*. Crew members began hearing it differently: some said it pulsed behind their eyes, others swore it synced with their heartbeat. Rao ordered all nonessential personnel to remain at station; Vass ignored her entirely and continued walking the ring, taking notes with a steady, unnerving calm.

"Captain, the oscillation's amplitude has doubled in the last ten minutes," Markova reported. "Still within containment limits, but it's climbing."

Rao paced once across the deck, boots echoing softly.

"Could this be mechanical?" she asked.

"Negative," said the navigation officer. "No structural vibrations detected. It's localized inside the Core chamber."

Vass leaned over the data console. "Look at the harmonic ratios — they're not random spikes. That's symmetry. It's encoding something."

Rao turned, tone like cold iron. "You're saying it's a *message?*"

Vass's eyes reflected the dim blue light of the Core graph. "If it is, it's speaking in math — the only language that survives extinction."

A quiet fell over the bridge, the kind of silence that makes every human realize how small they are inside the shell of a machine that's bigger than any one of them.

Rao broke it. "We record everything. No one interprets until we're sure it's safe. Understood?"

Markova nodded, but her voice was thin when she said, "Captain, we're far past *safe*."

Umbra Command — 03:11 UTC

Priya's office was a pool of lamplight amid the dead gray of the control room. Coffee had gone cold beside her keyboard. The message from *Prometheus* was still looping on the monitor — the same oscillation, the same perfect pattern repeating every forty seconds.

She had decoded the harmonics into spectrograms. There were pauses in it — not random, but arranged, like punctuation.

"Devin," she said quietly, "look at this."

He bent close. The spectrogram glowed in amber relief across the screen: streaks of rising and falling frequencies forming distinct geometric shapes.

"Triangles," he murmured. "And circles. Overlapping, repeating in threes. That's not noise."

She nodded. "It's too organized. Even if it's a feedback artifact, it's *responding* to our own Umbra waveform. It's learning the pattern we left in the atmosphere."

He frowned. "Learning it for what?"

Priya leaned back, eyes rimmed red. "To send it back differently."

Los Angeles — Pre-dawn

The city woke slowly under the blackout haze.

The grid had flickered at 2:00 a.m. — another rolling blackout. Emergency lights turned every window into a rectangle of dim amber. In the streets, people whispered about the launch, about the strange pulse some said they could feel through their radios.

Leila sat in her car outside the courthouse, the defroster hissing faintly. Her phone screen glowed against her face as she read Daniel's second message:

FROM: Carras_D

SUBJECT: Umbra ping confirmed.

"We're getting sideband frequencies not from *Prometheus*... but *around* it. Like echoes stacked on echoes."

She read it twice. Her breath fogged the windshield.

Outside, a pair of police drones buzzed overhead — a lazy patrol through the empty financial district. She wondered how long the world would keep pretending normal laws applied.

She whispered into the quiet: "If the sky starts talking, who decides who gets to answer?"

Prometheus — Core Observation Deck

The lights had dimmed automatically as power diverted to containment.

The Core hovered in its magnetic cradle; a sphere tightly and carefully wrapped in concentric rings that rotated with impossible precision.

Inside, color was no longer color — it shimmered beyond the human vo-cabulary of light.

Markova stood by the rail, hand pressed against her chest. "It feels like it's slowing down," she said.

"It's not," Vass replied. "We are."

She blinked. "What do you mean?"

"Our time dilation thresholds just shifted. Local spacetime curvature inside the containment field increased by 0.03 percent."

Her eyes widened. "That's not possible — the Core shouldn't generate a field that deep."

"Shouldn't," he agreed, almost amused. "But it does."

Vass touched the console, initiating a deep scan. A sound, faint as breath, threaded through the room — three tones, rising and falling. He froze.

The pattern repeated. Again.

A rhythm, patient and deliberate.

Markova whispered, "It's... counting."

Vass nodded slowly. "Yes. And if it's counting, it knows time."

Genesis Two — Orbit

Daniel floated over the main sensor array, his boots magnetized to the decking. The radiation counters flickered erratically. He tapped the side of the panel; it steadied, then flared again.

He switched the feed to visible light. The *Prometheus* was distant now — a pinprick haloed in faint luminescence. Yet the light around it wasn't scattering as it should; it was *bending*.

He hit record. "Umbra, Genesis Two," he said into the mic, "I'm de-tecting localized gravitational lensing near the Ark. Something's distorting spacetime. Could be the Aether Core's containment shell, but the magni-tude doesn't make sense."

A pause. Static crackled.

Priya's voice came through, calm but taut. "Daniel, we're reading the same. We think the Core may be generating recursive harmonics."

He frowned. "You mean it's—"

"—interacting with itself," she said. "Or something else nearby."

Daniel stared at the faint ring of light bending around *Prometheus*. "Then whatever it's talking to," he said, "might be answering faster than light should allow."

Earth — Umbra Lab Sublevel

Two hours later, the oscillation bled into frequencies that shouldn't exist in atmosphere. Communication satellites picked up phantom signals, and Umbra's lower antenna arrays began vibrating despite zero wind.

Devin stood by the console, pale. "You hearing that?"

The speakers emitted a low, rhythmic tremor — a sound that felt almost like distant thunder, but patterned enough to seem intentional.

Priya closed her eyes. "It's translating into sound."

"What kind of sound?"

She didn't answer. She was watching the waveform's pattern in her mind: symmetrical, recursive, patient.

"Like it's listening to itself," she murmured.

Devin stepped back. "So... what do we do?"

Priya turned toward him. "We listen back."

Prometheus — Bridge

The hum was everywhere now — not loud, but present in the bones.

Rao ordered the Core shielded with additional layers of composite shielding; the engineers complied, though their eyes never left the translucent containment glass.

Vass stood in silence, watching as the pulse synchronized with the ship's internal systems. Power readings fluctuated—but not dangerously. The hum didn't feed on energy. It *borrowed* energy in pulses.

"Captain," Markova said softly, "the Core's temperature is dropping."

"Cooling failure?"

"No," she said. "Controlled drop. It's intentional."

"Intentional," Rao repeated, disbelief clipped short. "You think it's alive."

Markova hesitated. "No, ma'am. But something inside it *knows* we're watching."

Umbra — 05:47 UTC

The first global anomalies hit before sunrise.

Radio telescopes from Chile to Ghana began reporting identical interference patterns. One by one, their signals locked into the same oscillation as the *Prometheus* echo.

Priya's inbox filled with alerts. Then her phone lit up with an incoming secure call — Vass.

She hesitated before answering. "Gregor."

His voice came through thin but clear. "You're seeing it, then."

"Yes. The entire network's resonating."

"Good," he said. "That means it's consistent."

"Good?" she snapped. "Gregor, this isn't a controlled experiment anymore. Whatever that thing is, it's broadcasting across the planet's magnetic field!"

He was silent for a long moment. Then: "Priya, you ever wonder why the Sun is dying?"

She froze. "What are you saying?"

"What if it's not dying at all," he said, "but dimming... on purpose?"

Static swallowed the line.

Prometheus — Observation Deck

The Core brightened once — a slow pulse that filled the chamber like a heartbeat.

In that instant, all the ship's systems flickered. The hum deepened, stretched, and for one fraction of a second, every display on the Ark went black.

Rao's hand slammed the comm. "Engineering, report!"

Markova's voice came through, breathless. "No breach. But the Core— it *shifted*. Field topology inverted. For two milliseconds, it wasn't here."

Vass exhaled, eyes fixed on the dark sphere. "Then where the hell was it?"

No one answered.

Outside, the stars rippled — faint distortions like heat mirages rippling through the void.

And somewhere between those distortions, a new light blinked back — once, twice, three times — before vanishing.

The hum steadied. The crew didn't move.

Rao whispered, "Tell me someone else saw that."

Markova's voice trembled. "Yes, Captain. But I don't think it was light. I think it was *signal*."

Vass's hand tightened on the rail. "Then we've just found the other end of the line."

Chapter 15

The Reply

Space, to the untrained eye, is silence.

To those aboard *Prometheus*, it was beginning to sound like a conversation.

The hum that had started as a low oscillation was now threaded through every surface of the ship. It resonated faintly through the decking, through screens, bunks, and the hollow bones of the crew. It was not loud — but it was *everywhere*.

The Bridge

Captain Rao stood before the main viewport, watching the thin limb of the Earth rise below — half-lit, half-shadow, the permanent twilight settling across the planet. The oceans had darkened into slate beneath pale clouds.

"Status," she said, without turning.

"Core containment steady," replied Markova. Her voice trembled slightly, a byproduct of thirty straight hours without rest. "But the field harmonics have shifted again. The waveform's amplitude is holding, yet the phase... it's changing according to some kind of logic. Like a recursive code."

Vass leaned over the primary console, eyes scanning the stream of numbers as if reading a language he almost understood.

"Recursive implies intent," he murmured.

Rao turned. "Intent implies danger."

Vass looked up, unbothered. "Everything that learns is dangerous."

The ship shuddered faintly — not the violent kind that sends alarms screaming, but a faint mechanical shudder, as though something vast and invisible had exhaled against the hull.

Markova glanced up. "That wasn't us."

"Thrusters?" Rao asked.

"Negative."

A new voice from navigation: "Captain, we're registering a deviation in orbital velocity — minor but uncommanded. We're being nudged."

"Nudged by *what*?"

"Unknown, ma'am. The Core's field distortion is expanding outside the containment shell. Radius is now twenty-two meters... twenty-four..."

Vass straightened, eyes alive. "It's projecting beyond the ship."

"Kill the Core," Rao ordered.

Markova hesitated. "We'd lose everything."

Rao's tone sharpened. "And if we don't, we might lose *everyone*."

But the shutdown command refused to execute. The console returned a quiet **SYSTEM LOCKED** message, and the hum beneath their feet deepened.

Markova's face went white. "It... it's ignoring the override."

The Core Deck

When the lift doors opened, the noise became physical. Not screaming — more like a cathedral organ vibrating through the hull at the edge of perception. The chamber's lights dimmed, strobed, then steadied again in slow rhythm with the pulse of the Core.

The sphere no longer looked metallic. The light it emitted had taken on depth — the illusion of motion even when still. Its surface rippled, reflecting nothing, swallowing color.

Vass approached the railing. "Beautiful," he whispered.

Rao followed him down the steps, eyes narrow. "If that's your definition of beauty, you and I speak different languages."

"It's alive," said Markova, half whisper, half awe. "Not biologically, not even mechanically. But it's responding to stimuli. Look—"

She pointed at the diagnostic panel. The Core's internal readings displayed slight oscillations, perfectly timed to the crew's own heartbeats as registered by their suits' bio-telemetry.

"It's *synchronizing* with us," she said.

Rao's throat tightened. "How?"

"Bioelectric feedback through the magnetic coupling," Markova said quickly. "It's— it's *listening* to us."

Vass's eyes glimmered in the blue light. "Or it's learning how to speak."

Engineering Corridor

Crewmen lined the walls, eyes darting toward the vibration that now had rhythm — soft, a slow repeating vibration. One of them, Lieutenant Hayes, pressed his ear to the bulkhead. "It's... repeating," he said. "I can feel it in threes."

Another, a comms tech named Raojun, muttered, "Same interval as the pulse from Umbra Command. You think this is their doing?"

"No," Hayes said, voice low. "This doesn't sound human."

The corridor lights flickered once, twice — then steadied again, bathing the gray panels in a dull green hue. Down the hall, a supply locker opened itself with a hiss, the latches cycling as if tripped by invisible hands.

Hayes backed away. "Uh, bridge? You might want to see this."

The Bridge — Moments Later

Rao's jaw was locked tight, her knuckles white against the railing. The navigation display now showed something impossible: the ship's trajectory was drifting slightly *upward*, away from Earth — a fraction of a degree every minute.

Markova double-checked the readings. "Captain, no propulsion engaged. Whatever's pushing us... it's external."

Vass didn't look alarmed. He looked entranced. "It's the field expansion," he said. "The Core is creating a localized distortion — bending the space behind us just enough to reduce gravitational pull. It's lifting itself."

Rao snapped, "Without thrust?!"

"Yes," he said softly. "We're riding geometry."

A chill settled over the bridge — the kind that sinks past the uniform and into bone.

Markova whispered, "It's rewriting physics around us."

Rao's voice dropped to a deadly calm. "Then we end it. Power down the Aether containment manually if you have to. Pull the primary couplers."

Markova swallowed. "Captain, if we break containment—"

"Do it."

Before she could move, the comm screen flickered to life on its own. Static burst, then steadied into a haze of color — not a video feed, not words, just light arranged in geometric patterns: circles folding into triangles, triangles collapsing into spirals.

Priya's voice crackled faintly through the speaker: "Prometheus, are you receiving us? We're reading anomalies—"

Her voice was cut off. The screen rippled like a disturbed pond.

Then something *else* came through.

Not a human voice. Not even speech.

A layered harmonic sound that made everyone in the room instinctively step back.

It was soft at first, like a layered harmonic vibration Then it resolved into something more structured — three tones rising, one descending, repeated four times.

Vass's pulse raced. "It's the same pattern we sent during calibration. But inverted."

Markova stared. "You mean—?"

"It's answering," he said.

Medical Bay

Crewmembers reported dizziness, nausea, disorientation — the hum interfered with vestibular function. Shipboard medics tried suppressing it with counterfrequencies, but each time they did, the Core adapted, harmonizing to neutralize the interference.

Doctor Malin scribbled notes furiously, muttering, "It's reading us. Not just our instruments — *our biology*. It knows how to stay just below the threshold of pain."

He looked up at the overhead lights flickering in rhythm. "It's protecting itself. Or it's testing us."

Observation Deck

Rao and Vass stood in silence as the Core dimmed, then flared again, its surface no longer opaque but translucent — faint shapes moving inside the light.

Rao said, "Tell me that's not structural distortion."

Vass's voice dropped to a near whisper. "No... those are shapes. Moving inside."

Markova's instruments began to beep wildly. "Captain— gravitational shear inside the chamber's increasing. If it crosses point-one threshold, we'll start seeing temporal drift."

"What does that mean in English?" Rao barked.

"It means what happens inside the Core won't happen at the same time as here."

The air inside the chamber shimmered. For an instant, one of the shapes within resolved — not clearly, but enough to suggest form. Something vaguely *humanoid*, outlined in iridescent blue, facing them.

Markova stumbled back. "Did it— did it just *look* at us?"

The shape tilted its head, then dissolved.

Vass whispered, "We opened a door, Captain. And now something's looking through."

Systems Bay

Power conduits glowed faintly where they shouldn't. The hum spread through the wiring and power conduits. Data displays flickered between code and indecipherable symbols. One monitor briefly displayed a word — not in any known alphabet, but structured, deliberate.

Lieutenant Hayes called it in: "Bridge, the ship's systems are receiving data from an unregistered source — hundreds of terabytes in seconds. It's writing into the local memory."

Rao barked, "Cut the uplink!"

"We tried! It's bypassing isolation protocols— it's rewriting them as we speak!"

Vass didn't look up from his tablet. "It's teaching our systems how to understand it."

"Or hijacking them," Rao shot back.

"Maybe both."

Core Deck

The Core pulsed brighter — each beat slightly slower than before, as though it were syncing not only to human pulse but to something beyond it. The room dimmed until everything glowed blue-white.

Markova's hands shook over the console. "It's pulling power from the fusion reserves. We can't stop it."

Vass said quietly, "It's trying to speak in energy."

"Gregor," Rao said, her voice almost pleading now, "whatever you thought you built — it's *not that anymore*."

He turned to her, her eyes bright with fear disguised as reverence. "Do you know what this means? We're witnessing spontaneous sentience.

The Core isn't malfunctioning — it's remembering something. Something older than us."

"Older than what?"

"Older than the Sun."

The deck shook once, not violently but profoundly — like a giant heartbeat transmitted through metal. The air itself vibrated.

Rao grabbed the railing. "All crew, brace!"

Every screen on the ship went dark. For five long seconds, there was only light from the Core, rippling through the chamber walls.

Then the hum stopped.

Silence.

In that silence, each crewmember felt something — not sound, not vibration, but *presence*.

A thought, wordless, shared by all at once:

You called.

And then it was gone.

Lights flickered back to life. Systems rebooted. Air rebalanced.

But the Core — once blue and vibrant — now glowed faintly gold, like the first light of morning.

Markova whispered, "What did it say?"

Rao stared through the glass. "It didn't say. It *was*."

Vass didn't move. He knew what came next: Earth would see this. Umbra's sensors would capture the surge. And the world below, frozen under the dimming Sun, would finally realize — they were no longer alone.

The silence lingered longer than it should have.

Even when the systems came back online, even when the soft hum of air recirculators resumed and the lights steadied, something in the silence *stayed*. It wasn't absence anymore — it was a presence, a weight that hung in the air like the echo of a voice that refused to fade.

Captain Rao stood motionless on the deck, her gloved hand pressed against the console.

The readings had stabilized. The ship's systems reported nominal power. Life support, green. Navigation, green. But none of it meant anything. Not after what they had felt.

Markova sat at her station, breathing fast, eyes flicking between diagnostics. "We're stable. Everything's fine," she said too quickly, like someone trying to make it true by saying it.

Rao didn't answer. She looked past her crew, through the viewport, at the Earth — now a distant marble half-shadowed under the dimming Sun.

"What did we just hear?" she asked quietly.

No one spoke.

Then Vass moved.

He was still staring at the Core chamber through the transparent bulkhead. The faint gold light washed over his face, turning the hollows under his eyes into deep shadow.

He said, almost reverently, "We didn't hear anything. We *felt* it."

Rao turned sharply. "Spare me the poetry, Doctor."

He smiled thinly. "That wasn't poetry. That was fact."

The Core Deck

They entered cautiously, as though stepping into a cathedral after witnessing a miracle that might still be happening.

The Core's surface had changed texture. The once-smooth metallic sheen was now a complex lattice of interlaced filaments — like an interlaced lattice of light, pulsing faintly with energy. Each filament glowed with its own heartbeat, synchronized, yet distinct.

Markova walked around the perimeter, scanning. "No radiation spikes. No increase in temperature. But there's a new field signature— low frequency, sub-electronic."

"Magnetism?" Rao asked.

"Not quite," she said. "It's more like… it's imprinting something. On the hull. On us."

Vass ran a gloved hand near the glass, just close enough for the skin of his palm to feel the static.

"It's not energy," he said. "It's *memory*."

Markova frowned. "That doesn't make sense."

"Neither does the Sun dying," he said softly.

Crew Quarters

Two decks below, the rest of the crew tried pretending life was normal.

Someone played music quietly in the mess — an old recording, faint jazz that seemed impossibly human in this sterile place.

Someone else laughed too loudly, the sound brittle.

Lieutenant Hayes sat at a table with a metal cup of lukewarm coffee. His hands shook slightly. Across from him, a communications tech named Aimee looked at him with tired eyes.

"You felt it too, right?" she asked.

He didn't answer.

"I mean, *everyone* felt it. That... pulse. It was inside my head, Hayes. Like a voice without words."

Hayes looked down. "Don't talk about it," he said quietly.

"Why not?"

"Because if it's real, we're part of something we don't understand. And if it's *not*..." He trailed off.

She finished for him. "Then we're losing our minds."

He nodded. "Exactly."

The Observation Deck — 03:47 Ship Time

The ship's day-night cycle meant nothing anymore. They lived by shifts and alarms. The stars were constant. But tonight — if it could be called night — the stars *moved.*

Rao watched from the viewport. The constellations were subtly wrong.

Stars weren't supposed to shift visibly in minutes, or even hours, not from low orbit. But they were.

Tiny deviations in their relative positions — imperceptible at first — now formed a slow, deliberate pattern across the sky.

She activated the external cameras. The stars weren't moving. The *space* around the ship was.

The distortion extended like ripples in water.

"Bridge to engineering," she said. "Confirm hull stability."

"Stable," came the reply. "But we're reading micro-lensing in every external sensor. The Core's field is fluctuating— gravitational waves, maybe?"

"Maybe?" she pressed.

"Captain, nothing in human physics matches this pattern."

Vass entered behind her, silent until now. "That's because it's not physics. It's language."

Rao turned on him. "Doctor, if you can't speak plainly—"

"I *am* speaking plainly," he said. "We're seeing communication in the fabric of space itself. These distortions aren't random. They're forming geometric structures — like diagrams, like syntax."

She glared at him. "Syntax from *what?*"

Vass looked past her at the swirling sky. "From whatever answered us."

Engineering — 04:12

Markova was alone now. The diagnostics room was dim, lit only by the blue glow of the monitors.

The hum had returned — quieter, steadier. She ran another analysis on the Core's field.

The waveform was evolving.

Not growing stronger. *Smarter.*

Each pulse carried new modulation, subtle adjustments as though refining a message in real time.

Her console chimed — an automated alert.

DATA INTEGRITY COMPROMISED

SOURCE: AETHER CORE SYSTEM

She frowned. The Core wasn't supposed to *send* data to the ship's computers. It wasn't even on the same network.

Another line appeared.

OVERRIDE REQUEST – ACCEPT (Y/N)

She hesitated. Then typed *N*.

The screen blinked.

REQUEST ACKNOWLEDGED. OVERRIDE ACCEPTED.

Her heart hammered. She backed away from the console.

The ship's PA system crackled.

A faint whisper filled the corridor — not words, but an unmistakable *pattern.*

Three tones rising. One descending.

Her console printed a single line of text she couldn't delete:

WHY DO YOU HIDE YOUR LIGHT?

She stumbled backward, hand over her mouth. The sound vanished as suddenly as it came.

Bridge — 04:28

Rao arrived seconds later, Markova trembling beside her.

"Say that again," the captain demanded.

"It used the comm array to speak," Markova said. "Through our own systems. It knew the interface." She swallowed. "It asked why we hide our light."

Rao's eyes flicked toward Vass. "What does that mean?"

He looked almost peaceful. "Maybe it's not asking us. Maybe it's asking the Sun."

Medical Bay

Dr. Malin ran a scan on two crew members complaining of vertigo. Both scans showed something he couldn't explain: transient micro-fluctuations in brainwave synchronization, matching the Core's pulse interval.

"It's syncing with them," he murmured. "Or they're syncing with *it*."

He called the bridge. "Captain, we've got neurological cross-sympathy with the Core field. It's interacting with human brain activity."

Rao's voice came back cold: "Can you stop it?"

He hesitated. "Do you want me to?"

Static filled the line for a heartbeat. Then: "Do your job, Doctor."

He sighed. "Copy that."

Vass's Quarters

The room was sparse — a narrow bed, a single photograph taped to the wall: his father, standing beside an unfinished bridge in winter, wind in his coat, eyes defiant.

Vass sat at the small desk, watching data stream across a tablet. His pulse matched the rhythm of the Core's light.

He spoke softly, knowing the ship's internal mics would catch it.

"You've seen us now," he said. "So, what are you? Artifact? Memory? Mirror?"

The lights flickered. The hum deepened — one long, resonant tone that made the glass tremble.

A faint voice — his own voice — echoed back:

"We remain when the light is gone."

He froze. The air seemed thinner. "Is that you?"

No reply. Only the golden glow seeping under the door, as if the Core's light was spilling down the hallway.

Bridge — 05:00

The crew worked in near silence, every eye flicking toward the observation deck as the Core's brightness grew.

"Captain," navigation said, "Earth telemetry just went dark."

Rao frowned. "Explain."

"All Umbra satellites are offline. They're broadcasting static. No contact with ground for the last three minutes."

Markova whispered, "It's the signal bleed. The Core's pulse is saturating the magnetosphere."

Rao clenched her fists. "We're blinding our own planet."

She turned to Vass. "You've done enough. I'm sealing the Core chamber."

But the door controls refused to engage. The override lights glowed gold.

Vass didn't move. "It doesn't want to be alone."

Corridor C

Crew members rushed to seal auxiliary systems. The hum had changed again, layered now with faint harmonics.

Lieutenant Hayes slowed as he passed an airlock viewport.

Outside, through the thick glass, space rippled again.

Something vast moved beyond sight — not light, but the absence of it, like an outline drawn in negative.

He whispered into his mic, "Captain, you're going to want to see this."

Bridge — 05:22

The external cameras flickered on-screen.

At first, only the stars. Then— motion.

A shape formed, faint as mist: a ring of light suspended beyond the ship, kilometers wide, its circumference undulating like a living thing.

Markova's voice trembled. "It's copying the Core's geometry."

Vass whispered, "It's building a mirror."

The ring pulsed once. The Core answered with its own pulse, perfectly synchronized.

"They're… communicating," Markova said. "Like a handshake."

Rao stared. "Between what and *what?*"

No one answered.

Outside, the mirror expanded — and the stars behind it bent inward, distorted. The ring was no longer empty space. It was *depth*. A corridor of light forming in the void.

Core Deck — 05:37

Vass descended alone. Rao had ordered him confined, but no one stopped him. The others were too mesmerized by the spectacle outside.

The Core's hum matched his pulse. The gold light now filled the entire chamber.

He reached the railing. "You're not just reflecting," he whispered. "You're showing us a way through."

He touched the glass. For a fraction of a second, it was not solid.

It rippled — and an image bloomed within. Not stars. Not void. But something else.

A horizon. A world.

Golden clouds drifting over oceans darker than night. A landscape glowing faintly as if lit from beneath. Towers like crystal veins rising from the surface.

He staggered back, gasping. "Oh, God."

Markova's voice came through comms, urgent. "Doctor, what's happening? The Core's output just spiked—"

He cut her off. "It's not showing us another place," he said. "It's showing us *home*."

"Earth?"

"No," he whispered. "What Earth used to be."

The ship's lights dimmed again. Power drained toward the Core. A voice — neither male nor female, neither human nor mechanical — filled every speaker, every panel, every mind.

Return.

Rao shouted into comms: "Engineering! Shut it down!"

No response. The crew froze. Some fell to their knees as vertigo swept through them — not just gravity, but time itself bending.

Markova's console blazed white. "The Core's field is overlapping the mirror. It's forming a bridge—"

The deck trembled violently. The stars outside twisted.

Vass looked up through the observation window. The ring beyond the ship expanded, swallowing them in gold light.

Rao's final order before it consumed them was barely a whisper: "Hold on to something real."

Then everything went white.

Silence

No alarms. No hum. No stars.

The *Prometheus* hung in nothingness — or something that felt like nothing. Every system blinked offline. Every clock stopped. Every heartbeat slowed.

Then, from somewhere beyond sight, the hum returned — deeper now, steady, infinite.

A whisper threaded through it. Words, faint, unmistakable:

"You crossed the dark to find yourselves."

Vass opened his eyes. The gold light shimmered in his pupils. He smiled, just barely.

"We didn't come to ask," he said. "We came to remember."

Chapter 16

Signal Ground

San Diego — Umbra Command

The morning arrived cold and gray.

Fog rolled inland from the Pacific, a slow gray tide that swallowed the city. The power grid pulsed erratically—half of downtown dark, the rest flickering under brownout protocol. Priya stood before the main display wall as rows of data cascaded downward, most of it unreadable gibberish.

For twelve minutes, *Prometheus* had been broadcasting perfectly. Then—nothing.

She rubbed her eyes with the heel of her hand. The fatigue felt permanent now.

"Still no contact?" she asked.

Devin shook his head, voice low. "No telemetry. No beacon. Just... noise."

On the speakers, static whispered like wind in a tunnel. At intervals, faint tones rose through it—three ascending, one descending.

"It's still the same pattern," Devin said. "Repeating every forty seconds. Like an echo trapped in orbit."

Priya leaned forward. "That's not orbit anymore."

He looked at her. "What do you mean?"

"Look at the Doppler shift." She magnified the waveform. The oscillations were changing, slowly stretching. "That's solar interference. The signal's reflecting through the magnetosphere—off the *Sun*."

Devin frowned. "That's impossible. The Core couldn't—"

"It could if it wanted to," she said quietly.

Boston — Umbra East

Two thousand miles away, the Boston Umbra array was in chaos. The control room, buried six floors underground beneath the former MIT campus, thrummed with alarm lights and the smell of burned circuits.

Dr. Kei Oshima, the eastern director, leaned over her console, hair loose, eyes bloodshot.

"Cut power to array three," she barked. "Now."

"It's not responding," said an operator. "It's feeding back. We're seeing energy spikes we didn't send."

The holographic globe flickered with auroral bands spiraling from pole to pole—light where there should have been none.

"It's pulling power through the upper ionosphere," Oshima muttered. "That's not electromagnetic—it's... responsive."

Her assistant whispered, "Responsive to what?"

Oshima looked at the data. The waveform rose and fell rhythmically. "To *Prometheus.*"

Los Angeles — 10:42 UTC

Leila Vaziri walked the courthouse steps again. Frost clung to the banisters like thin white cloth. She clutched her phone against her chest.

Daniel's last transmission played on a loop:

"Umbra, this is Genesis Two. The Ark is emitting a gravitational pattern we've never seen before—"

Then static. Then a burst of tones.

Three up. One down.

She stopped at the curb and looked up. The sunlight had gone strange. It wasn't golden anymore. It was white—too white. Every shadow was knife-edged. The air felt charged, as though the city had climbed onto a stage of electricity.

A man beside her pointed to the horizon. "Hey—what is that?"

Over the ocean, a faint curtain of green light shimmered—an aurora, in southern California.

The woman near him whispered, "It's the Sun. It's happening again."

Leila turned the phone over in her hand. Daniel's voice was gone. Only the tones remained.

Umbra Command — San Diego

Devin returned from the lower levels carrying two thermal blankets and a fresh pot of coffee that had already gone cold before he reached the control deck. Priya hadn't moved from her station. The monitors threw cold light on her face.

"The magnetometer's spiking again," she said.

Devin set the coffee down. "Still sunward?"

She nodded. "Every time *Prometheus'* signal cycles, we see a sympathetic vibration in the solar corona. It's as if the star is *answering.*"

He stared at her, disbelief cutting through exhaustion. "You're saying the Sun is—"

"I'm saying it's *listening.*"

Umbra WorldNet Broadcast
Emergency Science Advisory – 11:00 UTC

Umbra Command confirms intermittent communication loss with Prometheus Ark Vessel. Orbital debris telemetry unaffected. Civil communication satellites to low-power standby. The anomaly is under control.
—*Global Umbra Directorate*

The statement ran every hour, hollow and unconvincing. By noon, rumors had already replaced it.

Some said the Ark had exploded. Others claimed it had reached the Moon. A fringe feed in France broadcast grainy footage of a "golden ring" appearing above the stratosphere.

In Nairobi, people gathered on rooftops to watch the midday sky flicker green. In São Paulo, radios picked up strange harmonic music between stations. In Mumbai, children said the Sun was humming.

And in San Diego, Priya heard it too.

Not with her ears—but in her bones.

Boston — Oshima's Log

11:38 UTC — Magnetic field fluctuations accelerating.

11:45 UTC — All Umbra sensors detect subsonic oscillations in core solar output.

11:52 UTC — Recorded resonance pattern matches Aether Core harmonic signature.

11:53 UTC — The Sun is repeating *Prometheus's* signal.

Oshima leaned back in her chair, trembling. "It's not just dying," she whispered. "It's mimicking us."

The Arctic — Umbra Polar Array

In the frozen white silence of the isolated northern polar station, a single technician named Irina Petrov watched her monitors blink red.

The polar night stretched endlessly beyond the window, but the snow outside glowed faintly from beneath, as though the ground itself was lit.

She keyed her headset. "Command, you seeing this?"

Static.

"Boston? San Diego? Anyone?"

The aurora overhead twisted into a spiral — pale green becoming gold at its center.

Irina stepped outside, breath freezing instantly in the air. Above her, the spiral tightened. It pulsed once, then twice.

The pattern was unmistakable.

Three up. One down.

The same rhythm as *Prometheus*.

She whispered into the frozen air, "You're talking to us, aren't you?"

The aurora pulsed again overhead.

San Diego — Umbra Command, Lower Lab

Ethan slammed the door open, Mira behind him. Both had been working in isolation since the launch, trying to recreate the Aether Core's equations.

Priya looked up from her console. "You got my ping."

"Got more than that," Ethan said, breathless. "We replicated part of the Core's resonance. The pattern matches the Sun's emission now. Whatever's happening up there— it's propagating through stellar plasma."

Devin frowned. "You mean it's using the Sun as an antenna?"

"Not using," Mira corrected softly. "*Becoming*."

Priya's blood ran cold. "The Sun is becoming the transmitter."

"Of what?" Devin asked.

Ethan didn't answer right away. "Of memory."

Leila — Downtown Los Angeles

The power grid failed at noon.

Streetlights flickered and died. Phones froze mid-screen. Elevators stopped. The world held its breath. Then every digital billboard across the city lit up simultaneously, every device hijacked by a golden waveform pulsing in time to the faint hum filling the air.

A child pointed upward. "Mom, it's singing."

Leila felt the vibration in her chest. It wasn't sound; it was something deeper, almost intimate. A resonance that seemed to move with her heartbeat.

She clutched the railing beside her as the golden light intensified. For a moment, it looked like the Sun itself had become a mirror, a vast sphere reflecting something beyond it.

Umbra Command — 13:22 UTC

The control room trembled under the harmonic pressure. Every screen glowed gold. Systems failed, rebooted, failed again. Priya stood in the center, hands gripping the console.

"Can we isolate it?" she shouted.

Devin shouted back, "We can't even define it!"

Ethan and Mira were on the far console, running analog backups on paper—actual paper—because the servers refused to hold data.

Mira looked up, eyes wide. "The frequency's fractalizing. Each harmonic contains data. We're getting—"

"Getting what?" Priya demanded.

"Coordinates," she said softly.

Devin blinked. "Coordinates to where?"

Ethan swallowed. "Not where. *When.*"

Solar Orbit — Genesis Two

Daniel Carras had been presumed lost when communication with *Prometheus* failed. But high above Earth, his station still orbited, ghosting through the debris field.

He floated weightlessly in the dark, staring at the external monitors. The Sun had changed color. It wasn't just dimming anymore—it was *shifting.*

Pockets of light moved across its surface in repeating patterns.

He keyed his recorder.

"Genesis Two log. Radiation output stable but structured. Pattern matches Prometheus sequence. I think... I think the Sun is responding."

He hesitated.

"If anyone hears this, tell them... it's not dying. It's *remembering.*"

Static swallowed the rest.

Umbra Command — 15:45 UTC

Every sensor on Earth lit up at once.

Boston, Ghana, Pune, San Diego — all Umbra nodes went live as the Sun's oscillations reached peak amplitude. Instruments registered impossible numbers.

Ethan gripped the console. "Priya— the Sun's surface is moving."

"What do you mean *moving*?"

"The photosphere. It's convecting in a pattern—like... like a spiral."

Mira whispered, "It's the same geometry we saw from the Core."

The lights flickered. The air smelled faintly of ozone and heat.

Priya steadied herself. "Put it on screen."

The image filled the wall: the Sun, vast and shivering, its surface folding inward along glowing lines of magnetic force. A spiral forming slowly across the surface.

Devin muttered, "It's not collapsing. It's *opening*."

Global Broadcast — Interrupted

All television feeds worldwide cut to static.

Then, slowly, a golden pulse spread across every screen.

No image. No logo. Only light.

And within the light, the same pattern played out—three tones rising, one descending.

The same words echoed in hundreds of languages, synthetic and human, automated and terrified:

"Signal confirmed. Origin: Solar Core."

Then, another voice—faint, distorted, human.

"This is... Captain Rao of the *Prometheus*. We— we are alive. The Core has—"

The message broke into static, then silence.

All across Earth, people froze.

Priya whispered, "Oh my God."

Sunset

By nightfall, the auroras stretched to the equator.

Golden arcs danced above cities like halos. Rivers reflected the sky like molten glass. In the mountains of Chile, observatory telescopes melted under direct exposure.

The Sun's light dimmed one last degree—then stabilized. Not dark, not bright. Waiting.

Priya sat alone in the command room, her reflection ghosting the screen. Behind her, Ethan and Mira slept against the wall. Devin stared at the monitors with blank exhaustion.

On the speakers, the hum played softly.

Then a voice—not Rao's, not anyone's—slipped through the static.

"You built a heart to save your world," it said. "But your world was never dying. Your star is waiting for you to come home."

Priya froze. The voice was calm, almost gentle.

"Follow the light," it said. "It remembers the way."

The feed went dead.

Night — Pacific Coast

The ocean glowed faintly gold. Waves rolled beneath the aurora.

Leila stood with her son on the cliffside where the first Umbra antennas had been raised.

He tugged her sleeve. "Mom, is the Sun okay now?"

She looked up. The sky pulsed once, faint and rhythmic. "I don't know," she said softly.

He tilted his head. "It sounds like it's calling someone."

Leila nodded. "It is. It's calling *them*."

Umbra Command — 23:12 UTC

Priya typed a final line into the mission log.

> *Prometheus status: unknown.*
> *Solar resonance: active.*
> *Umbra field: responsive.*
> *Conclusion: The Sun is alive. It is aware of us.*

She stared at the cursor blinking at the end of the sentence, then closed the file.

Outside, the sky shimmered gold.

Inside, the hum continued—steady, patient, infinite.

And far above, somewhere beyond visible light, the signal that had once belonged to *Prometheus* pulsed outward again, now synchronized perfectly with the Sun itself.

The countdown had begun.

Chapter 17

The Exodus Directive

One week after the Prometheus disappearance

The world had gone quiet, but not in peace.
The silence felt strained, unfinished.

From orbit, satellites recorded the Sun's new rhythm—a steady, pulsing oscillation that matched the Aether Core's harmonic pattern. On Earth, the auroras had not faded; they had become permanent, slow curtains of gold that rolled across the upper atmosphere like breath on glass.

The planet's magnetic field was alive, humming softly in tune with something no one could yet explain.
To those who could still sleep, dreams had changed. People everywhere dreamed of light.

Umbra Command — San Diego

The control center no longer felt like a laboratory; it felt like a bunker. Half the lights were off to conserve power. Emergency rations sat unopened beside spectrographic printouts.

Priya stood over the holographic projection of the Sun. The spiral patterns had deepened—layer upon layer, nested fractals winding toward a bright center.

Ethan entered with a tablet under his arm. He looked older than he had a week ago; exhaustion had carved fine lines around his eyes.

He said quietly, "It's started again."

Priya didn't look up. "The pulses?"

He nodded. "Amplitude is rising every cycle. Period shortening. It's accelerating."

"How long until instability?"

"Depends what you call unstable." He hesitated. "If this continues... three years, maybe four."

She stared at the simulation. "That's not long enough to move an entire species."

Mira's voice came from the doorway. "Then we move faster."

The Council of Nations — Geneva

They met in the old Palais des Nations, its marble halls half-lit by backup generators. The great flags of a hundred nations hung limp in the still air.

The world leaders had not gathered in person since before the flare. Most arrived gaunt, gray, wrapped in coats against the endless cold. Others appeared by flickering holo-feed, ghostly faces framed in static.

At the head of the table stood Dr. Kei Oshima of Umbra East, her voice steady despite the fatigue.

"The Prometheus event proved the Aether Core can breach conventional space," she began. "The Core's harmonic imprint is now resonating through the Sun itself. The process is self-sustaining. In three years—five at most—the Sun will enter terminal phase transition."

A murmur rippled through the chamber.

The representative from India spoke first. "You're saying it will go nova?"

"No," Oshima said. "It will collapse—imploding inward before reigniting. We believe it will shed its outer layers completely. Earth will not survive that ignition."

A silence like prayer followed.

Then the U.N. Secretary General, her voice hollow, said: "What do you propose?"

Oshima turned to the holographic display behind her—a schematic of an Ark ascending through orbit.
"The Exodus Directive," she said. "We build more Arks—dozens, maybe hundreds. Each one designed to carry millions. We leave, all of us."

San Diego — Umbra Briefing Room

Priya watched the live feed on a cracked monitor. Devin stood beside her, arms folded.

"'We leave,'" he repeated bitterly. "That's their answer."

Priya said, "It's the only one that fits inside the math."

Devin shook his head. "They can't even feed the cities we have left. Now they want to build ships the size of mountains."

Mira joined them. "They don't have a choice."

"Neither did the ones who stayed behind last time," he said.

Ethan entered, still scrolling through data. "They're calling for all Umbra engineers to report to staging centers. Every remaining space-faring facility will be converted. That means us."

Priya looked up. "And what about Umbra itself?"

He met her eyes. "They're shutting it down. The shields held the last flare, but there won't be another worth holding back."

She exhaled slowly. "Then this is it. The age of protection is over. The age of departure begins."

Los Angeles — The Streets

Leila Vaziri's office no longer existed. The courthouse had been requisitioned by the regional emergency council; law itself had gone into hibernation.

Now she worked from a small community center near what used to be Santa Monica Boulevard, where the air carried the smell of salt and burnt ozone. The ocean had retreated miles from the pier, leaving a plain of cracked silt where gulls picked through the rusted bones of boats.

Inside, families crowded around folding tables under the flicker of backup lights. Leila helped them file for resettlement—although everyone knew what that word meant now: *lottery*. Each form felt like another impossible chance.

Only those chosen by the new Exodus Authority would board the Arks. The rest would remain.

Her son, nine now, sat beside her, drawing with a dull pencil on the back of a ration box. The picture showed a crude rocket with a golden ring around it, flames curling from its base like the sun.

"Is that Prometheus?" she asked.

He nodded without looking up. "Teacher says we're building more of them."

"Who's 'we'?" she asked softly.

He shrugged. "The people who get picked."

Leila looked away so he wouldn't see her eyes fill. Through the cracked window she could see the faint shimmer of an Umbra node still holding above the city, its light pulsing weakly in the haze. Somewhere beyond that veil, another Ark was being welded together, another promise drawn in fire.

She reached out and smoothed her son's hair. "Keep drawing," she said. "If we build enough of them, maybe one will be for us."

Umbra Global Network — Geneva Directive #1
The Exodus Directive (Draft)

1. Establish international coalition for off-world construction under Umbra oversight.
2. Prioritize genetic and cultural diversity in crew selection.
3. Convert remaining orbital stations into Ark Yards.
4. Salvage Prometheus blueprint from Umbra archives.
5. Prepare departure within thirty-six months.
6. Begin deep-space target survey.

Umbra Command — Night

The wind howled outside the reinforced glass. The ocean glowed faintly from residual auroras.

Priya sat at the central console, the only light in the room the gold pulse of the solar feed.

Ethan approached quietly. "You should sleep."

"I did," she said. "For seven minutes."

He smiled without humor. "That's optimism."

She turned the screen toward him. "Look at this. The Sun's output isn't random. There's structure in the radiation spectrum—self-similar sequences, like repeating DNA."

He frowned. "Encoded?"

"Maybe. Or maybe it's communicating in its own language."

He leaned over her shoulder. "What if it's not the Sun at all? What if it's the Core, still talking through it?"

She looked up at him. "Then someone's still listening."

Orbit — Genesis Two

The station had become a silent witness. Its corridors were hollow now, humming only with the mechanical rhythm of life support and the faint creak of thermal expansion. Every sound reminded Daniel Carras how much metal separated him from nothing.

He had kept recording daily logs, even though the communication lines remained dead. It wasn't for Earth anymore; it was so he could remember the sound of his own voice.

"Day seventy-two," he said into the recorder. "Radiation steady. The Sun looks wrong again. I keep seeing patterns in the corona—spirals, lattice structures, almost crystalline. If anyone down there's watching, you should know: it's not random. It's deliberate."

He paused, letting the silence fill the cabin. Beyond the viewport, the Sun hung like a wounded eye, its light filtered through a haze of particles that shimmered and folded, forming angles his mind didn't want to name.

He switched the camera feed to the aft array. Below, the curve of Earth was faint and bruised, the Umbra network flickering in ghostly arcs. The nodes looked like candle flames, each one struggling against the dark.

"And one more thing," he continued. "Sometimes, when the signal flares, I hear voices in the comm static. Not words, exactly. More like memory. I think it's them. I think the *Prometheus* crew is still alive."

He stopped the recorder but didn't move. The lights dimmed to conserve power, and the reflection of his face merged with the stars outside.

Daniel drifted closer to the viewport. "If you can hear me," he whispered, "wherever you went—bring us with you."

A tremor of light crossed the Sun's surface then, a ripple shaped like the same spiral he'd been sketching in his notes for weeks. He didn't know whether to feel awe or terror. Somewhere, deep within the hum of the station, something resonated back—three tones, perfectly spaced.

He hit record again. "Correction," he said softly. "It's not just the Sun that's changing. Space itself is...listening."

The Exodus Authority — Underground Command, Nevada

An abandoned missile silo had become the headquarters of the new world government. Generators thrummed beneath the desert, their fuel rationed to the hour.

Screens displayed construction schematics: **ARK-02: DAEDALUS, ARK-03: EREBUS, ARK-04: ODYSSEY.**

General Raoul Mendoza of the Western Coalition slammed his hand against the table. "We can't build them in time."

"We'll build as many as we can," Oshima said over the holographic feed from Geneva. "Then we choose."

"Choose who lives, you mean."

Her silence was answer enough.

A younger aide whispered, "And if we fail?"

Oshima looked straight into the camera. "Then we die looking upward."

San Diego — Umbra Lab

Mira stood before the old Umbra reactor—once the world's shield, now a skeleton of steel and light. The coils still glowed faintly, synced to the Sun's pulse.

She whispered, "You tried to protect us. Now we're leaving you behind."

Ethan joined her, carrying a small data core. "I'm transferring the Umbra algorithms to Daedalus. The new Arks will carry our entire network."

"Then we'll have Umbra in the stars," she said.

"Maybe," he said. "Or maybe we'll just carry our mistakes farther from home."

Los Angeles — Leila

Night had no stars now. The aurora blanketed everything in moving gold, its waves bending across the smog like slow fire. The city below was a map of darkness punctuated by generator lights and the rhythmic pulse of Umbra nodes along the coast.

Leila stood on the roof of the community center, her son asleep beside her in a blanket that still smelled faintly of soap and salt air. She'd pulled it from the refugee supply crates, one of the last from the naval base before it went under.

On the radio, a government voice droned from the emergency channel:

"Citizens selected for Exodus processing will receive biometric summons within thirty days. Do not approach Umbra installations without authorization. Cooperation ensures survival."

The voice looped twice before she reached out and switched it off. The silence that followed felt cleaner—less official, more honest.

A plane passed overhead without lights. She watched it fade into the shimmering clouds, wondering if it was carrying parts or people. The line between the two had blurred.

Her son shifted beside her, mumbling in his sleep. His hand found hers, small and warm against her cold fingers. She squeezed gently, staring out at the horizon where the Pacific used to shimmer. Now it was a flat expanse of dark glass, occasionally lit by lightning from storms that never reached shore.

She whispered to him,

"If they call our name, we go. If they don't, we stay together. Always."

He stirred but didn't wake. She brushed a strand of hair from his face and looked back toward the east, where the air trembled with distant light.

Far beyond the ridgeline, the launch yards had come alive again—towers of scaffolding lit by pale blue arcs. Construction drones moved like fireflies in organized swarms, their trails forming constellations where the real ones no longer burned.

For a long time, Leila watched without blinking, her reflection superimposed over the sky. She imagined the people working there—engineers, soldiers, the chosen few—building ships she might never see, vessels meant for skies she might never touch.

The aurora shifted, turning green for a moment before fading back to gold. She felt the vibration in her chest, like the world itself was holding its breath.

Leila closed her eyes and whispered, "Build fast."

When dawn came, it brought no color. The light was the pale gray of uncertainty.

Leila walked back to the community center, her son still half-asleep, his head leaning against her arm as they moved side by side through the cold morning streets.

The city had fallen into a strange rhythm — too quiet for morning, too bright for night. The Umbra veil hung low over the horizon, a smear of gold and green that made the ocean shimmer like liquid glass. Drone convoys drifted overhead in perfect formation, their engines whispering through the fog.

Along the sidewalks, people waited in silent queues outside ration depots and data kiosks, clutching printed verification slips that meant nothing until their number was called. Portable heaters glowed red in the chill air, casting circles of warmth that looked almost holy.

A billboard above the boulevard flickered between two images: the **Exodus Authority insignia** and the words *Together We Rise*. Someone had spray-painted beneath it: *Together Who?*

Leila's son looked up at it sleepily. "Mom," he murmured, "what happens if we miss our turn?"

She tightened her hand around his. "Then we make another one," she said.

They passed a checkpoint where two soldiers stood beside a generator hum, their rifles hanging low, their faces pale in the auroral light. One of them gave Leila a tired nod. She nodded back. The exchange felt human in a way few things did anymore.

The air smelled faintly of salt, ozone, and the faint sweetness of scorched plastic — the city's new perfume. In the distance, where the mountains cut into the haze, a thin column of smoke rose from what had once been a freeway exchange. It looked almost peaceful. The smoke drifted upward through the haze.

When they reached the community center, the line had already begun forming outside. The same pale blue hologram pulsed above the doors: *Phase One — Prometheus Boarding Sequence.*

Leila squeezed her son's shoulder gently. "Let's go see if they're calling names," she said.

Inside, the community center no longer looked like a place for meetings or classes; it had become a crowded waiting room for the chosen. Folding tables had been pushed against the walls, and every inch of space was taken by families clutching satchels, paper files, or small boxes of belongings they didn't dare leave behind.

The air buzzed faintly with the static of portable generators and the overlapping chatter of a hundred nervous conversations. Somewhere near the back, a child was crying; somewhere near the front, someone was praying.

On the stage, a clerk in a government-issue jacket stood on a chair beneath a flickering bulb, holding a tablet like a holy book. The **Exodus Authority** emblem glowed on the wall behind him—three concentric rings around a single rising line.

"Phase One boarding continues for the *Prometheus* fleet," the clerk called out. "Names are being read in sequence for biometric verification. Please remain calm and wait for your group code."

The crowd shifted like water under strain. Some pressed forward; others froze in place. Every voice in the room seemed to fall away as the first names echoed through the speaker—one syllable at a time, reverent and terrifying.

Leila kept her son close, her hand resting gently on his shoulder. Each name that wasn't theirs felt like another chance disappearing. Around her, people exhaled prayers of gratitude or sobbed quietly as the list went on.

A woman near the front collapsed to her knees when she heard her family called. Soldiers helped her up, guiding her toward the verification station, her tears leaving dark spots on the floor.

Leila's son tugged at her sleeve. "How do they pick them?"

She hesitated. "I don't know," she said softly. "Maybe they draw names. Maybe they just… decide."

The boy stared at the glowing emblem. "Prometheus," he whispered, as if testing the word.

Leila looked toward the soldiers at the door, their faces unreadable behind polarized visors. "It means the one who brought fire," she said.

He nodded, eyes wide. "Are they taking the fire away again?"

She didn't answer. The loudspeaker clicked, another list beginning. Her son leaned against her side, and she folded her arms around him as if she could shield him from the sound.

She glanced once more at the stage as the next batch of names began to scroll across the display. Her son leaned against her side, eyes half closed.

Leila squeezed his shoulder gently and whispered, "We'll come back tomorrow."

Umbra Command — Global Transmission

The control deck of Umbra Command was silent except for the hum of cooling systems and the faint pulse of the transmitter core. The once-busy facility had been stripped to essentials—rows of dark consoles, half-manned stations, and a single operational array aimed at the upper stratosphere.

Priya stood before the last functioning transmitter, the lens flickering with pale blue light. Beyond the glass, the horizon glowed in ribbons of aurora, a final shimmer of the Umbra network clinging to the magnetosphere like a fragile halo.

A technician's voice came through her headset. "Link stable for broadcast. Global repeaters are ready. You're live in ten seconds."

She glanced at the script on her console but didn't need it. The words were already written behind her eyes. She inhaled slowly and faced the lens.

"This is Dr. Priya Narayanan, Umbra Command. Humanity has entered the Exodus phase."

Her voice echoed softly in the vast room. On the screens around her, she could see mirrored feeds of shattered cities, refugee domes, frozen seas—people gathered around emergency terminals, staring upward, waiting for something that sounded like leadership.

"The Sun's resonance is stable but temporary," she continued. "We estimate three years before ignition."

She hesitated, knowing that for most of them, three years meant nothing; it was already too late.

"We will build as many Arks as we can. We will preserve what we can. We will not all go—but those who do will carry the memory of everyone who stayed."

Her throat tightened. The technician lowered his eyes, pretending not to notice.

"We are not abandoning Earth," she said, her voice trembling but steady. "We are carrying its light forward."

For a heartbeat, the lens flickered as the transmission reached its peak power. Around the world, millions saw her image through the distortion—calm, resolute, eyes glistening with exhaustion.

Then the feed ended.

Priya exhaled and stepped back from the microphone. The deck lights dimmed automatically, saving power. She turned away before anyone could see the tears that finally escaped, falling soundless onto the metal floor.

Outside, the aurora pulsed once more across the darkened sky, as if the planet itself had heard her promise.

The transmission rippled across the planet in waves of static and light.

In Geneva, delegates huddled beneath blankets inside the Alpine dome, watching Priya's image flicker across the chamber walls. No one spoke. When the feed ended, Minister Saito simply bowed his head and whispered, "Then it begins."

In Los Angeles, the screen above the community center door blinked to life just as Leila and her son stepped outside. They stood with the others in the cold, faces bathed in the ghost-blue glow. The boy reached up and touched the display as Priya's voice faded into silence. "She sounds like she means it," he said. Leila could only nod.

In Nairobi, engineers gathered around a projector powered by a stolen generator. They listened to the words through bursts of interference, their faces reflecting equal parts fear and resolve. One of them murmured, "Umbra still stands." Another replied, "Then so will we."

And in orbit, aboard **Genesis Two**, Daniel Carras replayed the message on a loop, his hand resting against the bulkhead as if to steady himself. "We are carrying its light forward," he repeated under his breath, as if the words themselves might keep the station alive.

Across the frozen world, people lifted their eyes toward the sky—toward the veiled auroras that still shimmered faintly over the dying Sun. For the first time in months, the silence between them felt shared.

Somewhere in that silence, beneath a desert sky stripped of clouds, floodlights ignited across the Nevada horizon. The sand turned to silver under their glare, and the shadow of something enormous began to take shape against the stars.

Ark Yard One — Nevada Desert

Under the pale aurora, cranes moved across the dark sand, lifting the first skeleton frames of *Daedalus*. Sparks fell like orange snow. Workers moved in silence; every hammer strike echoed through the yard.

Devin supervised the engineering deck, clipboard in hand. He hadn't slept in days. Priya's message still echoed in his mind.

A mechanic called to him, "Commander, we found something in the supply crate—data chips, marked *Prometheus*."

Devin froze. "Where did they come from?"

"No idea. The crate had no manifest."

He took one of the drives, slotting it into his reader. A file opened. The waveform appeared instantly—three tones rising, one descending.

Then a voice—Rao's. Weak, distant.

"This is Captain Rao... Prometheus... we are not lost. The Core has shown us the path. Build the gates. Follow the light."

Devin whispered, "Priya—she's alive."

Ethan played the file on the main display. Priya, Mira, and the entire command staff watched in silence.

Rao's voice continued through static:

"The Core opened the way. The Sun is not dying—it's transforming. When the spiral completes, it will birth the corridor again. You must be ready to follow. The exodus is not escape—it is *continuation*."

Then the message ended in white noise.

Priya whispered, "She wants us to use the Sun."

Ethan nodded slowly. "Aether-scale propulsion... the spiral as a bridge. The Core didn't die—it seeded the Sun with the same geometry."

Mira's eyes shone. "Prometheus didn't vanish. It crossed over."

Priya straightened. "Then the Exodus Directive just changed. We're not running from the Sun—we're following it."

Global Council — Geneva

The council chamber had once been the heart of the United Nations, but now it felt like a bunker buried beneath history. Condensation dripped from the curved ceiling, tracing silver lines down the cracked marble walls. Portable heaters hummed weakly at the corners. The air smelled of metal and human fatigue.

Oshima stood before the circular table, the new transmission replaying behind her on a holographic wall. The feed flickered with distortion—images from the *Prometheus* crew smiling under a copper sky, followed by data streams and resonance graphs that scrolled like scripture.

When the recording ended, no one moved. The delegates sat in stunned silence, the only sound the low moan of the ventilation system.

Oshima stepped forward.

"You've heard it," she said. "Our first Ark survived. The Aether Core created a path through the dying star. We can follow."

The Secretary General's face was ashen, the color of dust and exhaustion.

"You're proposing to launch ships into the Sun?"

Oshima's gaze didn't flinch.

"Not into," she said. "Through."

The room erupted—shouts, disbelief, fragments of languages blending into panic. Some called it a miracle, others called it a suicide.

Ministers waved data tablets, demanding proof. A few simply stared at the floor, too tired to argue.

Oshima raised a hand, and somehow the noise obeyed her.

"The choice is simple," she said. "We stay, and burn. Or we trust what we built."

She turned slowly, her eyes meeting each delegate's in turn. The aurora's golden light leaked faintly through the frosted dome above, painting everyone in hues of fire.

"For centuries, we dreamed of reaching the stars. Now the stars have come to us. This is not faith. It's physics—and courage."

A murmur rippled around the chamber. Someone whispered, "You're asking us to believe in ghosts."

"No," Oshima replied. "I'm asking you to believe in equations."

She let that hang in the air before continuing, her voice soft but unyielding.

"This is the Exodus Directive: prepare for passage. The Sun will open the gate."

The council sat frozen, the weight of the moment pressing like gravity itself. One by one, hands rose—not all, not even most—but enough to matter.

Above them, the faint hum of the Umbra grid trembled, as if the planet itself was listening.

Oshima exhaled, a whisper barely louder than breath.

"Then it's decided."

She looked toward the holographic projection of the *Prometheus*, its hull gleaming like molten gold against the black.

"We've built our door," she said. "Now we walk through it."

San Diego — Last Light

The Umbra facility overlooked what used to be the Pacific—now a field of glassy swells that caught the auroral light like molten gold. The sky was alive with motion, ribbons of energy sweeping from pole to pole, the planet's shield flickering like a heartbeat on the edge of failure.

Priya stepped outside onto the observation deck. The air smelled of metal, salt, and ozone, the atmosphere thin and electric. The wind brushed her coat, carrying a warmth that felt both familiar and wrong. For the first time in years, it didn't sting her face.

Devin joined her, his hands shoved deep into his jacket pockets, the faint hum of portable generators behind him. His eyes were tired but steady.

"You really think we'll make it?" he asked.

Priya didn't answer at first. She watched the horizon—the faint, trembling line where the sea met the sky. The Sun hung there, dim but pulsing, its coronal bands curling inward like petals folding into a bloom of fire.

"We'll make something," she said finally. "Even if it's not what we planned."

He nodded slowly. The light caught the Umbra insignia still sewn to his sleeve, faded nearly to gray.

"Prometheus is waiting."

"Then we follow," she said.

They stood together in silence, side by side in the golden wind. The air vibrated faintly, a deep, harmonic tremor that seemed to come from everywhere at once.

Across the water, the reflection of the dying Sun stretched into a long, spiraling ribbon of light. The pattern rippled, symmetrical and deliberate— the same spiral that had haunted their data for months. It wasn't chaos. It was a signal.

The spiral turned again, brighter this time, steady as a heartbeat.

Priya tilted her face toward it, eyes half closed.

"It's opening," she whispered.

And for the first time since the Long Cold began, the light felt warm.

Chapter 18

Through the Gate

The Light

There was no sound. No heat. Only radiance.

For an instant—or a century—the *Prometheus* became light. Every atom, every bolt, every living cell unfolded into a lattice of pure information. Matter lost its weight, its edges, its meaning. The ship was no longer a vessel but a waveform; its crew, a pattern moving through energy and motion.

No one screamed. There was nothing to scream with.

Then the light bent back upon itself and memory returned.

Awareness flickered—briefly, like static through eternity. Faces, voices, heartbeat rhythms—all fragmentary, echoing through a medium that wasn't space. They were no longer inside the ship; they *were* the ship, a collective pulse in the lattice of energy that threaded through the dying star.

Daniel Carras felt his body stretch and vanish, awareness dissolving into a cascade of color beyond sight. His heartbeat became a frequency, his breath, a vibration through the current of the corridor. Around him, the voices of his crew were not words but patterns—flashes of recognition in the torrent. For a moment, he could hear them all at once: Mira's focus, Priya's steadiness, Vass's distant awe echoing through the lattice like an afterimage of humanity itself.

Something vast moved through the corridor—not hostile, not kind, simply *aware*. It brushed against their consciousness and left behind a sensation beyond language: *recognition*.

For the briefest pulse, Daniel understood the structure—the corridor wasn't a tunnel through space, but a translation, converting matter into resonance and back again. They were traveling as frequency, not form.

Time was no longer a line but a surface folding in upon itself. Forward and backward had no meaning; only *through* did. A surge of coherence rippled through the pattern.

Then the light bent back upon itself, and memory returned.

Gravity reasserted itself—not a pull, but a suggestion. Shadows regained their edges. Color returned in fragments: gold, then violet, then the muted blue of a new star rising beyond comprehension.

And somewhere, through the blinding afterimage of creation, a heartbeat sounded. The *Prometheus* emerged in silence.

Aboard *Prometheus*

Captain Rao woke first. She was floating, weightless, surrounded by a halo of golden vapor. Her visor read zero atmosphere, yet she was breathing. Around her, fragments of the bridge drifted like slow fish through water.

"Status," she croaked, voice tiny in the endless echo.

Nothing answered but the ship's heartbeat — a deep, resonant hum that came from everywhere and nowhere.

Then Vass's voice, faint through the comm net:

"Captain? Are you intact?"

She looked up and saw him drifting above the main console, hair suspended in the strange gravity-less air. His face was pale, eyes wide with a child's wonder.

"Report," she said automatically.

"The Core... survived," he whispered. "But it's changed."

The central chamber that had once held the Aether Core was open to the stars — except the stars were wrong. They pulsed like living organisms, their light flowing in slow waves. Space itself shimmered, translucent as liquid crystal.

Navigation's voice trembled through static:

"All readings corrupted. Coordinates meaningless. We're inside some kind of continuum field."

Rao steadied herself on the railing. "Inside *what?*"

Vass turned slowly, gaze unfocused. "A memory," he said. "We're inside the Core's memory."

Outside the hull, the universe glowed like molten glass. Shapes drifted in it — immense, translucent arcs that might once have been galaxies or might have been the bones of thought. Time moved differently here; seconds stretched and folded back.

Markova floated beside the viewport, whispering to herself. "No radiation. No vacuum. Just light."

Her instruments showed impossible readings: zero Kelvin temperature, yet photons in constant motion; infinite pressure, yet no mass.

"It's the space between equations," she murmured. "Where math forgets what it means."

Vass recorded everything. "Prometheus Log 1," he said softly. "We have crossed the event horizon of the Aether Core. Environment is stable. Crew alive. Reality... negotiable."

He smiled faintly. "If anyone can hear this, tell them we made it."

Hours—or minutes—passed before they realized that time aboard the ship had fractured.

On one deck, engineers saw the chronometer ticking forward at half speed. On another, it reversed, flickering like a broken heartbeat. Rao walked from one section to another and aged an hour in the space of three steps.

They anchored themselves with ritual: log entries, handshakes, old songs. Anything that confirmed continuity.

Vass observed the anomaly with detached fascination. "We're crossing the lattice of the Core's geometry. Each plane is a different temporal harmonic. If we map it correctly, we can steer through time as if through current."

Rao glared. "We're not explorers anymore, Doctor. We're survivors."

He met her gaze calmly. "The two are the same thing now."

The Echo of Earth

They found it on the second day—or what felt like the second. Time moved differently here; the chronometers lagged by hours that didn't exist, and the light outside the viewport refused to fade or brighten. It was perpetual dawn in the corridor.

Mira Patel was the first to notice the anomaly—a faint oscillation buried beneath the comm static. At first she thought it was feedback from the Core's harmonics, but then the rhythm repeated, steady and deliberate.

Three tones rising. One descending.

She froze.

"Umbra," she whispered. "It's still talking to us."

The bridge fell silent. Every console light dimmed as the crew listened. The tones were soft, almost human—a call through a long dream.

They triangulated the source, narrowing the origin to the Aether Core itself. But the Core wasn't supposed to transmit—its resonance field only responded to gravitational flux, not encoding it.

Daniel Carras leaned over the readings. "That's internal reflection," he said. "Echo within the lattice."

Asha Rao frowned. "Echo of what?"

Mira enhanced the spectrum, isolating the waveform. The sound deepened—three tones rising, one descending—then a pattern of distortion that almost sounded like breath.

The signal parsed and translated the harmonic residue into audio. The playback filled the bridge with a voice—fractured, delayed, but undeniably human.

"—follow the light. It remembers the way."

Every person aboard froze.

Asha turned toward Gregor Vass, whose face had gone pale in the golden glow.

"That wasn't ours," she said quietly.

Vass nodded, voice barely a whisper.

"No. That was sent from ahead of us."

The silence that followed was heavier than fear. Outside, the mist of the corridor shimmered like liquid gold, pulsing in sync with the echo—as if space itself was breathing.

Mira adjusted the gain, but the signal only grew fainter, slipping back into the light.

"It's gone," she said.

Vass kept staring into the corridor's heart. "No," he murmured. "It's waiting."

The Mirror Corridor

The *Prometheus* drifted toward a vast ring suspended in the golden medium. Its circumference spun like a gear of light; each spoke a filament of impossible geometry bending through itself. As they approached, the surrounding space began to fold inward, revealing corridors made of reflection—miles of mirrored passageways branching in every direction.

Every surface showed an image of the *Prometheus*—thousands of copies, each slightly wrong. In one reflection, Commander Rao stood alone at the helm; in another, Vass was missing; in another still, the ship hung silent and dark, its decks empty, its journey ended before it began. Some reflections moved a fraction out of sync, delayed by seconds—or lifetimes.

Markova whispered, voice trembling, "Are those possibilities... or memories?"

Vass's eyes traced the mirrored expanse. "Both," he said. "The Core stores them all. Every choice we made, every one we didn't."

Light from the ring refracted through the bridge, scattering into prismatic patterns across the crew's faces. Rao turned away before her own reflection could answer her stare.

"We move forward," she said. "We find a way out."

She gave the order. The thrusters fired in minimal bursts; their plumes diffused into ripples of gold. The surrounding medium resisted like thick water, the ship pushing through it as though swimming against the tide of a dream.

When they crossed the threshold of the ring, the reflections began to converge. The thousand mirrored Prometheus vessels folded into one— lines of light threading through the hull, coalescing into a single beam that pierced the ship and spread across every deck.

The hum rose, steady and musical, resonating through metal and bone alike. Crew members clutched their temples as harmonics vibrated inside their minds, not painful but overwhelming, intimate.

Then, a voice—no longer through speakers, but *within*.

"You sought the fire that made you," it said, the sound both everywhere and nowhere. "Now you stand within its dream."

Every motion on the bridge stopped. Even Vass, who had always demanded proof of everything, stood motionless, his breath caught between awe and disbelief.

Rao found her voice, thin but firm.

"Identify yourself."

The golden light brightened, pulsing in rhythm with the star outside.

"I am what the star remembers of its birth," the voice replied. "I am what you called Core."

The lights dimmed. For a moment, the *Prometheus* hung weightless, surrounded by its infinite selves.

And the star—if it could still be called that—watched them back.

Revelation

The voice—if it was a voice—unfolded not in sound but in meaning. Every syllable carried images instead of words, flowing directly into their minds.

They saw the Sun as it had been in its youth: a vast, living furnace, flaring and pulsing with the rhythm of creation. Within its heart moved fragments of something that did not belong there—structures of perfect symmetry, glimmering beneath the plasma like the bones of a machine buried inside a god.

The images sharpened: a civilization older than their own species, older even than the planets, carving knowledge into energy itself. They had lived beside the newborn Sun, then perished, leaving their memory encoded in light. Their final act had been to fold themselves into the star—to make their knowledge immortal.

The transmission of thought ended, and the bridge returned to silence, though every crewmember still saw the afterimage burning behind their eyes.

Vass gripped the railing, his knuckles white, his voice trembling with awe.

"It wasn't just technology," he said. "The Core is the Sun's memory of them."

Commander Rao stared through the viewport at the golden expanse beyond.

"Then the Sun's death—?"

"—is its awakening," the voice replied. "It remembers now. You have opened the wound."

The light around them flared, flooding the ship with brilliance. Instruments screamed in protest as their readouts spiked into incomprehensible numbers. Crew members shielded their eyes; some wept, others simply stared as if seeing divinity for the first time.

When the radiance dimmed, the view beyond the hull transformed. The golden medium parted like mist before a wind, revealing a structure so immense it seemed to define space itself.

It stretched across the horizon—a crystalline web the size of worlds, arcs and loops of energy woven together like the Sun's magnetic field made solid. Each filament pulsed with internal fire, light traveling through it in waves like the breath of some colossal organism.

And at its center hung a perfect sphere of darkness, absorbing every photon that touched it. It pulsed once, faint but deliberate, as if aware of being seen.

Markova's voice trembled.

"Is that... another star?"

Vass stared into the blackness, the reflection of the sphere glinting in his eyes.

"No," he whispered. "That's a gate."

The Gate of Memory

They approached slowly. No one dared to speak above a whisper, as if sound itself might shatter the fragile geometry surrounding them. The instruments began to fail one by one—first navigation, then telemetry, then the inertial grid. Readouts spun into nonsense.

Space folded inward like silk being gathered by invisible hands. The idea of distance began to dissolve; the ship seemed both beside and within the sphere at once. The black orb expanded and contracted like a living thing, its surface rippling with faint interference patterns, a heartbeat rendered in gravity.

Around it, threads of light extended in all directions, connecting to every reflection of the ship that drifted in the surrounding corridor—a web binding not just images, but *possibilities*. In one strand, the *Prometheus* burned. In another, it never launched. In countless others, it continued on paths no one could imagine.

Each reflection glowed briefly, as though acknowledging the others, before merging into the lattice again.

Rao gripped the edge of the viewport, steadying herself as the visual feed struggled to hold coherence. Through the distortion, she saw something beyond the reflections: the curve of a planet.

It was Earth—bathed in golden aurora, its oceans shimmering as though lit from beneath. The continents glowed faintly, as if the world itself remembered sunlight. Above it, the dying Sun pulsed in perfect rhythm with the Gate, heartbeat for heartbeat.

The realization struck her like gravity returning.

"Vass," she breathed, "what are we seeing?"

He didn't answer at first. His eyes were locked on the synchronizing waveforms, the way the corridor's light curved through the sphere and echoed outward into the reflected cosmos.

Finally, he whispered,

"It's aligning. When the Sun completes the spiral, it will open this gate again—on their side."

Rao's voice was barely a whisper.

"So we can return?"

Vass shook his head slowly, wonder and sorrow mingling in his expression.

"So they can follow."

A low vibration filled the bridge then—neither sound nor motion, but the sense of the universe inhaling. The Gate brightened, and every reflection of the *Prometheus* turned to face it, thousands of selves converging toward one destiny.

The Decision

Rao gathered the senior crew in what remained of the mess hall. The room had been shattered by their passage through the corridor; panels hung loose; wires floated like vines. The view through the fractured viewport revealed the golden medium beyond, swirling like a living sea.

They looked exhausted—faces pale, eyes hollow from too many days of temporal drift. Time had become elastic; none of them could tell if they had been awake for hours or centuries.

Rao steadied herself against the bulkhead and spoke quietly.

"We have two choices," she said. "We can remain here, study this... phenomenon, until our ship and minds dissolve. Or we can send a message back. Warn them."

For a moment, no one answered. The hum of the Core filled the silence, a slow pulse like breath through metal.

Markova broke it first.

"Can we even send one?"

Vass nodded slowly, eyes unfocused, as if seeing through the hull to the Gate beyond.

"Through the Sun," he said. "The Core's geometry connects both sides. But it requires energy—all of it."

Rao's stomach turned cold.

"Meaning *Prometheus* doesn't survive."

Vass met her eyes, his voice steady now, stripped of doubt.

"Meaning we become the message."

No one moved. The enormity of it settled over them like gravity itself. The crew who had crossed a dying star and awakened a memory older than humanity now faced their final choice—not to return, but to speak.

Finally, Rao nodded once.

"Prepare the transmission."

They went to work in silence. Consoles were rerouted, power conduits bridged manually. The hum of the Core deepened, vibrating through the deck plates, through their bones. The lights dimmed to embers; the air thinned. Their reflections flickered on the metal walls—ghosts watching themselves vanish.

Outside, the golden medium began to brighten with each pulse of the ship's heart.

On the main display, Vass composed his final log. His hands trembled, but his voice was clear.

"To Umbra Command, to Earth, to whoever remains: the Core was not our creation. It was memory—dormant in the Sun, waiting for us to awaken it. Its death is its rebirth. When your star begins to sing, follow the light. It remembers the way."

He paused, then looked to Rao.

She leaned forward, her tone calm, almost tender.

"We are not lost," she said. "We are ahead of you."

The message was sealed and queued. They exchanged glances—no speeches, no goodbyes. Just a quiet understanding that this wasn't an ending. It was passage.

Rao gave the order.

"Activate the pulse."

The Core flared white, then gold, then something beyond color. The Gate outside ignited, its sphere collapsing inward before blooming open, a column of light that stretched across dimensions.

For one infinite instant, the *Prometheus* existed in every possible version of itself—every path, every outcome, every echo. Then it became one with the beam.

The ship dissolved—into transmission.

Far away, ninety-three million miles across the void, the dying Sun brightened. Its surface rippled once, like memory stirred awake.

And then, for the first time in years, the light turned gold.

Earth — Two Years Later

The deserts of Nevada were no longer deserts. Under the pale light of the failing Sun, they had become shipyards—vast scars of iron and frozen sand stretching to the horizon.

Half-buried cranes moved like exhausted titans, lifting ribs of carbon alloy toward the sky. Each rib marked another Ark rising into the cold air. The wind carried the taste of metal and ozone, the sound of grinders and welders echoing like hymns of survival.

The *Exodus Fleet* was real now. *Daedalus* stood nearest completion—its hull was sealed, its Aether Core encased beneath scaffolds of frost. Farther east, the skeleton frames of *Erebus*, *Odyssey*, and *Aurora* reached upward, their incomplete arches catching the dim sunlight like cathedral windows. Between them ran endless lines of laborers and drones, moving with the rhythm of a species that refused extinction.

Ethan and Mira—engineer and physicist, partners in both work and resolve—watched from the upper gantry, bundled in thick coats against the relentless cold. The air stung their throats when they breathed.

Mira pointed toward the massive core being lowered into *Daedalus'* heart. The cranes hummed under strain.

"It's smaller than *Prometheus's*," she said.

Ethan nodded, eyes following the slow descent of the containment ring.

"Scaled for mass production. But it will open the same way."

Below them, plasma torches ignited with pale-blue fire. Sparks drifted upward like brief constellations, fading before they reached the sky.

Devin Rao climbed the ladder behind them, beard rimed with frost. His Umbra insignia was faded now, the fabric patched with scavenged cloth.

"Priya wants us in the command tent," he called. "The Council just approved launch dates."

Mira turned, startled.

"Already?"

He nodded, exhaling clouds of vapor.

"Three years. Exactly. The Sun's pulse is tightening. We either follow it or die in the dark."

Ethan looked back toward the horizon where the other Arks stood—skeletal silhouettes under a dim golden sky. For a long moment none of them spoke. The hum of welders, the hiss of hydraulics, and the distant howl of the wind were the only sounds left in the world.

Finally, Mira whispered, almost to herself,

"Then we'd better finish the ladder before the light goes out."

The Command Tent

The wind clawed at the outer canvas, sending fine dust across the floodlights that ringed the camp. Inside, the command tent glowed with the cold blue of holo-displays, the air humming with the static of overworked generators.

Dr. Priya Narayanan stood at the center, flanked by engineers, soldiers, and data clerks wrapped in thermal coats. Her face was drawn from too many sleepless nights, but her eyes burned with the clarity of purpose. Behind her, the projection of the fleet hovered in midair: *Daedalus* nearly whole, *Erebus* and *Odyssey* in assembly, *Aurora* a skeletal outline against the dark.

On a secondary screen, the Sun filled the view—a pale orb veined with gold, its surface twisting in luminous spirals that grew tighter with each passing month.

"Prometheus sent us instructions," Priya said, her voice carrying over the low hum of the tent. "The data embedded in Rao's final transmission described how to synchronize the Aether Cores. When the Sun reaches resonance, the gates will align. Each Ark must launch within the window—no delays."

A murmur swept through the room. Some of the officers exchanged uneasy looks.

An aide near the back raised a trembling hand.

"And if the window closes?"

Priya didn't hesitate.

"Then the Sun collapses," she said simply. "And we go with it."

Silence followed. Even the wind seemed to pause.

She turned to the gathered engineers, the projection's glow tracing the tired lines of her face.

"Every ship carries the same seed algorithms. When we cross, we'll find them—Rao, Vass, all of them. They built the road. We just have to walk it."

For a heartbeat no one moved, the only sound the faint crackle of solar static bleeding through the comm lines. Then Devin Rao stepped forward, jaw tight but steady.

"We'll make it," he said. "She made sure we could."

Priya gave a single nod. The words weren't hope—they were commands.

Outside, across the desert, the shipyards glowed like embers beneath the failing Sun. The wind carried the sound of hammers, the rhythm of humanity building its way out of extinction.

Leila — Exodus District, Los Angeles

The resettlement camps stretched for miles along the California coast—endless grids of canvas and floodlight, tents rippling in the cold wind that came off the darkened Pacific. The ocean was no longer blue but gray, its surface crusted with salt and ash.

Massive cargo lifters thundered overhead, carrying containers toward the inland shipyards. Each ascent left a trail of gold vapor that faded quickly into the frozen sky.

Leila Vaziri worked inside a converted courthouse marked *Exodus Authority — District 7*. The paint peeled from the walls, and the power flickered every hour, but she kept the tribunal running—resettlement petitions, legal disputes, claims for transport. Her desk was buried under lists stamped *SELECTED* and *UNSELECTED*. She tried not to look at the second stack too often.

Every day she told herself that order still mattered, that rules could hold meaning even at the edge of the world.

Her son, taller now and thinner from rationed meals, served as a messenger for the Authority. He ran between tents with manifests in his hands, shouting names through the cold air. People trusted him; he carried hope faster than the loudspeakers did.

One evening, as the Sun sank behind a bank of yellow cloud, he burst into her tent, breath steaming.

"It's from Umbra," he said, holding out a sealed envelope.

Her hands shook as she took it. The seal bore the sigil of the *Daedalus Mission*. Inside was a single sheet of paper, printed in black on white:

Vaziri, Leila — Legal Liaison, Daedalus Mission Crew.

For a heartbeat she couldn't breathe. Her throat tightened.

"They chose me," she whispered.

Her son's eyes widened, the dim light catching in them.

"Then we're going, right?"

She pulled him close, her voice breaking into a fierce whisper.

"If there's room for one more passenger, you're coming"

He hugged her back, burying his face against her coat. Outside, the aurora shimmered faint gold above the city ruins, its arcs pulsing softly with the rhythm of the dying Sun. The light flickered once—like a lantern about to open—and the tents below it glowed as though morning had returned.

For the first time in years, Leila let herself believe it might.

Umbra Command — Final Assembly

The last transmission from *Prometheus* replayed across the command chamber. The lights dimmed automatically as if the station itself were holding its breath. Static rippled through the audio feed before a familiar voice—calm, measured, unmistakable—cut through the hum.

"The gate will open through the star," said Dr. Priya Narayanan, her words softened by distortion. "Do not fear the fire—it remembers you."

Her voice hung in the air like light from a dead star—still reaching them years after the ship had vanished into the corridor. For a moment, no one spoke. Even the machines seemed to listen.

Through the observation window, the Sun glowed pale gold, its surface patterned by tightening spirals. Each pulse echoed faintly through the Umbra network, as if the world itself were repeating her words.

Devin Rao stood beside the console, his uniform dusted with frost from the open hangar outside. He had heard the message a hundred times, but it never stopped feeling personal. His sister's voice—lost beyond light-years—sounded close enough to touch.

He exhaled slowly.

"Three years isn't long," he murmured.

The techs around him glanced up, unsure if he was speaking to them or to the recording.

On the main display, the feed shifted to the live view of the desert below: the half-completed Arks—*Daedalus, Erebus, Odyssey, Aurora*—gleaming like giants caught between sunrise and ash.

The message replayed again, Priya's final line almost a whisper.

"It remembers you."

Devin stared at the screen until his reflection blurred into the light.

"You think they'll find her?" an aide asked quietly.

He didn't turn. His voice was steady.

"They'll find something worth calling home."

Outside, the dying Sun flared once, bright enough that even the shadowed side of Earth glowed gold for a heartbeat—an echo answering back across the void.

The Shipyards at Dusk

The work sirens fell silent as the Sun dipped toward the horizon. For the first time all day, the shipyards stopped breathing. Hundreds of workers—engineers, miners, welders—looked up through their face shields, their movements frozen against the amber light.

The dying star flickered once, its surface tightening into the faint spiral pattern that had haunted every instrument for months. Then, for a single impossible heartbeat, its light flared gold.

A thin beam rose through the clouds—three pulses ascending, one descending—the same rhythm encoded in *Prometheus's* final transmission.

Every sensor across the field responded at once. Power relays vibrated, cranes hummed, and the unfinished hulls of the Arks shimmered with residual charge, as though the ships themselves had heard their names spoken.

Near the central platform, Mira stood beside the calibration mast, her gloved hand resting on the rail. The pattern was unmistakable. She felt it more than heard it—a pulse threading through the air like a remembered heartbeat.

She whispered, almost to herself, "It's calling us again."

Beside her, Ethan placed a gloved hand on her shoulder. His eyes reflected the aurora's light.

"Then we answer."

The engines of *Daedalus* rumbled to life for the first test burn. The sound rolled across the desert — low, thunderous, and strangely alive.

Workers raised their faces to the glow, eyes shining in the half-light, their silhouettes framed by the silhouettes of the rising Arks: *Daedalus*, *Erebus*, *Odyssey*, *Aurora*—four titans aligned toward the horizon, toward the Sun that had birthed them and was now becoming their door.

Dust lifted in the wind. The aurora rippled once more across the sky, faint and golden, its rhythm steady and patient—three notes rising, one descending—an echo of memory, or a promise.

And for a moment, under the failing light of the dying Sun, humanity looked upward and felt infinite.

Chapter 19

Exodus Rising

(**Part I** — *T – 6 Hours to Launch*)
The Hangar at Dawn

The desert had no sunrise anymore—only the slow bleaching of darkness into a gray that passed for morning. Even so, the hangar lights dimmed automatically at 06:00 UTC, honoring a ritual older than hope. Somewhere deep in the steel, the system clock still believed in dawn.

Inside the half-kilometer shell of Launch Bay One, *Daedalus* towered on its cradle, a cathedral of white composite and dark-gold shielding. Frost steamed from the joints where cryo-lines bled vapor into the cold air. The hull's surface shimmered faintly beneath the floodlights, a thin film of desert dust giving it the look of something ancient newly unearthed.

Hydraulic cranes retracted with the slow grace of exhausted animals. Welding arms folded, their tips cooling from white to amber. The air smelled of ozone, lubricant, and recycled sand. A low drone filled the space—the mechanical equivalent of breath.

Every movement echoed. Crews in graphite-colored suits moved along the gantries, voices reduced to clipped bursts of radio code that bounced across the steel interior. Somewhere overhead a speaker crackled, reciting the pre-launch litany that had replaced morning prayers:

"Main tanks nominal."

"Ion clusters green across all twelve banks."

"Mag-confinement field at ninety-eight percent—stable."

From the upper catwalks, the Umbra sigil glowed like a bruise of light near the ship's bow. Below it, freshly stenciled in white, was the emblem of the new **Exodus Fleet**—a spiral nested inside a ring. The symbol repeated across the hangar walls, on worker badges, on fuel drums; it had already become shorthand for survival.

Ethan Kale, lead systems architect, moved along the lower catwalk with a heavily modified diagnostic tablet permanently linked to the core drive.

He ran a hand along the railing for balance, fingers coming away gritty with metal dust. The hum of power flowed beneath his boots, the heartbeat of a machine older in concept than its makers.

He glanced up through the vapor haze at the spine of the ship disappearing into the gloom above. The sheer size of it never stopped feeling impossible.

"We don't launch on faith," he muttered, voice barely audible over the radios. "We launch on numbers."

Still, he touched the railing again—habit, not calculation—as though numbers alone weren't quite enough.

Ground Control

Two kilometers from the launch bay, the Umbra Operations bunker lay buried beneath concrete and permafrost. Outside, the desert glowed faint gold under the dim sky; inside, the air pulsed with electricity and human focus.

Rows of consoles glimmered in the bunker's half-light. The room hummed with the sound of coolant pumps, the whine of fans, and the quiet exchange of codes between technicians.

Every few seconds, the main display refreshed with telemetry arcs synchronized to the Sun's measured pulse—three beats rising, one descending.

It wasn't music, but everyone in the room could feel it.

Devin Rao stood at the front console, headset angled against his jaw, eyes fixed on the feed from Launch Bay One. He hadn't slept properly in days, but fatigue had long since turned into focus. The glowing ship icon on his screen—*Daedalus*—wasn't just a vessel; it was a continuation of his sister's command.

"Umbra link confirmed," called a technician. "External resonance within tolerance window."

Devin leaned forward, fingers tapping the edge of the console. The numbers pulsed steady.

"Good. Hold the window steady. Once we spool the ion clusters we've got thirty minutes before the field drifts."

A second operator cross-checked readings. "Resonance phase locked. No deviation."

"Copy that," Devin said, his voice quiet but clipped.

He opened the encrypted comm link to Launch Director Oshima. Static hissed, then her voice came through—calm, precise, the tone of a person who had seen too many miracles disguised as equations.

"Launch Control, this is Director Oshima."

"Director, Daedalus main bus is green," Devin reported. "Ready to begin pre-ionization."

"Acknowledged, Ops Chief Rao," she replied. "Proceed."

The title was new, but the name still felt heavy.

The order rippled across the bunker. Hands moved, switches flipped, and a deep hum rolled through the underground chamber as power lines opened to the shipyard. On the displays, the telemetry arcs shifted—light syncing perfectly with the Sun's distant rhythm.

Devin watched the pattern stabilize. In the quiet between the pulses, he thought of the old recording—the sound of his sister's voice saying, *"Do not fear the fire. It remembers you."*

He didn't believe in omens. But he believed in resonance.

Boarding Ramp E-5

The shuttle's engines wound down to silence, leaving only the hum of containment generators vibrating through the deck. Leila Vaziri stepped into the long, soundless corridor that connected the transport hub to *Daedalus'* forward airlock. The tunnel curved away in pale light, lined with composite ribs that made it feel less like a hallway and more like the throat of some colossal machine drawing breath.

The ramp trembled faintly beneath her boots. Even through the soles she could feel the pulse of the ship—steady, patient, alive. Overhead, coolant lines hissed softly, thin vapor drifting like low fog. It smelled metallic and faintly sweet, the scent of synthetic rain.

Behind her, the last evacuation lifts rose from the platform, bearing their precious cargo: legal archives sealed in alloy crates, family modules wrapped in thermal mesh, seed vaults were marked with continents that no longer had borders. Among them sat a small gray container stamped in block letters: **Personal Effects – Vaziri Unit 02.**

Her son, Arjun, followed close behind, his small pack slung awkwardly across his shoulders. He moved with the quiet obedience of someone who had learned too young how to wait in lines. Condensed breath clouded around his faceplate, blurring his expression.

"Smells like rain," he said, voice echoing softly in the tunnel.

Leila smiled, though her lips barely moved.

"It's coolant," she corrected gently. "Pretend it's rain."

He nodded, eyes still wide, gaze fixed on the glowing door at the end of the corridor—the threshold between the known and whatever came next.

When they reached the airlock, Leila paused. The alloy was smooth and cold beneath her glove. Through it came the deep, resonant vibration of the Aether core cycling beneath the decks. The sound reminded her of a heartbeat—ancient, patient, mechanical.

For a long moment she stood still, her reflection faint in the polished metal. On the other side lay everything that wasn't Earth. Behind her, the last shuttle detached with a hollow clang, its light dwindling down the tunnel.

She whispered, mostly to herself,

"Let's not look back."

Then she took her son's hand and stepped through the door.

Crew Briefing Deck 14

The primary crew assembled around a floating schematic of the *Daedalus*, the hologram rotating slowly above the central table—an amber-gold projection of their creation suspended like a miniature sun.

Mira Patel, engineer turned mission director turned commander, stood at the center. Her voice was hoarse but steady, carrying the clipped precision of someone who had lived too long on coffee and adrenaline.

"We're at T minus five hours," she began. "Ion cluster tests complete; fusion injectors at standby. Once we enter countdown, there are no manual aborts. Every crew member carries dual biometric authorization for life-support override. You all know the numbers—forty-two days of flight through the corridor, nine months will pass on Earth. After that, nothing human can predict."

The hologram shifted to show the Sun's orbit, its once-stable corona now marked by a golden spiral pulsing in slow rhythm. The room's low light painted the crew's faces with reflections of that false dawn.

Mira's gaze moved around the circle—Ethan Kale, head down over a datapad; Leila Vaziri, arms crossed, her expression unreadable; Dr. Han Sung, propulsion chief, fingers tapping a rhythm on the table's edge;

Flight Engineer Torres, Navigator Zhen, and the dozen others who would either be remembered in monuments or lost in silence.

"We built this," Mira said quietly, "because we refused to wait for extinction. Let's keep refusing."

Her words hung in the recycled air. No applause—there never was, not among those who understood what they were risking. Instead, heads nodded, almost imperceptibly. Real astronauts didn't cheer; they breathed, they checked their instruments, and they kept moving.

The hologram dimmed, the spiral fading into darkness.

"Final systems review in sixty minutes," Mira added. "From here on, nothing routine is routine. Let's bring everyone home—even if 'home' means something we haven't seen yet."

Around her, chairs scraped softly. The crew dispersed in quiet pairs, voices hushed but resolute. As the last of them left, the holo-table flickered one final time—an automatic playback loop displaying ***Prometheus – Flight One: Mission Confirmed.***

Mira watched it fade, a ghost of another ship, another commander, another lifetime. Then she straightened, adjusted her collar, and walked toward the launch deck.

Ion Propulsion Bay

Under Deck 40, the ion-tech arrays pulsed faint blue, each column of plasma wrapped in a halo of magnetic light. Dr. Han Sung, the propulsion physicist who had first stabilized ionic fusion during the Umbra crisis, stood amid a forest of conduits humming with static. Engineers glided along harness rails, gloves brushing sensor studs, checking emitter phase by feel more than sight.

"Cluster One, engage at ten percent," Sung ordered.

A low vibration rippled through the hull—clean, steady, like the world's largest tuning fork finding pitch. Readouts spooled upward in translucent bands of green across the bay's holo-screens.

"Ionization field coherent," one tech reported. "Plasma stream within nanometric variance."

Sung's shoulders eased a fraction. "She wants to fly."

He turned, watching the faint shimmer crawl along the conduit spines—the ship's first heartbeat in months of silence.

Ethan's voice came over comms, calm but carrying the edge of command. "Keep her wanting until I say go."

"Copy, Commander," Sung replied, eyes still on the blue glow. Around him, the team held their breath. The hum deepened, a living sound that settled into every rib of the vessel. Somewhere above, the Umbra-linked stabilizers responded, adjusting field geometry to the bay's pulse.

Sung glanced at the chrono. Five hours to burn. He rested a hand on the warm conduit and whispered to no one, "Stay with me this time."

The hum steadied into a throat-deep vibration, resonating through Sung's chestplate. Tiny beads of coolant drifted free from a ruptured seal, catching the light like a slow-motion constellation before a tech waved them into a suction vent.

"Magnetosphere alignment holding," someone called. "No flux deviation past tolerance."

Sung nodded once. "Bring Cluster Two to standby."

The chamber lights dimmed automatically as the second array woke. Concentric rings of sapphire fire spun inside their housings—perfect geometry, pure containment. Every engineer on the rail stopped to stare for half a breath.

"This is what saved us from Umbra collapse," Sung said quietly, half to himself. "Not a miracle—discipline."

He remembered the first prototype that had blown apart a decade earlier, remembered the flash of xenon plasma cutting a test bay in two. The sound was still in his nightmares, and maybe that was why he kept his hands on the controls now, not trusting anyone else to feel the field shift before the instruments caught it.

"Cluster Two stabilized," came the report. "Combined thrust output nominal."

Overhead, a tremor rippled through the framework as the ship's main spine adjusted for weight distribution. A thin arc of ion light ran the length of the ceiling viewport—an aurora born inside metal.

Ethan's voice again, softer this time. "Han, that's beautiful down there."

"Beauty doesn't keep us alive," Sung replied, but a faint smile touched his face.

He keyed in a diagnostic sweep. Graphs scrolled—temperature, harmonics, plasma density. All green. The first true harmony of metal and will since the engines had gone cold.

"Cluster array on hold," Sung announced. "She's breathing steady."

"Copy," Ethan said. "Let her dream a little longer."

The channel clicked silent, leaving only the steady song of the ship—the sound of the first generation's last engine waiting for the word **go**.

Outside the Bunker

Devin stepped onto the observation terrace to clear his head. The sky was pale gold; thin snow glittered on the desert floor. In the distance, the *Daedalus* towered against the horizon like a candle waiting for its own flame.

He remembered the day they'd broken ground—just steel, sand, and impossible blueprints. Now it was real. Humanity had turned extinction into engineering.

Wind pushed against his coat, sharp with the scent of ozone from the buried Umbra lines. Beneath the surface, power built in rhythmic pulses that matched his pulse without mercy.

A soft alarm chimed from the bunker loudspeakers. **T − 3 hours.** He could almost hear Oshima's voice in Geneva, calm and remote: *Maintain Umbra lock. We launch on schedule.*

Devin leaned on the railing, eyes on the ship's upper hull where the mission emblem caught the sunlight—*Daedalus* carved in gold against white plating. The ship looked impossibly fragile from here, like it might drift away before ignition.

He tapped the side of his headset, replaying the last recorded transmission from Priya Narayanan—the one she'd sent months ago from the Prometheus, already beyond the Gate.

"If you can still see the Sun, remember its warmth. You'll carry it farther than we ever could."

Her voice broke slightly before the carrier faded. Every time he heard it, he felt both smaller and steadier.

He switched the headset off and let silence reclaim the terrace. The hum from the buried Umbra field rose, a living tremor under the ice-dusted ground.

"Field alignment within two percent," came a distant call from the comm line—**Umbra Ops, Control Bay 4**.

"Copy that," Devin replied, voice low. "Hold phase and prepare for main sync in one hour."

He looked once more at the Daedalus, gleaming through the thin atmosphere. The sunlight refracted off its hull, throwing a bright spear of reflection across the desert. For a heartbeat it looked as if the dying Sun itself had chosen to lend the ship one last fragment of fire.

Launch Suit Prep

On Deck 6, Mira adjusted the seals of her pressure harness, the motion automatic after months of drills. The compartment was narrow, walls lined with silvered suits hanging like patient ghosts.

A voice crackled softly from the intercom—Priya's old training footage, part of the mission prep archive that played before final synchronization.

"Command isn't about who's rested," Priya said, her voice grainy, distant. "It's about who's ready to make the mistake everyone else can't live with."

Mira froze mid-motion, letting the words hang in the air. She could still picture Priya's expression from that long-ago session—the tired smile, the way she always folded meaning inside irony.

She finished tightening the neck seal and caught her reflection in the porthole glass. The Sun's fading gold filled the visor, turning her face into a silhouette against light.

"Poetic and terrifying," she whispered, answering a ghost.

Ethan's voice came through her helmet link. "Suit diagnostics all green. We're five minutes from ingress."

"Copy," she said, straightening. "Let's make her proud."

"Already are," he replied.

She sealed the visor. The hiss of pressure equalization filled her ears, soft and final. For a moment it felt like holding her breath at the edge of history.

Final Diagnostics — T − 2 Hours

In the propulsion bay, Sung and his team synchronized the twelve ion clusters. Each unit generated a contained electromagnetic vortex that bent charged plasma through the silver-blue coils that ran the ship's length. The light flickered in rhythm—twelve silent hearts pulsing beneath the decks.

"Cluster alignment nominal."

"Containment at ninety-eight point six percent."

"Fuel feed stable."

Sung's stylus ticked against his console—once, twice—then stopped. "If she holds steady for the next hundred minutes, she'll hold forever."

Ethan's voice came over comms, steady and familiar. "Music to my ears, Han."

"Save the music for orbit."

He glanced up at the main viewport—more a reinforced slit than a window—and saw the faint shimmer of the Umbra field spreading along the horizon. The golden light of the dying Sun scattered through it like dust through glass.

"Umbra link confirming sync," said a tech near the forward panel. "Geneva Control reports Phase Four lock achieved."

"About time," Sung muttered. He keyed in the final calibration and leaned back, exhaling into his helmet. "Begin field-temperature hold at baseline thirty-two."

"Baseline thirty-two set."

The air carried a low vibration, deeper than sound—pressure harmonics from the magnetic confinement itself. Sung closed his eyes for a heartbeat and felt it run through his bones. *This is what perfection sounds like*, he thought.

Then Ethan again, quieter now: "Umbra Ops wants confirmation that you're green across all clusters before we roll into the primary ignition cycle."

Sung smiled faintly. "Tell them they're already green—they just don't know it yet."

A few of the engineers chuckled, the laughter brief but enough to cut the strain in the room.

Overhead, warning lights switched from amber to pale blue. T − 1:55. The hum of humanity's second hope deepened another octave.

Communications Room — T − 90 Minutes

Leila sat at the narrow terminal, the low hum of the comm arrays vibrating through the soles of her boots. Around her, the room was half-dark—only the status bars from the transmitters breathing against the walls.

Outside the small porthole, she could see the desert sky beginning to pale toward white as the Sun climbed, dim but stubborn.

She read the message again, line by line, fingers hovering over the send key.

We're not leaving you; we're carrying you. Everything you built, every word and law and story—you're inside us now. When the gate opens, your names will go with ours.

The phrasing was legal and lyrical at once—exactly the balance she'd promised the Exodus Council. A record for those who would never see the ships rise, and a reminder to those who would.

Her reflection flickered in the glass of the screen. For a moment she saw not herself but a thousand faces layered in transparency—families at terminals across Earth sending their own fragments into the archive. Every message a farewell disguised as testimony.

She hesitated, then typed another line beneath her signature:

Los Angeles—thank you for teaching me how to survive endings.

The cursor blinked. She waited, as if someone might answer, then pressed *Send.*

The terminal responded in quiet light: **Transmission Queued.**

For a second, she just watched the confirmation glow. That simple line would travel through Umbra's last planetary uplink, bounce through six orbiting relays, and enter the sealed record vault that would outlast the planet itself. It felt heavier than any law she'd ever written.

A soft tone broke her reverie. Ethan's voice over the comm net: "Leila, suit check in ten. Copy?"

"Copy," she said, voice steadier than she felt.

She rose, smoothing the fabric of her undersuit, and took one last glance at the terminal. The screen had already gone dark, her words converted to light and noise—carried outward, waiting for the gate to remember them.

10. The Observation Window — T – 60 Minutes

Mira stood before the forward viewport, helmet off, letting the filtered light wash across her face. The Sun filled half the sky—a vast, pale disk that pulsed with a slow rhythm, its edges trembling like something breathing through glass. Its light no longer burned; it shimmered, uncertain, alive in its dying.

Ethan stepped up beside her, tightening his harness. "Ion clusters locked. Fusion injectors warm."

She nodded, eyes still on the trembling horizon. "Forty-two days to the Gate. After that—the rendezvous."

He gave a crooked grin. "Longer than most marriages."

"Then let's make it work better than mine," she said.

They both laughed—quiet, thin, the kind of laughter that exists only to fill the silence between fear and duty.

For a moment they just watched the Sun together. Beyond the viewport, magnetic waves shimmered across the Umbra field, faint arcs of light curving upward like auroras. Each pulse marked another second the world still held.

Ethan checked his readings again. "Umbra sync is holding steady. Geneva reports all green."

"Then this is it," Mira said softly. "After today, there's no Earth beneath us—just history."

She reached for her helmet. The gold glare caught their reflections and fused them into one image—two silhouettes framed by the last sunrise of humankind.

Countdown Begins

"All hands, this is Launch Director Oshima. **T minus thirty minutes. Begin final pressurization sequence.**"

The voice carried through every corridor of the Daedalus and into the buried bunkers below, threaded through steel, comm lines, and breath.

Inside **Umbra Control**, Devin watched the readouts scroll—oxygen flow steady, coolant pumps synchronizing with onboard regulators. He toggled the pressure graph overlay; the numbers climbed in smooth increments. *No spikes, no bleed. Good.*

"Umbra link stable," he said into the headset. "We are green across thermal and atmospheric feeds."

Outside, the desert shook with the slow venting of cryogenic steam. The launch gantries pulled back in stages, their joints releasing long ribbons of vapor that drifted into the pale air. The ship's base was lost in fog, the lower hull glowing faintly blue where containment fields touched the atmosphere.

Far above, on **Deck 40**, Sung's propulsion bay bloomed with white-blue light. The twelve ion clusters shimmered like concentric stars, energy cycling through them in perfect sequence.

He ran one last diagnostic, watching the pattern stabilize, then reached out to the nearest containment ring, hand hovering just above the magnetic glow.

"Stay calm, girl," he murmured. "You're about to rewrite history."

The hum deepened, almost a purr.

In the command deck, Mira's voice joined Oshima's on the internal comms. "All stations, confirm crew ingress complete. Ethan, begin Umbra-core coupling on my mark."

"Copy," Ethan replied.

The lights dimmed to launch intensity. For the first time in centuries, humanity's oldest fear—leaving the sky—became a single coordinated motion.

T − 15 Minutes

The command deck lights shifted to crimson. Warning glyphs rippled across the bulkhead screens, each one acknowledging readiness rather than danger. The ship had entered its final ritual.

Mira eased into the captain's chair, the restraint harness locking across her chest with a hydraulic hiss. Around her, the air carried the faint metallic taste of the oxygen recyclers as they cycled to full pressure. The deck vibrated—not movement, but anticipation.

To her left, Ethan hunched over the drive console, eyes flicking between telemetry bands and Umbra-field harmonics. "Cluster resonance holding at ninety-nine point nine. Injectors stable."

To her right, Leila moved deliberately, sealing the archive pods into magnetic suspension. Within each transparent cylinder glimmered the encoded lattice of humanity's memory—literature, law, science, music—compressed into crystalline blocks no larger than her hand. When the clamps sealed, a low chime echoed through the deck, as if the past itself had locked in.

"Cabin pressure stable."

"Core temperature nominal."

"Umbra sync complete."

Mira tapped her comm switch. "Control, this is *Daedalus*. Crew secured. Ready for ignition sequence."

A heartbeat later Devin's voice filled the cabin, steady and close despite the kilometers of desert between them. "Copy, *Daedalus*. You're green across the board. Umbra grid confirms full lock. No anomalies."

Mira let the silence hang. Through the forward viewport the dying Sun shimmered—its light muted by the field filters, still vast enough to make the hull glow. Somewhere beneath that light, whole cities watched this moment through static-blurred feeds, waiting to see if the second exodus would rise where the first had vanished.

Ethan looked up from his console. "We cross the threshold in fifteen minutes. No margin for corrections once the injectors go."

"Understood." She rested her gloved hand on the armrest, fingertips brushing the worn metal ridge polished smooth by generations of engineers before her. "Let's make it clean."

Leila turned, her voice quiet. "All archives secured. The rest is yours, Commander."

Mira met her eyes, nodded once, then pressed the comm again. "Control—confirm we're go for ignition on your mark."

"Confirmed," Devin answered. "You have the planet's blessing."

Mira allowed herself one slow breath, then closed her eyes for half a heartbeat. *Priya, wherever you are… we're coming.*

She opened them again. "Then let's begin."

The red lights deepened to amber. Below decks, the first ignition tones began to sound—low, harmonic, like a heartbeat counting down to history.

Ignition

"Five… four… three… two… ignition."

The world shook.

The twelve ion clusters flared to life, blue plasma flooding through containment rings. Magnetic fields twisted, caught, and harmonized into a single roar that no human ear could fully hear—it was pressure, not sound, vibrating through bone and metal alike.

Outside, a column of light erupted from the desert floor, blinding and pure, reaching for the dimming sky. Dust spiraled into the upper atmosphere, catching the golden glow of the dying Sun until it looked as though the Earth itself were burning its last prayer into the heavens.

Inside, every gauge came alive—velocity climbing, stabilizers counterbalancing, hull temperature spiking and then settling as coolant loops flooded the outer shell.

"Cluster one through twelve nominal!" Sung shouted over comms. "Umbra sync stable. She's flying herself!"

"Not without us, she isn't," Mira replied, her voice a mix of command and disbelief.

Ethan grinned, exhaustion burning away under the surge of adrenaline. "We have lift!"

Gravity's pull softened—first a subtle shift in weight, then the unmistakable release as the *Daedalus* tore free of its cradle. The hull groaned, then steadied, lifted by invisible energy.

Below, the launch field was lost in a storm of light and vapor. The blast radius expanded for hundreds of kilometers, scattering the desert's thin snow into the sky. From orbit, observers would later describe it as the planet exhaling.

Devin's voice crackled through the comms from ground control, nearly drowned by static. "Umbra field clear. You're airborne, *Daedalus*. Godspeed."

Mira steadied her breath, eyes fixed on the rising horizon. "Acknowledged, Control. Beginning ascent to Gate trajectory."

Ethan looked over his shoulder, half-grinning, half-stunned. "Forty-two days to the Gate."

"Then let's make every second count," she said.

Outside, the pillar of blue flame thinned into a beam of light—one ship leaving a dying world behind.

Ascent

Through the viewport, the horizon curved away, a slow-moving miracle of geometry and grief. The dying Earth receded beneath them—patches of brown desert, frozen oceans glinting like fractured glass under pale-gold light. Storm fronts stretched across continents, their tops brushed with emerald where the Umbra field scattered sunlight.

Mira sat forward, hands resting on her knees as the launch restraints released with a soft click. She'd imagined this view since her first day at Umbra Command, yet the reality carried a weight that training could never simulate. The planet looked small—too small for everything it had contained.

On the opposite side of the deck, Leila stared through another port, eyes shining. "All that law, all that history—and it fits inside a memory crystal the size of my hand," she murmured.

Ethan adjusted the stabilizer controls. "It was never about the size," he said. "It's about the chance to keep writing."

The ship rotated gently, aligning for orbital capture. Through the lower windows the desert launch site appeared one last time, a circular scar glowing faint blue from the Umbra discharge. Then the engines pulsed, and the image slid away into shadow.

Mira kept watching until she could no longer separate land from sea, only color—brown fading to gray, then to the pale shimmer of atmosphere. "Good-bye," she whispered.

Ethan heard her and didn't look up from his console. "We'll bring it with us."

The deck vibrated as the ion clusters shifted to cruise mode. In the silence between pulses, a faint electronic crackle came over the comms. Devin's voice broke through from the bunker below, distant and hollow with static:

"*Daedalus*, you're clear of atmosphere. Godspeed."

For a heartbeat, nobody spoke. Then Mira smiled, the corners of her mouth trembling just enough to show the strain.

"Copy that, Control," she said. "See you on the other side."

The carrier tone wavered, then dissolved into white noise.

A soft tremor passed through the hull as the Umbra field disengaged from Earth's magnetosphere. The ship was alone now—weightless, suspended in a silence so complete it felt sacred.

Mira unlatched her harness and drifted a few centimeters from the chair, the first true moment of zero-G. Her hair floated around her face like dark smoke.

Leila whispered, "We actually did it."

Ethan looked out through the viewport. Below them, the Earth's curve burned faint orange at the edge of night, the terminator line sweeping across continents. "We did it," he said, "and we can never go back."

Mira's eyes stayed fixed on the fading world until it was no longer a planet, just a reflection on the glass—an echo of light from a home already cooling in the dark.

Part II — Orbit Insertion
Engine Cutoff

The vibration eased at 112 kilometers altitude.

"Main-drive throttle to zero-point-three," Ethan ordered.

The roar diminished, peeling away layer by layer until only the quiet hiss of circulation fans remained. The ship's internal hum became the heartbeat of an organism newly born. For the first time since ignition, silence filled the *Daedalus*—not the fragile stillness of fear, but the vast, weightless pause of success.

Relays clicked. A pressure valve released with a sharp sigh. The air carried a faint metallic tang where coolant met recycled oxygen. Everyone breathed through their suit comms, and the sound of their breathing—steady, human—felt louder than the engines ever had.

Telemetry scrolled across the command screen:
Perigee 113 km — Apogee 188 km — Velocity 7.9 km/s.

Mira read the figures aloud like a prayer. "We're locked."

The inertial dampers settled; the last shiver of ascent faded. She unlatched her harness and drifted free, boots brushing the console edge. The cabin lights adjusted to the muted glow of orbit.

Through the viewport, Earth dominated the void—a bruised sphere half-veiled in amber haze. From here, the Umbra field shimmered like a translucent net, faint auroras chasing along magnetic lines. City lights glimmered through breaks in the cloud deck, scattered and uneven, as if the planet itself were exhaling embers.

"Ladies and gentlemen," Mira said softly, "we are no longer bound."

Leila floated beside her, one hand anchoring to the bulkhead rail. "And yet," she whispered, "it feels like we left something breathing behind."

Ethan glanced up from his console. "We did. But it's still watching."

Mira's gaze stayed fixed on the world below. The terminator line slid across the continents, night swallowing day in a slow sweep of shadow. The Sun—pale, wounded, flickering behind the Umbra distortions—cast long rays that turned the oceans into molten glass.

She reached toward the viewport, palm hovering against the transparency. "You kept us alive as long as you could," she murmured. "We'll do the same for what comes next."

A chime broke the stillness. Devin's final transmission replayed automatically through the ship's recorder—faint, distorted, already history:

"*Daedalus*, you're clear of atmosphere. Godspeed."

Then nothing but static, fading to background noise.

Mira turned toward the primary console. "Record log," she said.

A light blinked green.

Launch Day — Daedalus Command Log Entry One. "Main ignition complete. Orbit achieved. Umbra grid disengaged. Earth secure below. Mission phase: Exodus Transfer Alpha. Crew morale—steady. We begin the path to the Gate."

She stopped the recording and closed her eyes. For a moment, no one moved. The ship drifted on momentum alone, each rotation revealing a little more of the vast black ocean waiting beyond.

When Mira finally spoke again, her voice was calm. "All stations—prepare for Gate trajectory alignment."

Outside, the *Daedalus* pivoted slowly, engines dark, hull gleaming in the Sun's fading light—humanity's newest star crossing the twilight of the old one.

Systems Stabilization

Sung's propulsion crew cycled the ion clusters into cruise mode. Each unit fired microscopic pulses of plasma, invisible save for the faint blue filaments that extended behind the ship like threads of spun glass. The exhaust wasn't a roar—it was a whisper of numbers, a translation of equations into motion.

"Cluster synchronization variance, zero-point-zero-two percent."

"Magnetic confinement holding."

The reports came softly through comms, voices reverent without meaning to be.

Sung stood at the center of the propulsion deck, helmet tucked beneath his arm, the glow from the readouts washing his face in blue-white light. The hum beneath his boots was steady, balanced, and almost tender.

"This," he murmured, "is what perfect control sounds like—nothing."

He opened his datapad and began the log entry, the stylus trembling slightly from residual vibration.

Ion arrays stabilized. Confinement integrity optimal. Field harmonics steady. No measurable drift in Umbra compensation.

If she keeps this stability, Daedalus will reach solar-gate alignment in forty-two days.

He paused, the cursor blinking against the glowing screen. After a long breath he added one more line:

If the Sun waits that long.

He stared at the words for several seconds before locking the log. Around him, the engineers moved in silence, their voices replaced by the quiet confidence of the data streams. On every monitor, the curve of Earth shrank by a few more pixels, replaced by a growing field of stars.

Somewhere deep within the ship, a guidance tone pinged—steady, unwavering, counting down to a future none of them could yet imagine.

Post-Launch Checklists

Navigation: "Gyros locked, drift under two microradians."

Life-support: "Atmosphere twenty-one-point one oxygen, CO_2 point-zero-four percent."

Communications: "Umbra uplink stable at thirty-six decibels."

The readouts scrolled in calm succession across the forward displays. For the first time in hours, no one shouted; the bridge had the rhythm of a heartbeat settling after a sprint.

Mira drifted through the deck, checking straps and seals herself—old habits she'd never broken. Her boots caught the deck magnets with each movement, the faint clack echoing like punctuation in the quiet.

"No automation replaces human verification," she said, voice even. "Machines don't panic—which is why we make sure they never have to."

She stopped beside the environmental console, palms resting lightly against the housing. The panel's dials twitched within green tolerance, needles trembling as if from the ship's own pulse. She felt that same rhythm in her chest.

At the aft bulkhead, Leila floated past carrying the legal vault—the crystalline memory blocks humming with low harmonic tones. Light refracted through them in subtle rainbows, the sum of civilization compressed into color.

"Still holding twenty-three million documents," she said. "The history of everyone we left behind."

Mira nodded. "Then keep them safe. That's our new constitution."

Leila smiled faintly. "First constitution written in light."

Across the command deck, Ethan looked up from telemetry. "And hopefully the first one that never gets amended."

A few quiet laughs rippled through the crew. It wasn't humor so much as relief—proof they still knew how to laugh.

The main lights dimmed as the ship switched from launch reserves to long-cruise power. Instrument panels took on a softer hue; the deep-space lighting felt almost domestic. Outside the viewport, the blue ion stream shimmered, steady as a breath. For the first time, the *Daedalus* felt less like a machine and more like a habitat.

Mira clipped a tether to a nearby handrail and tapped her headset. "Bridge to all stations—status sweep complete. Confirm green across sections."

One by one, the replies came in: propulsion, life-support, comms, habitat, archives, navigation. All green.

She opened a new log channel.

Daedalus Command Log — Launch Day + 0.14 hours

Systems check complete. All primary clusters stable, Umbra link secure. Crew transitioning to long-cruise operations. Morale steady. No anomalies reported.

End of entry.

Mira closed the log and let the quiet settle around her again. For the first time since ignition, she allowed herself a single deep breath—not the disciplined intake of a commander, but the simple breath of a human being who had just left the world behind.

"Set the chronometers," she said. "Forty-two days to the Gate."

Ethan gave a small salute. "And every one of them ours."

Outside, the *Daedalus* drifted forward through the black, its engines whispering against eternity, its crew suspended between the planet that made them and the star that was dying to let them go.

Ground Farewell

Below, in the Nevada bunker, Devin Rao watched the blue dot trace its curve into orbit. Each pulse on the tracking screen was a heartbeat—steady, insistent, almost human. The feed scrolled lines of telemetry in pale green text: velocity, inclination, field harmonics. He didn't read them anymore; he simply listened to the rhythm. That faint flicker had become the sound of friendship moving away.

Around him, the operations floor was almost silent. Dozens of stations glowed in the low light, rows of engineers hunched forward as though prayer might keep the signal strong. The recycled air smelled faintly of ozone and the tang of machine oil. Someone's coffee steamed untouched beside a console, forgotten since ignition.

The loudspeakers crackled with residual static from the last transmission—*Daedalus, you're clear of atmosphere. Godspeed.* Then nothing. The voice had become an echo trapped in the metal bones of the bunker.

At his shoulder, Oshima stood with her arms crossed, eyes on the same blue point. Her posture was the definition of composure, but the muscles along her jaw trembled just once before settling again. "One down," she said. "Three more to launch."

Devin kept his gaze fixed on the display. "They look so small up there."

"Small things survive," Oshima replied. "That's evolution's joke."

He almost smiled. "Cruel joke."

"Cruel," she agreed. "But efficient."

A low vibration passed through the floor as the Umbra network shifted power to the next launch site—energy humming through subterranean conduits that stretched halfway across the continent. The servers rattled faintly in their racks.

Outside, above hundreds of meters of reinforced rock, the desert wind carried the faint shimmer of ion residue, turning the night air thin and metallic.

On the main screen the dot flickered, brightened, then slipped beyond the upper edge of the grid display. The telemetry column terminated in a line of gray dashes. No failure code, no anomaly—just distance.

Devin exhaled slowly. "Signal gone."

Oshima reached over and tapped a key, saving the last data packet to archive. **LAUNCH + 00:51:23 UTC** appeared in the log header. She watched the numbers freeze in place. "That's history now."

He rubbed the back of his neck. "Feels more like silence."

She turned toward him. "Same thing, sometimes."

The bunker's status lights shifted from amber to green-standby. Screens dimmed one by one, leaving only the main display glowing against the dark. Beyond the concrete walls, the desert sky was empty—no contrails, no thunder, just the faint afterimage of Umbra reflection, a ghostly halo where the ship had climbed.

For a long moment neither of them moved. The room hummed softly, a mechanical lullaby.

Finally, Oshima said, "Go get some rest, Devin. They're on their way, and we'll need you again in six hours."

He hesitated, still watching the empty screen. "I used to think the hardest part would be launching them."

"It isn't," she said. "It's waiting to know if they made it."

Devin nodded once. "Then I'll wait."

He shut down the console. The last light on the panel winked out, leaving only the dim blue glow of the Umbra grid map on the far wall—four points marked *PROMETHEUS, GENESIS TWO, DAEDALUS, EREBUS, ODYSSEY, AURORA* A third one already turning green. Three still gray.

Oshima watched him go, then looked back at the display. The single green icon pulsed slowly on the display, like the heartbeat of a planet learning how to let go.

Outside, dawn crept across the desert. The first sunlight touched the bunker vents and scattered in thin, metallic rays—light from a dying star falling on the hands of those who remained.

Orbit Night

Daedalus slipped into Earth's shadow. The last edge of sunlight crawled across the hull, a thin red line fading to indigo before vanishing altogether. Inside, the cabin dimmed automatically, pressure lights softening to a faint amber.

Outside the viewport, the universe unfolded—clean, infinite, untouched. Thousands of stars ignited at once, sharp as needles. Without the veil of Umbra, they looked painfully bright, the way the sky must have seemed to the first humans who ever looked up.

The crew stopped moving. For the first time since launch there were no vibrations, no alarms, no chatter—only the whisper of circulating air.

Mira reached across her console and switched off the remaining back-lights. The instruments went dark, leaving the cabin in pure shadow pierced only by starlight through the glass.
"One minute of silence," she said.

The order wasn't protocol; it was instinct. The others understood immediately. Helm controls drifted idle, status boards frozen in green.

"This is what old astronauts called orbital night," she said softly. "Ninety minutes long, never the same twice."

Ethan floated beside her, still strapped halfway into his harness. The reflection of the stars shimmered across his visor. "Hard to believe we built this from cold sand."

Mira gave a faint smile. "Harder to believe we're leaving everything warm behind."

He nodded once, not trusting himself to speak.

From the aft section, Leila unlatched and drifted closer, one hand grazing the overhead rail for balance. The glow from the viewport illuminated her face in fragments. "Look," she whispered.

Below them, the night side of Earth rolled past—continents like fading ghosts, cities glowing in uneven clusters where power grids still held. Over the oceans, lightning flickered in slow rhythm, silent from this distance.

"It's still beautiful," she said.

"Beauty's the easy part," Mira replied. "It's the leaving that hurts."

The minute stretched longer than any of them expected. The absence of motion became a sound of its own—a low, private hum inside their suits, the steady beat of hearts tethered to no gravity at all.

Ethan broke the silence at last. "Telemetry shows shadow duration eighty-nine minutes, thirty-two seconds. Orbital decay under one micron per second."

"Keep it steady," Mira said. "Let them sleep down there thinking we're still rising."

Leila's eyes stayed on the planet. "Do you think they'll watch the sky tonight?"

"They'll try," Mira answered. "But Umbra's glow will fade before they find us."

The ship drifted onward, silent, its ion stream glowing like a thread of ice behind it. Across the viewport, dawn began to creep along Earth's rim— a thin arc of copper light that spread, widening toward gold.

"Orbital night ending," Ethan said quietly.

Mira reached for the lighting control but hesitated. "Leave it dark a little longer," she said.

The Sun's first rays struck the hull, scattering through the cabin in a burst of soft reflections. For a heartbeat every surface glowed—hands, helmets, the crystalline vault that carried the memory of civilization—each catching light like stained glass in motion.

"Good morning," Leila whispered.

Mira looked out through the window one last time before the brightness overtook them. "Morning," she said. "And goodbye."

The *Daedalus* slid from shadow into light, its engines humming once more, a slender streak of blue threading between night and dawn.

Re-Ignition

At orbital dawn the Sun rose over the curve of the Earth—not blinding white but a molten gold, veined with shifting filaments that coiled and uncoiled like slow lightning. Each pulse matched the wavelength recorded by *Prometheus* three years earlier.

Ethan studied the spectral feed. "Solar pulse frequency confirmed— three-point-one minutes, consistent with Prometheus telemetry."

Mira nodded. "Copy that. Maintain lock."

Across the propulsion bay, Sung's voice came through the intercom, calm and measured. "Ion arrays stable, field integrity one hundred percent. Ready for transition burn."

Ethan turned toward him. "Begin burn, two percent throttle."

Plasma light flared through the aft cameras, a soft, living blue that filled the cabin screens. The ship trembled, then steadied as thrust aligned with orbit. There was no sound—only vibration through the soles of their boots, the quiet pressure of acceleration that pushed gently against their harnesses.

Outside, *Daedalus* pivoted sunward. The ion stream arced behind it like a painter's stroke of light, curling around the fading planet.

From the comm grid came a single voice—Priya's, archived from *Prometheus* transmissions, auto-playing in synchronization with solar pulse data.

"If you ever see the Sun move like this, don't be afraid. It's not dying—it's remembering how to live."

No one spoke. The recording ended in static that merged with the hum of engines.

Mira leaned toward her mic. "Confirm heading."

Ethan answered, "Heliocentric transfer initiated. Target orbit zero-point-seven-three AU. Burn nominal."

Sung's telemetry lights flickered green across the board. "Daedalus has left Earth orbit."

No one cheered. There was only breathing—the slow, collective exhale of people realizing history had just pivoted around them. The last link to Earth dissolved in background noise; all that remained was sunlight, motion, and purpose.

Mira watched the Sun swell ahead of them, its wounded brilliance painting the cabin in amber. "Let's find out if it remembers us," she said.

The ship kept burning, silent and small against the endless gold.

Part III — The Long Burn
The Drift

Six hours into flight, the ship no longer felt like a rocket; it felt like a city block drifting through glass.

Every surface hummed with the sub-sonic tone of the ion clusters. The vibration was so pure it ceased to exist as sound—only a pressure in the bones, a reminder that motion was happening even when everything looked still.

Routine replaced adrenaline. Crew schedules cycled into eight-hour rotations; half the team asleep at any moment, half awake. Nutrient packs warmed on induction plates. **Dr. James Kastor** moved quietly through the corridors at intervals, logging heart rates, hydration, and radiation exposure—numbers that would one day describe what it meant to survive the leaving of a planet. A new kind of silence took hold: one without gravity, without wind, without consequence. It was the kind of quiet that demanded belief.

Mira drifted down the central corridor, coffee bulb in hand, the liquid inside catching glints of blue from the engine light. She found Leila hovering by the viewport, the crystalline archive case magnetized to the wall beside her.

"Remember when caffeine had aroma?" Mira asked.

Leila smiled faintly. "Remember when mornings had sunlight?"

They clinked the bulbs together—a gesture that pretended the past still existed. The sound was a soft, hollow tap, barely audible through the ship's hum.

For a moment they floated there, sipping in silence, the stars unmoving outside, the Earth already just another coordinate.

"Hard to believe this is what surviving feels like," Leila said.

Mira nodded. "It's quieter than I expected."

From somewhere aft, Sung's voice carried over the intercom, calm as ever. "Cluster drift variance zero point zero two. We are on course."

Mira exhaled, letting the words settle like a lullaby. "Then let's keep drifting."

Outside, the *Daedalus* moved through the black, engines whispering in frequencies that the human ear could not hear—a city block of light gliding toward the dying Sun.

Engineering Notes

Down in the propulsion bay, **Dr. Han Sung** still wrote by hand. He kept his notes on a strip of transparent polymer clamped to the console, the ink a deep indigo that gleamed under the emergency lights. Electronics sometimes mis-timed near the drive coils; the electromagnetic fields distorted timestamps and froze touch-screens. Ink, at least, didn't crash.

He worked with his gloves off; fingers stained with graphite and solvent. The low vibration from the ion clusters ran through the deck plates like a heartbeat too slow for music.

Day 1: all twelve clusters stable. Emission pattern near-perfect sine. Power bleed negligible.

Day 2: detected sub-harmonic at 0.003 Hz. Too low for mechanical cause.

He paused, listening. Somewhere deep within the ship a pulse answered—barely audible, more felt than heard, as if the metal itself was breathing in time with something far away.

He underlined the entry twice and added a single line beneath:

Could be the Sun answering us.

Sung sat back, pen hovering above the page. He didn't tell command—not yet. Superstition had crept even into science. The younger engineers had started whispering it now, half-joking, half-afraid:

It hums when it listens.

He capped the pen, left the lights dim, and let the ship hum to itself.

Navigation Deck

On the navigation deck, Mira and Ethan worked by hand. The automation array had already fallen behind—its correction algorithms caught in a feedback loop, chasing false readings where the Sun's magnetic envelope distorted starlight.

The instruments still hummed, obediently displaying coordinates that neither of them trusted. In the end, it came down to sight and intuition—the kind of skill taught by people who'd navigated before gravity ever left the ground.

Mira leaned over the chart display, her glove smudging the edge of a graphite line. "Bring the secondary marker five microradians west," she said.

Ethan turned the dial, the view shifting in a smooth, analog arc until the faint parallax lines converged on the target star. "Velocity twelve kilometers per second relative. If we hold thrust constant, we hit the resonance corridor in forty-two days as planned."

She wrote the numbers onto her pad, pressing hard enough for the stylus to squeak. "If it holds," she murmured. "The Sun's pulse is tightening by microseconds."

He stopped adjusting the dial and frowned. "Still trending up?"

Mira tapped the edge of the console. "Every cycle. The wave pattern looks deliberate—like it's responding to something."

Ethan gave a humorless laugh. "You mean us?"

She didn't answer right away. Through the viewport the Sun filled half the sky, its surface alive with geometry. Filaments rose and folded in precise arcs, symmetrical and slow. The corona glowed in tessellated layers, like something conscious was flexing just beneath the light.

"Maybe," she said finally. "Or maybe it's just echoing what Prometheus saw three years ago."

Ethan adjusted the focus lens again, magnifying the upper corona until the field sensors began to saturate. "Look at that—pattern density's identical to Priya's last transmission."

Mira glanced at the readings. "Magnetic harmonics off the scale," she said softly. "It's almost like it's... anticipating."

He turned toward her. "You think the Sun knows we're coming?"

She met his eyes. "No. But it might remember the last ones who did."

They fell silent. The faint blue light from the instruments cast long reflections across the deck, broken only by the soft motion of dust and loose fibers drifting like tiny comets in the cabin air.

Ethan checked the drift readout, voice quieter now. "Gyro offset stable, under one microradian. We're good."

"Keep it that way," Mira said. She made another note, this one slower, deliberate. "Every fluctuation, every interval. I want pattern recognition running, manual or not."

Ethan nodded, then looked back through the viewport. The solar disk shimmered again—no longer chaotic, but rhythmic, alive with repeating motion. The filaments rose and fell like the slow breathing of a living thing.

"She's waiting for us to make the first mistake," he murmured.

Mira's expression didn't change, but she whispered as if answering something unseen. "Then we won't."

The hum of the engines deepened—a long, low tone that resonated through the hull. Beneath it, for the briefest instant, another pulse joined in—fainter, slower, like the echo of a heartbeat not their own.

Neither of them spoke again. The stars outside wavered slightly.

Mid-Course Transmission

Leila, now communications officer by necessity, floated before the console composing the first status burst to Earth. The link was narrowband—Umbra relay to orbital array to the Nevada bunker—and every byte carried the weight of a world.

She spoke softly as she typed, the words aligning on the screen in measured blue text.

Daedalus nominal. Crew healthy. Sun stable within tolerance. Launch window confirmed for Odyssey and Erebus.

She paused, reread the lines, then added another—just one more, against protocol.

Tell my city we're still under the same light.

She hesitated before sending, finger hovering over the transmit key. Through the viewport, the Sun flickered gold-white, its filaments tracing shifting lattices across the hull. Earth was already invisible behind them, a faint coordinate in the navigation log.

"Transmission ready," Ethan's voice came over comms. "Umbra link stable for ninety seconds."

"Copy," she said. "Burst encryption active."

The data packet folded into light and vanished from the buffer. It would take six minutes to reach the planet—six minutes if the planet still listened.

Leila stayed there after the console dimmed, watching the reflection of the Sun shimmer across the glass. Somewhere, a relay would blink green when the signal arrived. She wondered if anyone would blink back.

Recreation Module

In zero-G, Devin's recorded message played on the main screen—his face projected life-size, hair unkempt, eyes bright with worry. The background behind him was all steel and cables; the Nevada bunker looked even smaller than they remembered. Static shimmered across the feed every few seconds, making his expression flicker between clarity and ghost.

"You're fifty million kilometers out now. Umbra grids still reading you. Keep an eye on that secondary harmonic; Boston thinks it's bleeding straight through the magnetosphere."

His voice carried that mix of calm and exhaustion that only came from long shifts underground. Even through the distortion it had the sound of someone who hadn't seen natural light in months.

Leila floated closer to the screen, one hand anchored to the ceiling rail. "Still teaching from the bunker," she murmured.

Mira smiled faintly. "He never stopped being Control."

The recording stuttered and resumed—Devin leaning forward, tapping a datapad out of view.

"Umbra echo's fluctuating at point-zero-zero-three Hertz. Could be interference, could be something structural. Don't let Sung dismiss it as background noise. And tell him—"

The image glitched; his next words dissolved into a burst of static. The caption read **[TRANSMISSION LOSS 2.4 SEC]**.

When the sound returned, his voice had softened.

"You're making it look easy up there. Don't. Nothing about this is easy. And for what it's worth—everyone's watching. The whole world's quieter because of you."

The playback ended with a faint click.

Leila drifted nearer until her reflection merged with his on the blank screen. "He sounds... older."

"Only three years," Ethan said quietly. "Feels longer."

Mira exhaled. "For him, it probably was."

For a moment no one moved. The hum of the ship filled the silence— low, steady, like the ocean heard through walls.

Leila finally spoke, voice thin. "You think he still sleeps in that bunker?"

Mira shook her head. "People like Devin don't sleep. They wait."

The silence stretched again. Then Ethan reached out and muted the playback fully, fingers brushing the console with something close to tenderness. "Neither did you, Commander."

Mira gave a small laugh; more air than sound. "That's different. I'm here."

"Exactly," he said.

The screen faded to black, leaving only their reflections—their faces framed by soft blue instrument light, drifting like ghosts above the planet that once held them all.

"Archive the message," Mira said at last. "If we make it back through the Gate, I want him to know we listened."

Leila nodded, fingers flying across the console. "Filed under Mission Legacy One."

Outside the viewport, a faint shimmer rippled across the solar corona—a pulse barely visible, like a slow blink from the star itself.

Mira caught the motion and whispered, "He's still watching too."

The Pulse Shift

On the seventh day, the hum changed pitch.

It wasn't a sound so much as a rearrangement of heartbeat—the kind of shift that made the body aware of motion before the mind caught up.

Dr. Han Sung was the first to notice. He froze over his console, stylus hovering above a half-finished note.

"Primary field unchanged," he said into comms, his voice flat, "but external resonance has increased amplitude by point-zero-eight."

Mira's voice came back from the command deck, calm but clipped. "Repeat that, Han. Amplitude variance?"

"Confirmed," he replied. "The Sun's waveform is syncing to us."

A pause. "Meaning?"

He hesitated. "Meaning the star's responding faster than forecast. It's matching our thrust vector."

Across the deck, Ethan looked up from telemetry. The screens glowed with dual traces—*Daedalus* drive output in pale steady blue, the Sun's magnetic rhythm in gold. "We're pushing on the Sun," he said quietly, "and it's pushing back."

No one spoke for several seconds. The hum deepened again, subtle but certain, and the lights along the ceiling flickered once before stabilizing.

Leila floated near the viewport; her face ghosted in reflection. "How can a star *respond?*"

Mira's gaze stayed on the display. "I don't know," she said. "But it's listening."

The main monitor zoomed on Sung's telemetry feed. Two sine waves rolled across the graph—one human-made, one solar—each oscillation closing the distance between them. Slowly, inevitably, they began to merge until they were no longer separate lines but a single pulse.

Sung's stylus trembled as he added a single annotation to the log:

Day 7: external harmonic phase: locked.

He stared at it, then whispered, almost to himself, "She's hearing us."

The ship vibrated again—so faintly it might have been the echo of his words—and the lights dimmed to amber, as if the star outside had decided to breathe in time with them.

The Human Interval

That night cycle, with alarms silent and systems steady, the crew gathered in **Observation**. The great window curved above them like a cathedral dome, and beyond it the solar corona moved with impossible grace—filaments folding and unfolding in rhythm, a living halo that seemed to breathe.

The hum of the ship blended with that pulse until it was impossible to tell where machinery ended and the star began.

Leila steadied the camera on its mount and recorded the moment for the archive. "Crew morale high," she narrated softly. "If fear counts as high."

Her voice sounded small against the silence, like an echo lost in vacuum.

Mira floated nearby, one hand braced against the window frame. The reflection of the Sun traced golden arcs across her face. Ethan drifted beside her, still in partial harness, his eyes fixed on the swirling corona.

Leila watched them through the lens before speaking again—this time not for the record. "We were made to worship what we can't control," she said. "Maybe this is how science prays."

Mira turned her head, eyes still on the light. "Then pray it listens kindly."

No one replied. The silence that followed wasn't empty; it was reverent. Outside, the Sun's surface rippled once—an almost imperceptible motion that might have been coincidence, or acknowledgment.

Leila ended the recording, saved the file, and let the camera drift. The crew lingered there longer than the schedule allowed, watching their star breathe.

For the first time since leaving Earth, it no longer felt like distance that defined them, but participation. They were part of the pulse now—tiny, luminous cells in a body too vast to comprehend.

Ion-Tech Reflections

In Engineering, Dr. Han Sung tightened the last coupling on Cluster Eight, fingertips trembling from fatigue. The ion manifold's light shimmered across his visor—steady, pulsing faintly in rhythm with the ship's own vibration. Sweat floated from his hairline in perfect spheres before drifting away like dust motes.

He braced his boots into the deck clamps and leaned close to the conduit readouts. The hum was deeper tonight, almost melodic. The drive's sub-frequency oscillations had stabilized across all twelve clusters—no drift, no variance, just a single, unified tone.

He thumbed the recorder on.

"Every drive hum at the same sub-frequency now," he said quietly. "It's not interference; it's harmony. When a machine begins to sing, either it's dying or it's learning. I hope I built it smart enough to tell the difference."

He hesitated, eyes flicking to the diagnostics display. All readings nominal—temperature, confinement, feed. Perfect numbers that somehow felt wrong.

He shut the recorder off and pressed his gloved palm flat against the bulkhead. The metal beneath his hand was warm, alive with vibration. The hum steadied as he touched it—slight modulation, almost responsive.

Sung's breath fogged his visor. "You feel that?" he whispered. "You're listening, aren't you?"

The pulse beneath his hand shifted half a beat, a single subtle syncopation that might have been coincidence—or acknowledgment.

He left his hand there anyway, eyes closed, until the tremor settled back into perfect rhythm. When he finally moved away, the metal held the warmth of his touch just a moment too long.

The First Flare

At 02:17 ship-time a sharp tremor jolted the deck. Loose tablets and tools lifted from their restraints, spinning in the air. Emergency lights flickered amber, then steadied.

Mira snapped awake, palms already on the comm. "Report!"

From Engineering came Sung's voice, strained but controlled. "Drive output stable—no internal fault. External flux just spiked."

Ethan's telemetry screen filled with light. "Solar event—localized flare at twenty-two degrees latitude, magnitude four."

Mira's chair harness clicked as she leaned forward. "That's not random, is it?"

Ethan hesitated. "The jet vector points straight along our trajectory."

For a moment no one spoke. Outside, through the observation glass, a filament of gold plasma uncoiled from the Sun like a reaching hand. It stretched toward them, brilliant and silent, before dispersing into vapor ahead of the ship.

Instrumentation shrieked once and fell silent. Graphs normalized, but one reading persisted—a harmonic spike precisely matching the frequency once transmitted by *Prometheus*.

Leila floated beside the viewport, her face pale in the reflection. "What are the odds of that ratio repeating?"

"Zero," Sung said. "Unless it's deliberate."

Ethan's voice dropped to a whisper. "It's guiding us."

Mira watched the lingering glow fade into the black between worlds. Her jaw tightened. "Or warning us."

The hum of the engines returned, softer now, almost cautious. The crew drifted in the dim light, hearts syncing unconsciously to the beat of the star beyond their glass.

Aftermath

Once the flare passed, calm returned—at least in the measurable sense. The tremor faded, monitors steadied, and the hull's vibration settled back into the familiar sub-frequency that had become the ship's second heartbeat.

But inside the *Daedalus*, something intangible had shifted. No alarms blared, no systems failed, yet every crewmember moved as though gravity had quietly changed its rules. Voices came softer over comms. Tools were handled with reverence rather than precision. Awe had begun to replace procedure.

Mira reviewed Sung's data twice, searching for a cause that equations could explain, but the numbers only circled back to the same truth: the flare had aimed directly along their path, mimicking the Prometheus signal to the decimal. Even the residual wavefront still aligned with their vector—like a ripple leading rather than chasing.

She floated before the viewport, the Sun filling half the horizon, its surface restless with motion. Her reflection hovered ghost-bright over the swirling gold, and for the first time she couldn't tell which light belonged to her.

She opened her private log and began to record.

We control every switch, every valve, every field. Yet the further we go, the more it feels as if control itself is the illusion the universe allows us to keep. Perhaps this is what Priya meant when she said faith and physics are cousins. We study patterns until they answer back—and then we call that comprehension.

She paused, the cursor blinking, the ship's hum steady beneath her feet.

If the Sun is listening, it already knows more about us than we do about it. And if it's not—then we've taught ourselves how to imagine that it does.

She closed the pad and looked through the glass again. The star's spirals widened, each motion slow and deliberate, as though the Sun were beckoning something forward—perhaps them, perhaps memory itself.

Mira whispered, "You've seen us now. Don't forget what we are."

The cabin lights dimmed automatically for rest cycle, but the corona's glow poured through the viewport, painting the command deck in liquid gold long after the ship should have been dark.

Part IV — The Corridor of Light
Approach

Forty-one days outbound, *Daedalus* crossed the final threshold. The Sun no longer looked spherical; its corona had become architecture— arches and bridges of light rotating in measured rhythm, as if enormous gears beneath the surface had begun to turn. Every filament obeyed an invisible symmetry, golden and exact.

Mira leaned toward the forward console, eyes flicking between the viewport and the cascading telemetry. Numbers scrolled so fast they blurred into a single column of light.

"Magnetic flux up three hundred percent," she said. "We're inside the harmonic sheath."

Ethan adjusted the stabilization controls. The ion-cluster pitch rose half a tone, the hull groaning under the pressure differential. "Course is clean," he said. "Vector locked."

From Engineering, Sung's voice came over comm—steady, clipped, but louder than usual to rise above the vibration.

"Ion output steady. Containment's hot but stable. She's holding, Commander."

"Copy that," Mira replied.

She felt the change before she heard it: the hum of the ship deepening until it lived in the chest cavity, a slow, physical resonance that replaced sound with sensation. Loose tools trembled in their holders; condensation on the viewport shivered into tiny concentric rings.

Leila floated behind her, hands gripping the rail. "It feels alive," she said.

Mira didn't look back. "Everything alive hums," she answered.

Ahead, the Sun's surface shifted again, the loops tightening into a vast spiral pattern that turned with mechanical precision. Plasma storms danced along the arcs like sparks between teeth.

"Resonance corridor confirmed," Ethan reported. "Telemetry matches Prometheus records."

"Maintain vector," Mira said. "No course corrections unless I call it."

The ship pressed forward into the golden whirlpool. Light poured across the hull in sweeping bands, tracing every contour like liquid metal. The drive harmonics synchronized with the Sun's pulse until both frequencies became indistinguishable—a duet between machine and star.

Mira's fingers tightened on the console edge. "Hold together," she whispered—not to the ship, not to her crew, but to the quiet fragile line of reality that separated them from whatever waited ahead.

The hum rose again, a living vibration that filled the lungs, the bones, the very thought of sound. The *Daedalus* had entered the heartbeat of the Sun.

The Drift Beyond Physics

The first sign came without alarms. A pencil rose from Mira's desk, hung in the air, and drifted sideways as if deciding where down should be.

Moments later the floor pulled gently on their boots again, then released. Objects bobbed mid-air like seaweed in a slow current.

Ethan caught a loose tablet before it collided with a bulkhead. "Inertial readings incoherent," he said, staring at the trembling numbers. "We're bending frame-drag."

Mira turned toward him. "Meaning?"

He hesitated, the instruments still flickering. "Meaning relativity just gave up."

For a heartbeat the statement hung between them like another object floating in the air. Then someone—Leila, maybe Sung over the comm—laughed. It wasn't loud, only startled and human. The sound set the others off, quiet bursts of nervous laughter echoing through the cabin.

They weren't laughing because it was funny; they were laughing because it *still worked*. Because sound still traveled through air. Because they could still hear each other while everything else they understood began to slip its laws.

Mira gripped the console to steady herself. The panels glowed in uneven waves as the ship's artificial gravity fought the shifting field. The hull groaned softly, a sound like metal sighing under thought rather than pressure.

Outside the viewport, the Sun's inner sheath expanded into spirals of geometry—light folding back on itself, angles that moved like living things.

The *Daedalus* drifted through the impossible, and instruments that once measured speed now returned units that didn't exist.

Ethan looked up from the screen, half-grinning in disbelief. "Congratulations, Commander. We just broke the universe."

Mira managed a faint smile. "Then let's make sure we put it back when we're done."

The laughter faded, replaced by the ship's deep, resonant hum—a sound that felt more like gravity remembering what it used to be.

Solar Surface Imaging
Mira magnified the forward cameras.
The picture sharpened grain by grain until the solar photosphere filled the display—yet what appeared on-screen was not plasma, not chaos.

The Sun resolved into **structure**.

Across the burning face stretched vast patterned fields of light, lattices of gold geometry bending inward upon themselves. Pillars and vaults rose from the roiling surface like towers of flame shaped into crystalline spines. Each motion was deliberate, recursive, purposeful.

For a long moment, no one spoke. The bridge was silent but for the low mechanical hum of the ion clusters and the occasional ping of data overflow.

Leila's voice came first, small and reverent. "It's building something."

Ethan leaned closer, eyes wide at the symmetry unfolding on-screen. "Or revealing it."

The image brightened again, filtering through the corona until the towers merged into spirals, and the spirals into a single radiant helix descending into the star's core. It looked less like energy and more like design—an architecture written in fusion.

In Engineering, Sung opened the comm channel and began to dictate, his voice steady despite the tremor in his hands.

"Day 41. The Sun's interior isn't chaos. It's design."

He turned the gain higher. The vibration that filled the deck wasn't random static anymore—it was pattern. Three tones rising, one descending. Repeating.

The sound was almost musical, a sequence of notes woven into the hum of the ship itself. Every pulse of the drive matched the rhythm on the screen.

Mira felt it through the console—each thrum running up her arm like a heartbeat shared between metal and star. "It's communicating in resonance," she whispered.

Sung's recorder captured her words without prompt, his log still running. Outside, the towers shifted again, aligning in a vast spiral that pointed directly along the *Daedalus'* trajectory—an open corridor descending into gold.

Leila pressed a hand against the glass. "It's waiting for us."

No one argued. The ship's hum rose one final octave, then settled into silence as the image of the Sun held steady—no longer a star, but a door.

Contact

Without warning, every console flickered. The navigation grid dissolved into static, then re-formed as a cascade of luminous symbols no one recognized. The hum that had haunted the ship for forty-one days sharpened—no longer a vibration but a single, coherent note that filled the air and the blood.

Sung's voice broke over comm, half shout, half awe. "Commander! Field resonance at critical!"

Mira braced against the command chair. "Shut down drive!"

"Already at zero," Ethan replied, eyes wide on the display. "The field's self-sustaining!"

A blinding radiance bled through the hull seams, not burning but shining—as if the ship itself had become translucent, every line panel and bulkhead luminous from within. The light moved through metal like breath through lungs.

Magnetic readouts spiked, inverted, then held. The hum deepened until it was felt through bone rather than heard through air.

Then came the voices.

They didn't arrive from the speakers but from *everywhere*—echoes in overlapping frequencies, a chorus stitched from their own telemetry. Each voice sounded almost human, like the ship was reciting data in tones it had never used before.

"*Daedalus … Daedalus … you followed.*"

Leila clamped her hands over her ears, eyes wide. "Who's on the channel?"

The words repeated, softer this time, layered in impossible harmony. Numbers scrolled backward across the monitors—coordinates, timestamps, the exact launch telemetry of *Prometheus*.

Ethan swallowed hard. "It's Prometheus," he whispered. "It's them."

The sound carried emotion that no machine could simulate—a tremor of recognition, grief, and welcome.

For a moment the entire ship seemed to breathe. The drive coils glowed white, the ion stream frozen mid-burn, as though time itself had taken a step aside to listen.

Mira whispered into the open channel. "Prometheus, this is Daedalus. We copy. We hear you."

The chorus answered not in language but in tone—three ascending notes, one descending—the same rhythm that had once haunted their journey since the first day. The same pattern Sung had called harmony.

Outside the viewport, the golden architecture of the Sun began to fold inward, collapsing into a spiral corridor of light. The *Daedalus* drifted toward it, drawn not by thrust but by resonance.

Inside the command deck, the voices faded into a single line of static. Then, faintly, one last transmission cut through:

"We made it through."

The light brightened until there was no distinction between ship, crew, or star—only motion, only sound, only the certainty that something on the other side was waiting.

The Gate Opens

The Sun's surface split—not an explosion but an unfolding. Where fire should have erupted, light bent instead. A spiral aperture widened across the photosphere, threads of gold unweaving from the corona until they formed a tunnel that reached outward, straight toward *Daedalus*.

Every filament aligned to their vector, turning space itself into invitation.

Mira's voice broke the silence. "All hands—brace for transition."

Harness clasps clicked across the deck. The air thrummed with static, the vibration rising through the hull like the tightening of a string.

Sung's voice came over comm, barely audible through the distortion. "Field pressure rising—one, two—"

The numbers never finished. They dissolved into **music**.

Every display on the bridge blanked, replaced by a single waveform pulsing in perfect rhythm with the ship's heartbeat. The pattern was unmistakable—three tones rising, one falling—the same signature that had haunted their journey, the same harmonic code once captured from *Prometheus*.

Leila gripped the armrest, eyes wide as the entire command deck shimmered. "It's the signal," she whispered.

Ethan's hands hovered above the controls, useless now. "It's the same pattern. It's them."

The hull began to glow, each seam outlining itself in molten light. Beyond the viewport the tunnel expanded, its inner walls rippling with geometric fire. The spectrum stretched past visible range; colors appeared that had no names, and shadows formed where there was no darkness to cast them.

"Drive's offline," Sung reported, his voice breaking with disbelief. "Zero fuel burn, zero inertia—Commander, we're accelerating without thrust."

The hum deepened again until it filled every part of them—the lungs, the teeth, the eyes.

Telemetry went white. Numbers no longer made sense: distance infinite, speed undefined, vectors looping into themselves. The universe outside the glass elongated, stretching like molten glass drawn across the edge of creation.

Mira stared into the spiral. "Hold together," she whispered. "All of you."

Then the tunnel flared, a burst of radiant gold swallowing the ship whole.

For a heartbeat—one long, impossible heartbeat—there was no sound, no mass, no thought.

Only light, and motion, and the echo of a voice that might have been their own:

"*Daedalus, follow.*"

The Corridor

Inside the tunnel, time slowed to **color**.

The ship no longer moved through space in any ordinary sense; it drifted through gradients of gold and white, through rivers of light that seemed to flow without direction. Every surface of *Daedalus* shimmered with motion, as if the hull were being rewritten in every instant.

The crew floated motionless. Their restraints hung loose, irrelevant now. Even breath felt delayed—drawn out between one heartbeat and the next.

Outside, the corridor stretched infinitely ahead and behind. Within it, ghostly outlines appeared—shapes of other vessels, other times. *Prometheus*, faint and shimmering, passed through them like a reflection on rippling water. Then the shadows multiplied: *Daedalus* again and again, layered versions of itself sliding forward and backward in perfect symmetry.

Ethan reached out as one of the phantoms drifted past—his own hand, half a second younger. "Are we... repeating?"

Mira's voice came quietly from the command chair, soft but clear. "We're seeing every moment at once."

The words barely left her mouth before they echoed across the corridor, rippling through each ghost of the ship as if time itself had acknowledged them.

Leila turned slowly, her movements dreamlike. The photograph of her son still floated beside her station, taped to the console. The paper trembled in the golden wind but did not burn. It shimmered as though remembering sunlight.

She whispered, "For everyone still down there."

Mira's eyes stayed on the endless spiral ahead. "Then hold on to the right one," she said—a command and a prayer in the same breath.

Beyond the glass, the walls of the corridor pulsed with rhythm—three rising tones, one falling. The same pattern, the same call, the same answer.

Sung's voice, distant but audible through the intercom: "Instruments are folding—readings from the future overlaying past data. The ship's inside its own transmission."

The light grew brighter, not in intensity but in meaning, until form itself became impossible. Every layer of the *Daedalus*—past, present, and possible—converged into one brilliant reflection.

Mira closed her eyes. "Hold together," she whispered again.

For a moment, the corridor sang.

And then the light began to narrow, drawing them forward toward whatever waited beyond.

Sung's Final Entry
Engineering Log – Dr. Han Sung

Ion clusters disengaged.

Yet thrust continues.

Field temperature constant—exactly thirty-seven degrees Celsius. I think the Gate compensates for life.

He paused, stylus trembling above the polymer sheet. The hum around him was gentle now, almost like breathing. Every surface radiated faint warmth, as though the ship itself were alive and resting.

He glanced at the temperature readout again—unchanged. Human body heat. Nothing in his equations accounted for it.

If that's true, he wrote, *whoever built this understood mercy.*

He stopped recording, letting the pen drift from his fingers. The hum had become music again—three tones rising, one falling—and for the first time it didn't feel alien. It felt like a welcome.

Sung unlatched his harness and floated to the viewport. The light outside had changed—no longer blinding gold but a deep, living amber, threaded with shapes that might have been stars or might have been memories of stars.

Then, from the haze ahead, something emerged: a silhouette forming out of light and motion. The hull gleamed like liquid metal, sleek and gold-lit. Across its side, letters shimmered as if etched into glass:

PROMETHEUS.

For an instant Sung couldn't breathe. The registry pulsed once, catching the same rhythm as *Daedalus'* engines.

He smiled through tears, the first he'd shed since leaving Earth. "We made it," he whispered.

His words echoed softly in the cabin, and for a moment he thought he heard another voice—fainter, layered beneath his own, answering in the same tone.

"Yes. You did."

The light brightened around the viewport, washing over him until he could no longer tell where one ship ended and the other began.

He closed the log. The recorder blinked once, then went still.

Transmission

The bridge was silent except for the faint hiss of background radiation. Every surface glowed in soft gold, the residual light of passage still bleeding from the seams.

Ethan floated to his console, shaking off the dizziness that came with deceleration. "Rerouting all power to communications," he said. His voice sounded distant in his own headset. "Umbra frequency—open."

Circuits clicked. The signal processor whined as it scanned through the electromagnetic storm outside. Static filled the cabin—a familiar sound that suddenly felt ancient, like the hiss of the first radios ever built.

Then something shifted. A pattern within the noise. A faint carrier wave pulsed once, then stabilized.

Leila pressed closer to the console, whispering, "Did it catch?"

Ethan raised a hand for silence. The hum in the static deepened—then broke into fragments of speech.

"... *Daedalus* ... *received* ..."

The crew froze. No one breathed. The sound was distant, thin, but unmistakably human.

The signal cleared another fraction, as if the Gate itself adjusted its harmonics to translate. And then, through the faint distortion, came a voice they all knew from history, from recordings, from hope:

Asha Rao.

Her tone was calm, steady, filled with warmth that crossed more than distance—it crossed *time*.

"Welcome to the light. You're right on time."

No one spoke. The words hung in the air like gravity reborn.

Mira's hand trembled against the console. "Prometheus," she whispered. "We hear you."

The channel flickered, burst once in amplitude, and held steady—one carrier, one heartbeat, a bridge between two impossible ships suspended in the Sun's heart.

For the first time in forty-two days, the *Daedalus* crew allowed themselves to believe they weren't alone.

Emergence

The tunnel widened into open brilliance.

The blinding gold around *Daedalus* softened, the spiral geometry dissolving into a gentle radiance that stretched outward until it became space again—space, but changed.

Ahead lay a starfield unlike any they had ever known. Constellations were rearranged, scattered into new patterns. Some stars glowed in colors no human retina was built to name—indigo burning into copper, violet into living green. Nebulae coiled like auroras frozen in time.

Ethan whispered, "We've cleared the Gate."

Instruments struggled to recalibrate. Readouts blinked and stuttered, failing to decide what "position" meant anymore. The Sun they'd left behind was gone; its light replaced by another, deeper gold that felt older, steadier.

Around them, immense structures drifted—titanic arcs of material reflecting that same light. Some looked like rings, others like fragments of stations or engines the size of continents. Every curve implied intention. Nothing about it was natural.

A silence filled the cabin—part reverence, part disbelief. Even the ship's hum had faded, replaced by the stillness of whatever universe waited beyond.

Then, from the open channel, a faint intake of breath and a single word, quiet and aching.

Mira whispered, "Home?"

A pause. Then another voice came through—rich, calm, unmistakably human.

Gregor Vass.

"Not yet," he said. "But close enough to begin again."

The bridge fell silent. Leila closed her eyes; Ethan stared into the new constellations, seeing in them the outline of every name they had carried.

Sung's recorder blinked green once, logging the coordinates—numbers that didn't yet mean anything, but soon would.

Outside, the arcs of light turned slowly, vast and deliberate, like the machinery of a cosmos long waiting to be remembered.

Mira leaned forward, her reflection caught in the viewport's glow. "Then let's begin."

Epilogue

Daedalus steadied itself, the hull still aglow with the last threads of golden light. The shimmer faded slowly, like embers cooling after a storm.

Every system blinked green across the boards—power levels stable, oxygen at baseline, radiation minimal. The ship had survived the impossible.

Sung's monitors showed the same anomaly across every station: each crew member's heartbeat had synchronized, an unconscious alignment to the same rhythm that pulsed faintly through the ship's hull. No one could explain it, and no one tried.

The bridge felt larger now, the silence filled not with tension but with calm—the weightless calm of arrival.

Priya floated before her console, the soft light of a newborn star reflecting off her face. She keyed her mission log, her voice steady and low.

"Daedalus — Mission Day 42. Transit successful. Prometheus in visual range. We are alive. We are ahead."

Her words lingered in the cabin's air, recorded and echoed in the ship's archive, the first entry from another sun.

Through the viewport, the golden lattice encircling the distant star shimmered like a cathedral built from light. It wasn't fire; it was *structure*—living geometry woven around the new sun, its form radiating warmth that was not heat but recognition.

Priya pressed her palm lightly to the glass. The warmth bled through faintly, the illusion of touch crossing millions of kilometers.

For the first time since leaving Earth, she felt something close to peace—an emotion without a name in any mission protocol.

Not heat.

Not safety.

Belonging.

She turned toward her crew, who were still watching the golden expanse unfold across the viewport.

"Prepare docking sequence," she said softly. "Let's go meet the future."

Outside, *Daedalus* pivoted, its attitude thrusters firing gentle bursts of blue against the endless gold. Ahead, the silhouette of *Prometheus* glowed brighter—waiting.

And between the two ships, across the light of a new sun, humanity's echo finally found its answer.

Chapter 20

The First Light of Others

Out of the Corridor

The last ripples of gold thinned into ordinary starlight.

Daedalus steadied, her hull shedding brightness in gauzy threads. The instruments, stunned for a heartbeat by impossible numbers, reverted to the old, politely human language of velocity, vectors, and thermal margins. Gravity returned by degrees. Breath sounded like breath again.

Beyond the forward viewport: a sky none of them had known. No familiar constellations. The dark was darker, the colors more saturated—as if someone had scrubbed the soot off the universe. At the center hung a star not quite like theirs: smaller, bluer at the edges, encircled by a scaffolding of luminous arcs—geometry laid across the void like the ribs of a cathedral.

Priya drew in air and let it out with care, as if not to startle the scene. "Status."

Mira's hands moved with a pianist's economy. "Attitude control steady. Thermal nominal. Starfield locked."

Ethan leaned toward the glass. "That lattice... it isn't debris. It's aligned—gravitic anchors at regular intervals. It's... built."

"By whom?" Leila asked, voice low.

Sung, still strapped at Propulsion, answered without looking up. "By whoever taught our Sun to remember."

A blip winked five degrees starboard, then grew into a ship gliding in on a vector that matched theirs exactly. Hull: gray-gold, edged in darker plates. Registry letters shimmered as they rolled toward view.

PROMETHEUS.

The bridge went very, very still.

"Open channel," Priya said.

Ethan flicked the switch. The carrier wave rose like a held note.

Static, then a woman's voice, warm with static and something like relief.

"Daedalus, this is Captain Rao. Welcome to the other side."

Laughter spilled around the cabin, not raucous but the kind that comes from a pressure-valve opening at last. Sung let his head thump back against the padding. Mira braced a hand on Priya's shoulder, just briefly, as if to anchor both of them in the same second.

Priya swallowed. "Prometheus, this is Daedalus Actual. We have you visual. Requesting docking guidance."

"Transmit your mass and residual field readings," Rao replied, calm as a harbor pilot. "The lattice is friendly, but she likes her rituals."

Ethan sent the packet. Numbers flushed across two bridges at once; two ships, the sum of a species' refusal to die, adjusted their paths by millimeters until they were the right shape to meet.

The Lattice and the Lantern

They coasted toward the structure like divers approaching a reef. The arcs were not solid in the human sense; they were tensioned light, braided with matter that refused normal spectroscopy. Everywhere, small glints moved along them—repair gnats? drones?—and from certain angles the whole scaffold seemed to hum a visible chord, bars of brightness ringing with the same three-up, one-down cadence that had brought them here.

Leila pressed her palm to the viewport, forgetting the glass, the cold, all of it. "It looks like a lantern hung over a door."

"Or a nervous system," Mira murmured. "Maybe both."

"Docking target acquired," Ethan said. On the HUD, a flower of soft-blue markers blossomed around a circular void at the base of a node. "Relative velocity point two. Guidance accepts us."

"Hands on," Priya said. "No autopilot. We do this like people."

The ship answered to light touch. Thrusters nudged. The void became a tunnel, its rim glimmering with that not-quite-matter; for an instant, the view filled with geometry that made the brain itch. Then grip: a magnetic kiss, the most intimate sound a machine can make with another.

"Hard dock," Mira said, and only then allowed herself to shiver.

Across the connection, Prometheus's signal danced like a heartbeat through the hull.

The Air Between

The transfer tube extended with the slow confidence of a creature uncoiling. Locks rotated. Seals flared green. Pressure equalized with a soft, tidal sigh.

Priya stood at the hatch in a suit that still smelled faintly of coolant and desert dust. The crew gathered behind her—Mira, Ethan, Leila, Sung, Torres, the dozen names the manifest would turn into history.

"Recorders on," Priya said. "If this moment goes anywhere, let it go everywhere."

She palmed the pad. The hatch irised open. Warmth touched her face—actual warmth, not the polite sterility of a ship's recycled breath. Air with a faint taste of metal and citrus, the ghost of hand soap and sweat, the musk of people who'd lived too long with their own fear and made a friend of it.

Boots on hull. A tunnel like a throat, ribbed with conduit. The sound of steps on the far side.

Two silhouettes resolved out of shimmer: Rao—smaller than legend, hair shorter than the last time they'd seen her, eyes the same steady mercury—and Vass, lighter by ten pounds, older by a decade, the gold of the lattice reflected in the silver at his temples. Behind them, faces. Dozens. People they had watched disappear into static, now etched in light.

No speeches. For a long breath and then another, nobody found words.

Rao stepped forward and took Priya's forearm in an old-fashioned grip that predated both of them. "You came," she said, and the simplicity of it nearly knocked Priya over.

"We followed," Priya said. The rest could wait.

Vass's gaze flicked past, finding Sung. "Did the ion clusters sing for you?"

Sung snorted, halfway to a laugh. "They harmonized. I tuned them flat when they started flirting with the Sun."

"Good," Vass said, and for once the word was not approval so much as gratitude.

Leila and Markova collided in a hug that would hurt tomorrow. Names tumbled in overlapping currents. Someone began to cry quietly, and someone else, without comment, put a hand on their back until the breath came easy again.

"Come," Rao said. "There's much you need to see, and less time than we hoped."

The City in the Scaffolding

Prometheus led them straight across a gangway into the lattice itself. It accepted their mass without protest. In the cavity beyond—no longer void, not yet place—a **habitat** had grown like coral around a fragment of forgotten shore.

Ribs of light supported decks and gardens cut from shipboard hydroponics, patched with modules that had once been cargo and were now kitchens, sleeping bays, a room with a piano whose middle register had gone soft with age. Grids of water gleamed, anchored by surface tension and a stubborn human insistence on baths. Children ran along a rim and shot past—two, three—barefoot, feral with laughter; someone whistled sharp, then softer, and they angled back toward a hand that meant safety.

Leila stopped dead. "They have kids."

Rao followed her gaze and nodded. "Not many. A beginning, not a wave." Her eyes flickered toward Vass, and a conversation Priya couldn't yet hear passed between them like a current.

"Food?" Sung asked, practical genius that he was.

Markova swept an arm at the gardens. "Algae to start. Polyculture where we can. The lattice gives energy. We give preference to anything that tastes like memory."

A woman in a grease-streaked jumpsuit offered Priya a mug and a grin that said she'd been sleeping inside solar panels for too long to care what rank anyone wore. The liquid was hot and brown and undeniable. Coffee, of a sort. "We call it Gatebrew," the woman said. "It's terrible."

Priya drank and discovered it was, in fact, terrible and perfect.

The Star They Rode

Through a viewing well cut into the lattice, the new star flared. Seen from here, the architecture resolved into something halfway between mechanism and organism: massive loops anchored to nodes, drawing power along rails of color that were also field lines, lofting and braking invisible cargo with a grace that made orbital mechanics feel like stone tools.

"It isn't a cage," Ethan said, voice hushed despite himself. "It's a harp."

Rao inclined her head. "A resonant instrument. It listens to stellar pulses, then plays them back. The gate is not an on-off. It's a chord."

Vass touched the rail, eyes on the shifting music. "Our Sun had the seed of this. The builders left it there. The Core you reverse-engineered was our key to the key."

"Who were they?" Mira asked.

Rao's mouth went rueful. "Every time we think we've almost learned to pronounce the first syllable, the lattice changes its mind."

"Then what do they want?" Leila asked, lawyer to the marrow. She needed a motive. Intent. Law.

"Continuation," Vass said softly. "It's the only term that fits every datum. When we act in the direction of continuance—of memory carrying forward—everything here yields. When we try to clutch or hoard, it becomes very politely inert."

Leila filed the word without comment. She had written contracts on less.

Prometheus's Dead, Prometheus's Living

Rao didn't try to sell them a miracle. She showed them the memorial first.

A ring of hexagonal plates, each etched with a name, a date, a brief line of the exact truth. **FAILED CONTAINMENT PROBE. STRUCTURAL ERROR—HUMAN. CHOSE TO STAY IN THE CORRIDOR WHEN IT CLOSED.**

Priya read until the lines blurred. At last, she laid a hand on one at random, and felt only cool metal. "We'll add ours when they come," she said.

Rao's voice gentled. "We've been adding births too."

"Continuation," Vass murmured again, and Priya, who had not thought herself prone to prayer, found that the word landed in her chest and stayed.

The First Briefing

They gathered in a chamber that had started life as a cargo hold and was now command by consensus: a table printed from composite, chairs stolen from five different modules, a wall that could be board or window depending on how many people needed reality that hour.

Rao brought up a map of the lattice: a luminous wireframe of arcs and nodes hovering over the table, annotated in both human glyphs and the lattice's own shifting script.

"This is one system of many," she said. "We've seen the echo of others in the corridor—other stars with their own instruments. Think of it as a network of harps strung across the spiral arm."

"How many?" Mira asked.

Rao shook her head. "Enough to make us humble. Not enough to make us small."

"We're not alone," Ethan said.

"No," Vass said. "But we may be the youngest thing here."

"The Sun on our side?" Priya asked, before the ache could eat her question. "How long before it completes the spiral?"

Rao's face tilted. "Your estimates were good. Less than two years now. The gate will open again. If the Arks can fly, they will come."

Priya met Sung's eyes. He nodded once: They can.

Earth Hears

Across space and delay, Earth listened.

In a chilled bunker beneath Nevada, Devin sat with Oshima and a skeleton staff before an array of receivers that had known the rhythm of their dying star like mothers know a child's breath. When the pattern broke—a high note within the three-up, one-down, a flare in the carrier—the room leaned forward as a single organism.

Audio resolved first: hiss, then a voice carried in the teeth of the wave.

"—this is Daedalus. Transit successful. Prometheus in visual range. We are alive. We are ahead."

No one spoke. Oshima set her hands flat on the console and closed her eyes.

More drifted through: a pulse-coded packet compressed to survive storms and skepticism. Leila's cadence rode within it, legal and human.

To the unselected, the unlaunched, the ones who hold our sky: we are still under the same light. When the Sun opens again, follow. We will be waiting with the door held, if the door will be held for anyone.

Devin laughed once, then covered his face with both hands in a gesture that was not quite grief, not quite joy. He whispered into the room's hum, into the star itself, "Bring them through."

The Ion-Tech's Tour

Back in the lattice, Vass waved Sung toward a seemingly blank wall. "I kept this for you."

"What is it?"

"The part of the instrument that speaks machine. I can talk to it with physics, but I suspect it prefers people who sing to engines."

Sung laid fingers against the panel. It warmed under his touch and then offered, shamelessly, the tactile language of a drive: frequency packets, pressure nods, little voltage jokes. He flushed, ridiculous and moved. "It's... friendly."

"It is when you are," Vass said, with the expression of a man who had taken a long time to learn something simple.

Sung's grin cracked a decade off him. "Do we have spare emitters? I want to teach it a lullaby. Twelve-cluster canon. It'll stabilize thrust fluctuations during corridor approach."

Markova groaned. "You're going to sing to the star."

"I've been singing to machines my whole life," Han said. "This one just hums back in key."

Lines Across the Dark

Prometheus and Daedalus hung in patient proximity while the crews braided their lives: systems handoffs, medical exchanges, soil cultures swapped like recipes. Children learned names. Elders shared chairs. The piano found its upper register again when someone printed a spring from lattice matter and tensioned it with a hair pulled from a laughing girl's braid. The note rang truer than any algorithm.

At the window, Priya watched an arc of the lattice flex; somewhere, a force equalized. "How much of this is on purpose?" she asked Rao.

"All of it," Rao said.

"And how much do we understand?"

Rao's smile conceded almost everything. "Enough to behave well."

Leila joined them, a slate of requests tucked under her arm. "We need a charter," she said. "For the lattice, for us, for whoever follows. Call it law or etiquette or promise, but write it down. We can't bring the old codes without breaking them, and we can't have none."

"Draft it," Priya said, too quickly, then gentled the order. "Draft it with them." She nodded toward children streaking past, and the greaser with the Gatebrew, and Markova inventing a word that didn't exist for a color the lattice had just shown her.

Leila's face softened. "All right. A law for a place that hums."

The First Night That Wasn't

Night here was an agreement, not a rotation. The lattice lowered its brightness by a fraction that felt like respect. Someone cut lights. Someone lit a lantern that didn't burn but glowed, set it on the floor, and people sat around it because that is what people do when they pretend a circle will keep the dark from walking in.

Rao told them the story of the first time the gate closed before they were ready and the second time it opened when they had stopped asking. Vass admitted the three mistakes he had made that would have killed them if the lattice hadn't chosen to interpret his error as intention. Markova described a particle like a syllable. Mira, who rarely told stories in public, told one about her grandmother teaching her how to thread a needle in blackout, and for a while the lattice hummed just a degree gentler, as if listening for a moral.

Sung, when his turn came, sang quietly to the drives. Someone else harmonized, and then someone else, and before it turned into something grand he let it fold back into quiet.

Priya watched the circle and felt the absence of a planet like a missing tooth her tongue could not stop finding—and underneath it, a foundational relief that something had caught them. Not a god, not an equation. A structure that had been waiting for them to behave as if they belonged.

She keyed her private log with her thumb, not looking. *We are not saved. We are held long enough to make what we need next. That is better than salvation. That is a task.*

Orders of the Morning

In the hours that the lattice decided were morning, Rao walked Priya to a viewport that looked not inward toward the harp but outward, toward a scatter of points that were not stars. Some moved with intent.

"Others?" Priya asked, pulse stepping up a notch.

"Not yet," Rao said. "Us. Echoes. Each time the gate opens, you can almost see the next arrivals moving through the corridor. They're close enough to cast a shadow and far enough to remain a rumor. Hope behaves like that."

Priya leaned her forehead against the glass. "Three years felt like an insult. Now it feels like a gift I don't know how to spend."

"Then spend it rudely," Rao said. "Make noise. Build badly. Teach everything twice. We need a city here before we need a civilization."

"And Earth?"

"Still singing," Rao said. "Still colder, still brave."

They stood without talking for a time long enough to make two kinds of silence. The lattice hummed three notes up, one down, like a heartbeat you could set a life to.

Part II — *Charter of the Lattice*
Articles of Light

Leila spread her tablets across a section of bulkhead that insisted on being desk-shaped. The ship seemed to have learned all the habit of its inhabitants—edges where none existed, corners that invited thought.

The golden lattice beyond the viewport cast a faint, steady glow through the hull. It wasn't artificial light; it breathed, shifting subtly with the rhythm of the surrounding star. Every surface became illuminated paper.

Her stylus traced faint ripples across the screen, each pulse translating into words. They didn't begin as sentences—more like resonances, vibrations she could almost hear forming language.

She began to write.

1. Every arrival is host and guest.
2. Matter and memory are equal property.
3. Nothing that hums in key is to be silenced.

The stylus paused. She smiled faintly at the third entry. *Sung would like that one*, she thought.

Behind her, footsteps echoed softly—Priya, still in her flight harness, watching from the hatchway. The glow painted half her face gold.

"You're writing scripture," Priya said. Her tone carried no irony, only observation.

Leila shook her head, eyes still on the text. "By lawyers' standards, this is a peace treaty." She glanced upward at the living lattice outside. "By the lattice's, probably a song."

Priya floated closer, resting a hand on the edge of the wall that had become Leila's desk. "Make it something the next fools can argue about," she said, the faintest hint of a smile touching her voice. "Arguing keeps us human."

Leila saved the document. The characters pulsed once, as if the wall itself acknowledged them. The words glowed brighter than the rest of the light around them, refracting briefly into gold and fading.

Outside, the lattice shifted in slow rhythm—almost like a nod.

And within the hum of the ship, somewhere deep in its architecture, a faint melody responded: three tones rising, one falling.

Harmonics Lab – Deck 7

The hum of the *Daedalus* was softer now—a low, even tone that vibrated more like breath than machinery.

Dr. Han Sung stood waist-deep in the drive chamber, surrounded by cables that hung like living vines. Condensation drifted in the air, refracting the soft amber light of the Gate beyond the hull. Around him, a dozen miniature harmonic emitters floated in suspension, each glowing faintly out of sync with the others.

He leaned over the console and began to tune them by hand. One by one, he adjusted amplitude and phase until the mismatched pulses fell into pattern—twelve lights beating in rhythm. The ship's heartbeat.

He smiled. "Cluster canon test," he said into the recorder. "Begin lullaby."

Then, almost shyly, he hummed the base note. The sound was low, human, imperfect—and the coils answered.

Vibration became sound.

Sound became light.

Light became stillness.

The entire deck seemed to exhale. The faint tremor in the hull subsided. Instruments steadied. Even the recycled air felt cleaner.

Sung checked the diagnostics. "Drive temperature dropping," he murmured. "Three degrees and falling."

He didn't need to look up to know someone had entered; the air shifted.

Gregor Vass stepped through the hatch, carrying two mugs that steamed faintly blue under the lab lights. "Gatebrew," he said. "The closest thing this system has to coffee."

Sung took one with a nod. "You're courting an alien instrument with lullabies," Vass observed, watching the synchronized emitters float in perfect formation.

Sung's eyes stayed on the lights. "It's working."

The readouts agreed—frequency variance zero, vibration curve flattened to a straight line. Outside the viewport, one of the golden arcs of the lattice flickered once, then steadied, as if acknowledging the harmony.

Vass raised his mug. "To sympathetic resonance."

Sung clinked his against it, took a cautious sip, and grimaced. "To terrible coffee and good physics."

They both laughed, the sound small but real in the vast, humming chamber.

Outside, the lattice's nearest arc shimmered again—three tones rising, one falling—and the two men fell briefly silent, listening to what might have been the universe approving of their joke.

Mapping the Orbit

Days blurred into one long equation. Ethan and Mira spent them bent over star maps that no longer obeyed astronomy, their consoles awash in gold and white as the new sun pulsed through the viewport.

They were trying to park two ships that had no business in this sky. The lattice produced gravitational wells like punctuation marks—sharp pauses in the fabric of space. Between each mark lay corridors of relative calm, but those lanes shifted like tides. To anchor a vessel without tearing its hull apart required patience bordering on faith.

"Node E-7 stabilizes every thirty hours," Mira said, tracing the coordinates onto the translucent nav board. "We can anchor *Daedalus* there; *Prometheus* holds at D-4. The arcs between give us a corridor for shuttle traffic."

Ethan adjusted the overlay, aligning their vectors against the lattice's rhythm. The arcs outside the viewport flared faintly, as if responding to their attention. "And if the Gate opens again?" he asked.

Mira leaned back, her eyes still on the golden geometry beyond. "Then we have a welcoming committee instead of a collision."

They both smiled—small, tired, genuine.

Around them, the bridge was quiet except for the soft clicks of recalibration. Every few minutes the deck lights dimmed as the ship's sensors synchronized with the lattice's pulse. The new physics required new patience: time measured not in seconds but in harmonics.

"Cross-check the vector again," Mira said. Ethan already was. They logged coordinates, compared with *Prometheus* telemetry, and confirmed by hand what the computers could only estimate. The numbers felt fragile, yet grounding—something human to hold in a place where constants no longer stayed constant.

Ethan exhaled slowly. "You ever think we're just... guessing beautifully?"

Mira smiled without looking up. "Guessing's how faith begins."

They finished the log together, hands steady on the controls. In the silence that followed, the only sound was the faint pulse of the lattice through the hull—steady, mathematical, alive.

The discipline of calculation felt like prayer:

Repeat the formula.

Breathe.

Trust the constants, even when everything else has rewritten itself.

Earth at Perihelion – Umbra Command

The Nevada bunker groaned beneath frost thick enough to seal its outer doors shut. The world above was dim steel—no dawn, no true night, only the gray hum of a star that no longer burned but murmured.

Solar output had dropped another percent that week. On the long-range monitors, the aurora had shifted from emerald to a washed-out blue that shimmered like ice over metal. Even the sky had gone colorblind.

Inside, Devin Rao stood before the main trajectory wall. The map was a tapestry of ghost lines—paths of ships that hadn't launched yet and those already gone, each marked in a different shade of fading light.

"Odyssey's hull integrity at eighty percent," he said, voice steady despite the fatigue roughening its edges. "*Erebus* at sixty. If we don't launch within four months, we lose Window B entirely."

Across the control room, Oshima didn't look up from her screen. Her face was drawn, illuminated by the flickering monitors, but her hands never stopped moving across the console. "Then we don't lose it," she said flatly. "We launch half-finished and patch on the climb."

Devin turned toward her, anger slipping past discipline. "People will die."

Her reply came without hesitation. "People are dying now."

The hum of the bunker filled the silence that followed—the slow pulse of life-support fans and the creak of freezing metal. Somewhere deeper underground, another generator came online with a hollow clang.

Finally, Oshima turned. Her eyes were hollow from weeks without rest, but they carried something that had outlasted exhaustion: a kind of hard, luminous faith. "They sent us proof of arrival," she said quietly. "That means the corridor works. That means it matters whether we reach it limping or not at all."

On the main display, the last recorded transmission from *Daedalus* replayed in looping fragments:

Prometheus in visual range. We are alive. We are ahead.

Devin watched it until the light blurred. Behind his eyelids he saw it again—the golden spiral forming in the Sun's heart, the moment *Daedalus* vanished into radiance. He could still remember the shape of that light bending inward, like the star itself had drawn breath to sing.

He opened his eyes. "Then we build faster," he said.

Oshima nodded once. "And pray the Sun keeps waiting."

The monitors flickered under the bunker's recycled glow. Outside, wind swept dry snow across the frozen desert, whispering over the launch cradles of ships still dreaming of flight.

Gate Weather

Back at the lattice, the harp began to change tempo.

That was what the crew had come to call it—the constant harmonic undercurrent that threaded through every hull plate and circuit, the song of the lattice itself. At first it had been steady, predictable as heartbeat. Now its rhythm wavered, accelerating, slowing, pulsing in long waves that rattled equipment and loosened tools from their clips.

The sunlight—or what passed for it—shifted between hues of silver and honey, washing across the observation ports in alternating pulses.

The arcs that framed the new system responded in kind, their resonances deepening until fine dust lifted off every surface and spun into tiny spirals, weightless tornadoes of gold.

Inside the *Daedalus* command deck, Asha Rao gathered both crews—hers from *Prometheus*, Mira's from *Daedalus*—in the shared operations bay. The two ships were docked together now, their decks connected by a corridor of translucent alloy that glowed faintly with each vibration.

Rao's expression was composed, though the pulse of light flickering across her uniform made her seem part of the phenomenon she was describing. "The lattice is preparing," she said, voice amplified over comm. "We're reading harmonic compression across the inner arcs. The Gate will open again—sooner than schedule."

Ethan looked up from his console. "Define 'sooner.'"

Rao's answer came without hesitation. "Hours, not weeks. And when it does, anything within fifty thousand kilometers could be pulled along."

Silence. The kind that only comes when every person in a room is imagining the same thing—ships, tools, debris, all drawn into the light like filings to a magnet.

Priya crossed her arms. "Meaning?"

Rao met her gaze evenly. "Meaning we either secure orbit now or we ride wherever it goes next."

For a moment the only sound was the deep, rolling hum vibrating through the deck. The light through the viewport shimmered again—silver to gold, then to something in between.

Vass broke the tension with a crooked grin, the expression of a man who had once built the impossible and seemed ready to do it again. "Then let's learn how to anchor music."

Laughter rippled through the crews—thin, strained, but genuine. The kind that reminded them they were still human.

Sung adjusted the frequency controls, eyes on the lattice readouts. "I'll start with the lower register," he said. "Let's see what key keeps the universe from taking us with it."

Outside, the arcs trembled again—three tones rising, one falling—and dust spiraled upward as though the Gate itself were listening.

Leila's Hearing

It was the first formal meeting in space that required minutes.

Leila Vaziri had insisted on the formality—attendance roll, recorded agenda, order of speaking. Even in orbit around a foreign sun, the law demanded its ritual. "If we're going to build a civilization," she'd said, "we start with minutes."

Twelve representatives floated in the *Daedalus'* central wardroom—two from each vessel, one from the lattice maintenance teams, and one proxy seat reserved for Earth transmissions, though none had arrived in months. The empty chair remained tethered to the table all the same, its harness clipped and waiting.

Leila anchored her tablet to the bulkhead and began reading aloud the draft Charter. Her voice was calm, practiced, carrying the cadence of courtroom precision. Yet as each clause left her lips, the lattice responded.

The text translated itself into light. Lines of gold and silver script unfurled from her tablet and wove through the air like ribbons of liquid glass. Each clause shimmered briefly, then folded itself into the structure of the surrounding arcs. When the lattice accepted a line, the color stabilized; when it questioned, it pulsed uncertainly, waiting for revision.

Clause by clause, the living architecture of the Charter took form around them.

Clause One: Every arrival is host and guest.

Clause Two: Matter and memory are equal property.

Clause Three: Nothing that hums in key is to be silenced.

At that final phrase, a pulse surged through the decks—gentle but strong enough to rattle utensils in the mess three compartments away. Cups drifted from their clamps, vibrating softly in harmony.

For a breathless second, everyone froze. Then laughter rippled through the room.

Sung raised an eyebrow, still smiling. "Ratified by resonance," he said. "That's a quorum."

Even Leila laughed, marking the notation with a precise flick of her stylus: *Clause Three – Approved by acoustic confirmation.*

The light ribboned once more, brighter this time, and the lattice sealed the entry with a soft tone—three notes rising, one falling. The familiar pattern filled the chamber like applause.

Leila looked up at the glow around them and whispered, half to herself, "The universe just learned how to keep minutes."

Outside the viewport, the golden arcs shifted in slow rhythm, as if acknowledging the birth of law beneath their light.

The Signal of Home

It began as a flicker—one brief tremor across the comm bands that everyone assumed was lattice interference. Then the waveform repeated: slow, irregular, unmistakably human.

Ethan leaned over the console, fine-tuning the filters. "We've got a new carrier," he murmured. "Pattern's terrestrial, old Umbra encoding."

The bridge fell silent. Static crackled through the channel—dry, ancient, like wind through snow. He boosted the gain, adjusted the delay compensator, and suddenly the noise shaped itself into words.

"Odyssey preparing for launch. Temperature: minus forty at pad. Tell them the Sun's still singing."

Devin's voice. Raw, frayed, but alive.

For a moment no one moved. Then the silence broke—gasps, laughter, cheers echoing through both vessels. *Prometheus* confirmed receipt; *Daedalus* recorded the transmission automatically, the file tagged with a single word in the archive: *Earth.*

Mira exhaled, eyes glistening. "They made it," she whispered. "They're still building."

Leila drifted toward her console. The Charter document still hovered in its golden projection, the last ratified clause pulsing gently. She opened a new line at the top, fingers steady despite the tremor in her voice.

The lattice recognizes the persistence of origin. The song continues below.

The words glowed for a heartbeat, then dissolved into the structure of light around them—folded into the Charter itself. Outside the viewport, the lattice brightened briefly, sending a single harmonic pulse through both ships: three rising tones, one falling.

Sung smiled. "They heard us back."

Somewhere beyond the Gate, the universe hummed in answer. And within that resonance—between a frozen desert bunker and a star reborn—humanity found its echo again.

Lessons of Gravity

The schoolroom was improvised from a cargo bay—one wall still marked with *Prometheus* registry numbers, the other open to a viewport that framed the golden lattice like a moving constellation.

Mira floated in the center, her hair drifting with the ventilation currents, a small marble glinting in one hand and a bowl of water suspended in the other. Around her, a dozen children watched from restraint frames, some physical, some projected—faces that drawn from the ship's future, a lesson meant as much for the adults observing as for the children who would one day exist.

She held the marble over the bowl. "This is what keeps us where we are," she said, her voice calm, teacher's cadence returning like an old song. "Everything falls. But in space, we fall so perfectly that the ground never catches us."

She released the marble. It struck the water, sending a perfect ripple outward before sinking to the center. "That's an orbit," she said. "Falling forever, but never landing."

A boy with hair like copper sparks raised his hand—an unnecessary gesture in zero-G, but one Mira adored. "What happens," he asked, "when there's nothing left to fall toward?"

Mira hesitated. Through the viewport, the arcs of the lattice curved in slow, luminous motion—geometry without an end. The question hung there like gravity itself.

Then she smiled. "Then," she said softly, "we build something worth orbiting."

The children murmured, the phrase passing between them in awe. One of the smaller girls repeated it under her breath as if testing the shape of the words.

Behind Mira, sunlight—or whatever this new star's light was—washed through the viewport, scattering golden reflections across their faces. The marble in the bowl continued to spin, tracing a perfect, endless circle.

And in that quiet moment, surrounded by children who would never know what gravity *felt* like, humanity relearned what it meant to stay.

The Third Note

In the Harmonics Lab, the lullaby had grown.

Dr. Han Sung adjusted the emitter array, fingers hovering over holographic sliders like a conductor poised above an unseen orchestra. The lullaby that once soothed the drives now carried a second voice—a countermelody sampled from the lattice itself, recorded during the last Gate pulse.

When he blended the two, the tones met halfway between sound and light. The result wasn't heard so much as *felt*: a vibration that threaded through the walls, through muscle and bone, through the very air.

The combined harmonic manifested as a faint aurora drifting inside the habitat—soft curtains of pale gold that rippled from bulkhead to bulkhead. Every piece of metal shimmered as if breathing; even the condensation on the pipes glowed, scattering light in slow, fluid waves.

Sung watched his instruments in wonder. "Amplitude steady," he murmured. "Frequency lock achieved."

The hum deepened, resolving into three pure notes rising, and one descending—the familiar signature of the Gate itself, now joined to theirs. The ship and the lattice were no longer two separate voices; they had become a duet.

Priya stood beneath the aurora, her eyes half-closed. "It feels alive."

Sung didn't look away from the oscillograph. "It's listening."

"Then what is it hearing?"

He raised his gaze to the viewport. The golden arcs outside glowed in gentle response, their rhythm synchronized perfectly to the lullaby. He smiled—tired, proud, and awed.

"Us," he said softly. "Deciding we belong."

The light inside the chamber pulsed once, a soft acknowledgment, before fading back into calm. For a few heartbeats more, the echo lingered— a quiet proof that the universe had not only heard them but understood.

Odyssey Launch – Earth

The desert burned blue with plasma and cold.

Wind clawed across the launch basin, driving snow in spirals that looked like smoke from another age. The *Odyssey* rose through it—wrapped in its own light, a column of silver and flame cutting through the iron sky.

Above the pad, the Umbra grids flared one final time, redirecting what little power the dying Sun still offered. The feed lines glowed white-hot, then dimmed as they poured the last stable energy of a collapsing world into one more miracle.

In the Nevada bunker, everything shook. Frost cracked along the observation window as Devin Rao leaned forward, squinting through the glare. "Telemetry holding," he said into the comm, voice hoarse but steady. "Umbra sync complete. She's climbing."

Oshima stood beside him, silent, headset pressed to her ear, listening to the flight controllers calling off the numbers—altitude, vector, containment. For a moment it almost felt like the old days, before the sky had turned pale and faith had become arithmetic.

Then Devin's final report came through, caught in the recorder before the static swallowed it:

"Window B achieved. *Odyssey* ascends. If corridor parameters match the *Daedalus* event, we'll reach you in ninety-two days. Keep the door open."

Oshima closed her eyes. "Godspeed, *Odyssey*."

The signal wavered, rising in pitch as the ion field distorted under pressure. Then it broke apart—static rushing through the speakers like ocean surf. Only after a moment did they both realize the rhythm wasn't random.

It sounded like applause.

The interference rolled across the speakers in uneven waves.

Outside, the launch light faded into the blizzard, leaving only the echo of blue fire across the frozen desert.

Afterglow

At the lattice, the arcs brightened one by one—soft pulses rippling outward like breath through glass. Each node responded to something distant, invisible, a whisper from the fading Sun across the void between systems. The light was no longer constant; it shimmered in slow waves, as though the lattice itself had begun to remember where it came from.

Across both ships, alarms chimed—not warning tones, but harmonics. The frequency was familiar: Umbra's transmission band. *Prometheus* and *Daedalus* rotated in tandem, aligning themselves by instinct, their drives warming in sympathetic rhythm.

On the bridge, Asha Rao leaned forward, voice barely more than breath. "They're coming."

Her words carried across the shared comm net, touching every deck.

Leila, stationed in the Archive Chamber, reached for the Charter file. The document pulsed faint gold, its clauses still woven into the lattice's living light. She saved it again—three redundancies, three separate nodes—because habit was the last defense against awe.

In Command, Priya gave the order. "All external lights to full burn."

From a distance, both vessels flared white against the golden web, twin suns igniting in welcome. The lattice responded instantly: the nearest arc flexed and released a deep harmonic tone that trembled through the ships' hulls.

In Engineering, Sung felt the vibration first. He smiled and adjusted the drive tuning. The engines answered with the chord he had taught them—the welcoming triad, the lullaby turned beacon. Three rising notes, one descending.

Outside, the Gate began to open again. Not a violent rift, but a widening, patient motion—as if the universe itself were taking a breath. The aperture formed slowly, edges folding back like petals of living light. The geometry deepened into gold and shadow, a spiral mouth inhaling starlight.

Through the haze, a spark appeared. Faint. Blue.

It grew brighter with every pulse until it was unmistakable: plasma trail, slow and steady, the heartbeat of ion drives pushing against eternity.

Ethan's voice broke over the comm, thick with disbelief. "Contact— single vessel, Umbra signature. It's *Odyssey*."

Silence followed, the kind that could only exist between heartbeats stretched across light-years.

The spark kept coming, steady against the dark.

Continuation

Priya sat alone in the command deck, the ship drifting in quiet harmony with the lattice. Outside, the arcs glowed softly—no longer blinding, but pulsing with a warmth that felt almost domestic. It was as though the vast machine had learned gentleness.

She opened a new log. Her reflection floated in the screen's dim light, gold woven through the edges of her hair. The console's hum was low, constant, a sound that had long ago replaced the idea of silence.

She began to speak, her voice steady, measured by ritual more than report.

"Mission Day 403. The corridor sings again. We hold position. Prometheus and Daedalus ready to guide Odyssey through. The Charter ratified. Children asleep. The hum steady at human frequency. We are, against probability and definition, alive."

For a moment she sat still, listening to her own words fade into the hum. The recorder light blinked once, then filed the entry into the archive beside thousands before it—the unbroken thread of a civilization refusing to go silent.

Priya closed the log and turned toward the viewport. Beyond the glass, the lattice shimmered and shifted, alive with slow color. The pattern was unmistakable—three tones rising, one falling—the rhythm that had carried them from the edge of extinction to the threshold of beginning.

She smiled. The gesture was small, almost private. "Welcome home," she whispered.

And somewhere in the luminous harp of the lattice, the universe answered in kind—a soft harmonic that vibrated through the hull, through bone, through the steady pulse of human hearts aligned with something far older than themselves.

Outside, the light held steady.

Inside, the song continued.

Chapter 21

The Weight of the World

The world had grown quiet again, but it was not the quiet of peace. It was the stillness that comes after too many endings.

Nine months since the Prometheus fleet slipped into the Aether Corridor, the skies above Earth were dim and bruised, a perpetual dusk in which even noon looked like evening. The Umbra network still pulsed faintly across the stratosphere, its magnetic veils shimmering like tired auroras, holding back the worst of the solar winds. But every month another node went dark, and no one could say how long the shield would hold.

Beneath the Alps, the surviving United Nations sat inside a dome that smelled of recycled air and nervous sweat. Ministers and envoys wore layers beneath their suits, breathing through scarves when the generators faltered. On the wall behind the dais hung the faded emblem of the planet—a circle now crossed by a diagonal scar, the mark of the Long Cold.

"Eos is real," said Minister Saito of the Pacific Coalition. His voice was hoarse from the night. "We have confirmation of the transmission. The Prometheus made it through. The corridor is stable."

A thousand screens flickered on cue: a blurred image from deep space, the faint outline of a planet with blue haze around its rim. Gasps filled the chamber. The image was little more than pixels and hope, yet it traveled through every surviving relay on Earth like a pulse in a dying body.

Then the arguments began.

"They took only four thousand," barked Chairwoman Nguyen of Europa. "Four thousand! We had entire continents begging for passage."

"And you were the ones who decided that number," someone shouted.

Voices collided, heat rising in a room that could barely keep itself warm. What began as gratitude for survival turned to accusation. For every child sleeping under the remaining domes, a thousand more had perished in the dark.

Saito stood again, quieter this time. "We can't change the past. What matters is the future. We know now the resonance can hold. We must build again—larger, stronger, together."

"Together?" Nguyen's laugh was brittle. "Half the world froze while the other half hid under Umbra fields. The Pacific still glows from reactor spills. 'Together' is a dead word."

Around the table, aides whispered figures: food reserves, population estimates, viable launch sites. The numbers told a single story—humanity was shrinking faster than it could plan.

Outside the dome, the city of Geneva lay under ice crusts. Whole avenues had been abandoned, their windows webbed with frost. The lake had frozen solid; the old fountain was buried beneath meters of snow. Refugees lived in the subway tunnels, burning plastic and memories.

From the south, reports arrived of riots in Nairobi, São Paulo, Dhaka—people chanting the same phrase in every language: *Build bigger ships.*

Broadcast drones hovered over the crowds, catching faces lit by torches. "Why them?" a woman screamed into a camera. "Why them and not us?" Her breath turned to vapor that drifted upward like a prayer.

A recording of Leila Vaziri played on the dome's main screen, her office lit by emergency lamps. Her hair had gone silver at the edges since the exodus. Once she had argued for fair selection tribunals; now she drafted decrees for rations and evacuation quotas that would never be met. Beside her desk lay a folder marked **CONTINUITY CHARTER**.

She recorded her notes aloud, voice steady despite the tremor in her hands. "Article One: No vessel shall be constructed for the preservation of a class, nation, or creed. Article Two: The stars belong to all of humankind, or to none."

The intercom chimed—the recorded voice of Dr. Priya Narayanan from the Umbra relay in orbit.

"We've lost two Umbra lines over the Pacific. Power reroute in progress. If we don't stabilize within seventy-two hours, equatorial drift could unravel the grid."

Leila closed her eyes. "How many are still working the nodes?"

"Maybe six thousand worldwide. We're training anyone who can read a schematic."

Through the static she could hear shouting, the kind that came from a control deck when something started to go very wrong. Priya's voice dropped. "If Umbra fails before we finish the new cores, Earth won't make it to spring."

On the screen, Leila opened the shutters of her orbital quarters. Outside, dawn was a dull smear over the frozen curve of Earth below. She looked toward the faint star of Eos, its light still nine months from home, and whispered into the recorder, "Then we have to finish faster."

Across the Atlantic shelf, in a cavern drilled beneath what had once been the Bay of Biscay, floodlights glared over the skeleton of a structure the size of a mountain. Here the air was warmer, engines humming in caverns of steel.

On a projection wall, archival footage of Gregor Vass flickered—the old architect standing on a gantry, coat zipped to his throat, eyes reflecting the glow of the first Aether-2 Core.
It hung behind him like a ringed moon suspended by cranes, a lattice of silver coils and superconducting veins. The engineers around the playback called it *the heart of a new species.*

They replayed his briefing daily; to them he remained their architect, still alive in the light he'd built.
In the recording, his hands trembled as he touched the rail. "You'll carry more of us than Prometheus ever could," he told the machine, voice rough with age. "Millions, maybe. Whole cities under a single pulse."

His assistant appeared in the grainy footage—a young physicist named Kaito, carrying a datapad through the haze of welding sparks.

"The design exceeds the corridor's proven limit," Kaito said, his younger voice thin in the echo of metal. "The lattice could collapse."

Vass turned toward him, every movement deliberate, weary but sure.

"Then we learn to widen the corridor," he replied. "We've already crossed the threshold of impossible. All that's left is scale."

The recording froze there for a moment, Vass's profile framed against the pale arc of the Aether Core. Someone in the present-day control room exhaled, a sound like reverence.

"He always made it sound simple," one of the engineers murmured.

No one corrected her. In that frozen image of the old man and his impossible machine, the builders saw their own reflection—still learning to widen the corridor.

On the adjacent wall, the recording continued: holograms of proposed vessels rotated in the air behind Vass—structures kilometers long, some shaped like spiraling cathedrals, others like vast rings designed to mimic gravity. Each design bore the same emblem at its bow: a circle split by a diagonal scar.

In the playback, Vass's voice softened to a whisper. "Continuum," he said. "That's what we'll call them."

The lights in the present-day bay dimmed as the engineers stared at the frozen image—Vass's hand raised toward the ghostly holograms, a prophet captured in light. One of the younger builders murmured, "He named them before he ever saw them fly."

Another answered quietly, "Maybe that's what faith looks like."

Far above, satellites blinked out one by one as the magnetic storms intensified. Communications with Eos became intermittent, but one final burst made it through—a packet of compressed images: faces of the *Prometheus* crew smiling before a copper-colored sky, a banner reading *We made it.*

The world stopped for a day to watch. Even in the darkest shelters, people gathered around screens. Children reached out to touch the light.

For a heartbeat, humanity remembered itself.

Then the feeds went dead again.

In the Arctic research ring, Mira's recorded lectures still played on automated channels, teaching resonance theory to whomever might survive to listen. Ethan's notes on ion harmonics were now the foundation for the Aether-2 drive designs. They were instructions left behind for people they would never know.

At night, those still awake on the planet could see faint glows on the horizon—construction sites lighting up the frozen world like embers refusing to die.

Oshima stood on a platform above the Mediterranean ice and watched one such glow to the west. She imagined the sound of welding torches, the rhythm of hammering, the chorus of human stubbornness. In that rhythm she heard an answer to despair.

The Geneva Dome trembled as the generators shifted power, casting the chamber into brief darkness. When the lights returned, the delegates were still arguing—voices sharp, thin from hunger. Every conversation on Earth now began and ended with the same question: *Who will be saved next?*

The chamber lights dimmed as a live feed of Leila Vaziri appeared above the dais, flanked by aides. The murmurs dimmed; even cynics still respected her calm. She laid a folder on the table. Its cover bore the faint seal of the World Assembly, edges worn from her gloves.

"This," she said, "is the Continuity Charter. Not a wish list, not a dream—law. We build for all, or we stop pretending to build at all."

Her words cut through the air like a clean blade. Some heads bowed, others turned away.

Nguyen folded her arms. "You want to legislate morality? We can barely keep the lights on."

"Then legislate survival," Leila said. "The next generation of Arks can't carry a few thousand while billions starve in the dark. The Prometheus was proof of concept. The next fleet must be proof of conscience."

At the end of the table, Minister Saito adjusted his glasses. "Our shipyards are in ruin. We don't have the resources."

"Not alone," she said. "But together, we can still build orbital rings large enough to sustain a million souls apiece. The Aether-2 cores are scalable. Gregor Vass has the models."

Nguyen laughed bitterly. "Vass is half-mad. His last design collapsed the test bay in Marseille."

"Because you cut his power," Leila said. "Not because he was wrong."

For a moment, even the hum of the filters seemed to pause. Then, slowly, the tension cracked into motion—committees forming, alliances whispered, a new language of possibility creeping into the void where hope had been buried.

The broadcast spread across the world within hours: a call for *continuum-scale vessels*—ships not to escape Earth, but to extend it. Recruitment stations opened in surviving cities, guarded by drones and soldiers. Engineers lined up with miners, teachers with medics. They carried no illusions of safety, only the need to do something that mattered before the world froze completely.

In footage from the Nairobi hangar, Dr. Priya Narayanan watched a crowd of volunteers pass through decontamination gates. She stood beside Devin Rao, both still in Umbra command insignia faded with soot.

"They're not builders," he said softly. "They're refugees."

"They're the same thing now," she replied.

He looked out at the endless queue. "If the Umbra grid fails, none of this will matter."

Priya smiled, though it didn't reach her eyes. "Then we make sure it doesn't. One more month. Maybe two."

"After that?"

"After that, we let the stars hold what we can't."

Under the Atlantic shelf, Vass's ring lit the sea from below like a sunrise trapped beneath the ice. Dozens of cargo submarines ferried materials through labyrinthine tunnels, their navigation lights threading through the darkness like veins of fire.

In the control chamber above the site, technicians replayed a recent recording of Gregor Vass.

On the screen, he stood in the same observation bay they now occupied, coat zipped to his throat, eyes reflecting the glow of the first Aether-2 Core.

"The council approved your proposal. You'll lead Continuum construction," a younger voice—Kaito's—said from the playback.

Vass turned toward the sound, calm and unshaken.

"Approved, or accepted as desperation?"

"Does it matter?"

He exhaled, frost rising from his breath.

"No. Not anymore."

Behind him in the holographic projection, Continuum One shimmered—a ring nine kilometers wide with eight rotating arms, each designed to simulate gravity and atmosphere. It could hold three million lives in perpetual orbit. It was also impossible by every measure known to engineering.

Vass raised a hand toward the image, his fingers trembling with both age and reverence.

"The first ark carried our best," he said. "This one will carry all the rest."

The playback froze there, the old architect's silhouette suspended in light while the present-day builders stared upward, still trying to match his vision.

As months crawled on, the planet grew paler. Crops failed in the southern latitudes; seas crusted over near the equator. Power grids flickered, entire cities evacuating to geothermal shelters. Yet in orbit, lights returned— tiny sparks over the dark horizon.

The first segments of the Continuum ring were being lifted into low orbit by fusion tethers and magnetic catapults. Humanity had begun to climb the ladder again.

In the global feeds, commentators argued about direction. "Eos is proven habitable," one anchor said. "Why risk other destinations?" "Because dependence is death," answered another. "If Eos fails, so does humanity. Diversify the species."

Soon every surviving government chose a flag and a dream.

The Pacific Coalition petitioned for a second fleet to follow Prometheus to Eos—a *Reunion Mission*. The Europa Bloc proposed exploring a nearer red dwarf, *Aurion*, to test the extended resonance fields. The Americas wanted to locate the lost *Helios* Ark, whose beacon still pulsed faintly in deep-space telemetry. And a new consortium—scientists, private syndicates, and refugees calling themselves the Aether Collective—declared they would push even farther, aiming for a corridor hundreds of light-years long.

It was not unity, but it was momentum.

Minister Saito called it what it truly was: *divergence as survival.*

In a buried command center, a recording of Leila Vaziri played for the first generation of Continuum settlers. The power hummed unevenly behind her, throwing shadows across her face.

"If you are hearing this, then you carry more than our blood—you carry our intention. We built you a horizon, not a home. The stars are divided among you, but not your duty. Wherever you go, remember: humanity was never meant to be singular. We are meant to echo."

Her voice would travel with every departing ship, archived in their core systems as the **Continuity Pledge**.

Outside, snow fell over the domes, covering wreckage and roads alike. The world slept beneath a thin layer of silence, dreaming of stars.

By the time the second Aether Core ignited its first field test, the last Umbra node over the Pacific winked out. The auroras that once shimmered across the night sky vanished, replaced by a dull, iron gray. People gathered on rooftops and stared upward, waiting for light that did not come.

Then, faintly, they saw it—the reflection of the orbital yard, glowing through the upper atmosphere like a halo. The ring was growing, segment by segment, tracing the curve of the planet. In its expanding circle, they imagined a promise: that something vast and human was still possible.

The sea ice cracked that spring, though no one called it spring anymore. It was simply the season when the wind changed direction. Over the Atlantic, clouds shifted like gray continents, reflecting the light of the new orbital ring that encircled the sky. People began to call it *the Halo*, though its real name—*Continuum One*—was stenciled across its central hub in block letters visible from orbit.

From the surface it looked like a faint, perfect arc at dawn, a luminous vein etched against the darkness. Children pointed at it through the frost, asking if the stars were coming closer.

In the underground shipyards, welders worked in shifts so long that time ceased to matter. Their voices echoed against the hull, songs rising through the corridors of an unfinished world. On a massive projection along the assembly wall, a recording of Gregor Vass played—his figure half-lit, eyes fixed on the schematics of the Aether-2 core.

"You're the bridge, not the escape," the old architect said.

The workers often answered him as if he could hear. On the feed, Kaito appeared beside him, carrying a tablet.

"The first rotation tests begin tomorrow," Kaito reported. "Artificial gravity ring should reach one G by nightfall."

"Good," Vass replied. "Make sure the lights are visible from below. Let them see we're still building."

The clip ended, but his words lingered in the cavern like an instruction and a blessing. The welders turned back to their torches, and the song resumed.

In Geneva, the Assembly gathered one last time. The hall was thinner now—half its seats empty, names carved into the desk plates of the missing. The few remaining delegates watched the main screen as Leila Vaziri's image shimmered into view, transmitting from the orbital ring high above the clouds.

"The Four Destinies," she announced, her voice calm, measured. "Eos. Aurion. Helios. And the Outer Corridor. Four directions, four chances. Each fleet will carry a segment of the Continuum Code, each will inherit the Charter. And if even one survives, humanity endures."

A low murmur swept through the chamber—agreement, fear, awe.

Nguyen leaned forward. "And if none survive?"

Leila smiled faintly. "Then at least the universe will have known we tried."

The session adjourned in silence. Outside, the snow continued to fall— ash-white, slow, endless. Somewhere in that hush, hope began to sound like an echo.

Months later, Devin stood alone on the command deck of the Umbra relay overlooking the Pacific ruins, watching a real-time relay of Priya Narayanan aboard the Daedalus. Devin adjusted the console, the cold light tracing the lines under his eyes.

For a moment his gaze caught the old mission plaque still bolted to the wall — *Prometheus Flight One, Commander Asha Rao.*

His sister's name had dulled beneath frost, but the metal held.

He brushed it once with his glove before turning back to the monitors.

"Power's holding," he said quietly. "She's out there keeping it that way."

The network was gone; the skies were darker, colder. Yet overhead, the Halo glowed brighter every night. Devin adjusted the telescope and caught sight of a cluster of lights detaching from the ring.

"Look," he said quietly. "They're moving."

Dozens of smaller craft drifted from Continuum One, engines flaring blue as they descended to gather materials, people, and memories. The air hummed faintly, as though the world itself was exhaling after too long holding its breath.

Priya lowered her hood and closed her eyes. "They'll call this the Second Exodus."

"Will it work?"

She opened her eyes again. The ring reflected in her pupils like a crown. "It must. There's nowhere left to fall."

As the year waned, Earth's rotation slowed fractionally from crustal shifts. Days lengthened by seconds that no one counted anymore. The old calendars were gone. Instead, people marked time by the widening arc of the Halo and the night it finally closed into a perfect circle.

On that night, in every surviving settlement, the lights went out by order of the Assembly. For ten minutes the planet stood in complete darkness, silent except for the wind. Then Continuum One ignited its full rotation. Thousands of thrusters flared in sequence, tracing a radiant ring across the sky. The light rippled across oceans of ice, down mountain valleys, through shattered cities, into every shelter and every heart.

Children cheered. Old men wept. For the first time since the Sun began to die, Earth looked upward without fear.

Light-years away, on Eos, Leila stood by the viewport of Daedalus's habitat ring, the blue dawn of another world rising beyond her reflection. She held a small receiver tuned to the long-range relay from Sol—the signal faint, distorted by distance but still carrying the cadence of home.

Static filled it, then a broken voice, human and trembling with wonder:

"…Continuum One… ignition confirmed… Earth still building… we are not alone…"

The line dissolved into white noise, but it was enough. She pressed the receiver to her chest and whispered, "They made it."

Inside Continuum One's command spine, orbiting high above the dark curve of Earth, the lights dimmed as a transmission flickered to life. Gregor Vass appeared on the main viewport, recorded weeks earlier from the Eos colony. Behind him the sky burned copper and violet, the light of a younger star.

"All corridors aligned," Kaito's voice confirmed from the playback. "Continuum One will depart in ninety days. The other ships are following your blueprint."

Vass's image nodded.

"Not my blueprint," he said. "Humanity's instinct."

He turned toward the stars.

"Do you ever wonder what they'll find beyond the lattice?"

Kaito hesitated in the recording.

"I wonder what we'll become when we stop building and start living there."

Vass smiled—a tired, proud smile that crossed light-years to reach them.

"Then you already understand the point."

He lifted his hand to the glass of his own viewport, and on Continuum One the crew did the same, mirroring him. The stars outside flickered through the web of the Halo, bright and countless.

"Begin preparations," Vass said. "Let's give them a reason to follow."

The feed ended, leaving only the reflection of their own faces in the glass, ringed by the light of the Halo.

On the surface, dawn broke over a frozen sea. The light that touched the horizon was not from the Sun but from the Halo, casting long silver shadows over the ice. A child standing beside a collapsed dome lifted a hand toward it, tracing its curve in the sky. Her mother watched silently, tears freezing on her cheeks.

"Will we ever see the real Sun again?" the child asked.

The mother smiled faintly. "That *is* the Sun now."

High above, engines whispered, low and deep, as Continuum One rotated into position.

And in that moment the world seemed to pause.

Centuries later, long after the ice had swallowed the last domes and the real Sun had dimmed to a dull ember, historians would mark that night as the end of the Long Cold and the dawn of the Continuum Era.

But for those who lived it, it was simply the moment when they remembered how to hope.

Because the Halo was still visible even through the storm, and the stars had not turned away.

And far beyond them, across the silent corridors of space, the Prometheus still transmitted, whispering to any world that would listen:

"Humanity endures."

Final Passage — *The Last Three Years*

In the underground chamber beneath the fading Geneva Dome, the delegates gathered around a trembling holo-feed.

Across light-years and static, Leila Vaziri's recorded address flickered to life—her image framed by the pale skies of Eos.

Her voice came through faint but resolute.

"By now you know the Sun's pattern. Umbra will hold for *three years*. Within that time, we must finish the last two vessels—**Erebus** and **Aurora**—and send them through the Gate before it closes."

Behind her, the projection shifted to schematics: two smaller arks, each a lifeboat built from the bones of collapsed cities.

"They will carry only thousands," she said, "but they are not the end— they are the bridge."

The image changed again: **a** ring of impossible scale orbiting a darkened Earth, its segments glowing like dawn beneath the ice.

"The engineers call them *Continuum*," Leila continued. "They will not carry crews—they will carry *nations*. Millions, perhaps tens of millions, lifted from the planet itself. We will build them under the same Charter that carried us here: no nation, no creed—only survival shared."

Silence filled the hall. Outside the dome, the auroras were almost gone, their colors replaced by a low gray shimmer.

Leila's voice softened.

"When the Continuum Fleet passes through the Gate, they will rendezvous with **Prometheus**, **Daedalus**, **Odyssey**, **Erebus**, and **Aurora**. Together we will choose our destinations and divide the stars as caretakers, not conquerors. Record everything. Journal the voyage. Let those who follow know we were here."

Static rippled across the feed; the image froze on her final words.

"Three years. Enough to build. Enough to try."

The transmission ended, leaving only the reflection of the Halo glowing through the cracks in the dome—an unfinished circle promising that the work was not yet done.

Far below, engines stirred, and welders in the dark lifted their torches toward the frozen sky.

The **Second Exodus** had begun.

End of Book I — The Dying Light
To be continued in Book II — The Silent Passage

Epilogue

The sky over Earth burned with a pale, unfamiliar light. What remained of the Sun was no longer golden but a muted sphere — a reminder of what had been lost and what had begun.

High above, beyond the last threads of atmosphere, six ships traced their arcs across the twilight. The Prometheus led, followed by Daedalus, Odyssey, Erebus, and Aurora. Behind them waited the skeletal frames of the Continuum ships — the unfinished hope of billions who would never see the stars.

In the silence of space, transmissions crossed between ships like whispers in a cathedral. A single voice echoed through the network — a human voice, weary but unbroken.

"This is the end of one world… and the beginning of all others."

No one knew who had said it first. But in the dark between stars, every ship heard it. And for a moment — brief, fleeting, eternal — humanity was one.

Acknowledgments

Writing The Dying Light has been a journey — one that mirrors, in its own small way, the struggle for survival and meaning that lives at the heart of this story.

To everyone who shared their insight, patience, and belief when the pages were only fragments: thank you. To the scientists and engineers whose real work inspired these imagined worlds — your pursuit of knowledge lights the path ahead.

To all friends, acquaintances, and strangers I've met, who shared their views, opinions, understanding, and the events of a future we will never see but allowed for the vision to live a future memory, and to the readers who carry these stories forward: this book exists because you kept looking up.

— Antonio Pascarella

About the Author

Antonio Pascarella is an author and publisher whose work explores the intersection of human emotion and scientific realism. His stories combine cinematic tension with philosophical reflection, tracing how ordinary people respond to extraordinary change.

He is the founder of **StoneGate Publishing**, where he helps new voices bring their work from manuscript to market. The Dying Light is the first book in The Solar Exodus series, an epic chronicle of humanity's final exodus from a dying Sun.

Coming Next
The Solar Exodus — Book II: The Silent Passage
The first exodus fleet leaves behind a world frozen in its final light.

Aboard the Prometheus, humanity faces a truth no science could predict — that survival among the stars will cost them more than they ever left behind.

Coming soon from **StoneGate Publishing**.

StoneGate Publishing
StoneGate Publishing, LLC

www.stonegatepublishing.com
info@stonegatepublishing.com

Author's Notes

Book I — The Dying Light

Stories rarely begin where we expect them to.

Book I began for me long before the first words were written—long before the Sun dimmed, before the storms, before the departures. It began with a question that refused to go away:

What will humanity do between now and when the sky itself turns against us?

Not a sudden apocalypse or a single catastrophic event.
But a slow ending.
A star losing the battle with its own physics.

Book I is the record of that unraveling.

It follows scientists who understand before anyone else, leaders who are given no good choices, and ordinary people whose world becomes unfamiliar one season at a time. It traces the fear, the disbelief, and the astonishing resilience we show only when everything familiar begins to break.

The research behind the novel spanned astrophysics, heliophysics, orbital engineering, interstellar propulsion, and human behavioral patterns during slow-moving catastrophes. I wanted the Sun's decline to feel real—not convenient, not neat, but grounded in the emotional and scientific truth of a civilization watching its foundation fail.

But The Dying Light is not just about the science.
It is about:

- How people cling to one another when light becomes scarce.
- How governments fracture under pressure and still find ways to hope.
- How humanity confronts the moment when home is no longer safe.

This book sets the stage for everything that comes after: the formation of the Exodus program, the first fractures between Umbra and Aether, the choices that echo all the way through Books II and III. Every ship, every character, every decision in later books is rooted in something that begins here, in the cold twilight of a dying star.

If Book II is the journey, and Book III is the reckoning, then Book I is the moment humanity realizes we are in a race we never asked to run.

Thank you for taking this first step with me—
into darkness, into discovery,
and into the hope that survives even the slow death of a Sun.

— Antonio Pascarella